HIRAMIC BROTHERHOOD

Ezekiel's Temple Prophecy

William Hanna

Matador
9 Priory Business Park,
Wistow Road, Kibworth Beauchamp,
Leicestershire. LE8 0RX
Tel: 0116 279 2299
Email: books@troubador.co.uk
Web: www.troubador.co.uk/matador
Twitter: @matadorbooks

ISBN 978 1788032 704

British Library Cataloguing in Publication Data.
A catalogue record for this book is available from the British Library.

Printed and bound by CPI Group (UK) Ltd, Croydon, CR0 4YY
Typeset in 10.5pt Aldine401 BT by Troubador Publishing Ltd, Leicester, UK

Matador is an imprint of Troubador Publishing Ltd

Justyna

A very special friend

Prologue

"When you tear out a man's tongue, you are not proving him a liar, you're only telling the world that you fear what he might say."
George R.R. Martin, *A Clash of Kings*

1

Tuesday, 1 December

Little Venice, London, England

Journalist and documentary filmmaker Conrad Banner was a habitual early riser who, since Freya Nielson had moved in to live with him, always took time before getting out of bed to think how lucky he was as he marvelled at the serenity of her angelic face – a serenity that would no doubt dissipate when she woke up to face the challenge and at times less than pleasant realities of being a freelance photojournalist recording "man's inhumanity to man." Conrad got out of bed quietly so as not to wake her, slipped on his dressing gown, and crept downstairs where in the kitchen he switched on the pump espresso coffee machine for his first caffeine fix of the day. Minutes later he was sat at his desk with laptop open checking his inbox. Amongst some 15 notifications there were a couple from Adam Peltz and Sami Hadawi in Jerusalem. Peltz was a Jew involved with an Israeli organisation of archaeologists and community activists who were concerned about the use of archaeology by Israel to facilitate political objectives through various organisations of which the most prominent was the Israel Antiquities Authority (IAA). Sami was a Palestinian Christian who though unlicensed, was nonetheless a knowledgeable tourist guide with a roguish but spontaneous, endearing, and defiantly irrepressible grin despite the humiliating and hazardous hardships of life under an oppressive occupation. But of prime importance for Conrad was an email from his father Mark in Beirut, whom he had asked for general advice and ideas for a title regarding the documentary Conrad was planning to make about Jerusalem and the current conflict on the Haram al-Sharif/Temple Mount.

Dearest Conrad,

As always glad to hear that you are both keeping well. Freya is an adorable and very special young lady deserving of all that you have to give, and much more. Equally pleased to learn that since your return from Jerusalem you have resolved to make a documentary about the tragedy of Palestine and am flattered you have asked for my advice and suggestions for a title. As requested, I have given the matter some thought and in view of the fact that the concept of a "Promised Land" is a central tenet of Zionism that is coupled with a Judaic yearning for the building of a "Third Temple" on Temple Mount – I will collate all the information I have about the Hiramic Brotherhood of the Third Temple and send it to you later this week – I can think of nothing more appropriate than a title with a biblical connotation such as The Promised Land and Ezekiel's Temple Prophecy.

"I will bring them out from the nations and gather them from the countries, and I will bring them into their own land. I will pasture them on the mountains of Israel, in the ravines and in all the settlements in the land."
Ezekiel 34:13 (written between 593 – 571 BCE)

As an atheist I have never given any credence to the Bible with its prophets who were generally presented as having received revelations from God Himself which they subsequently penned for posterity. Such prophetic passages which supposedly foretold or predicted what was to come, were interspersed throughout the Bible with the most frequently cited being from Ezekiel, Daniel, Mathew 24/25, and Revelation.

While some biblical prophecies were conditional with either the conditions implicitly assumed or explicitly expressed, others were depicted variously as being direct statements from God, or were expressed as the privileged though deliberately portentous perceptions of their alleged authors who were credited with inexplicable prophetic powers.

Believers in biblical prophecy engage in exegesis, the critical explanation or interpretation of a text, and hermeneutics, the theory of text interpretation of scriptures which they believe contain descriptions of global politics, natural disasters, Israel's emergence as a nation, the coming of a Messiah, a Messianic Kingdom, and the Apocalypse.

So as you work on your film, and with that in mind, you will have to clearly demonstrate the downside of biblical prophecy which is that it has often been hijacked and exploited by fraudulent religions and questionable ideologies as justification for actions and policies that if impartially examined by an international criminal court or tribunal would be adjudged as being in violation of the Geneva Conventions – comprising of four treaties and three additional protocols – and tantamount to crimes against humanity.

One of the most ever successful fraudulent exploitation of biblical prophecy was and still is being currently perpetrated by the much vaunted "only democracy in the Middle East" which as an Apartheid Zionist Jewish state cites biblical narratives to justify both its arrogant disregard with impunity for every one of the 30 articles of The Universal Declaration of Human Rights, and for its ethnic cleansing of the Palestinian people which, incidentally, is defined as a crime against humanity under the statutes of both the International Criminal Court (ICC) and the International Criminal Tribunal for the Former Yugoslavia (ICTY).

Israel's ethnic cleansing has involved the systematic forced removal of indigenous Christian and Muslim Palestinians from Palestine with overwhelming military force so as to make it ethnically homogeneous. Such cleansing has included the removal of physical and cultural evidence in Palestine through the destruction of homes, social centres, farms, and infrastructure; and the desecration of Palestinian monuments, cemeteries, and places of worship.

Your film should argue that concocted biblical narratives alone, are insufficient to justify brutal colonisation and ethnic cleansing of a territory supposedly promised to the Jews by God himself. It should also make apparent that the perpetration of crimes against humanity in Palestine is being assisted by highly organised and abundantly financed Jewish lobby groups; by a consistent mainstream media's unforgivable portrayal of the brutal Jewish colonisers as the victims; by an unconscionable demonisation of the indigenous population; and by the ruthless suppression of freedom of speech through the exploitation of "anti-Semitism" and the "Holocaust" to silence and criminalise criticism of Israel throughout the world.

The extent of Zionism's Nazification of our freedoms was recently illustrated with the interrogation by British anti-terrorism police of a pupil who wore a "Free Palestine" badge and wristbands to school. Rather than encouraging their pupils to learn about and support human rights, teachers reported the boy to the police for what can only be described as his commitment to the Universal Declaration of Human Rights which starts off by categorically stating that "all human beings are born free and equal in dignity and rights. They are endowed with reason and conscience and should act towards one another in a spirit of brotherhood." But supporting such sentiments where Palestinians are concerned, is now apparently a crime in Britain. The teachers' action in this case was reminiscent of Nazi Germany when the roles were reversed with the Hitler Youth Movement grooming schoolchildren to report any "subversive" talk or action by their teachers, friends, neighbours, and even their own parents. In Britain, the existence of a Zionist Thought Police is now a reality and their suppression of free speech is killing off what little is left of British democracy.

The onerous task you have undertaken is fraught with many dangers that should not be underestimated so that you and Freya must take all necessary precautions to ensure your safety. It is not for me to question your decision to allow Freya to accompany you, but it is a decision which you may wish to reconsider. Also remember that you have already been stigmatised as an enemy of Israel by virtue of your surname and its association with my alleged "anti-Semitic" newspaper articles and books. By simply raising the question of Israel's criminality, you will *automatically be accused of anti-Semitism and of wanting to do to the Jews, what Israeli Jews have with cheerful chutzpah been, and still are doing to the Palestinian people with impunity.*

Finally, you must neither surrender your principles like most of the mass media's petrified "presstitutes," nor lose heart because as a journalist you have a responsibility to both your own conscience and the rest of humanity whose liberties are gradually but surely being curtailed. As was once observed by Christopher Dodd, the American lobbyist, lawyer, and politician: "When the public's right to know is threatened, and when the rights of free speech and free press are at risk, all of the other liberties we hold dear are endangered."

Love and best wishes, Mark.

The White House, Washington, D.C.

"Arrogant slime-ball," the President said angrily at his Oval office desk as he slammed the telephone receiver back into its cradle, "that guy's a certifiable lunatic," he said referring to the Israeli Prime Minister.

The Chief of Staff – who had just witnessed the President's expressed disapproval over the fact that during the past month Israeli forces had killed 142 Palestinians, and injured a further 15,620 – was sympathetic but not particularly impressed. He had heard and seen it all before and knew only too well that when the Israeli PM came to Washington, both leaders would carefully conceal their mutual animosity when in front of the cameras with the President mealy-mouthing all the obligatory and reassuring pro-Israel soundbites regarding the Jewish state's security "requirements" and its right do whatever was necessary to "defend itself."

The Chief of Staff had long been reconciled with such unconditional U.S. support for Israeli aggression despite the fact that token Palestinian resistance to it – epitomised mostly by stone-throwing youths and children who on flimsy evidence could be jailed for up to 20 years for their symbolic defiance – was a justified reaction to an oppressive, brutal and illegal occupation. Such well rehearsed geniality between the two leaders would be followed up by meetings where hundreds of millions of dollars of additional aid would be pledged to Israel as a token of America's unconditional love and fealty to an Apartheid war criminal state. As far as the Chief of Staff could make out, it was always more convenient for the American government to pay off the bellyaching Israeli blackmailers in hope that they would stop chanting their tiresome mantra about the Holocaust and go away. As was observed in *The Jerusalem Post* by Reuven Ben-Shalom – who served for 25 years in the Israel Defence Force as a helicopter pilot; in various international relations positions including director of Israel-US military cooperation; and as director of the International Fellows Program at the Israel National Defence College – "We get so carried away in presenting our case that listening to us is sometimes exhausting, depressing, boring, and annoying."

During the visit the Israeli leader would no doubt also scoop up a pile of large amount cheques from the Wall Street fraternity of financial felons and deep pocket Jewish billionaire members of the world's wealthy one-percenters; would be grovelled to by a bicameral Congress consisting mostly of quislings totally controlled by the American Israel Public Affairs Committee (AIPAC); and would receive fawning praise from compliant media whores – especially in *The New York times* – to the applause of the brainwashed and blinkered American public. George Orwell's *Nineteen Eighty-Four* with its portrayal of perpetual war, omnipresent government surveillance, and public manipulation was now a flourishing reality in the land where the star-spangled banner was no longer fluttering in triumph "O'er the land of the free and the home of the brave."

In view of the President's current agitated mood, the Chief

of Staff reluctantly gave him the Presidential Daily Briefing (PDB), a top-secret document compiled by the Director of National Intelligence whose office combined intelligence reports from the Central Intelligence Agency (CIA), the Defence Intelligence Agency (DIA), the National Security Agency (NSA), the Federal Bureau of Investigation (FBI), and other U.S. intelligence agencies. Today's Briefing, as had been the case for the past few months at the President's request, also contained a summary of Israeli media reports which were invariably not well received by the President who was often portrayed as being anti-Semitic and an enemy of Israel.

U.S.-Israeli relations had been at an all time low for some time as a consequence of continued Jewish settlement building in the illegally occupied Palestinian territories; mischievous Israeli efforts to derail the the Iran nuclear negotiations; and the stalled charade of Israeli-Palestinian peace talks. During his presidential campaign in July 2008, the President – apart from pledging not "to waste a minute" in tackling the Middle East conflict if elected president – had also asserted "you and I, we're gonna change this country, and we will change the world," to the ecstatic chants of "yes we can," all of which would eventually prove to be yet another example of how the hopes of the American people had triumphed over the reality of their past experience of broken promises by treasonous politicians who sold their souls to AIPAC.

So despite his election marking a new era of expectation and his having been prematurely awarded the Nobel Peace Prize the following year, the President had not only failed to deliver on any of his pledges for peace and a better world, but had actually expanded war powers well beyond those of his semi-literate predecessor George W. Bush by establishing precedents that made it even easier to use lethal force abroad without congressional approval.

Just like all his recent presidential predecessors, the

President had been very quickly taught that as far as the Middle East was concerned, it was Israel through AIPAC which dictated U.S. Middle East policy and not the White House or Congress. Israel had made that point by launching the barbaric Operation Cast Lead in Gaza – which started on December 27, 2008 and ended on January 18, 2009 – just two days before the President's inauguration on the twentieth.

"What have you got for me?" a testy President asked as he took the morning's briefing papers and started reading the summary of Israeli media reports which included a controversial revelation that Israel was the major purchaser of oil produced and sold by the Islamic State of Iraq and Syria (ISIS) which was producing between 20,000 and 40,000 barrels a day in those two countries to generate between $1m and $1.5 million in profits; that one of Germany's largest department store chains – with over 100 branches and 21,000 employees – had removed Israeli products from its shelves in response to new EU labelling regulations; that members of the extreme right, anti-Arab assimilation group Lehava had protested against a Christmas tree decorating event – intended for Jerusalem's Christian population – which they claimed was targeting Jewish children; that after meeting the Russian President in Paris, the Israeli PM had said that Israel would continue to protect its interests by acting in Syria to prevent the transfer of game-changing weaponry to Hezbollah; and that according to the Jewish Agency, almost 30,000 Jews – the largest influx in 15 years – had moved to Israel in 2015 as part of the continuous aliya that was necessary for the gradual but constant encroachment on Palestinian territories with new illegal settlements.

The Chief of Staff had been part of the White House pantomime of supposedly opposing Israeli settlement building, while legislation – initiated and backed by the insufferable AIPAC – was in the pipeline for a trade bill that would contain a provision lumping together Israel and "Israeli-controlled

8

territories." So even though such legislation would contravene longstanding U.S. policy towards Israel and the occupied territories, including Israel's illegal settlement activity, the President would sign the bill. Dubbed as The Trade Facilitation and Trade Enforcement Act, the bill was designed to strengthen enforcement rules, address currency manipulation, and bolster efforts to block evasions of trade laws. The bill would also include a clause addressing politically motivated acts to limit or prohibit economic relations with Israel by targeting corporate entities or state-affiliated financial institutions who engaged in the Boycott, Divestment and Sanctions (BDS) campaign against Israel.

The provision would place the U.S. firmly on record as opposing BDS and supporting enhanced commercial ties between the U.S. and Israel while passing into law solid anti-BDS negotiating objectives for American trade negotiators. Furthermore, within 180 days of the bill becoming law, the US administration would be obliged to report to the Congress on global BDS activities, including the participation of foreign companies in political boycotts of the Jewish state. Apart from providing legal protections for U.S. companies operating in Israel, the bill would also conflate Israel proper with contested occupied Palestinian territories contrary to long-standing hypocritical U.S. policy stipulating that settlement activity was an obstacle to achieving peace and a two-state solution.

The extent of the AIPAC-led pro-Israel lobby's control of the U.S. Congress became evident when even the much cherished First Amendment of the Constitution – "Congress shall make no law respecting an establishment of religion, or prohibiting the free exercise thereof; or abridging the freedom of speech, or of the press; or the right of the people peaceably to assemble, and to petition the Government for a redress of grievances" – was threatened by Congresspeople with one vowing to destroy the mounting grassroots BDS campaign against Israel by pledging to weaken the First Amendment: "Free speech is being used in our country to denigrate Israel and we need to actively fight against that … "

The President – whom more than 90 percent of Israeli people disliked – was accustomed to this kind Congressional pandering to Israel whose Jewish population while mostly claiming to favour a two-state solution, and thus, Palestinian statehood, was actually lying to pollsters and disliked the President because of fear that he might be serious about ending Israel's occupation of the West Bank and the blockade of Gaza. Consequently, though Israeli fears – of Iran, of rocket attacks, of world isolation and abandonment – were hardly plausible, such fears nonetheless served both as a source of consolation for Israel's collective conscience and as justification for its continued occupation and oppression of the Palestinian people.

"What are they up to now?" The president asked as he finished reading the media reports and moving on to the PDB which the Chief of Staff had made a point of always reading first and which contained the report of suspicions that the Israeli secret service had been behind a series of mysterious yet highly sophisticated cyber-spying attacks on decisive negotiations over Iran's nuclear programme held at luxury hotels across Europe between Iran and the P5+1 nations of China, France, Russia, the United Kingdom, and the United States, plus Germany. Swiss security agents had raided Geneva's luxury President Wilson hotel – where some of the talks were held – and as suspected, discovered evidence of Israeli cyber spying.

After having eventually finished reading the daily briefing, the President sank wearily in his executive black leather high back chair with a sense of frustration. Following his reelection for a second term in 2012, the President had expressed the view that "We want to pass on a country that's safe and respected and admired around the world, a nation that is defended by the strongest military on earth and the best troops this world has ever known, but also a country that moves with confidence beyond this time of war to shape a peace that is built on the promise of freedom and dignity for every human being." Despite the proclamation of such noble sentiments about "freedom and dignity for every human being," the reality was that with American aid and complicity, "freedom and dignity" were still being denied to the Palestinian people after almost 70 years.

The President had long been reconciled to the fact – irrespective how many international and human rights laws Israel violated – that so long as AIPAC continued to have the American government by the balls, then the U.S. would continue with American taxpayer money to provide unconditional support for a racist Apartheid state whose arrogant conduct with boundless impunity on the international stage was intended to dispossess the Palestinian people of their land so as to facilitate illegal Jewish settlement in keeping with Zionism's ideological objective for a "Greater Israel." Despite all that, more than half of all U.S. global aid was given to Israel.

Even worse than the betrayal of the American people by its politicians, was the surrender of the great American Dream – Democracy, Rights, Liberty, Opportunity, and Equality – by the American people themselves: a people who tended to subscribe to the ideology of American Exceptionalism; a people of whom according to a Gallup/Harris poll, a full 73 percent were incapable of identifying their home country – let alone the location of other countries – on a map; a people no longer capable of accepting any irrefutable fact that did not conform with their own blinkered bias; a people devoid of the capacity to think beyond their indoctrination by a mainstream media of which 90 percent was controlled by only six corporations either owned or run by Jewish interests; a people no longer prepared to ask difficult questions or to regard obvious government and media propaganda and lies with suspicion; a people nurtured on racial antagonism and the need for constant wars against the ever present and deviously fabricated "threats" of terrorism; a people whom the rest of the world regarded as the greatest threat to human rights and the attainment of global peace; and a people who had lost all moral and political perspectives of how they, as a "superpower," should by their own example be leading and benefiting the rest of humanity.

Despite the status and trappings of his position, the Chief of staff had decided to tender his resignation because of disillusionment and a troubled conscience which cried out for unshackled governance with integrity where in the corridors of power the anguished wails of "We the People" would not be drowned out by the corrupting whispers of bribe-laden special interest lobbyists: lobbyists whose democracy subverting influence had been further enhanced by a U.S. Supreme Court ruling (a 5 to 4 decision) that struck down the limit on the total amount of money wealthy donors could contribute to candidates and political committees. So now, more than ever before, the millionaire/billionaire one-percenters could buy politicians and control government policies to the detriment of the vast majority who had yet to learn that the only difference between a democracy and a dictatorship is that with the latter you don't have to waste time by going to the ballot box.

Foggy Bottom Neighbourhood, Washington, D.C.

It was evening and in the sitting room where – having already melodiously mellowed the mood with Kaori Kobayashi's jazz saxophone sounds – the digital music system was now playing her *Nothing Gonna Change My Love for You.* The previously hovering wisps of cigarette smoke had dispersed leaving only the faint but distinct gaseous aroma of incinerated Virginia tobacco; the crystal champagne flutes from which a 2004 vintage had been sipped, lay empty on the ornate glass top coffee table next to the drained and upturned bottle in the silver plated ice bucket; and as a final flourish to the love nest setting, a trail of hurriedly discarded items of male and female designer clothing led from the black soft leather sectional sofa to the bedroom where on the upholstered bed the naked couple were pressed hard against each other in a passionate embrace.

The brunette's sun-bed tanned curvaceous hourglass figure was firm with a good muscle tone indicating regular workouts and attention to diet. Her impressively proportioned bust and hips were matched by a beautifully defined waist that gracefully curved down and outwards towards those hips which were perfectly aligned with gently rounded shoulders framing sizeable but nonetheless perky breasts. Her rounded bottom was symmetrical with the beautiful side and front profiles of an upper body that matched the length of her raunchily shaped legs. Every enticing inch of her was a picture of balance, harmony, and ethereal sensuality.

The middle-aged man on the other hand was carrying some flab that was more pronounced around his slightly sagging midriff. Despite that, his body had retained some vestige of what must have once been a fine physique before the ravages of time and debauched living had taken their toll. Nonetheless, like most men in positions of power he had an overactive libido which coupled with with the confidence that came with his position made him recklessly willing to chance his luck against the odds of having his illicit encounters being discovered irrespective of how, when, where, or with whom they might occur. Because of this perceived omnipotence he invariably assumed that other people would always do his bidding so that sexual compliance from women – who were in any case fascinated by men in positions of power – was something he expected and took for granted. The phenomenon was not restricted to men but was equally applicable to women of prominence for whom having authority over others was also the ultimate aphrodisiac.

The brunette suddenly tossed her head back, provocatively disengaging her tongue from their torrid embrace and instead began to kiss him gently as she worked her way downwards from his chin towards his crotch where her darting tongue taunted, teased, and titillated his testicles and caused his aroused manhood to throb with salacious expectation. Such expectation was then rewarded as she lightly stroked his upstanding manhood with well manicured fingernails while her lascivious tongue and lips performed sensual magic on one who was undoubtedly the promiscuous husband of a probably outwardly demure but socially ambitious hellcat of a wife whose priorities did not include nurturing or enhancing marital sexuality.

After what seemed like an age of agonising concupiscence for the man, the woman straddled him in a kneeling position, held his erection in her right hand and used it to gently massage her vulval lips which were already moist with the anticipation of welcoming his well endowed manhood into the pleasurable depths of her femininity. She could not help but smile to herself as she recalled her teenage years and wondered what Rabbi Amos Rosenfeld – a family friend and frequent visitor to their Brooklyn home – would have thought of her now. He used to frequently remind her that irrespective of what she chose to do in life, to always make sure she was in control and on top of any situation: which was precisely what she was now doing as she determined the position, the pace, and the procedure by which she would transport this besotted and deluded individual to that realm of coital cornucopia which most men dream about but very few actually experience.

As his breathing quickened and his moans grew more desperate, she finally relented and slowly but surely lowered herself onto his throbbing penis which she enveloped with her warm and wet love nest. There was no way this was going to be some casual *wham, bam, thank you mam* encounter because she had spent months using Ben Wa balls to conscientiously exercise her vaginal muscles so as to become an expert in the art of vaginal muscle control which many Oriental women had mastered as part of becoming highly proficient lovers. She could now hold a man's penis tightly with her vagina; she could by powerfully squeezing and releasing his penis give him the vaginal equivalent of fellatio; she could delay his ejaculation if he was about to reach the point of climax prematurely; and she could use her vaginal muscles to pleasure him in a variety of amazing and mind-blowing ways – and she did.

The fact that they were both virtually motionless on the bed belied the extent of their euphoria because despite the apparent lack of robust movement, all her well exercised vaginal muscles were delivering tidal waves of gratification to every sinew of the man's body whose head was now intoxicated with sheer, unadulterated rapture. As their rate of breathing quickened and the sound of their triumphant moans heightened, so too did the pace of the vaginal contractions whose pleasure providing effects were further enhanced by the woman's subtle but sensational circular movement of the hips.

Under the circumstances even the strongest of wills would have failed to stem the irresistible onrush of a jubilant climax and as this couple's fevered passion hurtled towards a sexual Armageddon, he clasped her hips tightly with both hands and responded to her enthusiastic acceleration of movement with macho-impelled thrusts that were deep, hard, and rapid. With each thrust her body convulsed with a long, loud, exultant shriek akin to that of a woman giving birth to a child. Their bodies arched and writhed wildly against each other as they sought to wring out every last smidgeon of sensual satisfaction from their physical endeavours until finally with a fanfare of frenzied sighs and squeals an explosion of unimaginable delight engulfed them and left them drained in a crumpled heap on the sweat and semen soaked Egyptian cotton bed sheet. Though such clandestine trysts were often a necessary part of the brunette's work, it was not work that she in any way regarded with abhorrence.

While tens of thousands of other potentially dangerous liaisons were simultaneously being played out within hotel rooms and private accommodations in different cities, towns, and villages all over the world, this particular one had taken place in Washington DC's Watergate Complex: a notorious address where corporate predators, Machiavellian miscreants, and an "I am not a crook" U.S. president had in the past met their Waterloos due to some caper, criminality, or cloak-and-dagger conspiracy.

The satisfied but now exhausted man dozed off momentarily, blissfully oblivious to the fact that the evening's sexual shenanigans were not an unwitting and incidental progression from last week's chance encounter with the brunette, but part of a predetermined scheme carefully orchestrated and executed as the direct consequence of world events including a spate of what many people regarded as being long overdue decisions recognising the historical existence of a Palestinian people who were deserving of justice, human rights, and a state of their own. Such decisions – despite furious Israeli threats accompanied by the inevitable endless reminders of the Holocaust – had recently included recognition of Palestinian statehood by a number of European nations; the provision of Palestinian observer status at the International Criminal Court (ICC); a vote of recognition by the European parliament; and the Geneva Conventions' invocation of Palestinian rights by 126 countries urging Israel to halt illegal settlement construction in the West Bank and East Jerusalem.

The Geneva Conventions which governed the rules of

war and military occupation had not on this occasion been attended by Australia, Canada, or the U.S.A. – countries whose far from exemplary past colonial governance had included racial discrimination, rampant exploitation, and heartless ill-treatment of indigenous populations which in some cases constituted premeditated genocide. Such overtly pro-Palestinian developments were now threatening to delay, or perhaps even completely thwart the Judaic dream of erecting the "Third Temple" in accordance with the biblical prophecy of Ezekiel.

Consequently drastic measures were required including the ramping up of *hasbara* – a Hebrew word literally meaning "explanation," but actually covering a wide range of propaganda activities promoting the positive aspects of Israel as a counter to negative press and public perceptions – to reinforce the misconception that Israel was "the only democracy in the Middle East" and had only been "defending itself" with "the most moral army in the world" during last summer's brutal destruction of Palestinian life and property in Gaza with overwhelming state of the art weaponry against a people without a single tank, warship, or fighter jet aircraft with which to defend themselves.

Nonetheless Israel would continue through its powerful Zionist Jewish lobby organisations to reinforce its tactic of gagging anyone who spoke up and actively opposed Israeli policies; would continue to push for Jewish lobby inspired legislation criminalising criticism of Israel; would continue to oppose and undermine pro-Palestinian activist criticism of the Jewish state's enforcement of Apartheid; and would continue to maintain its modus operandi of blackmail, bribery, and bullying supported by false flag operations to retain Western collusion in the deliberate rewriting of a Jewish history from one that portrayed Jews as being dependent and at the mercy of others, to one that instead had Jews as being independent and in control of their own destiny in a Jewish state whose establishment and survival necessitated gradually but positively denying the Palestinian people of their own history and homeland so as to forcibly and illegally facilitate the expansion of Jewish settlement.

Many observers and commentators had noted that during its pursuit of that goal, Israel had developed a righteous "self-defence" philosophy that combined all elements of military occupation and law enforcement to oppress the Palestinian people. It was a philosophy that had come to personify the character of settler Israeli Jews and their racist mentality as a "chosen people" exempt from accountability for their actions. Another consequence of this righteousness was the growth of a state of the art military-security industrial Goliath voraciously dependent on trade with other countries for whom population pacification was also an essential necessity for their governments. As far as the Israelis were concerned, it mattered not to whom they sold their tools of death and destruction – including governments who tortured, terrorised, murdered, or were even anti-Semitic – so long as such sales served to make a profit and forged alliances with those rogue states so as to curtail their criticism of Israeli policies.

The success of Israel's military-security industrial Goliath had to a great extent been due to the fact that the equipment sold had already been cold-bloodedly field tested in Gaza and the West Bank on "guinea pig" captive Palestinians of whom since 1967 some one million had also experienced arbitrary Israeli arrest and detention that was deliberately designed – with stressful conditions of confinement, painful methods of restraining detainees, long periods of isolation, beatings, degradation, intimidation, and threats against detainees and their families – to deprive them of their dignity and impair their physical well-being.

Israelis had been, and still were, able to perpetrate their

crimes against humanity with impunity because they had successfully managed to continue portraying themselves as the innocent victims of anti-Semitic terrorism against which they were defending themselves in a perpetual war. To further facilitate tolerance of their crimes by Western democracies, Israelis had exploited terrorist acts against Western nations to formulate the "clash of civilisations" perception in which Western nations and Israel shared civilised values that required an endless war against the uncivilised Islamic terrorists. So long as such spurious perceptions prevailed, Israel could then maintain its ethnic cleansing of Palestine under the guise of self-defence while inducing the rest of the now Islamophobic Western world to fight an ever present "terrorist threat" that served Israel's purpose of dividing and destroying its Middle East Muslim neighbours.

> " ... it is the leaders of the country who determine the policy and it is always a simple matter to drag the people along, whether it is a democracy or a fascist dictatorship or a Parliament or a Communist dictatorship ... Voice or no voice, the people can always be brought to the bidding of the leaders. That is easy. All you have to do is tell them they are being attacked and denounce the pacifists for lack of patriotism and exposing the country to danger. It works the same way in any country."
> **Hermann Goering (as told to American psychologist Gustav Gilbert during the Nuremberg Trials)**

It was, as he then was, former Israeli Prime Minister Benjamin Netanyahu who – following the September 11, 2001 attacks in the United States – confirmed the usefulness of this perception by saying "it's very good ... Well, not very good, but it will generate immediate sympathy ... strengthen the bond between our two peoples, because we've experienced terror over so many decades, but the United States has now experienced a massive haemorrhaging of terror." Meanwhile then Prime

Minister Ariel Sharon – another notorious war criminal – repeatedly placed Israel on the same ground as the United States by calling the assault an attack on "our common values … I believe together we can defeat these forces of evil."

By September 19, 2001, Aman – the supreme military intelligence branch of the Israeli Defence Forces – had begun circulating claims that Iraq was behind the 9/11 attacks, a blatant lie that helped neoconservatives to convince Americans that the War on Iraq was justified. This lie was further reinforced by an even bigger Israeli inspired falsehood that Iraq possessed weapons of mass destruction with then British Prime Minister Tony Blair – an Israeli asset and now widely regarded as a war criminal but still at large – becoming embroiled in the claim that Iraq could launch weapons of mass destruction within 45 minutes of an order being given. Such lies had served to infect Western perceptions with Israel's Perpetual War Syndrome which had to date resulted in tens of millions of innocent people in the Middle East and elsewhere to be continually traumatised, displaced, and in many cases simply killed.

Israel's apparent beneficence in offering to help "defeat those evil forces" was part of Zionism's contrivance to lull Americans in particular and the West in general into believing that apart from sharing their values, Israel was also their staunchest ally … An ally, however, that with the help of hundreds of Jewish organisations and numerous Zionist-neoconservative officials occupying strategic positions, had constantly pushed the West into fighting "Islamic terrorism" in an endless conflict where hateful contempt and heinous disregard for humanity prevailed above all else … An endless conflict in which Conrad Banner and Freya Nielson would soon become embroiled as witnesses to a brutal extrajudicial killing that confirmed Israel was now a nation lacking in any sense of principled morality. Conrad subscribed to the observation once made by the British lawyer and jurist

Judge Devlin (1905-1992), that "an established morality is as necessary as good government to the welfare of society. Societies disintegrate from within more frequently than they are broken up by external pressures."

2

Friday, 4 December

Little Venice, London, England

London's Little Venice – a large pond created in the 1810s as the meeting point between the Regent's Canal and the Paddington Arm of the Grand Union Canal – was the setting for a willow tree covered islet that served as a waterway roundabout known as Browning's Island. The islet had been named after the English poet and playwright, Robert Browning, who had lived nearby and was credited with having coined the name "Little Venice." Browning had formed one of history's most famous literary unions when in 1846 he married the older poet Elizabeth Barrett with whom he remained until her death in his arms while they were in Florence in June 1861. The neighbourhood with picturesque tree-lined streets, grand Georgian and Victorian terraces, and moored houseboats on its waterways, was still an oasis for peaceful solitude where it was possible to pause, step back, and for a while escape the pressures of modern day city life.

But even the tranquility of Little Venice and the passage of time had failed to diminish Conrad Banner's mounting outrage since Israel's Operation Protective Edge in the Gaza Strip last summer which killed thousands of men, women, children, and elderly civilians; caused massive civilian displacement and destruction of property and vital services; reinforced Israel's air, sea and land blockade of 1.8 million Palestinians who were collectively punished; and compounded an already existing humanitarian crisis in which people the world over – including Jews in diaspora who insist on their own inalienable rights – had been complicit with silent and icy indifference to the horrendous suffering of those beleaguered Palestinian people. To make matters worse, reconstruction of vital infrastructure had been virtually nonexistent; the more than 100,000 people displaced, were still homeless; and the near-daily Israeli breaches of the ceasefire – consisting of frequent military incursions, and attacks on fishermen and farmers – only served to make life even more intolerable. Conrad's increasingly resolute adoption of the Palestinian cause had occurred after reconciliation with his estranged father, Mark, whose articles and books he had begun reading.

While the disapproval of human rights activists over that summertime's barbaric bloodbath had been evident in Europe and other parts of the world, in the U.S., Israel's occupation of the collective American mind was relentlessly maintained by American politicians and the mainstream media's hypnotic incantations of "Israel has a right to defend itself." The long-term dehumanisation and massacre of Palestinians had not only occurred inside Palestine, but also elsewhere in refugee camps – such as Lebanon's Sabra and Shatila where the infamous 1982 massacre was facilitated by Israel – had remained a regular feature of Israel's brutal policy of colonising Palestine and displacing its indigenous people.

It was after Sabra and Shatila that Israel was forced to intensify its offensive of defending itself against negative publicity which was achieved with assistance from a mostly Jewish controlled American media portraying Israel as a brave "David" defending itself against a Palestinian "Goliath." Such portrayals were repeatedly drummed into the American psyche wherein they took root and had flourished ever since. Conrad felt that unstinting U.S. government support for Israel with billions of taxpayer dollars – not to mention endless hypocritical

U.S. vetoes of UN resolutions condemning Israel – could not have been possible without the institutionalised compliance of the American people themselves.

Conrad's eventual acceptance of the fact that Israel's ethnic cleansing of Palestinians was a calculated and ongoing policy, had prompted him to visit Jerusalem for ten days during late September to explore the possibilities for filming a documentary which he had now decided would be titled *The Promised Land and Ezekiel's Temple Prophesy*. Since returning from Jerusalem he had spent most of his time in acquiring as much background information as possible so that he could work on the project within the context of actual historical facts rather than the propaganda perceptions propagated by a dysfunctional pro-Israel educational system and a biased mainstream media.

It was while doing his research that he came across a reference to the Rothschild Banking Dynasty which led him out of curiosity into digging further and learning of that family's pivotal role in not only instigating World Wars, but also in influencing the course of numerous events that had, and still were, adversely affecting the lives of billions of people in a world where half of the world's wealth was owned by just one percent of the population; where the wealth of that one percent was approaching $120 trillion, or almost 70 times the total wealth of the bottom half of the world's population; where the wealth of the world's 85 richest people surpassed that of the bottom half of the world's population; where seven out of ten people lived in countries with economic inequality which had continually increased in the last 30 years; and where the fortunate and very wealthy minority had bought political power that served their own acquisitive interests as opposed to the urgent requirements of the far less fortunate majority.

Conrad's research revealed that it had all begun in 1743 when a son, Mayer Amschel Bauer, was born in Frankfurt to Moses Amschel Bauer – a money lender and proprietor of an accounting house – who was an Ashkenazi Jew. Ashkenazi Jews were descended from the medieval Jewish communities along the River Rhine from Alsace in the south to the Rhineland in the north. Ashkenaz was the medieval Hebrew name for that German region and consequently Ashkenazim or Ashkenazi Jews were literally "German Jews." Many of these Jews migrated, mostly eastwards, to establish communities in Eastern Europe including Belarus, Hungary, Lithuania, Poland, Russia, Ukraine and elsewhere between the 11th and 19th centuries. They took with them and diversified a Yiddish influenced Germanic language written in Hebrew letters which in medieval times had become the lingua franca among Ashkenazi Jews. Although in the 11th century, Ashkenazi Jews comprised only three percent of the world's Jewish population, that proportion had peaked to 92 percent by 1931 and now accounted for about 80 percent of Jews worldwide.

During the Dark and Middle Ages – when the Bible was viewed as being the principal source of knowledge and ultimate arbiter in matters of importance – the Christian Church's stubborn opposition to usury was consequently based on biblical and moral rather than sound commercial considerations. Such opposition was also repeatedly reinforced with legal restrictions to the extent that in 325 the Council of Nicaea banned the practice among clerics. During Charlemagne's time as Emperor (800–814) the Church extended the ban to include laymen with the assertion that "usury was as a transaction wherein more was required in return than was given." Centuries later, the 1311 Council of Vienne in Southern France – whose principal function was to withdraw papal support for the Knights Templar on the instigation of Philip IV of France who was in debt to the Templars – declared that persons daring to claim that there was no sin in the practice of usury would be punished as a heretics.

Subsequently in 1139 Pope Innocent II summoned the Second Lateran Council at which usury was denounced as a form of theft requiring restitution from those who practiced it so that during the next two centuries, schemes to conceal usury were strongly condemned. Despite all such pronouncements, however, there was a loophole provided by the Bible's double standard on usury which conveniently permitted Jews to lend money to non-Jews. As a result, for long periods during the Dark and Middle Ages, both the Church and civil authorities permitted Jews to practice usury. Many royals, who required substantial loans to finance their lifestyles and the waging of wars, tolerated Jewish usurers in their domains so that European Jews – who had been barred from most professions and ownership of land – found moneylending to be a profitable, though at times, a hazardous profession. Money lending therefore came to be regarded as an inherent Jewish vocation.

In the Old Testament, God allegedly said to the Jews: "[He that] Hath given forth upon usury, and hath taken increase: shall he then live? he shall not live . . . he shall surely die; his blood shall be upon him" (Ezekiel 18:13), and "thou shalt not lend upon usury to thy brother; usury of money; usury of victuals; usury of anything that is lent upon usury. Unto a stranger thou mayest lend upon usury; but unto thy brother thou shalt not lend upon usury, that the Lord thy God may bless thee in all that thou settest thine hand to in the land whither thou goest to possess it." (Deuteronomy 23:19 – 20).

So while Jews were legally permitted to lend money to Christians in need, the Christians themselves resented the idea of Jews making money from Christian misfortunes by means of an activity biblically prohibited with the threat of eternal damnation to Christians who understandably came to view Jewish usurers with a contempt that gradually nurtured the roots of anti-Semitism. Such contempt and opposition to Jewish usury was frequently violent with Jews being massacred in attacks instigated by members of the nobility who being in debt to Jewish usurers, cancelled their debts through violent attacks on Jewish communities with accounting records being destroyed.

While such treatment of moneylenders may have been unjust, they were also made scapegoats for most economic problems for many centuries; were derided by philosophers and condemned to hell by religious authorities; were subject to property confiscation to compensate their "victims"; were framed, humiliated, jailed, and massacred; and were vilified by economists, legislators, journalists, novelists, playwrights, philosophers, theologians, and even the masses. Throughout history major thinkers such as Thomas Aquinas, Aristotle, Karl Marx, J. M. Keynes, Plato, and Adam Smith have invariably regarded moneylending as a major vice. Dante, Dickens, Dostoyevsky, and Shakespeare's "Shylock" character in *The Merchant of Venice,* were but a few of the popular playwrights and novelists who depicted moneylenders as villains.

Moses Amschel Bauer, however, lived at a time and in a place where he was allowed a degree of tolerance and respect for his business which at its entrance boasted a red, six pointed star that geometrically and numerically represented the number 666 – six points, six triangles, and a six-sided hexagon. This seemingly innocuous sign, however, was destined to subsequently play an important role in the birth of both Zionist ideology and the state of Israel. That destiny had its seeds sown during the 1760s when Amschel Bauer worked for an Oppenheimer-owned bank in Hanover where his proficiency led to his becoming a junior partner and social acquaintance of General von Estorff. On returning to Frankfurt to take over his dead father's business, Amschel Bauer recognised the potential significance of the red sign and accordingly changed his surname from Bauer to Rothschild because "Rot" and "Schild" were German for "Red" and "Sign." The six pointed star, with cunning and determined Rothschild family manipulation, was to eventually end up on the Israeli flag some two centuries later.

On subsequently hearing that his former acquaintance General von Estorff had been attached to the court of Prince William of Hanau, Rothschild deviously renewed their friendship – on the pretext of selling Estorff valuable coins and trinkets at discounted prices – with the confident knowledge that it would lead to an introduction to Prince William himself who was delighted by the prospect of buying such rare items at a discount. By also offering a commission for any other business that the Prince might bring his way, Rothschild became a close associate of the Prince and ended up also doing business with other royal court members on whom he invariably lavished nauseating praise to ingratiate himself as he had done with Prince William:

"It has been my particular high and good fortune to serve your lofty princely Serenity at various times and to your most gracious satisfaction. I stand ready to exert all my energies and my entire fortune to serve your lofty princely serenity whenever in future it shall please you to command me. An especially powerful incentive to this end would be given me if your lofty princely serenity were to distinguish me with an appointment as one of your Highness' Court Factors. I am making bold to beg for this with the more confidence in the assurance that by so doing I am not giving any trouble; while for my part such a distinction would lift up my commercial standing and be of help to me in many other ways that I feel certain thereby to make my own way and fortune here in the city of Frankfurt."

Rothschild was eventually in 1769 engaged by Prince William to oversee his properties and tax collection with the permission to hang up a business sign that boasted "M. A. Rothschild, by appointment court factor to His Serene Highness, Prince William of Hanau."

Over two decades later in 1791 in America, Alexander Hamilton – first Secretary of the Treasury, influential member of George Washington's cabinet, and an adroit Rothschild agent – facilitated the setting up of a Rothschild central bank with a twenty-year charter called the Bank of the United States. Hamilton was to be the first of a long line of U.S. politicians who to this day still betray their own country by selling out for a fistful of dollars to facilitate Jewish interests.

Meanwhile back in Europe, Napoleon Bonaparte – French Emperor from 1804 to 1814 – declared his intention in 1806 of removing "the house of Hess-Kassel from rulership and to strike it out of the list of powers." This forced Prince William to flee Germany for Denmark while entrusting an estimated fortune of some $3,000,000 to Rothschild for safekeeping. That same year Mayer Amschel Rothschild's son Nathan Mayer Rothschild married Hannah Barent Cohen, the daughter of a wealthy London merchant and started moving his business interests to London.

When First Baronet Sir Francis Baring and Abraham Goldsmid died in 1810, Nathan Mayer Rothschild by default became the leading banker in England while his brother Salomon Mayer Rothschild departed for Austria to set up the M. von Rothschild und Söhne bank in Vienna.

Back in the U.S. the charter for the Rothschild's Bank of the United States ran out in 1811 and Congress voted against renewal with Andrew Jackson – subsequently to become the 7th U.S. President (1829–1837) – stating that "if Congress has a right under the Constitution to issue paper money, it was given them to use by themselves, not to be delegated to individuals or corporations." This led to an unamused Nathan Mayer Rothschild replying that "either the application for renewal of the charter is granted, or the United States will find itself involved in a most disastrous war." Jackson countered with "you are a den of thieves, vipers, and I intend to rout you out, and by the Eternal God, I will rout you out." Rothschild's reaction was a promise to "teach those impudent Americans a lesson. Bring them back to colonial status."

Consequently Britain's declaration of war on the U.S. in

1812 was unsurprisingly backed by Rothschild money with a view to causing a U.S. accumulation of war debt that would force it to surrender and thereby facilitate renewal of the charter for a Rothschild-owned U.S. Bank. That same year Mayer Amschel Rothschild died and his will set out specific instructions for the House of Rothschild to follow including the fact that all key positions in the family business were to be held only by family members; that only male members of the family were allowed to participate in the family business – Mayer also had five daughters – so that the spread of the Rothschild Zionist dynasty without the Rothschild name also became global; that the family was to intermarry with it's first and second cousins so as to preserve the family fortune; that no public inventory of Mayer's estate was to be published; that no legal action was to be taken with regard to the value of the inheritance; and that the eldest son of the eldest son was to become the head of the family, a stipulation that could only be overturned when the majority of the family agreed otherwise. This came into effect immediately and Nathan Mayer Rothschild became head of the family while Jacob (James) Mayer Rothschild left for France to set up the de Rothschild Frères bank in Paris.

As to the fate of the $3,000,000 that Prince William of Hanau had given to Mayer Amschel Rothschild for safekeeping, the 1905 edition of the Jewish Encyclopaedia states in Volume 10, page 494, that:

"According to legend this money was hidden away in wine casks, and, escaping the search of Napoleon's soldiers when they entered Frankfurt, was restored intact in the same casks in 1814, when the elector (Prince William of Hanau) returned to the electorate (Germany). The facts are somewhat less romantic, and more businesslike."

The implication being that the money was never returned by Rothschild with the encyclopaedia adding that "Nathan Mayer

Rothschild invested this $3,000,000 in gold from the East India Company knowing that it would be needed for Wellington's peninsula campaign," with Nathan then making on the stolen money "no less than four profits."

In 1815 the five Rothschild brothers exploited the policy of funding both sides in wars by providing gold for the armies of both Wellington and Napoleon. Because of their ownership of banks throughout Europe, the Rothschilds had a unique network of covert routes and fast couriers who were the only agents permitted to travel through the English and French lines. This meant that they were kept posted on the war's progress which enabled them to buy and sell on the stock exchange in accordance with the intelligence received.

British bonds were at that time called consuls and Nathan Mayer Rothschild instructed his employees to start selling them so as to make other traders believe that the Britain was losing the war and cause them to start panic selling that would see the value of the consul plummet. Rothschild's employees were then instructed to discreetly begin purchasing all available consuls. When it eventually became apparent that Britain had actually won the war, the value of consuls rose to an even higher level than before and the Rothschilds ended up with a return of approximately 20 to one on on their investment.

This gave the Rothschilds total control of Britain's economy and with Napoleon's defeat helped London become the financial centre of the world which required the setting up a new Bank of England under the control of Nathan Mayer Rothschild who boasted "I care not what puppet is placed upon the throne of England to rule the Empire on which the sun never sets. The man who controls Britain's money supply controls the British Empire, and I control the British money supply."

Such control enabled the Rothschilds to replace the method of shipping gold between countries by instead utilising their five European banks to establish the system of paper debits and credits that is still in use today. Having taken control of the British money supply, the Rothschilds proceeded to aggressively pursue renewal of their charter for a central bank in the United States of America. That bank, was was to become the Federal Reserve Bank and part of the Federal Reserve System which in effect controlled and implemented the monetary policy of the country: a country where a duped people had failed to recognise that they were not citizens in a democracy, but rather wretched subjects in a declining plutocracy where the widening divide between the very rich who had made it, and the very poor who never would, had irrevocably damaged American social structures and shattered all illusions of the quintessential American dream …

A dream that had metamorphosed into a nightmare where over 42 million American adults of whom 20 percent hold high school diplomas, cannot read; where 50 million more can only read at a fourth or fifth-grade level; where some 30 percent of the nation's population is illiterate or barely literate; where the number of illiterates is increasing annually by an estimated two million; where over 30 percent of high school graduates and 42 percent of college graduates never read a book after they leave school; where 80 percent of the American families will not buy a book this year; where most of those illiterates will not bother to vote; where those illiterates who do vote, will do so on the basis of the worthless slogans of reassuring political propaganda that compensates for their lack of cognitive and critical thinking skills; and where even those who are presumably literate retreat in droves into the malignant consequences of living in an image-based culture.

> *"For the present age, which prefers the sign to the thing signified, the copy to the original, representation to reality, the appearance to the essence … illusion only is sacred, truth profane."*
> **Ludwig Feuerbach (1804–1872)**

3

Saturday, 5 December

10th Arrondissement, Paris, France

The Café on the Rue Martel was the second one within the 10th. arrondissement that Malek Bennabi had visited during the past week and as on the previous occasion his contact, Pierre, was already seated at one of the tables with feigned absent-mindedness toying with what was left of his coffee and Pain au chocolat. Without showing any sign of recognition Malek sauntered over to the table and gestured enquiringly towards one of the empty seats before sitting down and placing his canvas holdall under the table next to a similar one belonging to Pierre. Neither of them spoke and shortly after Malek had ordered and been served with his *café noir,* Pierre asked the waitress for *l'addition,* left eight euros in the saucer as payment and gratuity, rose from the table, picked up Malek's holdall instead of his own, and without so much as a glance at Malek, nonchalantly walked out of the café.

As Malek sipped his coffee he unobtrusively made a mental note of the other customers so that when he left the café he could check he was not being followed. Despite his lack of concern over such a possibility due to his unreserved contempt for France's largest and most powerful intelligence agency, the Direction générale de la sécurité intérieure – General Directorate for Internal Security (DGSI) – Malek nonetheless always took precautions to remain well below their security radar. The DSGI was charged with wide-ranging responsibilities including counterespionage, counterterrorism, countering cybercrime, and surveillance of potentially threatening groups, organisations, and social phenomena.

When he had finished his coffee some fifteen minutes later, Malek left the café and walked southwards on Rue Martel which being somewhat narrow, enabled him to easily remain aware of what was going on around him as he was also wearing a pair of rear vision surveillance sunglasses. He turned left on Rue Des Petites Ecuries, walked to the nearby Chateau D'eau Metro station, and caught a Line 4 train to Château Rouge in the 18th arrondissement where he lived in a very modest studio apartment in the Arab Quarter just off the Boulevard Barbès.

Once in the apartment, Malek dropped the holdall on the floor, took the iPhone from his pocket, and viewed the photos he had taken of the room before going out. He always took some photos before leaving so that on his return he could check that nothing had been disturbed and that there was no sign of entry. After satisfying himself that nothing had been moved and that the drawers he had randomly left partly open were exactly in the same position, he deleted the photos, drew shut the window curtains, and switched on the light.

Malek put the holdall on the table, unzipped it, took out the large manila envelope which he already knew contained €20,000 in fifty Euro notes. He then took out the oblong-shaped parcel and unwrapped it to reveal a Czech-made VZ58 assault rifle – a gas operated, magazine fed, selective fire weapon capable of firing 800 rounds per minute – with shoulder sling, folding steel stock, and two empty lightweight alloy magazines with 30 round capacities. After expertly checking that the mechanism was oiled and operating smoothly, he carefully rewrapped the weapon in its tan-coloured heavy wax paper and placed it with the money back in the holdall which he was about to deliver to the brothers Aziz and Rashid Gharbi whom he had already previously supplied with one other similar VZ58 and two empty magazines. Nearer to the day scheduled for the attack, he would pick up another holdall with 120 rounds of ammunition along with an untraceable mobile phone, wires, detonators, and C-4 (RDX) plastic explosive which as he was aware was recommended in Al-Qaeda's standard curriculum of explosives training and was the explosive of choice for terrorist attacks.

Malek glanced at his watch to confirm he still had plenty of time to make his one o'clock meeting with the brothers who were somewhat unbalanced fanatics born of Algerian immigrant parents whom he had recruited for the forthcoming operation. The brothers – from a deprived area on the edge of the 19th arrondissement with no expectation of having a stake in French society – were ill-educated, frequently unemployed, marginalised, and had been initially dependent on petty crime before progressing to drug dealing and armed robbery. They had become potential terrorists after being motivated and radicalised by a charismatic revolutionary guru figure at a mosque in 19th arrondissement. Malek always made a point of meeting them at the conveniently located Marché Barbès, under the elevated Line 2 La Chapelle metro station on the Boulevard of the same name. Being mostly an enclave for Arabs and Africans, the market's frenetic bustle every Wednesday and Saturday provided an ideal and safe environment for their periodic furtive meetings.

Since coming to Paris two years earlier with a false passport as a British born citizen of Algerian parents, part of Malek's cover had included working in a wine bar on the Rue de Dunkerque in the 18th arrondissement. His fluency in Arabic, credible knowledge of the Koran, and a passionate interest in Middle Eastern politics had enabled him to gradually become firmly embedded within the Muslim Arab community.

Before being sent to Paris as a "sleeper," Malek had earned his spurs by attending a terrorist training camp run by the

Tehrik-e-Taliban Pakistan (TTP) in Pakistan where groups of about twenty men were trained at any given time. Enrolment in such militant training programs was quite difficult especially for foreigners who – as a result of security breaches leading to casualties including innocent civilians from U.S. drone strikes – were understandably suspected of possibly being spies. For those who passed the screening process, each day's training invariably began with morning prayers towards Mecca followed by a talk on the important significance of jihad. Physical drills and operational training were then provided during the day by veteran jihadists, or occasionally by former members of Pakistan's Directorate for Inter-Services Intelligence (ISI). Recruits were taught how to handle small arms such as AK-47s, PK machine guns, and rocket-propelled grenade launchers (RPGs). They were also instructed in tactics for attacking military convoys and for planting mines. Better than average students such as Malek were also given additional specialised training in bomb-making and operational security. Evening training sessions were reserved for indoctrination that included hours of viewing videos of Western atrocities against Muslims so as to reinforce the recruits' motivation for a jihad.

Of all the various religious and secular terrorist movements, Jihadi terrorism was regarded as being one of the most dangerous because it combined Islamic ideology with Islamic texts – which being open to different interpretations – allowed jihadi terrorists to adopt an extremist interpretation to justify their use of gratuitous violence under the pretence of preserving Allah's rule, defending Islam, and creating a Caliphate (a form of Islamic government led by a caliph). That, however, was not the sole reason behind the rise of jihadism and the more than likely main motivational factors included the historical, the ideological, the socio-cultural, and the political narratives.

The historical narrative concerned the Middle Ages (5th – 15th centuries) superiority of the Muslim world which was more advanced militarily, philosophically, and scientifically than was Christianity or other leading civilisations. Consequently the rise of Western Christianity as an enlarged and very powerful imperialistic civilisation proved to be the main factor contributing to the decline of a once formidable Islamic world. For Jihadists, therefore, the use of violence to defend Islam was a justified means of opposing Western globalisation.

Ideologically, by endeavouring to motivate and collectively unify different individuals with the common purpose of protecting Islam, jihadi terrorism legitimised the pursuit of its objectives, and paved the way for jihadists to employ violence for the achievement of their goals. Such extremist interpretation of Islamic texts by Jihadists, however, had the negative effect of providing critics of Islam with the opportunity to claim that jihadism was an extension of the intolerant and violent religion of Islam.

The defence of Islamic socio-cultural values also served as a motivational factor for the emergence of jihadism whose adherents viewed and reacted to the world in accordance with a perceived set of ideas, institutions, values, regulations, and symbols. Because the concept of "community" was very dominant amongst Muslims, they did not regard themselves as individuals but as part of the community that could legitimately use violence in opposing Western influence and power.

The political narrative which told of the injustice and suffering endured by Muslims was another important factor helping to motivate and contribute to the rise of jihadi terrorism which regarded Western colonialism as being responsible for demolishing the concept and possibility of a political reunification of the Muslim world under a worldwide Caliphate rule. The West, led by the U.S., was also blamed for the deliberate Israeli instigated division of the Arab world with "regime changes" that favoured Western geopolitical and economic interests; for the continued humiliation and persecution of the Palestinian people by Israel; for the U.S.-led Western imperialism that inflicted unjust and severe hardships on the world's Muslims with the presence of Western troops in countries such as Afghanistan, Iraq, and elsewhere in the Muslim world; and for its unconscionable support of reprehensible and repressive Middle Eastern regimes such as that of Saudi Arabia.

Saudi Arabia's regional mischief, on the other hand, was designed to retain the House of Saud royal family's complete control over the nation's oil wealth and people. This secretive dynasty, consisting of thousands of descendants of Muhammad bin Saud, his brothers, and the current ruling faction of descendants of Abdulaziz bin Abdul Rahman Al Saud, enjoyed the power of an absolute monarchy with no political parties or national elections. Any challenging political activity or dissent was severely dealt with by a judicial system that lacked jury trials and observed few human rights formalities. Those arrested – usually not given a reason for their arrest or access to a lawyer – were subjected to abuse and torture that lasted until a confession was extracted. The freedom of thought and action for Saudis was further restricted by the attentions of the *mutaween* – government-recognised religious police – whose warped sense of morality frequently intruded on citizen privacy and crossed the bounds of sanity. The idea of an "Arab Spring" in neighbouring countries had therefore been an abhorrent concept for the Saudi rulers who took steps to ensure the contagion of freedom did not cross over onto Saudi territory.

Consequently Saudi Arabia, with covert Israeli assistance, was causing chaos and bloodshed in Middle Eastern and North African countries by providing millions-of-dollars-worth of armaments to Al-Qaeda and other Takfiri networks – Muslims accusing other Muslims of apostasy – that were destabilising and destroying once proud civilisations in Iraq, Lebanon, Libya, and Syria by fomenting sectarian unrest. By serving its own interests, Saudi Arabia was also unwittingly helping to fulfil Israel's desire for political instability and chaos (divide and conquer) in the predominantly Muslim countries that surround it. From the Saudi perspective, Israel's existence as a state served to have Gulf state Arab populations focus on Israel as the enemy rather than their own autocratic monarchies who were not legally bound or restricted by constitutions.

Saudi Arabia's motive for interference in Syria for example, was its desire to neutralise Iran's regional influence. All that talk about supporting democracy in Syria was just a political pantomime with the actual objective being the installation in Damascus of a regime subservient to Saudi Arabia – which in turn meant being subservient and subject to the geopolitical control of the U.S., Israel, and tag-along allies who constituted the hostile imperialist thrust against Iran. Britain, France, and the U.S. had in the meantime continued to diligently claim that they were supporting "a pro-democracy uprising" – a euphemism for regime change – in Syria which of course was to be expected from those who hypocritically assert they were "championing" freedom and human rights. Such claims, however, were nothing more than a Western criminal conspiracy that also happened to both coincide with Israel's plans and to to serve the interests of the crude, feudal-style Gulf state dictators whom the West cherished for their equally crude oil. The jihadist cause was consequently one in which Malek Bennabi was wholeheartedly involved and especially with regard to current plans for teaching the West a lesson with another terrorist attack.

8th Arrondissement, Paris, France

After exchanging holdalls with Malek and leaving the café, Pierre – a man whose unremarkable features and manner ensured that he was invariably unnoticed – walked to the nearby carpark on Rue Du Faubourg-Poissonnière where he picked up his somewhat undistinguished Renault Clio and drove to his apartment in the Quartier de l'Europe in the 8th Arrondissement. Despite his deferential manner, Pierre nonetheless very firmly discouraged any sociality with his neighbours in the apartment block. He did not own his apartment which like numerous others in cities all over the world had been either rented on a long term lease or purchased outright for Mossad's use. The apartment's door had been explosive-proofed, the windows blast resistant, and the glass was capable of deflecting scanners. Pierre was a Mossad *katsa*.

Mossad was the Israeli intelligence service responsible for planning and carrying out special operations beyond Israel's borders; covert overseas activities including intelligence gathering; development and maintenance of special diplomatic and other advantageous relations; preventing the development and procurement of non-conventional weapons by nations deemed to be hostile to Israel such as Iraq and Iran; preventing terrorist acts against Israeli targets abroad; bringing Jews "home" from countries where there was no official Aliya Jewish Agency for Israel; and producing strategic, political and operational intelligence.

Pierre had been given his latest assignment in Paris six months earlier because of previous false flag operation successes when his fluency in Arabic, French, and German stood him in good stead variously as a businessman, software sales representative, freelance photographer, and even travel guidebook author while using different aliases, "washed" passports, and biographical details meticulously compiled by Mossad researchers. His value and success as an agent were primarily due to feline characteristics which included a patient predatory instinct, a sense of perception for human strengths and weaknesses, and inordinate powers of persuasion which were essential qualities for the successful manipulation of people.

It was those qualities which had enabled him for more than a decade to be Mossad's most effective agent in helping to covertly establish the Islamic State of Iraq and Syria (ISIS) with recruitment, weapons supply, financial support, and the ideology that played a crucial role in providing terrorists with both the initial motive for action and the lens through which they focussed on their selected targets.

Such targets – considered to be legitimate and deserving of being attacked – included both individuals and institutions perceived as being opposed to the ideologically-based tenets and moral framework of ISIS. Ideology-based propaganda also provided terrorists and the rest of the world with justification for the use of barbaric violence by transferring – as it does with Israel's "self-defence" justification for criminal brutality against the Palestinian people – the responsibility onto their victims who were portrayed as having "forced" their attackers to respond violently.

As a consequence of a zionist controlled/intimidated mainstream media and an invariably somnambulant general public in the West, hardly anyone ever questioned why Israel was primarily and apoplectically concerned over Palestinians, Iranians, Syrians, and the Lebanese, rather than with al-Qaeda, al-Nusra, and ISIS? Why did such groups wage wars against Israel's Arab enemies but not against Israel itself? To begin with, the head of Muslim Brotherhood responsible for leading the war against the Syrian regime happened to reside not in Beirut, or Cairo, or Riyadh, or Tehran, but in Tel Aviv. The reality was that by providing medical aid, basic weapons training, and outright military assistance, the highly principled state of Israel was more of a benefactor and friend to Muslim terrorist groups than were the Arab regimes that Israel regarded as its mortal enemies. Furthermore, according to a think tank contracted to NATO and the Israeli government, the West should not destroy the extremist Islamist group ISIS – which was committing genocide and ethnically cleansing minority groups in Syria and Iraq – because the so-called Islamic State "can be a useful tool in undermining" Iran, Hezbollah, Syria and Russia.

Israel's covert instigation by Mossad of death squad invasions across the Arab world were carried out by religious fanatics, semi illiterate savages, and insane criminals with little knowledge of Islam who nonetheless ironically retained their avowed hatred for Israel because they were either ignorant of the fact that Israel was their main sponsor, or were simply incapable of comprehending anything beyond what they were told by their manipulative leaders who were regular recipients of Israeli benevolence which political incorrectness could only describe as "blatant Israeli bribery." In reality the only consideration and main motivation for most Jihadists was the prospect of receiving the proverbial "thirty pieces of silver" without bothering to ask questions

Consequently Israel's penchant for blackmailing, bribing, or buying recruits for its strategy of "smoke and mirrors" had enabled it to cunningly create Hamas – its supposed archenemy – for the purpose of disuniting the Palestinian Liberation Organisation (PLO) and Fatah; had enabled it to become directly involved in implementing Islamic terrorism in other Middle Eastern countries; and had enabled it to establish "fake" al-Qaeda groups within territory under its control so as to justify its ill-treatment of the Palestinian people.

So despite being apparently engaged in lethal hostilities with Hamas, it was the Israeli government of then-Prime Minister Menachem Begin which in 1978 – in a calculated attempt to undermine the PLO and Yasser Arafat's leadership – approved the application of Sheik Ahmad Yassin to establish a "humanitarian" organisation known as the Islamic Association, or Mujama. The fundamentalist Muslim Brotherhood formed the core of this Islamist group which eventually blossomed into

Hamas with help from Israel which – according to current and former U.S. intelligence officials – began in the late 1970s to give direct and indirect financial aid to Hamas so as to use it as a counterbalance to the secular PLO by exploiting a competing religious alternative. Israelis were also known to have hosted and directed terrorist mercenary training camps in their own country in order to produce tailor-made mercenaries for use in the Arab world.

Before being transferred to Paris, Pierre had been instrumental in initiating an operation that involved Ansar Beit al-Maqdis – the Champions of the Holy Site, or Champions of Jerusalem – a militant group from the Sinai Peninsula that operated from within Sinai-Rafah. The group – which was reportedly affiliated with the regionally active Muslim Brotherhood whilst simultaneously pledging allegiance to ISIS – had for many months intimidated civilians on both sides of the border with lethal attacks. As a consequence of these attacks, the Egyptian army had ordered the evacuation of civilians inhabiting the town of Rafah that was located between the Egypt-Gaza border.

By evacuating Rafah and enforcing a buffer zone along the 12 kilometre-long border, Egypt hoped to secure the border, stop the flow of arms to militant groups, and prevent further attacks in the peninsula. Egypt's buffer zone affected over 10,000 residents, swallowed up much farming land, and cut through both neighbourhoods resulting in thousands of Egyptians and Gaza Palestinians becoming homeless. Egypt's action – yet another example of it's continued disregard for the plight of Palestinians – had also effectively shut Gaza's last remaining crossing into the outside world with Rafah itself being divided between Gaza and Egypt. Israel welcomed the creation of the zone which mirrored its own enforcement in 2001 of a similar zone around Gaza that was a three kilometre wide strip taking up 44 percent of Gaza's territory.

Though the much-hyped Mossad was relatively small compared to many other intelligence services, it had enhanced its operational effectiveness by building a network of overseas assets and sayanim (volunteer aides/helpers) who assisted in local intelligence gathering and espionage operations. Sayanim were unofficial Jewish foreign operatives who were recruited on the emotionally charged premise that by providing Israel and its agents with assistance and/or support as and when required within the capacity of their own professions – be they, bankers, businessmen, civil servants, community leaders, corporate managers, doctors, journalists, politicians etc. – they would be helping to save Jewish lives. Sayanim, whose ranks included members of Boards of Deputies for Jews, the highest governing bodies of the national communities, were not paid for their services which they simply performed out of a sense of devotion and duty to Israel.

Katsas, or field intelligence officers, amongst other duties, supervised the sayanim whose help could range from the humdrum to that of strategic importance such as providing accommodation, medical care, logistical support, and finance for operations. Sayanim kept in regular contact with their *katsa* supervisors whom they regularly provided with local news and information including gossip, rumours, items on the radio or TV, articles or reports in newspapers, and anything else that might be of use to Mossad and its agents. Sayanim also collected technical data and all kinds of other overt intelligence.

Despite being regular and supposedly upstanding members of their communities, sayanim were nonetheless leading double-lives by being closely involved with the Mossad intelligence network. Such involvement – especially in the U.S. where questions of loyalty have been raised as a result of many prominent American Jews also having Israeli citizenship – had resulted in diaspora Jews being accused of having a stronger allegiance to Israel than to their native countries. Criticism of this nature was simply dismissed by Jews as being anti-Semitic. Intelligence sources had estimated that the global sayanim network numbered in excess of 100,000.

Assets on the other hand, unlike the sayanim, did not have to be Jewish and have included former and current British prime Ministers, former and current French Presidents, former and current parliamentarians in European countries, and certainly most members of the bicameral U.S. Congress. The use of assets – or unofficial "agents of influence" who worked in politics, the media, or other significant professions – enabled Israel to have influence exerted on its behalf to the extent of ensuring that its illegal actions and policies were always viewed in political circles and reported by the media in the most positive and glowing terms. Mossad's perceived success and renown – like that of Israel itself – was to a great extent due to its being allowed get away with the kind of illegal activities that would not be tolerated from the intelligence agencies of other countries.

Pierre's Paris assignment was the implementation of another Israeli false flag operation which inevitably would appear not only as anti-Semitic, but also as an Islamic terrorist assault against the cherished "freedoms" which hoodwinked Western citizens believed they enjoyed. As a result of Pierre's involvement in such operations, he knew from experience that success was dependent on a number of important factors including a command structure with shadowy, unidentified individuals who instigated and financed the operation; recruitment of one or more low IQ simpleton fall guy or guys whom the mainstream media would focus on as the alleged perpetrator/perpetrators as was the case with Lee Harvey Oswald in the assassination of President John F. Kennedy in November 1963; the use of highly trained professionals who while organising and instigating the attacks, personally remained anonymous and unseen so that culpability was attributed to the fall guys; and finally an essential control of, or influence over the corporate mainstream media whose compliance in releasing misinformation served to deceive the general public into believing that the low IQ simpletons were the ones responsible rather than the unseen, elusive instigators and their professional operatives.

Israel's chutzpah ability to conduct such operations with impunity was substantiated by the fact that even when its false flag operations had failed or been exposed, it had escaped retribution while still gaining some degree of success as was the case with the Lavon Affair, an Israeli covert operation codenamed Operation Susannah conducted in 1954 in Egypt and involving recruitment of Egyptian Jews to plant bombs inside Egyptian, American, and British-owned civilian targets, cinemas, libraries and American educational centres. The bombings were to be blamed on the Muslim Brotherhood, Egyptian Communists, nationalists, and sundry malcontents with a view to creating an environment of violent instability that would induce the British government to retain its occupying troops in Egypt's Suez Canal Zone. As it turned out the only casualty of the operation occurred when the bomb one of them was carrying to place in a movie theatre prematurely ignited in his pocket and led to the group's capture, the eventual suicide of two of the conspirators, and the trial, conviction, and execution of two others.

Though the operation was a failure, it nonetheless served Israel's purpose by triggering a chain of events in Middle East power relationships that have reverberated to this day including the initial public trial and conviction of the eight Egyptian Jews who carried out the false flag operation; a retaliatory military incursion by Israel into Gaza that killed 39 Egyptians; a subsequent Egyptian–Soviet arms deal that angered American and British leaders who consequently withdrew previously pledged financial support for the building of the Aswan Dam;

the announced nationalisation of the Suez Canal by Egypt's President Nasser in retaliation for the withdrawal of that support; and the ensuing 1956 failed Tripartite invasion of Suez by Israel, Britain, and France in an attempt to topple Nasser. In the wake of that failed invasion, France had expanded and accelerated its ongoing nuclear cooperation with Israel, which eventually enabled the Jewish state to build nuclear weapons despite opposition by U.S. President John F. Kennedy in whose subsequent assassination Israel's Mossad was involved.

More than a decade later on June 8, 1967, deliberately unmarked Israeli fighter aircraft and Navy torpedo boats had attacked the USS Liberty – a naval technical research ship in international waters north of the Sinai Peninsula – killing 34 crew members, wounding 170 others, and severely damaging the ship with a view to blaming the Egyptians for the attack so as to bring the U.S. into the war on Israel's side. Israel's explanation that the vessel was thought to have been Egyptian was subsequently repeatedly contradicted by the ship's American officers who were certain that Israel's intention was to sink them; by an Israeli lead pilot who claimed to have immediately recognised the ship as American, to have informed his headquarters but was told to ignore the American flag and continue the attack, to have refused to do so and on returning to base was arrested; by the then U.S. Ambassador to Lebanon who confirmed that the Embassy's radio monitoring had heard that pilot's protestations; by a dual-citizen Israeli major who was in the war room and asserted that there had been no doubt whatsoever that the USS Liberty was American; by a former Navy attorney involved in the military investigation of the attack who claimed that the enquiry had been instructed by President Johnson and Secretary of Defence Robert McNamara to "conclude that the attack was a case of 'mistaken identity' despite overwhelming evidence to the contrary"; and by a former Chiefs of Staff chairman who after spending a year investigating the incident concluded that it was "one of the classic all-American cover-ups ... Why would our government put Israel's interests ahead of our own?"

The assault, however, had to this day remained as the only maritime incident in U.S. history where U.S. military forces were killed without there ever being an investigation by the U.S. Congress or justice for the victims and their families. The American government's treacherous failure to properly investigate the attack, had sent a clear message to the Israelis that if the American government – led by a gutless President Johnson who was fearful of ending up like his predecessor John F. Kennedy – did not have the courage to punish them for the murder of American servicemen, then they could get away with anything.

The failure by a U.S. government to fully investigate an attack against America was subsequently repeated on a much larger scale in the case of the September 11, 2001 – known as 9/11 – coordinated attacks on symbolic U.S. landmarks including the twin towers of the World Trade Centre (WTC) in New York's Lower Manhattan. Though regarded as symbols of American power dominating the New York skyline, the WTC buildings were not only costing the New York Port Authority millions of dollars in upkeep while tenancy was declining, but were also posing a serious health hazard resulting from their steel beams having been sprayed with fireproof asbestos decades earlier during construction. So after years of litigation which it lost in 2001, the Port Authority became liable for the removal of the asbestos which could have cost it $billions. But despite that liability, Larry Silverstein – a Jewish businessman, owner of Silverstein Properties, and a very close friend of Benjamin Netanyahu – engineered purchase of the WTC months before 9/11 for a paltry $115 million through fellow Zionist billionaire Lewis Eisenberg, Chair of the Republican National Committee and head of the New York Port Authority.

Silverstein then made a habit of having breakfast and coffee with his daughter every morning at the WTC's spectacular "Windows On The World" restaurant, but luckily for him on the morning of September 11, 2001 he just happened to have an appointment with a dermatologist. Equally fortuitous for Silverstein, was the fact that he had already not only doubled the buildings' insurance coverage, but had also made sure that such coverage included acts of terrorism so that with Judaic chutzpah he then filed a law suit against the insurance company demanding double payment since two planes had crashed in the WTC's twin towers. Silverstein was then blessed with more unbelievable good fortune when virtually all 9/11 litigation was funnelled through the court of Judge Alvin Hellerstein, who like Like Silverstein and Eisenberg, was also a rabid Zionist with close ties to Israel. Needless to say Silverstein's claim was acknowledged by the court and he was paid $4,550,000,000.

Coincidentally, Hellerstein's lawyer son and sister had both emigrated from the U.S. to orthodox Zionist settlements in the Occupied Territories. Both Hellerstein and his son used to work for the well-known Jewish law firm of Stroock, Stroock & Lavan LLP who apart from having a long history of representing the Rothschilds and other high-level Zionists, also teamed up with the Civil Court, Legal Aid Society, and City Bar Association to establish a project in response to thousands of small businesses that were physically damaged or otherwise disrupted by 9/11.

In a 2002 Public Broadcasting Service (PBS) documentary "America Rebuilds," Silverstein admitted to complicity in the controlled demolition of WTC-7, a 47-story skyscraper that collapsed in 6.5 seconds and for which he collected a further $861 million from insurers. Demolition experts have since contended that the manner of the collapse of all WTC buildings could only have occurred with the buildings having been wired for demolition and there is no shortage of information on the internet showing Israeli involvement with Israeli/Jewish fingerprints all over the 9/11 attacks.

Apart from Silverstein, a few of the other Jewish players in the 9/11 saga included Ronald S. Lauder – a member of the board of directors of New York's privatisation committee – who pushed for privatisation of the WTC; Lewis Eisenberg – Chairman of the New York Port Authority – who authorised the lease of the WTC complex to Silverstein; Jules Kroll – owner of Kroll Associates – which had the contract to run security at the WTC; Jerome Hauer – who ran Kroll Associates – and had run Mayor Rudy Guiliani's office of emergency management from 1996 to 2000; Rabbi Dov Zakheim – of System Planning Corporation which possessed the technology to take over planes and fly them by remote control – who while Pentagon comptroller from May 4, 2001 to March 10, 2004 oversaw the disappearance of two large sums of money from the Pentagon with Some $2.3 trillion being reported missing by Secretary of Defence Donald Rumsfeld; Michael B. Mukasey – the judge who oversaw the litigation between Silverstein and insurance companies in the wake of 9/11 – and ensured that Silverstein was awarded billions of dollars; Michael Chertoff – a dual U.S.-Israeli citizen – who was assistant attorney general for the criminal division of the Justice Department before becoming Director of Homeland Security; Richard Perle – otherwise known as the "prince of darkness" – who was the Chairman of Pentagon's Defence Policy Board at the time of 9/11 and had previously in the 1970s been expelled from Sen. Henry Jackson's office after the NSA caught him passing classified documents to Israel; Paul Wolfowitz – who was Deputy Defence Secretary – and a member of the Defence Policy Board in the Pentagon at the time of 9/11; Eliot Abrams – a key National Security Council Advisor despite being convicted of lying to congress in the Iran/Contra Affair but later pardoned by President Bush – who was associated with criminal Zionist/

Pro-Israel think tanks AEI, PNAC, CSP, and JINSA as well as Perle, Feith, Wolfowtiz, and Bill Kristol.

Shortly before 9/11, over 140 Israelis were arrested for suspected espionage with many of them posing as art students. The suspects had targeted or penetrated military bases, the DEA, FBI, Secret Service, ATF, US Customs, IRS, INS, EPA, Interior Department, US Marshal's Service, various U.S. attorneys' offices, secret government offices and even the unlisted, private homes of law enforcement/intelligence officials. Most of the suspects served in military intelligence, electronic surveillance intercept and/or explosive ordinance units. Dozens of Israelis were arrested in American mall kiosks selling toys, acting as a front for a spying operation. Sixty detained suspects worked for the Israeli company AMDOCS which provided most directory assistance calls and almost all call records and billings services for the U.S. by virtue of its contracts with the 25 largest U.S. telephone companies.

Following 9/11, New York Mayor Rudolph "Rudy" Giuliani initiated the immediate removal with some 120 dump trucks of 1.5 million tons of still smouldering debris – containing body parts and vital evidence which was destroyed – with much of the mangled steel being hurriedly sifted and sold at a discount price to the Chinese firm Baosteel thereby preventing a thorough crime scene investigation of an attack that had caused the largest loss of life and property damage in U.S. history. Giuliani subsequently lied and changed his story about having received a warning about the collapse of the twin towers which he did not pass on to others.

Another consequence of 9/11 was the health hazard to the thousands already present at the scene and to the first responders from the emergency services who were engulfed by the poisonous spew of asbestos, benzene, cadmium, lead, mercury, and other particulates from which many are still suffering and continuing to die from cancer despite repeated reassurances at the time from Christine Todd Whitman, the administrator of the Environmental Protection Agency, that the air was safe to breathe with the level of contaminates being low or nonexistent: an audacious lie to which she has clung tenaciously to this day.

Suppression of the truth was orchestrated by the Bush administration with the President holding out for 441 days until November 27, 2002 – while actively resisting an enquiry and urging Senate Majority Leader Tom Daschle to limit an investigation by Congress – to establish a commission to investigate the tragic events of that day. The fact that the President wanted to limit the scope of any enquiry was confirmed by his initial choice of the megalomaniacal Henry Kissinger as Chairman whose squirming over the question of conflict of interest led to him to ingloriously step down. Undeterred, the Bush administration then collusively snuck in Zionist Jew Philip Zelikow – a former member of the previous Bush administration's National Security Council – as the dictatorial Commission Executive Director who by hiring all the Commission's staff and restricting the information available to its members, in effect exercised a criminal and subversive control over the direction and scope of the investigation. Henry Kissinger's replacement as chairman – former Republican Governor of New Jersey Thomas Kean – subsequently described the Commission as having been deliberately set up to fail by being, amongst other things, severely underfunded and rushed.

Unbeknown to other Commission members at the time was the fact – which did not become common knowledge until the final months of the Commission's investigation – that Philip Zelikow had authored a 31-page document in September 2002 entitled "The National Security Strategy of the United States" that had been submitted by the Bush administration to Congress. The document advocated that the U.S. must build and maintain military defences beyond challenge; must ensure that efforts to meet U.S. global security commitments and the protection of Americans were not impaired by the potential for investigations, inquiry, or prosecution by the International Criminal Court; and must declare a War on Terrorism Itself because "the enemy is not a single political regime or person or religion or ideology. The enemy is terrorism – premeditated, politically motivated violence perpetrated against innocents." Zelikow's document, which was a fundamental reversal of U.S. containment and deterrence principles, had obviously been written with Iraq in mind and it was uncanny how – whether by coincidence or design – that the occurrence of 9/11 and subsequent events just happened to fit in with Israel's plan for the division and destruction of its main Arab rivals in the Middle East.

In his book *At the Centre of the Storm: My Years at the CIA,* George Tenet, the agency's former director stated that on the day after 9/11, he ran into Richard Perle, a leading neoconservative and the head of the Defence Policy Board, coming out of the White House. Tenet claimed that Perle turned to him and said: "Iraq has to pay a price for what happened yesterday. They bear responsibility." This, was despite the fact Tenet stated, that "the intelligence then and now" showed "no evidence of Iraqi complicity" in the attacks. A s a result of the ensuing and incessant instigation of Zionist-neoconservatives within the ranks of the American government, the U.S. led the illegal invasion of Iraq.

The New York Times reported that when "asked tonight what the attack meant for relations between the United States and Israel, Benjamin Netanyahu, the former prime minister, replied, "It's very good." Then he edited himself: "Well, not very good, but it will generate immediate sympathy." He predicted that the attack would "strengthen the bond between our two peoples, because we've experienced terror over so many decades, but the United States has now experienced a massive haemorrhaging of terror."

Pierre's planned attack against an ostensibly Jewish target in Paris was to be a follow-up to the Israeli PM's arrogant and ominous warning that the French parliament would be making a "grave mistake" if it voted for recognition of a Palestinian state. The attack was intended to help forestall the recent increase in European public opinion support for a Palestinian state – the very thought of which was incompatible with the Zionist Apartheid ideology of a Greater Israel (Eretz Yisrael) for Jews only – by fanning the flames of Islamophobia which would in turn hamper and discredit Palestinian aspirations. Though Pierre had no illusions about the forthcoming Paris attack matching the propaganda benefits Israel derived from 9/11, he was nonetheless confident that a series of far more modest attacks in Paris and other European cities would achieve the objective of further entrenching abhorrence for, and fear of Islam as the religion of hate amongst the blinkered and brainwashed Western masses, and impel France into becoming a militarised state rife with suspicion, fear, and racial hatred.

4

Sunday, 6 December

London, England

The Chief Executive of The Board of Deputies of British Jews did not usually go to the board's office in the north London mews on Sundays, but today was one of those exceptions because of the current campaign to discredit the British Labour Party – whose new leader had in the past described Israeli politicians as "criminal" and criticised the BBC's coverage of Palestine – by accusing it of being rife with anti-Semitism. She was about to start work when she received a phone call from the Board's Communications Officer telling her to go online to check out Mark Banner's latest article about Israel. She wasted no time in doing so and was outraged by what she read.

Israel's Historic Tendency For Blackmail, Bribery, And Bullying

Mark Banner
Sunday, 6 December

On 26 November 1947, when it became apparent to Zionists and their supporters that the UN vote on the Partition of Palestine would be short of the required two thirds majority in the General Assembly, they filibustered for a postponement until after Thanksgiving thereby gaining time to threaten the loss of aid to nations such as Greece – which planned on voting against – into changing their votes. U.S. President Truman, who was also threatened with loss of Jewish support in the upcoming Presidential election, later noted that:

"The facts were that not only were there pressure movements around the United Nations unlike anything that had been seen there before, but that the White House, too, was subjected to a constant barrage. I do not think I ever had as much pressure and propaganda aimed at the White House as I had in this instance. The persistence of a few of the extreme Zionist leaders – actuated by political motives and engaging in political threats – disturbed and annoyed me."

On 29 November 1947 the UN voted for a modified Partition Plan – despite Arab opposition on grounds that it violated UN charter principles of national self-determination – recommending the creation of independent Arab and Jewish States with a Special International Regime for the City of Jerusalem. The resolution's adoption prompted the 1947/48 conflict including atrocities by Zionist terror gangs whose genocidal brutality was responsible for the murder of thousands of unarmed Palestinian civilians and the forced exodus of more than 750,000 others. At the time, the consensus of world opinion was that Israel's contentious creation had been permitted as a conscious and wilful act of Holocaust compensation which included toleration of its crimes against humanity. Since then, Israel has steadfastly adhered to that successful tactic of blackmail, bribery, and bullying to suppress and silence – with accusations of anti-Semitism and Holocaust denial – any criticism of its blatant human rights violations and arrogant disregard for international Law.

The fear of being branded an anti-Semite is now a universal phobia which Zionist Apartheid Israel reinforces with

Gestapo-style vigilance that has permeated through corporate media outlets, parliaments and universities. This is most evident in the United States where the American Israel Public Affairs committee (AIPAC) is active on college campuses with a Political Leadership Development Program of pro-Israel activities including reports on faculty members, students, and college organisations critical of Israeli policies. The "miscreants" – exposed in AIPAC's College Guide and the pro-Israel Campus Watch – are then subject to harassment, suspension, or even dismissal.

AIPAC's lobbying of the U.S. government includes provision of in-depth policy position papers focusing on Israel's illusionary strategic importance to the United States. The Congressional Record is monitored daily and comprehensive records are kept of all members' speeches, informal comments, constituent correspondence, and voting patterns on Israel-related issues. AIPAC itself estimates that well over half of Congress and Senate members (who place Israeli interests above those of their own country) can always be relied upon for unflinching support. Every year some 70 to 90 of them are rewarded with "AIPAC-funded" junkets to Israel. The irony behind AIPAC's erosion of American democracy is that it is in effect financed – with almost $4 billion annual U.S. aid to Israel – by American taxpayers of whom 50 million are living below the poverty line with 47 million of them receiving food stamps.

The insidious cancer of AIPAC is also being spread with more free junkets by "Friends of Israel" groups in most European parliaments; by the Australian Israel & Jewish Affairs Council (AIJAC); and by the recently formed South African Israel Public Affairs Committee (SAIPAC) which will endeavour to silence criticism by a people already familiar with the iniquities of Apartheid.

Furthermore, the mainstream corporate media – apart from being mostly owned or influenced by friends of Israel – is also fettered by the fear of offending the Zionist lobby which insists that even the term "Apartheid Israel" is anti-Semitic. This stranglehold on the media is tightened even further by Zionist media watch organisations such as Committee for Accuracy in Middle East Reporting in America (CAMERA) and Britain's BBC Watch, who waste no time in vilifying any negative reports on Israel.

Despite being a nation in a profound existential crisis, Chutzpah Israel continues claiming to be a Jewish social democracy with exemplary ethical values. Such claims serve as a smokescreen for the endless lying, cheating, stealing, and murdering while ensuring a lack of accountability for its heinous crimes by undermining the process of Western democratic governance. Instead of unconditionally condemning Israel for its latest assault on the Palestinians in Gaza, Western leaders confirm they have been bought to betray the moral values of their constituents by mealy-mouthing the false premise of "Israel's right to defend itself" as a Jewish state.

Israel has no such right – God-given or otherwise – because for almost 70 years it has been the aggressor with a genocidal brutality matching that of the Nazis. Zionism's goal of creating a "Greater Israel" requires the "Final Solution" expulsion of non-Jews even if it means that – as was recently enunciated by the Israeli Interior Minister – "Gaza should be bombed into the Middle Ages." During World War Two, innumerable lives and resources were expended to defeat Nazism. Yet today, nothing is done while an even more insidious form of evil slowly destroys the concept of democratic governance and what little is left of human decency.

The time has come for the "Silent Majority" to finally give voice to their outrage – without demonstrations or violence – by repeatedly emailing their elected representatives. Lowlife politicians who have their inbox regularly swamped with thousands of emails will quickly realise that ignoring the will of the majority to serve minority Zionist and corporate interests alone, will not be enough to get them reelected. The Palestinian people should not be made to continue paying for the West's guilt complex over the Holocaust.

5

Wednesday, 9 December

Talbiyah, West Jerusalem

Despite being comfortably retired in his $1.5 million upmarket garden apartment – with bespoke fitted furniture, a swimming pool, and a well-watered garden with manicured lawns – on Disraeli Street in West Jerusalem's wealthy neighbourhood of Talbiyah where important government officials lived, Abe Goldman nonetheless always got up at seven every day for a leisurely morning coffee while catching up with the latest news and then assiduously reading his emails. As a South African born and raised Jew, Goldman was already familiar with the ramifications of being an unwelcome colonist in an Apartheid state where displacement and oppression of the indigenous population was an essential element of colonialism that had to be continually justified to the rest of the world by controlling and influencing its perception into accepting the unacceptable.

Goldman's meteoric rise in Johannesburg had followed his graduation with a degree in mercantile law from the University of the Free State Faculty of Law in Bloemfontein. After spending three years with a commercial law firm he had joined the legal department of a mining conglomerate that controlled some 1,200 subsidiaries involved in everything from anthracite coal mining to the exploitation of the Zulu culture for tourism purposes.

His opportunity for career advancement had then fortuitously occurred in the early sixties when the United

Nations Security Council condemned Apartheid and established a voluntary arms embargo. As the range of sanctions against South Africa increased and persisted, it became imperative for both the Afrikaner government and business conglomerates to somehow circumvent the embargoes by finding both alternative sources of supply and export markets. Israel was consequently the most obvious first choice not only because of its South African Jewish business connections, but also because of the fact that both nations shared similar sociopolitical challenges.

During the early years that ensued its creation as a state, Israel had maintained friendly relations with numerous anti-apartheid African nations whose support at the UN General Assembly Israel required to counter Arab Muslim opposition. As African nations, however, gradually ceased supporting Israel whose Apartheid policies were viewed as being even harsher than those of Afrikaner South Africa, Israel was forced to seek an alternative African ally and it was with South Africa that an alliance of shared interests began to materialise. To start with both states had been established on land stolen from an indigenous majority; both were outnumbered and surrounded by enemies who had to be disunited and kept at bay with military force; and both were subject to regular condemnation by UN resolutions which in Israel's case were always vetoed by its superpower ally and politically lackadaisical lackey, the United States.

As pursuance of a trade alliance was of vital importance, Goldman was dispatched on his first ever trip to Israel on an exploratory mission as an unofficial envoy for both the South African government and corporate business interests. His most pressing objective was to secure from Israel a lifeline supply of munitions that were essential for the continued suppression of the South African Black majority. At one stage Israel had even agreed to sell South Africa nuclear weapons, but the offer had been eventually declined because of the prohibitive cost involved. Apart from brokering a munitions supply agreement which included using Israel as an intermediary to purchase arms from other countries that were otherwise off limits to South Africa, Goldman was also instrumental in arranging for South African agricultural products to be sent by air cargo flights to Israel where they would be repackaged and re-exported as being of Israeli origin. Such *Israeli* products would then end up on the shelves of major European supermarkets in contravention of the embargoes.

Goldman's service to the Afrikaner nation was finally acknowledged in 1983 when he became the only ever non-Afrikaner to become an honorary member of the Afrikaner Broederbond (Brotherhood) secret society which had been founded following the Second Anglo-Boer War of 1899 when the depression, severe droughts, and crop failures had forced many Afrikaners to work in the cities and mines as underclass labourers – a situation that served to heighten racial tensions which in those days existed between Afrikaners and Britons rather than Whites and Blacks. Enforced anglicisation of Afrikaner culture and the debate over whether or not to fight alongside the British in the First World War were also causes for debate and division amongst the Afrikaner people. It was therefore during that period of doubt and disillusion that the Afrikaner Broederbond was established in 1918 to work for the unification of the Afrikaner people and to bring about the Afrikaner National Party's eventual election victory in 1948.

Though Goldman had been impressed by how the destinies of many could be determined in secrecy by the conniving will of a few – because they were unseen, unheard, and unknown – he nonetheless realised that White minority rule through suppression of a Black majority would sooner or later have to come to an end. So as far as he had been concerned, Afrikanerdom was doomed to failure because it was evident to him that what Jews were getting away with in Palestine, the

Afrikaners could never hope to continue getting away with in South Africa. Afrikaners, unlike Jews, had not been the victims of a Holocaust that had been endlessly publicised, globally promoted and ruthlessly exploited; Afrikaner past suffering – a mere 26,000 (10% of the entire Afrikaner population) had died in British concentration camps during the Boer War – was not on a comparative scale to the Holocaust to have accumulated either the amount or kind of international sympathy that would condone continued human rights violations against an indigenous population; Afrikaners, unlike Israelis, lacked the benefit of having the support of U.S vetoes at the United Nations Assembly; Afrikaners did not have a dedicated global network of well financed lobbyists who could buy political influence, control mainstream media reporting, and suppress negative public opinion; and Afrikaners did not have Western politician agents of influence befouling the democratic process on their behalf while perfidiously supporting a concocted biblical Judaic pretension to the "Promised land."

By February 1987 Goldman had begun making arrangements to take advantage of the Israeli Law of Return, a basic tenet of Zionist ideology which granted every Jew in the world – including those who like their ancestors had never been to or had any connection with Israel – the right to settle in a land from which indigenous Palestinians had been terrorised and forcibly expelled by Zionist paramilitary forces. As a result there were now some seven million Palestinian refugees with no such "right of return" and who as stateless individuals were also being deprived of all the basic human rights that Zionist controlled Western governments were constantly and sanctimoniously claiming to be fighting for. In July 1988, Goldman and his family *returned* to Israel and became Israeli citizens. They had simply moved from one Apartheid state to another whose far more barbaric Apartheid policies had been piously packaged and sold to the world as the only principled democracy in the Middle East and staunch ally of Western nations some of whom had once been, or to some extent still were, colonial masters.

Shortly after settling in West Jerusalem and setting up his own law practice – and as a natural progression from his brief secret society experience in South Africa – Goldman joined the Holy City's only English-speaking Masonic Lodge. Freemasonry and Judaism had long shared a fixation with Solomon's Temple with Masonic lore alleging that Masonic origins dated back to the time of the legendary Hiram Abiff (referred to as Huram in the Bible), who as an architect and master artificer was an allegorical character with a prominent role in a play covertly enacted during initiation ceremonies into the Third Degree of Freemasonry.

"King Solomon sent to Tyre and brought Huram, whose mother was a widow from the tribe of Naphtali and whose father was a man of Tyre and a craftsman in bronze. Huram was highly skilled and experienced in all kinds of bronze work. He came to King Solomon and did all the work assigned to him."
1 Kings 7: 13-14

In the Masonic drama Abiff is murdered while visiting the temple by three dissatisfied and envious Fellow Crafts whom Abiff had refused to raise to the level of Master by divulging the Master Mason's secret password. Abiff's subsequent restoration to life was in keeping with the age-old storyline based on the legend of the ancient Egyptian god, Osiris, who after being murdered by his ambitious and jealous brother, was resurrected by his wife Isis who after various hazardous adventures then gave a "virgin birth" to a son Horus who subsequently avenged his father's murder. Consequently the concept of the "virgin birth" became an essential element for the creation of divine beings and Isis herself became the personification of that great feminine capacity to conceive and to give birth to new life. Drawings and sculptures depicting Isis suckling her child became the model for the Christian Madonna and Child, and many of the qualities that were originally attributed to Isis were then given to the Mother of Christ. In order to supplant popular pagan deities, the Christian Church Fathers had to ensure that their own man-made Christian idols had characteristics similar to those of the existing pagan deities whom they were intending to replace.

This trinity of Osiris, Isis, and Horus – which despite being a figment of creative human imagination – also became the obligatory prototype for other man-made gods. The portrayal of an eminent man or deity who as a member of a trinity, first perishes as the victim of an evil deed, and then resurrects into a greater glory, is by now an all too familiar theme that is featured in the lore and rituals of cults, secret fraternal organisations, and diverse religions including Christianity's trinity of Father, Son, and Holy Spirit.

So it was of no surprise that after retiring from his law practice in 2004, Goldman, maintained his contact with government officials to many of whom he was a confidante and policy advisor. Also because of his having been influenced by his time in South Africa, his Masonic membership, and his dedication to Judaism's dream of a Third Temple, Goldman cofounded the Hiramic Brotherhood of the Third Temple whose members were obliged to take solemn vows to work tirelessly for fulfilment of a dream that was based on a very tenuous link to the past.

Silwan, Occupied East Jerusalem

Various threadbare carpets covered the floor of the sitting room which contained an old wooden cupboard with several drawers; a large raffia basket bag for Miriam Hadawi's embroidery, a coffee table with a worn and stained top; a couple of padded folding chairs that had seen better days; a small bookshelf with a tattered Bible, several small religious statues, some well-thumbed reference works, a few children's books in English which Sami Hadawi was encouraging his children to learn, half a dozen framed family photographs; and an old sofa bed on which the children slept. As was the case every morning without fail, Sami Hadawi, his wife, and two children sat around the table with heads bowed as Sami thanked God for breakfast – usually consisting of the slightly leavened pita flatbread and homemade humous – which Sami and his wife knew was inadequate nourishment for growing children but were nonetheless fortunate enough to have. According to the United Nations International Children's Emergency Fund (UNICEF), many Palestinian children were anaemic with high levels of stunting due to protein-deficient diets. This was the consequence of the ever increasing difficulties of being able to obtain or afford basic protein foods such as chicken, fish, meat, and nutrient dense vegetables of which about half of Palestinian children were regularly deprived.

Because he was a man with limited means and few employment opportunities, Sami was unable to give his children all that he would have liked, so he tended to overcompensate by showering them with his genial nature and a great deal of love. He had spent his entire life in the East Jerusalem Palestinian neighbourhood of Silwan which following the 1948 war, had fallen under Jordanian occupation until 1967 when East Jerusalem was invaded and had since remained under Israeli occupation. The medieval Arab geographer Al-Muqaddasi (c. 945/946 – 991) who after an excellent education and a pilgrimage to Mecca decided to study geography – and for a period of over twenty years travelled through islamic countries – had referred to Silwan as "Sulwan" where it was said that on the Islamic holy Night of 'Arafah the water of the holy well Zamzam, in Mecca, came underground to the water of the Spring of Siloam.

Since the Israeli government zoned as "open green space" virtually all unbuilt-upon land of Palestinian East Jerusalem following the 1967 invasion and forbade Palestinians from living in Jewish West Jerusalem, there was already insufficient space to accommodate them all even without having Palestinian homes appropriated or demolished to make room for Jewish settlers. This policy of deliberate displacement of Palestinians – despite the Fourth Geneva Convention which states that "the Occupying Power shall not deport or transfer parts of its own civilian population into the territory it occupies" – was described in the book *Separate and Unequal: The Inside Story of Israeli Rule in East Jerusalem* by Amir Cheshin who as an Advisor on Arab Affairs was one of the architects of the post-1967 policy:

" … *Israel's leaders adopted two basic principles in their rule of East Jerusalem. The first was to rapidly increase the Jewish population in East Jerusalem. The second was to hinder growth of the Arab population and to force Arab residents to make their homes elsewhere. It is a policy that has translated into a miserable life for the majority of East Jerusalem Arabs … Israel turned urban planning into a tool of the government, to be used to help prevent the expansion of the city's non-Jewish population. It was a ruthless policy, if only for the fact that the needs (to say nothing of the rights) of Palestinian residents were ignored. Israel saw the adoption of strict zoning plans as a way of limiting the number of new homes built in Arab neighbourhoods, and thereby ensuring that the Arab percentage of the city's population – 28.8 in 1967 – did not grow beyond this level. Allowing 'too many' new homes in Arab neighbourhoods would mean 'too many' Arab residents in the city. The idea was to move as many Jews as possible into East Jerusalem, and move as many Arabs as possible out of the city entirely. Israeli housing policy in East Jerusalem was all about this numbers game."*

Palestinian continuity, heritage, and rightful claims to East Jerusalem were consequently being gradually undermined by the illegal placement of interspersed, fortified, and guarded Jewish enclaves which were then expanded and linked as part of the plan to displace indigenous Palestinians and establish Jewish presence in all of Jerusalem. Apart from Israel's demographic considerations, Silwan's Palestinian population of approximately 45,000 was also victim to an Israeli reinvention of the area as "The City of David" with a visitors' centre having been built to provide some legitimacy for an assertion that lacked any archaeological or historical evidence.

Impudent Israel's "creative" tactics for helping Jewish settlers take over Palestinian land ranged from audacious fraud and forgery to military seizures for "security needs" or the "public good" to the use of outdated Ottoman laws. In order to facilitate transference of Palestinian land to Jewish settlers without having to purchase the land, Israel created and institutionalised a number of official ploys including "seizing land for military needs" which saw over 40 settlements being established on thousands of acres of privately-owned Palestinian land following the 1967 war; use of expropriation orders for "the public good"; enforcement of Ottoman land laws which stipulated that land not worked continuously for three straight years would automatically return to the state; funding of land takeovers, wherein the money is generally transferred through the World Zionist Organisation's Settlement Division or local and regional settlers councils; and by not enforcing laws against settlers and institutions that illegally and forcibly took over private Palestinian land.

Israel's proclivity for contemptible underhand tactics of bringing the entire area of East Jerusalem under Jewish control included accelerated efforts to confiscate Palestinian land and demolish Palestinian homes; procuring from Arab collaborators false documents so as to designate Palestinian houses as being "absentee properties"; the deliberate neglect of community services such as education, the economy, development, infrastructure, housing, and recreational facilities by Israeli authorities despite the high taxes paid by East Jerusalem Palestinians; the allocation of much of Silwan to the Jewish settlers – without offering it for tender – by the Israel Lands Authority and the Jewish National Fund; the discreet provision of tens of millions of dollars by Israeli government ministries; the use of public funds to finance the settlers' legal expenses; and the "Judaisation" of East Jerusalem by means of private settler organisations such as El Ad.

Following its establishment in 1986, El Ad had since been aggressively responsible for Jewish settlement in the area; for managing "The City of David" park construction; for cooperating with The Custodian of Absentee Property – established by The Absentee Property Law of 1950 – to facilitate Palestinian land confiscation and transfer ownership to Jewish settlers; for taking control of Jewish National Fund property for token prices and without having to bid competitively; for provoking – with the assistance of the Municipal Police – armed Jewish settler violence against unarmed Palestinians and their children; and for controlling the archaeological excavations that started soon after the occupation of East Jerusalem. Archaeological excavations were of vital importance to the Israeli government which sought to justify its Palestinian home demolitions through bogus historical and religious claims to the land by establishing a bogus Israeli-defined "Holy Basin" zone around the Old City.

Sami and his family, like most Palestinian families in Silwan, lived in constant fear with regards to the legal status of their land, their residency, and their property rights. They led a day to day existence full of uncertainty and bewilderment at how they could be in such a precarious situation as the rest of the world stood by and tolerated what was being done to them by the Israel. In 1948 – in the shadow of the Holocaust and the reality of millions of homeless refugees – the UN General Assembly had adopted the Universal Declaration of Human Rights with the assertion that "disregard and contempt for human rights have resulted in barbarous acts which have outraged the conscience of mankind, and the advent of a world in which human beings shall enjoy freedom of speech and belief and freedom from fear and want has been proclaimed as the highest aspiration of the common people … All human beings are born free and equal in dignity and rights."

The declaration – ratified by Israel with a Hebrew version available on the Knesset's Internet home page – was based on the inalienable right of every person to freedom and equality "without distinction of any kind, such as race, colour, sex, language, religion, political or other opinion, national or social origin, property, birth or other status." The proclamation put special emphasis on freedoms of thought, conscience, religion, expression and most of all the right to a nationality.

Despite the existence of such a righteous Declaration, a misnomered humanity – still hungover from World War Two and experiencing pangs of conscience over the Nazi persecution of the Jews while mostly forgetting the millions of non-Jews who died – stood idly by while armed Jewish terror gangs ethnically cleansed more than 500 Palestinian towns and villages and forced the exodus (the heartstring tugging Hollywood film *Exodus* was about Jews, not Palestinians) of more than 750,000 unarmed Palestinian men, women, and children whose barbaric treatment by Israel was now referred to as the *Nabka* (catastrophe).

It was perhaps ironic that the first use of the term "Nakba" in reference to the Palestinian displacement was by the Israeli military. In July 1948, when the Arab inhabitants of Tirat Haifa refused to surrender, the IDF made use of leaflets written in excellent Arabic to urge as follows: "If you want to be ready for the Nakba, to avoid a disaster and save yourselves from an unavoidable catastrophe, you must surrender." Shortly afterwards, in August 1948, the Syrian intellectual Constantin Zureiq published his essay *The Meaning of Disaster* with the assertion that "the defeat of the Arabs in Palestine is not simply a setback or a temporary atrocity. It is a Nakba in the fullest sense of the word." He also addressed the Arabs of the Middle East and implored them to respond to the terrible disaster that had hit them because he obviously felt that the Nakba affected the entire Arab world and not just the Palestinian people.

Though the Palestinian people had in no way been responsible for the Holocaust – they did not even offer to fight on the side of the Nazis as did the Zionists – the freedom worshiping and hypocritical West led by a not so Great Britain, was prepared to offer Palestine and its people as placatory compensation to the Zionist cause. So today, after almost seventy years of pernicious, persistent, and unjust persecution, 7.1 million displaced Palestinians worldwide had remained as the most protracted and largest of any refugee problem.

In the meantime, while Western Governments and the mainstream media with their combined double standards and hypocrisy spectated at leisure while Israel pursued its Zionist Master Plan for a Greater Israel, the Palestinian people would continue to be ethnically cleansed as stateless prisoner refugees on their own land and in adjoining Arab states; would continue being subject to air, sea, and land blockades that prevented the import of essential foods, medical supplies, and construction materials; would continue being routinely arrested, detained, and/or violently interrogated; would continue to be subject to Nazi-style arbitrary arrest, beatings, torture, and indefinite imprisonment without charges or due process for up to ten or more years without knowledge of when or if they will ever be released under Israel's Administrative Detention Orders; would continue to see their children being systematically targeted and detained by the military and police who subject them to violent physical and verbal abuse, humiliation, painful restraints, hooding, threats with death, physical violence, and threats of sexual assault against themselves or members of their family, and denial of access to food, water, and toilet facilities; would continue to be subject to having their freedom of movement denied by travel restrictions, separation fences, walls, checkpoints, and roads built for Israelis only; would continue to be subjected to attacks against themselves and their property – including the burning of their olive groves which are the only means of livelihood for many – by deranged savages from illegal Jewish settlements; would continue to have their lands illegally expropriated; would continue to have their pre-1967 territories gradually diminished as more and more illegal Jewish settlements are established; would continue to have their natural resources including water stolen or as in the case of the latter deliberately contaminated; would continue to be made homeless by having have their properties demolished; would continue to "live" under the constant threat of yet more barbaric Israeli military assaults; and finally, they would continue to be amazed at how supposedly civilised societies including diaspora Jews could be witness to all of this while in effect tolerating, approving of, and being complicit in such barbarous inhumanity.

Furthermore, to add insult to injury, many Palestinian victims of home demolitions by Israeli security forces were subsequently informed by the Israeli occupation authorities that they had to pay for the cost of the demolitions. One such example concerned Al-Araqeeb – an old Palestinian village in the lands occupied by Israel in 1948 – which successive Israeli governments had subsequently refused to recognise. That had resulted in the village not being connected to local public services; had been knocked down by the Israelis 92 times; and now its residents were subject to a demand by Israeli authorities that they pay the two million New Israeli Shekels (around €460,000 / £360,000 / $515,000) cost of the demolitions. As this was the cost of just one demolition, residents are faced with the probability of further costs for other demolitions with some 40 other Palestinian villages such as Al-Araqeeb also facing the same fate.

Even before its bribed and paid for inception as a state, Israel had no intention of peaceful coexistence with its neighbours; no intention of honouring UN resolutions or respecting international law including human rights; and certainly no intention of considering a two state solution. Israel's first Prime Minister David Ben-Gurion, was not the first Zionist to believe in the abolition of partition and the Jewish occupation of all Palestine. Theodor Herzl, the founder of modern Zionism, was of the opinion that "we shall try to spirit the penniless [Arab] population across the border by procuring employment for it in the transit countries, while denying it any employment in our own country … Both the process of expropriation and the removal of the poor must be carried out discreetly and circumspectly." Such sentiments were later to be echoed by other prominent Zionists.

"Take the American declaration of Independence. It contains no mention of territorial limits. We are not obliged to fix the limits of the State."
Moshe Dayan, *Jerusalem Post*, 08/10/1967.

"The settlement of the Land of Israel is the essence of Zionism. Without settlement, we will not fulfil Zionism. It's that simple."
Yitzhak Shamir, *Ma'ariv*, 02/21/1997.

"In strategic terms, the settlements (in Judea, Samaria, and Gaza) are of no importance." What makes them important, he added, was that *"they constitute an obstacle, an unsurmountable obstacle to the establishment of an independent Arab State west of the river Jordan."* **Binyamin Begin, son of the late Menachem Begin and a prominent voice in the Likud party writing in 1991. Quoted in Paul Findley's *Deliberate Deceptions.***

On that basis, successive Israeli governments had for decades gone along with the "Peace Talks" charade so as to play for more time while pursuing the Zionist goal of by any means driving out the Palestinians and stealing their land. There never had been any Israeli intentions for a two-state solution, for peace, or for granting legal and human rights to the Palestinian people. Yet despite such irrefutable facts for all to see, Western hypocrisy, double standards, and political correctness – instilled by the fear of being accused of anti-Semitism and Holocaust denial – continues to prevail instead of a realistic recognition that Israel is a lying, cheating, conniving, thieving, murdering, racist, Apartheid state whose existence is dependent not only on the brutal denial of human rights in Palestine, but also on the subversion of democracy and the right to free speech in other countries.

Consequently for Sami Hadawi and his family life was a day-to-day struggle for survival without any hope of relief from poverty or of looking forward to a better future. As Sami did not have a a real profession he earned a meagre living as a tourist guide and every morning – seven days a week – he would walk from Silwan to the Old City's New Gate where he would wait in the hope of being engaged by tourists coming from their luxurious West Jerusalem hotels to see the Old City. During the summer months between June and September when visitor numbers peaked, he would do fairly well, but times were otherwise lean for the rest of the year. It was during September that he had met and befriended Conrad Banner who was due to return to Jerusalem and had promised to employ Sami during the filming of his documentary. By finally having some definite income to actually look forward to, Sami and his stoic wife, Miriam, would this Christmas be able to provide their two children, Anton and Hanan, with a few basic nutritional treats that most Palestinian children were routinely denied along with their basic human rights as called for in the 1924 Declaration of the Rights of the Child.

While the Declaration may have asserted that "whereas mankind owes to the child the best it has to give," the stark reality was just the opposite. In 1960 – in just one year alone – the death of 18,900,000 children exceeded the estimated Jewish Holocaust death toll by more than three times. Yet because there is no "child mortality industry" similar to the "Holocaust industry," awareness of and concern for the plight of children received relatively little if any attention. So while humanity likes to periodically appease its collective conscience with reaffirmation of its concern and respect for the dead by commemorating those who died for their country, their is no such concern or respect for the hundreds of millions of children who have died due to indifference, neglect, hypocrisy, double standards, and certainly immoral if not also illegal wars.

During the Second World War – the bloodiest war in humanity's history – an estimated 60 million people died, which, spread over six years, meant that the death toll was more than 10 million people per year. At that time, more than 20 million children were dying annually so that child mortality had been comparatively far more deadly than the most terrible war in history. Currently, a very sad excuse for humanity – including those God chosen Jewish people who after the Holocaust vowed "never again" – has for almost seven decades displayed an amoral and criminal indifference towards the extensively documented and video recorded ethnic cleansing of the Palestinian people whose children are deliberately targeted by immigrant invaders who like a plague of locusts leave nothing but desolation and destruction in their wake.

One of Miriam's responsibilities – after Sami had left for his early walk to the New Gate – was to accompany their children on the often hazardous journey to the Silwan Elementary school in the neighbourhood of Ras Al-Amoud. This involved "running the gauntlet" of Israeli occupation forces and illegal Jewish settlers who deliberately deploy to verbally abuse, spit on, attack, or endeavour to prevent Palestinian children from getting to school. This was a well established and calculated Israeli strategy not only in Silwan, but also throughout the Occupied Palestinian Territories.

After returning home, Miriam spent most of the day embroidering – an important part of Palestinian identity – before walking back to Ras Al-Amoud neighbourhood to pick up the children. By selling her hand embroidered purses and handbags to a retailer for between 15 and 25 Israeli New Shekels, Miriam was able to augment the family's meagre income. Her persistent application to this craft in the midst of a persecuted, tragic, and turbulent existence for the Palestinian people, helped to keep alive the tradition and beauty of Palestinian embroidery which despite sharing certain aspects of textile arts with neighbouring Arab countries, nonetheless had its own style and special uniqueness that was easily recognisable around the world as being of Palestinian origin.

Books on international embroidery were unanimous in recognising traditional Palestinian embroidery as being the prime example of such work emanating from the Middle East. It was a traditional craft that had developed from the traditional Palestinian costume which contained historical data documenting centuries of textile-art development in the region, an art form that had somehow persisted and survived to the present day. Whether one considered the ancient traditional simple cut of the thobe, the history of headdresses and accessories, the wondrous variety of embroidery styles, the stitch variations, or the ancient origin of patterns and motifs, one was deeply impressed with the historical richness of a legacy dating back thousands of years, and which affirmed the antiquity of Palestinian existence and the survival of an ancient heritage. While embroidering, Miriam usually indulged herself by praying quietly – in what she called her time with God – which was something that poor people without hope frequently resorted to doing. But what was the use of seeking succour from an Almighty God who had turned His back on her, her family, and her people while instead allegedly "choosing" the Jews and promising them Palestine.

6

Friday, 11 December

National Headquarters of the Israel Police, East Jerusalem

The Israel Police headquarters used to be in in Tel Aviv, but following Israel's 1967 smash-and-grab-territory war, Israel made a statement of intent by moving the headquarters to a newly established East Jerusalem site – a complex of government buildings named after the former Prime Minister and known as Kiryat Menachem Begin – located between Sheikh Jarrah in the north, Mount Scopus in the east, and Ammunition Hill in the west. The fact that this year alone had seen a "revolving door" arrival and departure of three different General Police Commissioners had required Abe Goldman making yet another visit to discuss Temple Mount policing with the latest Commissioner – hastily brought in from Shin Bet – whose recent appointment by the Prime Minister and Public Security Minister had more to do with having someone who was loyal rather than efficient.

Goldman hoped the new Commissioner's previous experience with Israel's domestic security agency would enhance control of the current Palestinian unrest on the Mount. Known by its Hebrew acronym "Shabak," Shin Bet was one of the world's most powerful security agencies with historical links to the Zionist paramilitary groups whose violence against Palestinians was rampant prior to Israel's creation. The agency had since become infamous for the torture and killing of Palestinian detainees with the UN Committee Against Torture condemning it for the illegal and violent use of interrogation techniques that were still being used to this day.

Though the meeting with the rotund, moustached, and kippa-clad Commissioner had been cordial, Goldman remained unimpressed by a man who during his short tenure had proved controversial by making a distinction between Jewish and Palestinian bereavement with the preposterous and obviously racially motivated assertion that "Israel sanctifies life, our enemies sanctify death." Furthermore, he had taken a decision to conceal from the public a recommendation by police investigators that the Prime Minister's wife should be indicted concerning irregularities in the running of the prime minister's households. Goldman's request for the meeting was to ensure that strict Temple Mount policing would be at least maintained if not increased to facilitate opportunities and protection for Jews visiting the site: a deliberate policy of ever increasing Jewish presence that would ultimately favour the Hiramic Brotherhood of the Third Temple's main objective.

Goldman had established the Brotherhood as a rogue cell within the cloaked secrecy of Freemasonry, but without the organisation's official sanction. Though the Masonic members of this cell were dedicated exclusively to covertly assisting fulfilment of the envisioned building of the Third Temple – as described in the Book of Ezekiel – their dedication was based on questionable biblical narratives as explained in *The Book of the Commandments* by Maimonides – a preeminent medieval Sephardic Jewish philosopher, astronomer, and one of the most prolific and influential Torah scholars and physicians – which included commandment details and the instructions given by God Himself to the Jewish people on the day following Yom Kippur (Day of Atonement) on Mount Sinai: "The Creator commanded us to erect a chosen House for His service, where the sacrificial offerings will be brought for all time. And the processionals and festive pilgrimages will be conducted there three times a year."

The commandment to build the Temple was recognised as one of the 613 mitzvot (commandments) for which there was a perpetual Judaic obligation to fulfil. The great Judaic sages had maintained that rebuilding of the Holy Temple in accordance with the dimensions, characteristics, and attributes of the Second Temple, was a definite commandment for the people of Israel. Such disputable and probably fraudulent Biblical commandments, however, do not constitute sufficient justification for the illegal and invariably brutal and destructive appropriation of Palestinian land and property. It would appear that whenever the ancient Jewish scribes wanted to enhance or legitimise the nature and history of the Jewish people and their actions, they had no qualms about falsely ascribing the source of their self-aggrandising claims to God Himself.

It was for example claimed that Haram al-Sharif/Temple Mount in Jerusalem's Old City, was Judaism's most sacred site with the Jews referring to it as the Temple Mount or Mount Moriah (Har HaMoriya). For Muslims it was the third holiest site after Mecca and Medina and they referred to it as Haram Al-Sharif (the Noble Sanctuary) and to the mosque as "the Farthest Mosque," also known as Al-Aqsa and "Bayt al-Muqaddas" in Arabic. Muslims considered the Al-Aqasa compound to be holy because they had been taught that the mosque was the first Qibla – the direction Muslims face during prayer – in Islam's history and that it was the place from which the Prophet Mohamed made his miraculous *Isra and Miraj* (two-part) night journey from Mecca to Jerusalem prior to his ascension to heaven. The narrative had him travelling on a winged steed to the "Farthest Mosque" where he led other prophets such as Moses, Abraham and Jesus in Muslim-styled prayer that thereby clearly implied his prominence over all other Abrahamic prophets. In heaven he had a rare but brief meeting with God who provided him with instructions to be relayed back to the Muslim faithful.

The Hebrew Bible and Judaic narratives assert that the Al-Aqsa compound was associated with three Biblical mountains whose locations, though undetermined, were nonetheless of paramount importance: Mount Moriah where the binding of Isaac allegedly occurred (Genesis 22); Mount Zion (2 Samuel 5:7) where the original Jebusite (a Canaanite tribe) fortress and "the City of David" supposedly once stood; and the Temple Mount where the Third Temple was to be erected on the same alleged spot as that of Solomon's First Temple in Jerusalem which in Hebrew was called *Yerushaláyim* and *Qods/Qadas* in Arabic.

The First Temple was supposedly built by King Solomon – whose reign c. 967 – 931 BCE – was during an alleged "Golden Age" when Israel was at its height. Solomon was the man who after requesting and being granted wisdom from God ((1 Kings 3:11 – 12), proceeded to have seven hundred wives and three hundred concubines (1 Kings 11:3). Despite the time consuming responsibility of keeping so many women satisfied, Solomon apparently still found time and energy to write and is credited with being the author of much wisdom literature which was characterised by proverbs intended to teach about both divinity and virtue. In reality there was no evidence of a "Golden Age"; no evidence that the Israelites were a great nation; and no evidence of great cities with magnificent structures.

The character of Solomon, or Sun God of On, was the Israelite version of the Egyptian sun god, Re of Heliopolis. Even what little was recorded about Solomon was not written until some two thousand years later so that no records contemporary with his reign exist. The Hebrew Bible asserted that the building of Solomon's Temple was achieved with assistance from King Hiram of Tyre (part of present day Lebanon) who provided quality materials; skilled craftsmen, and the legendary architect Hiram Abiff. For such benevolent assistance Solomon was obliged to pay King Hiram an annual tribute of 100,000 bushels of wheat and 110,000 gallons of pure olive oil (1 Kings 5:11). To date, however, no archaeological evidence has been discovered for Solomon's Temple and the only reference to what might have been contemporary with its supposed existence comes from the Hebrew Bible. Even architectural descriptions of this First Temple lack any specific information and appear to have been compiled on the basis of the combined characteristics of other temples in Egypt, Mesopotamia and Phoenicia.

The present day location of Haram al-Sharif/Temple Mount and the state of Israel are therefore ideologically based on narratives of the Hebrew Bible which in its fraudulent translation into Greek at the renowned Library of Alexandria – by 70 Jewish scribes commissioned by King Ptolemy II the Greek monarch of Egypt at the time – included relocating the arena of the Biblical narratives from North Yemen and Southern Arabia to Egypt and Palestine. Qades, as mentioned in the Hebrew Bible, was one of 179 Yemenite mountains – making the country one of the most mountainous regions on the Arabian Peninsula – 80 kilometres south of the modern day city of Taiz which has no connection whatsoever with Jerusalem.

In its account of Solomon's God-given wisdom and "Golden Age" reign, the Bible recounts how the legend of his wisdom was so widespread, that Bilqis, the Queen of Sheba, travelled to Jerusalem to learn from this great man (1 Kings 10:2). Bilqis was one of a long line of matriarchal Sheban queens that ruled over the entire Sinai Peninsula which had enjoyed a genuine "Golden Age" with fabulous wealth derived from the Caravan Road that served as the main route for the transportation of frankincense, myrrh, gum, gold, textiles, Ivory, and important spices that were essential for religious and funerary functions as well as food preservation. It was unlikely that Bilqis would have stooped to travelling for any distance to pay homage to some other monarch. It is far more likely that this imagined link with Bilqis was just another Hebrew scribal concoction to enhance Solomon's legend and establish his supposed existence as fact.

The veracity of any such claims must therefore be judged in terms of the alleged Jewish Exodus from Egypt, the subsequent wandering in the desert for 40 years, and the relation of those events to the reality of present day Zionist Israel. To begin with, fundamental Zionist ideology is primarily concerned with the historically connoted Hebrew word *Aliyah* (ascent), which means travelling or migrating upwards to where the promised land of Israel was purportedly situated. It would therefore not be unreasonable to conclude on the basis of available facts and recent scholarly research that those migrating Jews did not do so from Egypt – in accordance with the flagrant concoctions of the Hebrew Bible – but from somewhere south of the Levant where ancient Arabia and the Yemen were situated.

By diligently chronicling the geography of ancient Arabia and Yemen, and studying classical Arabic historians of the first six centuries of Islam, it became evident to scholars that the actual theatre of Israelite Biblical narratives was in those Arabian locations with their mountains, valleys, and tribes. One does not have to be a brilliant scholar or researcher to uncover the fact that in its initial references to "Egypt," the Hebrew Bible used the name "Mizraim." which was a small, unremarkable village located along the ancient Caravan Road in southern Arabia from where Israelite narratives such as that of Moses had evolved.

More extensive research had also revealed that the ancient Israelites were not a people who had escaped from bondage in Egypt before wandering in the wilderness for 40 years and then conquering the promised land. The fact is that just as modern day Arabia is of strategic importance because of its wealth from oil and natural Gas, ancient Arabia was equally important because of its strategic location on the ancient Caravan Road from India, Yemen and the East African Horn to Iraq, Egypt, the Mediterranean coast and Greece. Neither the Caravan Road nor the ancient Silk Road – which were the main trade routes for the ancient world – terminated in or crossed Palestine.

Because of its value to the camel caravans that travelled for weeks and months across the Arabian Peninsula, the Caravan Road required protection and services which were provided by the Arabian tribes inhabiting the southern and western coast who in return benefited by providing food, water and other supplies to the travelling traders. Not all Arabian tribes, however, were fortuitously located to benefit from the Caravan Road and some tribes inhabited the mountainous area of North Yemen where hardships and lack of opportunity for honest living prevailed. Consequently, those less fortunate tribes – the Israelites being one of them – were forced to resort to frequently attacking and robbing the caravan traders of their valuable cargo. Furthermore the Caravan Road was also of such strategic value to both the Egyptians in the west and the Assyrians and Babylonians in the East, that it became essential for them to control Arabia which consequently became the target for most of the Egyptian and Assyrian military campaigns aimed at securing the Caravan Road.

Apart from doubt as to the origin of the Israelites, there was also evidence – which numerous people continue to obstinately disbelieve – that the Israelite God, YHWH, had a female consort and that the early Israelite religion only adopted the concept of monotheism during the Israeli monarchy's period of decline and not as claimed on Mount Sinai. It was as a consequence of the ancient Israelites' unflattering background that Hebrew scribes felt obliged to write a whitewashed history that would lend divine authority to a people desperate for a legitimate ethnic identity and a land of their own. Scientific researchers within the interlinked fields of the Bible, archaeology, and the history of the Jewish people, are now agreed that the reality relating to the emergence of Jews as a people in Palestine is poles apart from the concocted but nonetheless prevailing narrative which Israel was currently endeavouring to reinforce by exploiting archaeology to deny the indigenous Palestinian people of their history and replace it with their own.

Archaeology in Palestine had not begun to develop until the late 19th and early 20th centuries along with the archaeology of cultures such as those of Egypt, Mesopotamia, Greece and Rome. There was, however, a tendency amongst many archaeologists – who were in any case excavating for spectacular evidence of the past on behalf of the leading museums in Berlin, London, and Paris – to perhaps dishonestly connect and use archaeological discoveries as substantiation for biblical myths.

Because the conditions in ancient Palestine had never been conducive to the burgeoning of extensive kingdoms that were once host to impressive palaces, shrines, and temples such as those discovered in Egypt and Mesopotamia, its archaeology had consequently not been enthused over by leading museum initiatives, but by religious motives so that the main impetus behind the research in Palestine was its links to the Holy Scriptures.

Excavations had begun in Jericho and Shechem (Nablus) were biblical researchers hoped to find the remains of the cities mentioned in the Bible. Such archaeological research was energised by the efforts of an American, William Foxwell Albright (1891 – 1971) – an archaeologist, biblical scholar, philologist, and ceramics expert – whose stated approach was to use archaeology as the principal scientific means to refute critical claims against the historical veracity of the Bible narratives including those of the German Wellhausen school whose criticism of the Bible had prompted the view that it posed a danger to German Jewry.

This school of biblical criticism – of which Julius Wellhausen was the leading exponent and which had begun developing in the second half of the 19th century – challenged the historicity of Bible narratives and claimed that they had been deliberately devised during the Babylonian exile. Bible scholars, and particularly those in Germany, asserted that Hebrew history was a continuous series of events starting with Abraham, Isaac, and Jacob; that the sojourn in Egypt, the bondage, and the exodus; that the conquest of the land and the subsequent settlement by the tribes of Israel, were no more than a much later reconstruction of events with a theological agenda for a specific purpose.

Albright on the other hand believed that the Bible was a historical document, which, despite undergoing more than a few editorial and translational stages, was still a reliable reflection of ancient reality. He was certain to an almost fanatical degree that excavating the ancient remains of Palestine would provide positive proof of Jewish history in that land. Consequently the biblical archaeology that ensued in the footsteps of Albright and his disciples resulted in a series of extensive excavations at important biblical tells (mounds) including amongst others, Ai, a Canaanite royal city which according to the to the book of Joshua in the Hebrew Bible was conquered by the Israelites on their second attempt; at Beit She'an, whose ruins are now the Bet She'an National Park; at Beit Shemesh, where the modern Israeli city of Beit Shemesh was founded in 1950; at Gezer, formerly a Canaanite city-state in the foothills of the Judaean Mountains; at Gibeon, a Canaanite city north of Jerusalem that was conquered by Joshua; at Jericho, in the West Bank and now under Israeli occupation since 1967; at Tel Hazor, the site of ancient Hazor, located north of the Sea of Galilee; at Tel Lachish, now an archaeological site and an Israeli national park; at Tel Megiddo, which with its exaggerated historical importance is now protected as Megiddo National Park as well as being a World Heritage Site; and at Jerusalem, which Jews now claim as the eternal capital of Israel. So by enthusiastically adopting a biblical view of the excavations, archaeologists managed to ensure that every new discovery would somehow contribute to a jigsaw that conveniently matched the biblical narrative of the past including the Patriarchal Age of Abraham, Isaac and Jacob (Genesis 12–50).

This less than honest approach to archaeology inevitably brought about a situation where the profusion of archaeological discoveries – rather than substantiating the biblical narratives – instead served to discredit their credibility by creating inexplicable anomalies. Researchers for example had difficulty agreeing on which archaeological period matched the Patriarchal Age; agreeing on when Abraham, Isaac and Jacob actually lived; and agreeing on when was the Tomb of the Patriarchs in Hebron was purchased to serve as a burial place for the patriarchs and the matriarchs.

According to biblical chronology, Solomon built the First Temple some 480 years after the exodus from Egypt (1 Kings 6:1) to which a further 430 years had to be added for the sojourn in Egypt (Exodus 12:40) which along with the extraordinary lifespans of the patriarchs produced a 21st century BCE date for Abraham's move to Canaan. No evidence has, however, been unearthed to correspond with such a chronology. In the 1960s Albright suggested that Abraham's wanderings should be assigned to the Middle Bronze Age (22nd-20th centuries BCE), but Benjamin Mazar – regarded as an authority on the Israeli branch of biblical archaeology – proposed that the historic background of the Patriarchal Age should be a thousand years later, in the 11th century BCE "settlement period." Such proposals were rejected by others who viewed the historicity of the narratives as being ancestral legends narrated during the time of Judea's Kingdom.

As for The Exodus from Egypt, the wanderings in the

desert, and the Mount Sinai narrative, there were no Egyptian documents to substantiate such claims and while some Jews may have been expelled from ancient Egypt, it is highly unlikely that the number expelled was anywhere near the number claimed by Jewish scribes. If such a momentous event had actually occurred – 600,000 people in those days would have represented at least a quarter of Egypt's population – then surely it would have warranted being diligently recorded or at least mentioned. Numerous Egyptian documents do, however, mention the custom of nomadic shepherds entering Egypt to camp in the River Nile Delta during periods of drought and the scarcity of food, but such harmless incursions over a period of many centuries were frequent rather than a solitary, exceptional event.

Furthermore, researchers have continuously endeavoured to locate Mount Sinai and the desert encampments of the wandering tribes, but despite considerable efforts, not a single site has been located to match the biblical narrative. Because the main events in the history of the Israelites are not substantiated by either archaeological discoveries or non-biblical documentation, most historians are agreed that the stay in Egypt and the events of the subsequent exodus may have occurred to a negligible number of nomadic families whose story was embellished to accommodate the needs of a nationalist ideology.

Even the historically important narrative of how the land of Canaan was conquered by the Israelites is subject to doubt as a result of the difficulties encountered in trying to locate the archaeological evidence to support this biblical contention. Excavations by different expeditions at Jericho and Ai – cities whose conquest is conscientiously detailed in the Book of Joshua – have yielded nothing apart from the conclusion that during the agreed upon period for the conquest in the late part of the 13th century BCE, there were no cities in either location and certainly no walls that could have come "tumbling down." In response to this lack of evidence, a variety of feeble explanations were offered including the suggestion that Jericho's walls had been washed away by rain.

Almost half a century ago, biblical scholars put forward the idea that the conquest narratives should be viewed as nothing more than mythical legends because with the discovery of more and more sites it had become apparent that the locations in question had at different times simply petered out or been abandoned. It was therefore ultimately concluded that there was no factual evidence in existence to support the biblical narrative of a conquest by Israelite tribes in a military campaign led by Joshua.

While the biblical narrative exaggerates the extent – "great cities with walls sky-high" (Deuteronomy 9:1) – of Canaanite city fortifications conquered by the Israelites, the reality was quite different with excavated sites uncovering only remains of unfortified settlements consisting of a small number of structures that could hardly be regarded as cities. It was consequently evident that urban Palestinian culture in the late 13th century BCE had disintegrated over a period of hundreds of years rather than being the result of military conquest by the Israelites.

Furthermore, the authors of the biblical descriptions were either unfamiliar with, or deliberately ignored the geopolitical reality in Palestine which was subject to Egyptian rule until the mid-12th century BCE. Egyptian administrative centres were located in Gaza, Japho (Jaffa), and Beit She'an with evidence of numerous Egyptian locations on both sides of the Jordan River also being discovered. The biblical narrative fails to mention such prominent Egyptian presence and it is evident that the scribes were either unaware of, or deliberately omitted an important historical reality so that archaeological discoveries have demonstrated the biblical scenario of "great" Canaanite cities, impregnable fortifications with "sky-high walls," and the heroism of a few Israelite conquerors assisted by God against the more numerous Canaanites, were all theological reconstructions devoid of factual foundation.

Even the phased emergence of the Israelites as a people was subject to doubt and debate because there was no evidence of a spectacular military conquest of fortified cities, or evidence as to the actual identity of the Israelites. Archaeological discoveries, however, did indicate that starting some time after 1200 BCE which is identified with the "settlement" phase, hundreds of small settlements were established in the central hill region where farmers worked the land or raised sheep. As it had already been established that these settlers had not come from Egypt, it was proposed – because graves had been discovered in the hills area without settlements – that they were were pastoral shepherds who wandered throughout the region maintaining a barter economy with the valley inhabitants by exchanging meat for grains. With the gradual disintegration of both urban and agricultural systems, however, those nomadic sheep herders were forced to produce their own grains which necessitated the establishment of more permanent small settlements.

"Israel" is mentioned in a single Egyptian document dating from 1208 BCE, the period of King Merneptah, which states "plundered is Canaan with every evil, Ascalon is taken, Gezer is seized, Yenoam has become as though it never was, Israel is desolated, its seed is not." By referring to the country by its Canaanite name and mentioning several of the kingdom's cities, Merneptah had provided evidence that the term "Israel" was given to one of the population groups residing in Canaan's central hill region toward the end of the Late Bronze Age, where the Kingdom of Israel was later to be established.

Archaeology also played a role in bringing about a change in reconstructing the reality of David and Solomon's "united monarchy" period which the Bible describes as being the height of the economic, military, and political power of the ancient Israelites with David's conquests followed by Solomon's rule having created an empire stretching from the Gaza to the Euphrates River: "For he controlled the whole region west of the Euphrates, from Tiphsah to Gaza, all the kings west of the Euphrates" (1 Kings 4:24). Archaeological discoveries at numerous sites, however, prove that the imposing buildings and magnificent monuments attributed to that era were nothing more than functional but unremarkable structures.

Of the three cities mentioned among Solomon's amazing construction achievements, Gezer proved to be only a citadel covering a small area and surrounded by a less expensive casemate wall consisting of two thinner, parallel walls with an empty space between them; Hazor 's upper city was only partly fortified – about 7.5 acres from total of some 135 acres – which had been settled in the Bronze Age; and Megiddo covered a small area with what would have been huts rather than actual buildings and with no indication whatsoever of having had a fortified wall.

Further contradictions also arose as a result of excavations in Jerusalem – the united monarchy's alleged capital – where extensive excavations over the past 150 years have uncovered some impressive remains of the cities from the Middle Bronze Age and the Iron Age II (the period of the Kingdom of Judea). Apart from some pottery shards, no remains of any buildings from the united monarchy period have been found. In view of the existence of preserved remains from earlier and later periods, it may be concluded that Jerusalem in the time of David and Solomon was no more than a small "city" with at most a small citadel for the ruler, but certainly not the capital of an impressive empire as described in the Bible.

As they were obviously aware of the 8th century BCE's wall of Jerusalem and its culture of which remains had been discovered in different parts of the city, biblical authors were able to transfer that scenario back to the age of the united monarchy.

It may be assumed that Jerusalem's more prominent status was acquired following the destruction of its rival, Samaria, which had been besieged for three years by the Assyrian Sargon II before finally falling in 722 BCE.

Apart from justified doubts about historical and political details of the biblical narrative, questions regarding the doctrines and worship of the Israelites were also raised including the date at which monotheism was adopted by the kingdoms of Israel and Judea. For example in Kuntilet Ajrud in the southwestern part of the Negev hill region, and Khirbet el-Kom in the Judea piedmont, Hebrew inscriptions were discovered that mention "YHWH and his Asherah," "YHWH Shomron and his Asherah," "YHWH Teman and his Asherah." The authors were obviously familiar with a pair of gods, YHWH and his consort Asherah, and had sent blessings in the couple's name. These inscriptions from the 8th century BCE suggest the possibility that monotheism, as a state religion, was in reality an innovation of the Kingdom of Judea's era following the destruction of the Kingdom of Israel.

Archaeological discoveries had proved to be consistent with the critical school of biblical scholarship's conclusions that David and Solomon might have been tribal kingdom chieftains who ruled over small areas with the former in Hebron and the latter in Jerusalem so that from the outset they were not only separate, independent kingdoms, but also at times adversaries. Consequently the much plugged united monarchy narrative is an imaginary historiographic concoction written at the earliest during the time of Judea's Kingdom whose actual name has remained a mystery. What was astonishing about all of this, was the fact that a nation-state of the Jewish people – including the highly intelligent Abe Goldman – was citing such blatant biblical fallacies as justification for its current illegal and always brutal appropriation of Palestinian land, property, and resources.

Yaakov Katzir was an Ashkenazi Jew from Russia who in the strictest sense of the word, was not a Semite because diligent, impartial research would reveal that the word "Semite" had no relation with any particular religious group or ethnicity, but with a group of Semitic languages including Amharic (spoken by Ethiopians and Eritreans in lands formerly known as Abyssinia); Arabic (spoken by Arabs and others in Muslim countries because it is the language of the Qur'an); Aramaic (spoken mostly by the Chaldeans of Iraq, some Catholics, and Maronite Christians at least liturgically if not socially); Hebrew (spoken by Israelis, some Jews, and others outside of Israel); and Syriac (spoken by some in various parts of Syria and the Middle East).

Linguistic experts also point out that Abraham, the father of the Arabs and Jews, did not speak Hebrew, but Aramaic which was then the language of the land. Genuinely genetic Jews were from Spain, Portugal, North Africa and the Middle East and were known as "Sephardic," a word derived from the Hebrew "Sepharad," which relates to Spain. Sephardic Jews, because of familiarity with their own history and the true meaning of the word "Semite," tend to avoid using the term "anti-Semitism" because it is basically utter nonsense. Alternatively, Ashkenazi Jews who exploit Israel's Law of Return – Israeli legislation passed on 5 July 1950, giving Jews the right of return, the right to live in Israel, and the right to acquire citizenship – have no connection to Palestine as was observed by H. G. Wells in his *The Outline of History:* "it is highly probable that the bulk of the Jew's ancestors 'never' lived in Palestine 'at all,' which witnesses the power of historical assertion over fact."

Even the long held hypothesis that Ashkenazi Jews were descended from the Khazars – a multiethnic kingdom that included Iranians, Turks, Slavs and Circassians who allegedly converted to Judaism as ordered by their king – has been discredited by studies proving a maternal lineage derived largely from Europe. According to new evidence from a recent study of mitochondrial DNA – which is passed on exclusively from mother to child – Ashkenazi Jews were descended from prehistoric European women with no connection whatsoever to the ancient tribes of Israel. This also contradicts the persistent notion that European Jews were mostly descendants of people who left Israel and the Middle East some 2,000 years ago.

Under the heading of "A brief History of the Terms for Jew" in the 1980 Jewish Almanac, the following statement is made: "strictly speaking it is incorrect to call an Ancient Israelite a 'Jew' or to call a contemporary Jew an Israelite or a Hebrew." Despite all that, in 1970, Israel extended the right of return, entry, and settlement to include people of Jewish ancestry along with their spouses while in the meantime continuing to forcibly expel and persecute indigenous Palestinians who have no such right as inhabitants of refugee camps and what are effectively concentration camps such as Gaza and the West Bank.

Because the Hiramic Brotherhood of the Third Temple meetings were held on the third Thursday of every month, Yaakov Katzir was allowed by special arrangement to visit the Western Wall Tunnels – the most extensive archaeological-tourism project in the Old City – on the preceding Friday so that he could provide his fellow members with a progress report on the excavations which had been ongoing since 1969. The Brotherhood's forthcoming meeting was of particular importance because an invited guest of honour from the Sanhedrin Council, would be attending. The recently reestablished Sanhedrin – which was the supreme council, or court, in ancient Israel – consisted of elders (judges) whose last binding decision in ancient times appears to have been in 358 with the adoption of the Hebrew Calendar.

Katzir, however, was only interested in one particular excavation which was being conducted with absolute secrecy.

Consequently with With the Western Wall Tunnels being open to visitors on Sunday to Thursday from seven in the morning until six in the evening, and until noon on Fridays, certain tasks relating to that covert and arguably illegal excavation were only possible after closing time on Friday and all day Saturday, the Jewish Sabbath. Katzir always arrived before closing time and mingled with the team of sworn to secrecy diggers who were supposedly employees of the Western Wall Heritage Foundation.

Work on this particular excavation had begun almost a year and a half earlier with the construction of a state of the art trapdoor over a vertically dug shaft that was easily covered and rendered invisible. The trapdoor was situated directly opposite the Cotton Merchants' Gate – which along with the market was built in the fourteenth century by the Mameluke Emir Tankiz – and in line with the Dome of The Rock. The nine-foot vertical shaft was fitted with an aluminium ladder leading into a 20-foot square chamber that served as a utility room from which the tunnelling was carried out. Disposing of the excavated material and bringing in galvanised steel sheeting, pipes, and mud sills for shoring up the tunnel's roof, presented a problem, and some elaborate ploys and precautions had to be taken to avoid attracting unwelcome attention or suspicion.

The tunnel was headed towards the assumed location of the Well of Souls which some believed may have in the past, or may even still contain the mythical and yet to be discovered Ark of the Covenant containing the original Ten Commandment tablets that God allegedly gave to Moses on Mount Sinai when the ancient Israelites were wandering in the desert. The word ark was an outdated predecessor of the modern word arc and was derived from the Latin arca, meaning a box, chest, or coffer, so that items kept concealed in such containers were regarded as being arcane while something deeply mysterious was an arcanum as in alchemy and the Tarot (from the Italian tarocchi).

A depository for document preservation was an *archive,* with objects of antiquity being *archaic.* Consequently the excavation and examination of archaic objects was known as *archaeology.*

There were, however, some Biblical confusion over the stone tablets with for example Exodus 40:20 stating that "he took the tablets of the covenant law and placed them in the ark, attached the poles to the ark and put the atonement cover over it," while actual reference to the Commandments comes from a later retrospective in Deuteronomy. It was apparently at that point that the Israelites before carrying the Ark into Jordan were reminded by Moses of its great power, and of the earlier events on Mount Horeb. He recalled how the stone tablets, written upon with God's finger, were those which he had thrown on the ground and broken before their eyes. He then recounted how he had been ordered to hew two more tablets – on which was to be written that which had been written on the initial tablets – and that it was those tablets that he had placed in the Ark.

The assertion that the original stone tablets on which God had written were in fact not the ones placed in the Ark, had understandably been the cause of some dismay because the Ark narrative was based on that very premise which Judaic scholars reluctantly acknowledge to be factually suspect. In order to reconcile this troublesome issue, a compromise was conceived in the Middle Ages by theologians who concluded that there must have been two Arks: the one that Bezaleel built (Exodus 31), and the replica containing the tablets broken by Moses. It was nonetheless stressed that it was Bezaleel's original Ark that eventually came to rest in Solomon's Temple. The fate of the replica with the Commandments has since been an issue which Jewish historians have religiously avoided broaching and it was left to an Ethiopian Christian fraternity to exploit the fable.

One of several surviving misconceptions about Moses was the belief that he wrote the Pentateuch (Genesis, Exodus,

Leviticus, Numbers, and Deuteronomy) despite the fact that scholars have long known that they were not only written by different scribes in Jerusalem, but also during different time spans from probably towards the end of the post-exilic period – between the end of Jewish exile in Babylon in 538 BCE and 1 CE – with a view to creating a mythic history for a Hebrew nation based on the customs, pronouncements and legends of other nations. It was during that period some 700 years after Moses had passed away that Deuteronomy was written in a way that suggested the words were coming straight from the mouth of Moses. This was also the case with Exodus and was part of creating folklore that would substantiate the Israelite invasion of Canaan narrative by alleging it had been the will of God with Moses supposedly stating "and when the Lord your God delivers them before you and you defeat them, then you shall utterly destroy them. You shall make no covenant with them and show no favour to them" (Deuteronomy 7:2); "but thou shalt utterly destroy them namely, the Hittites, and the Amorites, the Canaanites, and the Perizzites, the Hivites, and the Jebusites; as the Lord thy God hath commanded thee" (Deuteronomy 20:17); "the Lord your God himself will go over before you. He will destroy these nations before you, so that you shall dispossess them, and Joshua will go over at your head, as the Lord has spoken" (Deuteronomy 31:3). Today in the 21st century, the Palestinian people are still being dispossessed of their land, are still being deprived of their culture, and are still being ethnically cleansed with arrogant impunity in accordance with the contrived concoctions of ancient Hebrew scribes.

The consensus of scholarly opinion is that such accounts were derived from four different written sources which were brought together over a period of time to produce the first five books of the Bible in a composite form. The sources were referred to as J, the Jahwist source (from the German transliteration of the Hebrew YHWH); E, the Elohist source;

P, the priestly source; and D, the Deuteronomist source. Consequently the Pentateuch (referred to by Jews as the Torah) was comprised of material gathered from six centuries of folklore which had been combined to provide a conceivable narrative of both God's creation of the world and His relationship with people in general, and Jews in particular.

There was also an apparent contradiction regarding the Ark's portable sanctuary, the Tabernacle of the Congregation, whose elaborate details as described in the Priestly ("P") Pentateuch do not resemble the far simpler description of a mere tent with one Elohist ("E") account stating that "now Moses used to take a tent and pitch it outside the camp some distance away, calling it the 'tent of meeting.' Anyone inquiring of the Lord would go to the tent of meeting outside the camp" (Exodus 33:7). This is in stark contrast to the Priest description which has a magnificent Tabernacle located in the middle of the camp with attendants and Levite Guardians. This version of the Tabernacle – which subsequently came to be viewed as the one replicated in Solomon's Temple – had its heavy plank walls draped with thick linen and goat skins and was complete with a Brazen alter, furnishings, hangings, rings, and other adornments. A hardly portable and altogether different sanctuary from the simplicity of the Elohim tent sanctuary.

It should also be noted that by the first-century Gospel period there was still no single combined Judaic text available and that only a collection of different individual texts existed as was demonstrated by the discovery of scrolls in the caves of Qumrân located some two kilometres inland from the northwest shore of the Dead Sea. Such scrolls were for use in synagogues rather than for availability to the general public. The first combined set of texts to be recognised as a Hebrew Bible did not exist until after the fall of Jerusalem to the Romans in 70 CE with the Old Testament being written in a Hebrew style consisting only of consonants. This led to a Greek translation

– referred to as the Septuagint (from the Latin *septuaginta:* seventy) because seventy-two scholars were responsible for the translation – to cater for the increase in Greek-speaking Hellenist Jews. During the fourth-century CE, St. Jerome produced a Latin translation referred to as the Vulgate that was subsequently used by Christianity. Unfortunately impartial scholarly research and evidence strongly suggest that the Septuagint Greek translation of the Hebrew narratives – actually undeserving of being referred to as a Bible – were a rather crude forgery whose pernicious deception has to this day continued brainwashing gullible multitudes and deleteriously affecting the fate of humanity.

By about 900 CE, Jewish scholars known as the Masoretes – because they appended the *Masorah,* a collection of traditional notes to the text – produced from the old Hebrew text a new form known as the *Codex Petropolitanus.* So irrespective of whether it is the Masoretic text, the Latin Vulgate, the English version, or other language translation, the reality is that they are all of the Current Era and as such have suffered from translational and interpretational adjustments by scribes committed to presenting a narrative – even if it necessitated stretching the truth – that would serve as a common religious conviction for the unification of a people desperate to establish and preserve a unique identity in the face of discriminatory oppression. It is equally important to recognise that historic references to the Ark in the book of Exodus and onwards through most of the Old Testament were frequent and included accounts of its pivotal role in the Israelites' conquest of Canaan; its apparent power to kill without warning all those who disobeyed the rules for its handling; and the fury of its unleashed power to cause tumours on a pandemic scale.

Since then it has been variously conjectured by historians and scholars that the Ark may have been taken away and destroyed; intentionally concealed under the Temple Mount;

removed from Jerusalem before the Babylonian invasion; taken to Ethiopia by the Ethiopian prince Menelik I the supposed son of King Solomon and the Queen of Sheba; relocated by Jewish priests during the reign of Manasseh; or simply miraculously removed by divine intervention. Though the last known allusion to the Ark being in the Temple dated from 701 BCE when the Assyrian king Sennacherib surrounded Hezekiah's forces in Jerusalem, its existence and destruction or removal from the Temple remains subject to much debate.

Despite the lack of certainty regarding the actual existence of the Well of Souls – or even the Ark of the Covenant – its location was claimed to be on Haram al-Sharif/Temple Mount below a natural cave under the rock upon which according to Jewish tradition Abraham prepared to sacrifice his son Isaac, and from where Islamic tradition maintains Muhammad ascended to heaven. While knocking on the floor of the cave elicited a mysterious hollow sound, renowned nineteenth century British explorers Charles Wilson and Sir Charles Warren believed that the resounding echo was due to some small fissure below the floor and they failed to either prove or disprove the existence of such a chamber.

Though there had never been any officially organised archaeological exploration of the site or Haram al-Sharif/Temple Mount itself – which is under control of the Waqf Muslim religious trust – it was known to be riddled with a network of some forty-five cisterns, chambers, tunnels, and caves. Shimon Gibson, senior fellow at the W. F. Albright Institute of Archaeological Research in Jerusalem, who with colleague David Jacobson wrote a definitive review – *Below the Temple Mount in Jerusalem: A Sourcebook on the Cisterns, Subterranean Chambers and Conduits of the Haram Al-Sharif* – said that "since the 19th century, no Westerner has been allowed access to the subterranean chambers on the Temple Mount … I would have liked to disguise myself as a local Waqf worker and infiltrate these sites, but I wouldn't want to run the risk of creating an international incident." Taking that risk was no longer an issue for a great many Israelis.

According to biblical accounts, the Ark – which was constructed with gold-covered shittah-tree wood (acacia) known to the ancient Egyptians as the Tree of Life with importance in traditional medicine and in many cases containing psychoactive alkaloids (hallucinogens) – had been hidden in a chamber under Haram al-Sharif/Temple Mount. If that were the case, then it was unlikely for it to have survived the adverse and damp conditions. It was Shimon Gibson's opinion that "the Ark probably would have disintegrated. Unless, of course, it had holy properties. But I, as an archaeologist, cannot talk about the theoretical holy properties of a wooden box." Even if that were the case, then surely there would still be some presence of either the gold that covered the Ark, or of the gold pot that contained manna, the "bread of the wilderness" which God gave to the 600,000 children of Israel when they were going from Egypt to the Promised Land.

As far as Yaakov Katzir was concerned, the discovery of the Well of Souls or any chamber under Temple Mount, would vindicate his own fanatical enthusiasm for the Hiramic Brotherhood's commitment to the building of a Third Temple; would justify the belief in his Jewish supremacism as inculcated by his upbringing and military service; and would inflame his Jewish nationalistic fervour and hatred for non-Jews while exploiting the Holocaust as justification for violence and discrimination against Palestinians, African migrants, and even Ethiopian Jews. Yaakov's conscience was in fact not at all troubled by the current Israeli racist violence against Ethiopian Jews whose claim of having the Ark of the Covenant in Ethiopia, he vehemently ridiculed as "nigger nonsense which they should take back with them to Africa."

Ethiopian tradition maintained that the Ark of the

Covenant was preserved in the ancient holy city of Axum. The Ark had apparently been kept for centuries in the Church of Mary of Zion, where the emperor Iyasu was recorded as having seen and spoken to it in 1691. Currently the Ark is allegedly kept in the Chapel of the Tablet, built adjacent to the church during the reign of the last emperor, Haile Selassie. It was said to be entrusted to a single guardian, who burnt incense and recited the Biblical Book of Psalms in front of the Ark. No one – kings and bishops included – was allowed to approach the ark other than the guardian who was not only a monk, but also a virgin serving the Ark until as he approaches his own death, he appoints a successor.

The classic account of Ethiopia's Ark comes from a medieval epic, *The Glory of Kings* (Kebra Nagast), written in the Ge'ez Ethiopian language. It describes how Bilkis, the Queen of Sheba, on hearing of King Solomon's immense wisdom, traveled to Jerusalem so as to acquire more knowledge and wisdom on how to better govern her own people. Being much impressed by both her beauty and intelligence, Solomon began desiring to have a child by her: a desire not driven by lust, but by an apparently unselfish aspiration to fill the earth with sons who would serve Israel's God. It was claimed that Bilkis did have a son who as a grown man travelled from Ethiopia to visit his father in Jerusalem. After anointing his son as king of Ethiopia, Solomon instructed the elders of Israel to send their own sons to Ethiopia to serve as counsellors. As they were unhappy at the prospect of never again seeing Jerusalem and its Temple, the young Israelites decided to take the Ark along with them. *The Glory of Kings* narrative asserts that it was in fact the Ark itself that decided to leave Jerusalem because the Jews had ceased to practice the faith revealed to them by God.

An alternative version of the visit by Bilkis, has her being welcomed with fanfare, festivities and a tour of the great buildings including the Temple which filled her with awe and admiration. On being captivated by her beauty, Solomon – who was said to have accumulated three hundred concubines and seven hundred wives – proposed marriage which a flattered Bilkis accepted. Following several subsequent visits to the Temple, however, Bilkis insisted on meeting the architect of such magnificence, and when brought before her, she found the architect Hiram Abiff's appearance and manner totally beguiling. On regaining her composure she not only questioned Hiram at length, but also defended him against Solomon's evident ill will and rising jealousy. When she asked to see the men who had built the Temple, Solomon protested at the impossibility of assembling the entire workforce consisting of apprentices, fellow-crafts and masters. But Hiram, jumping up on a large rock so as to be better seen, described with his right hand the symbolical Tau, and immediately all the workmen hastened from the different works into the presence of their Master. Bilkis was so impressed by such a display of authority that she realised she was in love with the great architect and regretted her promise to Solomon. She eventually got out of her pledge to Solomon by removing the betrothal ring from his finger while he was under the influence of wine.

This raises the questions of when *The Glory of Kings* was written, and when the tradition of the Ark being in Ethiopia began. It was known from coins and inscriptions that the ancient kings of Axum were pagan until the 4th century at which time they converted to Christianity – which was declared the state religion in 330 – with no record in existence of either their having claimed descent from King Solomon or of their being associated with the Ark of the Covenant. The earliest report of the Ark's presence in Ethiopia appears towards the end of the twelfth century when an Armenian in Cairo, Abu Salih, wrote in Arabic that the Ethiopians were in possession of the Ark of the Covenant which was carried by descendants of King David's family who had blond hair and red and white complexions. While some historians have justifiably claimed that Abu Salih was mistaken in asserting the Ark had been carried by Europeans rather than by Ethiopians, his account cannot be discounted because he may have relied on the authority of the Bible's *Song of Solomon* which states that Solomon had white and red cheeks and hair like fine gold.

Despite all such arguments and theories, it had to be ultimately recognised that the historical facts relating to King Solomon's lifetime (c. 1011 – 931 BCE) were loosely based on various legends from Egypt, Phoenicia, and southern Arabia where the land of Sheba had flourished from the Caravan Road.

Any honest examination by archaeologists and scholars of available facts would conclude that the Israelites were unlikely to have been in Egypt, could hardly have wandered in the desert for forty years, had lacked the military means to conquer the Promised Land, and consequently could not have passed it on to the twelve tribes of Israel. None of this, however, was going to discourage those intent on the complete Judaisation of East Jerusalem for the building of a Third Temple as fulfilment of a cherished aspiration for a united Jerusalem as the undivided and eternal capital of the Jewish people at the expense and obliteration of the indigenous Palestinians, their culture, and their history.

Respect for the rights of others – non-Jews in general and Palestinians in particular – was not a matter of much concern for Katzir who from early childhood had been taught that non-Jews (goyim) were evil people to be feared and regarded with suspicion because of what they had done in the past; had been inculcated with racist and invariably false precepts that encouraged an extremist, hatred and fear of the outside world; had consequently developed a siege mentality that precluded the possibility of tolerance for, and coexistence with other ethnic groups; and had come to regard himself as being one of the perennial victims whose "victimisation" was to be nurtured and used as a weapon against non-Jewish enemies. Katzir's tendency for vicious retribution was something that Conrad and Freya were destined to soon encounter in Jerusalem.

7

Saturday, 12 December

Beirut, Lebanon

The Committee to Protect Journalists' announcement that 69 journalists had been killed while on the job during the past year disturbed Mark Banner, but did not surprise him. Syria was where the most journalists had died with a total of fourteen, while France was second with nine; forty percent died at the hands of Islamic militant groups such as Al-Qaeda and the Islamic State; and more than two-thirds of the total killed had been singled out for murder. Such news, however, was not about to deter Mark and as usual he emailed his latest article to his London news agency.

Zionism's Ultimate Weapon:
The Exploitation of Anti-Semitism

Mark Banner
Sunday, 13 December

Differentiating between Zionism and Judaism requires recognition of certain basic facts. To begin with, Theodor Herzl (the founder of Zionism) was an atheist whose personal awareness of Jewishness appears to have been awakened during the 1894 trial, wrongful conviction, and imprisonment on Devil's Island of Alfred Dreyfus, a French artillery officer of Alsatian Jewish descent accused of spying for Germany. In his diaries, Herzl makes no secret of his intention to use Jewish suffering as a means of furthering Zionist ideology. His vision for a Jewish state had nothing to do with " … I will also bring them back to the land that I gave to their forefathers and they shall possess it" (Jeremiah 30:3). Herzl had actually considered various other locations such as Uganda and Argentina for his Zionist state and his view of Zionism and Judaism was more akin to that of Chaim Chassas who in 1943 in the Zionist newspaper, *Ha'Arutz*, said:

> *"Zionism and Judaism is not one thing but two different things. And of course two contradicting one another. Zionism starts at the place where Judaism is destroyed … one thing is certain, Zionism is not a continuation or healing of wounded Judaism, but rather an uprooting."*

Zionism has never had any qualms about the loss of Jewish lives so long as that loss furthered the cause of Zionism. In the book *51 Documents: Zionist Collaboration with the Nazis*, editor Lenni Brenner, uses actual historic documents to demonstrate the betrayal of Jews by Zionists – before during, and after the Holocaust – even to the extent of offering to fight for the Nazis on the understanding that after Germany won the war, Zionism would be rewarded with Palestine.

> *"If I knew that it was possible to save all the children of Germany by transporting them to England, and only half by transporting them to the Land of Israel, I would choose the latter, for before us lies not the numbers of these children, but the historic reckoning of the people of Israel."*
> **From Israeli historian Shabtai Teveth's book on Ben-Gurion.**

Zionist Apartheid Israel's deliberate long-term policy of periodic military attacks against the largely unarmed Palestinian people – including the current cowardly and barbarous assault which even the Nazis would have struggled to match – has absolutely nothing to do with "self defence" because even the pitiful Hamas rocket attacks are rendered ineffective by Israel's American taxpayer-funded Iron Dome Missile Shield. The real reason for such attacks is to fulfil Zionist ideology by avoiding any kind of negotiated peace that might forestall the illegal Israeli land grabs and ethnic cleansing required for the creation of a "Greater Israel" devoid of Palestinians. To add insult to injury, these unashamed Zionist savages also have the barefaced audacity to refer to Palestinians as "animals" and to themselves as "God's Chosen People." History has repeatedly shown that whenever one ethnic group regards itself as being superior to others – be it a "Master Race" or a "Chosen People" – then after much death and destruction it will eventually perish as was the case with the Third Reich.

Zionist Israel's evil racist intentions have remained constant ever since its inception with its primary founder and first Prime Minister, David Ben-Gurion emphatically stating that "We must use terror, assassination, intimidation, land confiscation, and the cutting of all social services to rid the Galilee of its Arab population." This "Father of the nation" and now (if there is an afterlife) guest of the Devil, must be very proud of the tenacity with which his "God-Chosen" compatriots have stuck to their task by pillaging and murdering their way southwards into the West Bank and Gaza Strip.

The successful selling to the world of blatant Israeli lies and fabricated justifications has been achieved by an assault on all possible fronts including the gross distortion of archaeological facts and Biblical narrative.

"Appropriations of the past as part of the politics of the present … could be illustrated for most parts of the globe. One further example which is of particular interest to this study, is the way in which archeology and biblical history have become of such importance to the modern state of Israel. It is this combination which has been such a powerful factor in silencing Palestinian history."

Keith W. Whitelam, *The Invention of Ancient Israel: the silencing of Palestinian History,* Routledge, London, 1996.

"De-Arabising the history of Palestine is another crucial element of the ethnic cleansing. 1500 years of Arab and Muslim rule and culture in Palestine are trivialised, evidence of its existence is being destroyed and all this is done to make the absurd connection between the ancient Hebrew civilisation and today's Israel. The most glaring example of this today is in Silwan, (Wadi Hilwe) a town adjacent to the Old City of Jerusalem with some 50,000 residents. Israel is expelling families from Silwan and destroying their homes because it claims that King David built a city there some 3,000 years ago. Thousands of families will be made homeless so that Israel can build a park to commemorate a king that may or may not have lived 3,000 years ago. Not a shred of historical evidence exists that can prove King David ever lived yet Palestinian men, women, children and the elderly along with their schools and mosques, churches and ancient cemeteries and any evidence of their existence must be destroyed and then denied so that Zionist claims to exclusive rights to the land may be substantiated."

Miko Peled, Israeli peace activist and author (Born Jerusalem, 1961)

The most successful Zionist ploy has been to equate itself with Judaism and to hijack and hide behind Judaic aspects starting with sacred emblems such as the Menorah and then to demean the memory of the Holocaust whose constant, cynical invocation is used to silence criticism of barbaric Israeli crimes and even to evoke illusionary justification for the cold, calculated genocide of the Palestinian people.

> *"Israelis and American Jews fully agree that the memory of the Holocaust is an indispensable weapon – one that must be used relentlessly against their common enemy … Jewish organisations and individuals thus labor continuously to remind the world of it. In America, the perpetuation of the Holocaust memory is now a $100-million-a-year enterprise, part of which is government funded."*

According to Israeli author Moshe Leshem, the expansion of Israeli power is commensurate with the expansion of the "Holocaust" propaganda.

> *"Ever since the Jews invented the libel charge of "anti – Semitism" in the 1880s. It was first published in the Jewish Encyclopaedia (1901 Vol. 1, p. 641), and has been built up with Jewish money, organisations, propaganda and lies (such as the Holocaust – Holohoax), so that now the word is like a snake venom which paralyses one's nervous system. Even the mention of the word "Jew" is shunned unless used in a most favourable and positive context."*

Charles A. Weisman, *Who is Esau-Edom?* Weisman Publications, 1966.

The continued use of "anti-Semitism" as a weapon against its critics – even to the extent of the recent invention of a "New anti-Semitism" – is essential for the survival of Zionism because it serves to deflect attention from the lying, cheating, stealing, murdering, war profiteering, blatant violations of international law, and barbaric crimes against humanity. Yet despite such overwhelming and irrefutable evidence of Israel's unabated criminality, Jews everywhere continue to decline from equating Zionism with Judaism, and most of those who do recognise the difference, lack the courage to say so; the corporate mass media continues to refuse to do the right thing by unconditionally reporting the facts; so-called political leaders – led by the U.S. President and Canada's noxiously obsequious Prime Minister – continue with blinkered eyes to fawn over and commend Israel's ethnic cleansing of the Palestinian people; and as for the most of the rest of us, by quietly accepting Israel's propaganda lies, we become complicit in its crimes while obediently supping from a Zionist trough that is overflowing with Palestinian blood.

8

Tuesday 15, December

Little Venice, London, England

Several events over the the past few years had dramatically changed Conrad Banner's life with the first being his meeting and falling in love with Freya Neilson. The second event of significance was the death of his grandfather which was followed six months later by that of his grandmother. Their demise had served to bring about a reconciliation between him and his father, Mark. The rift between them had occurred sixteen years earlier when Mark – an author and journalist with numerous British and international journalism awards for covering the Middle East – took up residence in Beirut where Conrad's mother was not prepared to go and live. The breakdown of the marriage had been followed by an inevitable but fairly amicable divorce with Conrad remaining in England with his mother and consequently drifting apart from his father.

The grandparents last will and testament had stipulated that their estate – including their house in the desirable location of Little Venice – be divided equally between Mark and Conrad who both agreed not to sell the family home where Mark had grown up as a child and Conrad had enjoyed many weekends and summer holidays. They had instead decided that Conrad would take up residence in the house where Mark's room had always been kept for whenever he visited London. It was a convenient arrangement that also enabled them to occasionally spend some time together. As

Mark usually made a point of spending Christmas in London, they had, along with Conrad's mother who had not remarried, managed to celebrate last Christmas together as a family for the first time in many years.

This year, however, Conrad had decided that the video documentary he was about to start filming in Jerusalem should include the Holy Land's Christmas celebrations on December 25th. Apart from the December celebration for Catholics and Protestants, there were further Christmas celebrations on January 6 for the Orthodox Christians, and January 19 for the Armenian Orthodox in Jerusalem. The topic of Conrad's documentary was going to be Israel's improper use of archaeology to de-Arabise, to invalidate, and to gradually destroy any evidential basis for the existence of a Palestinian people and instead to legitimise Israel's claim to all the Holy Land by creating unsubstantiated claims for the alleged existence of an ancient Jewish civilisation that would justify the current land-grabbing Jewish state of Israel.

On his previous exploratory visit to Jerusalem Jason had met and befriended Sami Hadawi, and Adam Peltz, with whom he had discussed his plans for the documentary. Peltz had explained that despite its alleged "aim to increase public awareness and interest in the country's archaeological heritage" while ostensibly engaging in scientific activity, the Israel Antiquities Authority (IAA), had failed to provide any easily accessible information about either the locations or objectives of its ongoing excavations, the scope of its activities, or the nature of its finds. Frequently the available information about tunnel excavations was provided after the fact through a communiqué from an IAA spokesperson and not reported transparently while the work was in progress. It sufficed to say that such lack of transparency heightened suspicion of irregular activities that might harm archeological discoveries in order to advance the covert activities for political objectives.

This morning Conrad was at his desk listing everything that would be required for the forthcoming trip to Jerusalem. He had decided on a compact rig that could be carried in one camera bag and was easy to walk and move around with including a PCM recorder designed for use with his choice of a digital single-lens reflex camera which, unlike a camcorder, could also shoot excellent stills; lenses including 18-35 f1.8, 50mm f1.8, and 200mm f3.5; LED lighting kit; a fluid head tripod; a 24-inch slider; and a shoulder rig. Having the right equipment was only a small part of documentary film making which included not only a technical familiarity with the equipment, but also competence in storytelling, scriptwriting, editing, production, and of course an exhaustive research of the subject which Conrad had been doing by reading about the evolving history of Judaism and its connection to Jerusalem.

According to approximate Biblical dates starting with Abram/Abraham – a key figure in the three monotheistic religions of Christianity, Islam, and Judaism – who allegedly lived in the socially advanced city of Ur of the Chaldees in Babylonia (now Iraq), it was sometime around 2091 BCE (Genesis 12) that he got the "call" from God/Yahweh/Jehovah in a verbal communication to "go from your kindred and your father's house to the land that I will show you." Conrad was soon to discover that this would prove to be the first of many alleged communications to the Jewish people from God who was apparently callously indifferent towards all the other human beings whom He had created: "So God created mankind in his own image, in the image of God he created them; male and female he created them" (Genesis 1:27).

So as his father Terah had recently died at the hard to believe age of 265 – having begat an offspring at the age of 190 – 75 year-old Abraham and his wife Sarai/Sarah departed for Haran (now Syria) to gather possessions and people before being led by God to Canaan where despite the presence of the Canaanites, God commits to giving Canaan to Abraham's offspring thereby enabling the Hebrew scribes to insinuate the twin concepts of a "Chosen People" and "Promised Land" – concocted concepts which Conrad noted had survived to this day and were being cited as justification for the displacement of an indigenous Palestinian population to facilitate establishment of a "Promised Land" for the Jewish people.

Unfortunately famine had apparently struck Canaan causing Abraham to leave for Egypt for a period of time before in due course returning to once again have God promise him and his descendants the land in perpetuity. Then despite being in his nineties and without the benefit of either Viagra or oysters – Venetian-born Giacomo Girolamo Casanova, the renowned lover, used to breakfast on fifty oysters – Abraham somehow managed to make Sarah's handmaiden, Hagar, pregnant with the child subsequently being named Ishmael sometime around 2080 BCE (Genesis 16:15).

It was years later that the postmenopausal Sarah became miraculously pregnant when Abraham was ninety-nine and after giving birth to Isaac in 2066 BCE (Genesis 21), demanded that her rival Hagar be expelled into the wilderness along with her son Ishmael. Despite some initial hesitation Abraham finally relented after receiving God's assurance that since Ishmael was his son, he would also make of him "a great nation." Arabs have subsequently claimed descent from Ishmael who features in the Quran as Ismail, a prophet and ancestor of the Prophet Muhammad.

Following Sarah's death at the age of 127, Abraham acquired from the local Hittites – along with the right to govern the area and establish Isaac as his heir – what is now the "Cave of the Patriarchs" at Hebron, known to Muslims as the Sanctuary of Abraham or the Ibrahimi Mosque where more recently in 1994, Baruch Goldstein, a deranged American-Israeli member of the far-right Israeli Kach and Kahane Chai, opened fire on Muslim worshippers killing 29 and wounding 125 others before being overpowered and subsequently dying from his wounds.

Ensuing Biblical events included the destruction of Sodom and Gomorrah whose main sin appears to have been either consensual or forced anal sex between two men with which the word "sodomy" had become synonymous; the turning of the wife of Lot (Abraham's nephew) into a pillar of salt; and the conspiring of Lot's two daughters to become pregnant by their father while he slept after drinking wine.

Isaac then had twin sons of whom Jacob – later renamed "Israel" by God – deviously cheated Esau out of his birthright; had four wives with whom he fathered twelve sons including the more favoured Joseph with his "coat of many colours" whose jealous brothers sold into slavery in Egypt; and where Joseph following sundry trials and tribulations wins the respect of the Pharaoh and goes on to become "governor of the whole land of Egypt" (Genesis 41:43).

During Canaan's drought, Israel and his other sons journeyed to buy grain in Egypt where they were received by Joseph who initially concealed his identity before finally revealing himself and forgiving his brothers. The brothers settled in Egypt where their thriving descendants become an affluent, influential minority known as "Hebrews" or "Israelites." They were, however, eventually enslaved because of the Pharaoh's allegation that the Hebrew people "are more numerous and more powerful than we" (Exodus 1-12): an allegation that established the long lasting concept of "separateness" and "victimisation" of the Jewish people

The Pharaoh, in due course, allegedly ordered all newborn Hebrew boys to be killed but the mother of the infant Moses born around 1525 BCE (Exodus 2) first hides and then floats him on the River Nile in a wicker basket where he is eventually found and adopted by an Egyptian princess. After being raised amongst the Egyptian aristocracy, Moses eventually learns of his Hebrew lineage, flees to the land of Midian on the Arabian Peninsula, and encounters the "angel of the Lord" in the form of a burning bush (Exodus 3:2) through whom he is ordered by God to lead his people out of slavery which Moses did by demanding of the Pharaoh, "Let my people go" (Exodus 8:1).

When the Pharaoh refuses, God smites the Egyptians with pestilence that forces the Pharaoh to relent and allow the Hebrews to leave. The Pharaoh then sends his troops in pursuit of the Hebrews who on reaching Red Sea are saved when God parts the seawater to enable Moses and his people to escape while the pursuing Egyptians are drowned as the seawater resurges.

Because Moses as a character was conceived with the Egyptian name *Thutmose* or *Ahmoses* and was based on a collection of different myths – including that of the Egyptian demigod Heracles of Canopus who was drawn from an arc in the Nile bulrushes and grew up to perform many great deeds before eventually dying on a mountaintop – the illusionary nature of his persona casts doubt on his actual existence.

The narrative regarding the parting of the Red Sea appears to have come courtesy of the ancient Egyptian Goddess Isis, who on learning the location of the chest containing the body of her murdered husband Osiris, simply parted the waters for her journey to Byblos in Lebanon, thereby also providing the story line for Bindumati (Kali as the mother of bindu or Spark of Life) who miraculously crossed the River Ganges.

Even the part about Moses being given the tablets of stone by God on Mount Sinai has echoes of the Canaanite "God of the Covenant," Baal-Berith, with the tablets' Ten Commandments following those of the Buddhist Decalogue. In ancient times such commandments were generally given by a deity on a mountain top as was the case with the Greek Titan Queen of heaven, Mother Rhea of Mount Dicte (in Crete), and Zoroaster who received his tablets on a mountaintop from Ahuru Mazda.

What also puzzled Conrad was that while Joseph's brothers were able to journey to Egypt in a relatively short period of time, 600,000 Hebrews somehow managed – despite the logistic impossibility in those days of providing food, water, and shelter for so many – to wander aimlessly for 40 years in a small triangular peninsula with an area of some 23,000 square miles situated between the Mediterranean Sea to the north, and the Red Sea to the South.

It was sometime around 1406 BCE that Joshua – who was one of twelve spies sent by Moses to explore the land of Canaan and became leader after Moses died – leads the Hebrews into the land of Canaan, which was inhabited by various peoples including Amorites, Edomites, Hittites Jebusites, Perizzites, Philistines, and others whom Joshua is ordered by God to exterminate – an order which contradicts the numerous biblical claims that God is all merciful. The conquest is achieved through various miraculous events, such as the parting of the River Jordan and the Battle of Jericho during which the city's walls fell when the Hebrews blew their trumpets. Then on God's command the triumphant Hebrews slaughtered every man, woman and child in the city.

Having supposedly conquered the "Promised Land" with its pagan city of Jerusalem, the Hebrews then spent generations under the governance of "judges" – who were in fact shamans such as Deborah, Gideon, Samson and Samuel – before deciding to appoint a king contrary to the interpretation by some that such action would be an affront to God's direct rule through the divinely inspired judges. Nonetheless a character named Saul – whose existence is questioned by many historians – becomes king to govern from around 1043 BCE before eventually falling on his sword in a suicide so as to avoid capture in the battle against the Philistines. Saul's son-in-law, David, then took over to first govern from Hebron for seven years and then from Jerusalem for 43 years.

The first mention of Jerusalem in the biblical narrative occurs when in the Battle of Gibeon, Joshua defeats Jerusalem's king (Joshua 10:5) and brings the city under Hebrew control by asking God to cause the sun to stand still – an astronomical impossibility – so that the fighting might be concluded in daylight which God obligingly and miraculously agrees to do (Joshua 10:12). Conrad also learnt that Jerusalem – first mentioned in the 20th-19th century BCE Egyptian execration texts – had been founded by the proto-Canaanite people long before the existence of anything resembling Judaism at some time between 4500-3500 BCE and was known as Daru Shalem in dedication to the god of dusk, Shalem. The city was then ruled from approximately 1500 – 1200 BCE by pharaohs from Memphis in Egypt with the Canaanites acting as their proxies. Even after pharaonic rule had ended, Canaanite monarchs continued to exercise control over the region where Canaanite culture and beliefs prevailed despite the gradual absorption of some religious practices that were later to be linked with Judaism.

The end of Solomon's reign, so the narrative goes, witnessed a split into the two kingdoms of Israel and Judah with the former eventually being twice attacked by the Assyrian Empire in 732 and in 720 BCE. The allegation that its population was dispersed led to the subsequent concoction about the tribes of Israel being "lost" in numerous faraway places. Judah's Hezekiah with his capital in Jerusalem, however, managed to negotiate peace with the Assyrians. It is at this stage that a Biblical narrative finally has an alternative non-Biblical corroboration as to the existence of King Hezekiah (c. 716 – 686 BCE) by Assyrian sources. The Bible narrative cites him as the king who established the worship of the one God/Yahweh/Jehovah while banning worship of pagan deities from the Temple. It was also thought by many scholars that Josiah, Hezekiah's great-grandson and Judah's king (c. 640 –

c. 610 BCE) codified the Hebrew scriptures with most Old Testament texts now believed to date at the earliest from the seventh century with the probability that Judaism itself also dated from that period.

Nonetheless, Judah eventually succumbed to the Neo-Babylonian Empire with the fall of Jerusalem around 590 BCE when presumably the First Temple was destroyed and some of the population deported to spend decades in the exile known as "the Babylonian Captivity." The exiles were consequently exposed to the Zoroastrian concepts of an afterlife, a heaven, a messianic saviour, and cosmogonic and eschatological Zoroastrian myths wherein men played the leading and most positive roles. What is now known as "Judaism" was probably the result of that cross-cultural encounter at which time the Psalms 19 and 137 "by the rivers of Babylon," were probably conceived.

In 539 BCE the Persian king Cyrus of the Achaemenid Empire, having conquered Babylonia, permitted the exiled Judaeans to return home and rebuild their temple but many declined the opportunity and instead continued enjoying the benefits of the society to which they had become attached. The land now regarded as "Judaea" fell under Persian rule until 330 BCE when it was conquered by Alexander the Great and remained under Greek control until the 167 BCE revolt by a Judaean rebel group known as the Maccabees. It was while under Greek control that the "Second Temple" in Jerusalem became a centre for the evolving Jewish religion but there was no independent "Jewish state" until the emergence of the Hasmonean dynasty rule that lasted for about a century before being succeeded by the Herodian dynasty which accepted Roman over-lordship in 63 BCE and gave way to full Roman rule in 92 CE.

Due to previous deportations – that incidentally also affected many other ethnic groups – voluntary migrations, or simply the necessity of travel for the purpose of trade, Judaean communities were already widespread and to be found in Mesopotamia, Egypt, Cyrenaica (Libya); Spain, Greece, Rome, and in what is now northern Turkey. After the death of Jesus, Jerusalem became host to a cosmopolitan community with Jews and Gentiles who hailed from far and wide including those on pilgrimage.

The First Jewish-Roman War (66 – 73 CE) consisted of a determined Judaean revolt against Roman rule that ended in the destruction of the Second Temple and the forced exile or enslavement of thousands but did not constitute a full-scale expulsion. The Kitos War (115 – 117 CE) and Bar Kokhba Revolt (132 CE) witnessed further expulsions that also included Christians who were considered a sect within the Judaean religion and were consequently banned from living in Jerusalem which subsequently became a pagan city where Judaeans were a minority amongst a population of Greeks, Romans, Syrians, and numerous others. So on the Basis of what he had so far learnt, Conrad concluded that there had never been an actual Jewish state let alone an "eternal capital" of "Israel" and any claim to the contrary was a blatant distortion of actual historical facts.

It was after the series of Jewish-Roman wars and the expulsions that Christianity started "shedding" its Judaic heritage by usurping elements of pagan sun worship by switching its sacred day of observance from Saturday, the Jewish Sabbath, to Sunday, the state's sacred and "venerable day of the sun." Further changes included "adoption" of the aureole of light that crowned the sun god's head for use as the Christian halo, and Christ's birthday was changed from January 6 to December 25 in keeping with the sun's rebirth celebration. Such usurpation paid off and by the fourth century CE Christianity became the official religion of the Roman Empire with the result that many Judaeans forsook their identity as the "Chosen People" and instead embraced the new faith. So while they may have remained ethnically Judaean, they had nonetheless surrendered the progeny of their predecessors to whom God had supposedly given entitlement to a Promised Land.

Jerusalem thus became a fully Christian city landmarked by the Church of the Holy Sepulchre, the Greek Orthodox Church of St. John the Baptist, and the Church of St. Mary with the latter being built by the Emperor Justinian. Many Judaean Christians subsequently converted to Islam after the Muslim conquest of Palestine was completed in 635 CE. Consequently a great many modern Palestinian Arabs have more DNA in common with the ancient Judaeans than do the European Jews who currently claim a "Jewish right of return" to their *ancestral* home.

As a Muslim city with the magnificent al-Aqsa Mosque being built on Temple Mount in the eighth century, Jerusalem became the third most sacred city in the Islamic world after Mecca and Medina and has remained as a symbol of Islam for more than twelve centuries of Muslim rule which was briefly interrupted by the Christian Crusaders' "Kingdom of Jerusalem" from 1099 to 1187 during which it once again became mainly Christian. It was, however, a Christian interlude which Saladin the Magnificent – a merciful Muslim Kurd leader renowned even amongst Christians – ended by defeating the Crusaders at the decisive 1187 Battle of Hattin and thereby paved the way for the recapture of Palestine for the Muslims. He mercifully allowed the Crusaders to retreat with dignity; confirmed the right of Christians to visit Jerusalem on pilgrimage; restored the rights of the Greek Orthodox community that had been suppressed by the Roman Catholics; and was consequently thanked by the Byzantine emperor for protecting the Orthodox churches. Muslims then resumed their rule of Jerusalem until the defeat of the Ottoman Empire in World War One. The revelations after World War Two of the Nazi death camps and atrocities rightly generated immense global sympathy for Jews which Zionists ruthlessly exploited – through the creation of a "Holocaust Industry – to achieve their goals in what can only be described as a betrayal of the Jews whom they were claiming to defend and represent.

This was made evident by Israeli author Moshe Leshem who in his book *Balaam's Curse: How Israel Lost its Way, and How it Can Find it Again,* asserted that Israeli power was commensurate with the expansion of "Holocaust" propaganda: "Israelis and American Jews fully agree that the memory of the Holocaust is an indispensable weapon – one that must be used relentlessly against their common enemy … Jewish organisations and individuals thus labour continuously to remind the world of it. In America, the perpetuation of the Holocaust memory is now a $100-million-a-year enterprise, part of which is government funded."

9

Thursday, 17 December

Jerusalem Technology Park, Malha, Southwest Jerusalem

During his military service Yaakov Katzir used to be an elitist and loose canon warrior for the Maglan which with Sayeret Matkal was one of the IDF's two Special Operations units. The Sayeret Matkal was a highly secretive special-operations brigade shrouded in a mythic status for its swift, surgical operations in Egypt, Lebanon, Jordan, and the 1976 daring rescue of 103 Jewish hostages in the hijacked plane at Entebbe Airport in Uganda. Hebraic hate for, and homicidal intent towards Arabs within the ranks of the Sayeret Matkal was sufficiently honed to enable those wishing to pursue a political career – such as prime ministers Ehud Barak and Benjamin Netanyahu – to do so without having to read the odious *The King's Torah,* in which rabbis Yitzhak Shapira and Yosef Elitzur – the rabbis of the occupation and arbiters of Jewish law from the Od Yosef Chai Yeshiva in Yitzhar – wrote that "the ban on killing a gentile does not stem from the intrinsic value of his life, which is not essentially legitimate as such." The book reads like a rabbinic instruction manual outlining acceptable scenarios for killing non-Jewish babies, children and adults with the assertion that "it is clear that they will grow to harm us."

Maglan commandos had been equally effective with no recognised limits as to behaviour while boasting a record of impressive covert operations in Lebanon including the 2006 Second Lebanon war which many Israelis now regard as not having been particularly successful because 121 Israeli soldiers and 44 civilians were killed with some cities and rural communities suffering a barrage of more than 4,000 rockets causing some 200,000 Israelis to flee their homes in the north while seeking shelter elsewhere. Exceptional strategic intelligence had, however, enabled the Israeli Air Force to launch devastating strikes in which Hezbollah's arsenal of long-range rockets were destroyed.

Katzir with other members of the Maglan had planted sophisticated listening devices – just one of the many surveillance tools at Israel's disposal – to eavesdrop on, and track movements of the Lebanese militant group's communications. Such forays into Lebanon by the IDF's elite commando units were not always "clean operations" because whenever Lebanese civilians were accidentally encountered during high-priority missions, they had to be killed so as to avoid causing a major political scandal resulting in embarrassment for Israel. Such tragic encounters were written off in Hebrew military jargon as a *mikreh muzar,* or "strange incident." More recently In a related matter, Israel's military chief, had revoked the "Hannibal Directive" which called for Israeli troops to prevent their comrades from being captured even if it meant killing them as had been the case on several combat occasions in Gaza.

Disposing of "troublesome" Palestinians was consequently not a problem for Yaakov Katzir, a sturdily built five foot eight inch man with short dark hair and recognisably pronounced dusky Semitic features. Since finishing his military service and becoming a member of the Hiramic Brotherhood of the Third Temple, his dedication to the cause had, to put it mildly, been unreservedly fanatical.

The Brotherhood's monthly meetings were held in the boardroom of an Israeli technology company located in the Malha Technology Park. As a neighbourhood in southwest Jerusalem – and part of the Ottoman Empire since 1596 until the British Mandate for Palestine came into effect in 1923 – Malha was known as al-Maliha up to the time of the 1948 Palestinian Nabka or "catastrophe" when some 530 Palestinian villages were destroyed by Zionist paramilitary forces who were also responsible for many massacres including that at Deir Yassin. News of such massacres and other atrocities had been responsible for causing much of the fear and panic that forced some 750,000 Palestinians to flee their homes many of which were then either destroyed or unceremoniously taken over and occupied by Jewish emigrants.

Even though files in the Israeli archives relevant to that forced exodus had, according to Israeli law, long ago passed their time as being classified, they had nonetheless – along with those already declassified – been reclassified as "top secret" and kept sealed and hidden from the eyes of researchers. Prevention of access to such archived, controversial, and embarrassing material – including reports of massacres, rapes, and other atrocities committed by the so-called "most moral" Israeli fighters – had been prompted by the publication of books by historians who had sought unsuccessfully to uncover the true facts.

Surprisingly, however, one file referred to as "The Flight in 1948," had somehow managed to escape the Israeli censor's cloak of secrecy to reveal documents dating from 1960 to 1964, that detail how the sanitised Israeli version of events had evolved. It was apparently under Prime Minister David Ben-Gurion's leadership, that leading scholars in the Civil Service were entrusted with the task of presenting evidence in support of Israel's position that, rather than being expelled, the Palestinians had left of their own accord.

Evidently Ben-Gurion had, as Israel's first prime minister, recognised the importance of the historical narrative and that Just as Zionism had concocted a narrative justifying Jewish presence in Palestine, then those Palestinians who had lived there before the violent intrusion of Zionism, could themselves also endeavour to present their own "Catastrophe" narrative of how some 750,000 of them had been terrorised and forcibly expelled to become refugees. It was therefore Ben-Gurion's opinion that such Israeli narratives were of foremost importance in Israel's diplomatic efforts to legitimise its own existence as a means of countering the Palestinian national movement. If for example the Palestinian claim of their having been expelled from their land was accepted as being an irrefutable fact, then the international community would regard a Palestinian desire to return to their homeland as being justified. If on the other hand the international community "bought" the false Israeli narrative that the Palestinians had left of their own accord after being persuaded by their leaders to do so with a promise of return following victory by the Arabs, then the international community would be less inclined to be sympathetic to their cause.

A majority of historians – whether Zionist or otherwise – are now agreed that in at least 120 villages the Palestinian inhabitants were forcibly expelled by Jewish paramilitary forces; that in half the villages the inhabitants fled because of the battles and were subsequently prevented from returning; and that only in a few cases did villagers leave as a result of being instructed to do so by their leaders. Though much Israeli archive material relating to the Palestinian Nabka remains classified, the information uncovered was still sufficient to establish that in most cases senior commanders of the Israeli paramilitary Forces had ordered Palestinians to be expelled; had ordered their homes to be blown up; and that not only had Ben-Gurion been kept informed, but that he had also actually given prior oral or written authorisation.

Though available Israeli documents do not provide a clear answer as to whether or not there was a deliberate plan to expel Palestinians, the fact remains that "New Historians" – Israeli historians who have questioned the validity of traditional versions of Israeli history, including Israel's role in the 1948 Palestinian Exodus and Arab willingness to discuss peace – such as Benny Morris, have maintained that Ben-Gurion had a specific plan to drive out the Palestinians for the creation of a Jewish homeland. The following is from the leaked censored version of Yitzhak Rabin's memoirs, published in the *New York Times,* 23 October 1979:

> *"We walked outside, Ben-Gurion accompanying us. Allon repeated his question, What is to be done with the Palestinian population?' Ben-Gurion waved his hand in a gesture which said 'Drive them out!'"*

Despite evidence to the contrary, an Israeli public relations onslaught ensued with such barefaced lies claiming "We did not expel Arabs from the Land of Israel … After they remained in our area of control, not one Arab was expelled by us," and "In vain did we cry out to the Arabs who were streaming across the borders: Stay here with us!" Contemporaries with government or paramilitary force connections during the conflict were fully aware that hundreds of thousands of Palestinians were being expelled and prevented from returning to their homes, and recognised that such facts needed to be kept a closely guarded secret.

As a consequence of mounting pressure in the early sixties from U.S. President Kennedy and UN General Assembly intentions to deal with the Palestinian refugee issue, Ben-Gurion convened a meeting of upper echelon politicians including Foreign Minister Golda Meir – on record as having said "There is no such thing as a Palestinian people … It is not as if we came and threw them out and took their country. They didn't exist" – to reiterate his belief that the issue of Palestinian refugees was mainly one of public perception *(hasbara)* which would persuade the international community that the refugees had fled on their own accord and had not been expelled.

Ben-Gurion had gone on to stress that "first of all, we need to tell facts, how they escaped. As far as I know, most of them fled before the state's establishment, of their own free will, and contrary to what the Haganah told them when it defeated them, that they could stay. After the state's establishment, as far as I know, only the Arabs of Ramle and Lod left their places, or were pressured to leave." The Haganah was the pre-independence army of Jews in Palestine.

Ben-Gurion had therefore firmly established the framework within which the subject was to be addressed even though some of those present were fully aware of the factual inaccuracy of his assertions. Moshe Dayan – who after 1949 had himself ordered the expulsion of Bedouin from the Negev – was for example one of those present who knew for certain that the Arabs had not left "of their own free will." Ben-Gurion had also explained that Israel must tell the world: "All of these facts are not known. There is also material which the Foreign Ministry prepared from the documents of the Arab institutions, of the Mufti, Jamal al-Husseini, concerning the flight, that this was of their own free will, because they were told the country would soon be conquered and you will return to be its lord and masters and not just return to your homes."

This narrative of Israeli "innocence" was backed up by dishonest Israeli historians who claimed that Palestinian refugees numbering no more 500,000 had left voluntarily in response to calls from their leaders reassuring them of a quick return after victory; they denied that the Jewish Agency, predecessor to the Israeli government, had deliberately planned the exodus; and they further maintained that the few and regrettable massacres such as occurred at Deir Yassin, were the result of extremist action by soldiers from Menachem Begin's Irgun and Yitzhak Shamir's Lehi. Yet despite these acknowledged atrocities by extremists under the leadership of Begin and Shamir, both these war criminals subsequently became prime ministers of a criminal state that has consistently claimed the highest of moral values while condemning the morality of any other nation that dares to question what many regard as being Israel's monstrous ethnic cleansing.

Zionism's narrative of the 1948 War started off by stating that the Arab-Jewish conflict in Palestine was ignited following the passage of the November 1947 United Nations partition resolution which called for the establishment of two separate Arab and Jewish states. Despite the painful sacrifices entailed, the Jews nonetheless accepted the UN plan which the Palestinians, the neighbouring Arab states, and the Arab League rejected. Furthermore, Britain, towards the end of its Mandate in Palestine, endeavoured to frustrate the establishment of the Jewish state as envisaged in the UN plan. Following expiry of the Mandate and the proclaimed establishment of the Israeli state, five Arab nations sent their armies into Palestine with the determined intention of strangling the Jewish state at birth. The ensuing struggle was one of a Jewish David against an Arab Goliath in which the newborn Jewish state fought a desperate, heroic, and ultimately successful battle for survival against overwhelming odds. During that conflict, hundreds of thousands of Palestinians fled to the neighbouring Arab states in response to orders from their leaders and despite Jewish entreaties to stay and prove that peaceful co-existence was possible. Following the war, Israeli leaders continued with all their might to earnestly seek peace but there was no one to talk to on the Arab side whose intransigence was alone responsible for the political deadlock which was not broken until Egypt's President Anwar Sadat visited Jerusalem in 1977.

The Israeli version of the Nabka as seen from behind rose-tinted kosher glasses was, however, subsequently challenged by the "New Historians" who apart from Benny Morris' *The Birth of the Palestinian Refugee Problem, 1947–1949,* also included Ilan Pappé's, *Britain and the Arab-Israeli Conflict, 1948–1951;* Avi

Shlaim's, *Collusion across the Jordan: King Abdullah, the Zionist Movement and the Partition of Palestine;* Tom Segev's, *1949: The First Israelis;* Hillel Cohen's, *The Present Absentee: Palestinian Refugees in Israel Since 1948;* Baruch Kimmerling's, *Zionism and Territory: The Socioterritorial Dimensions of Zionist Politics;* and Simha Flapan's, *The Birth of Israel: Myths And Realities.*

The general consensus of opinion from those "New Historians" was that Britain's intention was to prevent the establishment of a Palestinian state, rather than one for the Jews; that the Jewish forces outnumbered and outgunned the combined regular and irregular Arab forces fighting in Palestine; that the greater majority of Palestinians did not choose to leave but were forcibly expelled; that there was no monolithic Arab war agenda because Arab rulers were deeply divided – and still are – among themselves; and that attempts for a political settlement were frustrated by Israeli rather than by Arab intransigence. The irrefutable reality of Israel's tendency to lie and cover up its criminality had since become the hallmark of a nation hell-bent on total displacement of the indigenous Palestinian population; the establishment of all Jerusalem as Israel's undivided capitol; and the building of the Third Temple.

Despite all the research and the conclusions arrived at by Benny Morris and other "New Historians" that the Jewish state of Israel came into being as a consequence of the ethnic cleansing of Palestine, Benny Morris has lately succumbed to that tendency of those Israeli Jews – who having either criticised or acknowledged the truth of Israel's criminality – subsequently decide to recant the irrefutable truth and discard their self-respect and honour.

"The greatest way to live with honour in this world is to be what we pretend to be."
Socrates

Being the only member of the Hiramic Brotherhood employed as a full-time salaried Brother, Katzir was always the first to arrive shortly after six in the evening to prepare the boardroom for the monthly meeting. He placed his briefcase on his designated chair at one end of the long burr oak veneered boardroom table – which today would be occupied by the Sanhedrin guest of honour – before proceeding with his routine of first closing the floor to ceiling vertical slat blinds, unlocking the sideboard storage credenza, and emptying its contents onto the table in preparation for their arrangement according to the prescribed positions.

Half an hour later, Katzir glanced at his watch and noted that the members would soon start arriving dressed in their black suits, white shirts, and black velvet kippah skullcaps. They would then put on their Masonic aprons which in this instance had the Brotherhood's emblem of the Masonic square and compasses set within the Star of David. Katzir paused and surveyed the length of the table to ensure everything was in place. In front of each of the 29 chairs he had placed a notepad and ballpoint pen, a small bottle of still mineral water, a disposable plastic glass, a pack of pocket tissues, and the laminated A5 size card from which at the start of the meeting the Brothers would in unison reaffirm their vows which ended with Ezekiel 43:4-7.

"Son of man, this is the place of my throne and the place for the soles of my feet. This is where I will live among the Israelites forever. The people of Israel will never again defile my holy name – neither they nor their kings – by their prostitution and the funeral offerings for their kings at their death."

At the top end of the table by the window where Abe Goldman sat – as Chairman, Goldman was referred to as Master Hiram Abiff – lay a model of the Third Temple made of wood. The opposite end was occupied by a brown leather bound Hebrew Bible. The centre of the table was taken by an electric golden seven-branched Menorah. The Menorah, an ancient symbol of Judaism and the emblem of the modern state of Israel, was said to have been used in the ancient desert Tabernacle or sacred tent that housed the Ark of the Covenant whenever the Israelites camped during their very unlikely 40 years of wandering in the desert.

Having satisfied himself that everything was in place, Katzir opened his briefcase, took out printed copies of the evening's agenda whose main points included the Chairman's forthcoming fundraising trip to Washington and the issues to be raised in his meetings with officials of AIPAC; discussion of measures to counter recent global trends that supported recognition of a Palestinian state that might impede the rebuilding of the Third Temple; ways of increasing global awareness and acceptance of the need to rebuild the Third Temple by ensuring predominance of the narrative on the internet; full exploitation of the recent agreement between Israel's Ministry of Education and Wikimedia to promote students' multi-lingual writing and re-writing of history, geography, and science topics in Wikipedia which could be achieved by choice of words, information given or omitted, and the sources cited; taking a more active role in the Annual Wikipedia Academy Conference where Israelis received Wikipedia training and encouragement; increasing cooperation with the Israeli public relations organisation Committee for Accuracy in Middle East Reporting in America which had been editing Wikipedia since at least 2008; increased involvement with the Jewish Internet Defence League which claimed to be the "cutting edge of pro-Israel digital online advocacy"; and the increased coverage of Third Temple objectives in the "digital diplomacy" of the Ministry of Foreign Affairs' funded *hasbara* team of paid workers who posed as ordinary surfers while promoting Israel's version of the Middle East conflict on talkback sections of websites, internet chat forums, blogs, Twitter and Facebook.

After Katzir finished placing a copy of the agenda in front of each member's seat, he took out a file from his briefcase marked "Conrad Banner" and placed it on the table where he would be sitting next to the guest of honour from Sanhedrin. Conrad had come to the attention of the brotherhood as the result of intelligence obtained by one of the shadowy right-wing Israeli group such as Ad Kan – who's stated goal was "to restrict the ability of action and expose the real face of Israel's delegitimisation organisations" – which had some of its members infiltrate left-wing and human rights groups to obtain information about their members and activities with a view to attacking their anti-occupation campaigns. One such member had infiltrated Adam Peltz's organisation and had consequently learnt of his association with Conrad who planned on returning to Israel to make a documentary film about Jerusalem including the incendiary topic of the "Third Temple" on Temple Mount. Katzir with help from his security service contacts and their agents in London, had managed to compile a comprehensive dossier on Conrad whom he would be monitoring during his forthcoming visit to Jerusalem.

Today's honoured guest was going to reaffirm the Sanhedrin's support for the vital importance of building the Third Temple for the Jewish people and the state of Israel. The earliest mention of the Sanhedrin was recorded by Josephus – a Romano-Jewish scholar, historian and biographer (37 – 100 CE) – who wrote of a political Sanhedrin convened by the Romans in 57 BCE. Hellenistic sources invariably depicted the Sanhedrin as a political and judicial council headed by the country's ruler. Tannaitic sources – rabbinic works written from about 10 – 220 CE – describe the Great Sanhedrin as a religious assembly of 71 sages who met in the Chamber of

Hewn Stones in the Temple of Jerusalem. They constituted the supreme religious body in the Land of Israel during that time and had their own equivalent of a police force with powers to arrest people, as was the case with Jesus Christ.

Though the Sanhedrin heard both civil and criminal cases with apparent authority to impose the death penalty, during the New Testament period that authority was restricted to the Romans, which was why Jesus was crucified – a Roman punishment – rather than being stoned in accordance with Mosaic law which was given specifically to the nation of Israel (Exodus 19; Leviticus 26:46; and Romans 9:4). The law consisted of the Ten Commandments, the ordinances, and the worship system, which included the priesthood, the tabernacle, the offerings, and the festivals (Exodus 20–40; Leviticus 1–7; 23).

The Sanhedrin's eventual dissolution was the consequence of continual persecution by the Roman Empire coupled with the surging aspirations of Christendom. Efforts to reestablish the Sanhedrin, were initiated in 2004 in the form of a provisional body awaiting integration into the Israeli government as both a supreme court and upper house of the Knesset. Though the Israeli secular press regarded this new body as an illegitimate fundamentalist organisation of rabbis, the organisation nonetheless claimed to enjoy recognition and support from the entire religious Jewish community in Israel, and had stirred debate in both religious and secular circles.

Since its reestablishment, the Sanhedrin had supported the Temple Institute whose "ultimate goal was to see Israel rebuild the Holy Temple on Haram al-Sharif/Temple Mount in Jerusalem, in accord with the Biblical commandments." Haram al-Sharif/Temple Mount was unfortunately already occupied by three Islamic monuments from the early Umayyad period: the al-Aqsa Mosque, the Dome of the Rock, and the Dome of the Chain.

In supporting the Temple Institute, the Sanhedrin had called upon all groups working in the area of Temple Mount and in Temple related activity/research to begin preparing detailed architectural plans for the construction of the Holy Temple with a view to its establishment in its proper place; had stated its intention to establish a forum of architects and engineers whose assignment would be to implement the Council's decision, so that detailed working plans could effectively be brought to an operational stage; had asked the Jewish people to contribute towards the acquisition of materials for the purpose of rebuilding the Holy Temple; had ruled that such contributions would be considered as "chulin" – that is non-sacred – for the purpose of the planning and construction of the Temple; and had suggested that the gathering and preparation of prefabricated, disassembled portions of this building to be stored and ready for rapid assembly.

In anticipation of the Vatican's impending intention to sign a treaty with the "state of Palestine" in the hope that it would lead to improved relations between Israel and the Palestinians, the Sanhedrin planned to put the Pope on trial in absentia for such recognition. The Sanhedrin's seemingly outrageous presumption to interfere in international affairs including the exertion of authority over the Pope, was based on the Sanhedrin's assertion that "God in heaven is listening and obeys the Sanhedrin because the Torah interpretation is in the hands of the Sanhedrin here in this physical world, not in the heaven in the hands of the angels." The Sanhedrin rabbis also believed that they were not just a court for Jews, but were commanded by God to right injustice wherever it appeared, regardless of the religion or the country. Impartial observers of such hypocritical presumption may well ask why while obeying God's command, the Sanhedrin had apparently overlooked the necessity of first righting injustice and punishing crimes against humanity in their own blood-soaked backyard.

Hozrim LaHar ("Returning to the Mount") – another far-right Israeli group advocating Jewish sovereignty on Jerusalem's Haram al-Sharif/Temple Mount – had also added fuel to the fire by announcing that Jewish worshipers would be paid 2,000 shekels (about $500) to violate a ban on Jewish prayer on the Mount. The announcement appeared to have been deliberately timed to heighten the tensions on the Mount which were already at an all time high with Muslim threats to start a third intifada as a result of provocative Israeli incursions on the holy Muslim site.

While it was up to organisations such as the Sanhedrin and the Temple Institute to promote and implant within the public conscience the vision of a rebuilt Third Temple, it was up to the government itself to maintain the illegal occupation with its ethnic cleansing while declaring that a united Jerusalem was the eternal capital of the Jewish people; to exploit archaeology and concocted biblical narratives to deny Palestinian history and heritage so as to de-Arabise Palestine; to use spurious excuses and laws to expel Palestinians from areas around Haram al-Sharif/Temple Mount such as Silwan and replace them with Jewish families; to build a park adjoining Silwan and claim it was where King David built a city even though there was no archaeological or historical evidence of either his or such a city's existence; to orchestrate periodic controversial and confrontational visits to the Temple Mount that provoked Palestinian resistance which in turn provided an excuse for excessive and violent Israeli retaliation; to permit provocative visits to Temple Mount by Jewish settlers escorted and protected by police and the army while preventing Muslims from accessing their holy sites; and to incite in the not too distant future a violent confrontation where live ammunition and incendiary weapons would be used to cause the calculated fiery destruction of the Islamic monuments whose ashes and rubble would then be quickly cleared away for the immediate and rapid construction of the Third Temple. In the meantime the building and availability of luxury apartments in Jerusalem was advertised globally as being ready "for immediate occupancy in the vibrant heart of this sacred city ... Jerusalem – the heart's desire of Jews worldwide for generations, is now closer to you than ever before."

Possession was, after all, nine-tenths of the law which was why by driving out Palestinians and replacing them with Jewish families would ensure that there would never be a state for the Palestinian people whose only sin was to be the indigenous occupants of a land coveted by Zionism. Despite being Palestine's indigenous people, the Palestinians were nonetheless being denied – while the world watched in shameful silence – the protection of national and international legislation that provides indigenous peoples with a set of specific rights based on both their historical ties to a particular territory, and their cultural distinctiveness from other populations. Such legislation was based on the conclusion that certain indigenous people were vulnerable to exploitation, marginalisation, and oppression by nation states formed from colonising populations or by politically dominant, different ethnic groups.

A special set of political rights in accordance with international law were therefore set forth by international organisations such as the United Nations, the International Labour Organisation, and the World Bank. The United Nations had issued a Declaration on the Rights of Indigenous Peoples to guide member-state national policies to collective rights of indigenous people such as culture, identity, language, and access to employment, health, education, and natural resources.

A defining characteristic for an indigenous group is that it had preserved traditional ways of living, such as present or historical reliance upon subsistence-based production – based on pastoral, horticultural and/or hunting and gathering techniques – and a predominantly non-urbanised society. In contravention of such recognised international laws, Israel had with arrogant impunity deprived the Palestinian people of their sovereignty, environment, and access to natural resources: not to mention their legal and human rights. Katzir, like many Israeli Jews, shared the view of one speaker for Chabad – a movement promoting Judaism and providing daily Torah lectures with Jewish insights – that "the only way to fight a moral war is the Jewish way: Destroy their holy sites. Kill men, women and children (and cattle)."

10

Friday, 18 December

Little Venice, London, England

As their flight to Tel Aviv was at 08:15 a.m. tomorrow from Heathrow Airport, Conrad and Freya had spent most of the morning packing before walking to a nearby canal side pub for a pint and some lunch. On their return home, Freya busied herself with phone calls including one to her mother while Conrad resumed reading his notes on the Rothschild Banking Dynasty.

It was in 1821 that Kalmann (Carl) Mayer Rothschild was dispatched to Italy where he ended up doing a substantial amount of business with the Vatican which Pope Gregory XVI recognised by conferring upon him the Order of St. George. This was followed-up in 1822 with the emperor of Austria bestowing upon the five Rothschild brothers the title of *Baron,* which Nathan Mayer Rothschild declined to adopt, and in the following year the Rothschilds took over the Catholic Church's worldwide financial operations.

Five years later in 1827 Sir Walter Scott's nine-volume *The life of Napoleon* was published with a claim in volume two that the French Revolution was orchestrated by Adam Weishaupt's Illuminati and financed by Europe's money changers – an allusion to the Rothschilds.

President Andrew Jackson in 1833 began transferring federal funds from the Rothschild controlled Bank of the U.S. into democratic banks resulting in a subsequent 1835 failed assassination attempt on his life for which he later blamed the Rothschilds. The Rothschilds then acquired the rights to the Almadén quicksilver mines in Spain – quicksilver was vital for refining gold and silver – which being the biggest concession in the world, gave the Rothschilds a virtual world monopoly.

After many years of infighting, President Andrew Jackson finally succeeded in 1837 to rid America of the Rothschilds' central bank by preventing renewal of their charter, and Nathan Mayer Rothschild died with control of his bank being passed on to his younger brother, James Mayer Rothschild. During the following year the Rothschilds sent Ashkenazi Jew August Belmont – who at the age fourteen had joined their banking house in Frankfurt – to America to rescue and resuscitate their banking interests

Despite their setback in America, the Rothschilds managed in 1840 to become the Bank of England's bullion brokers with agencies in California and Australia. In 1841 President John Tyler's veto of the act to renew the Rothschild's Bank charter for the U.S. resulted in his receiving hundreds of death threats. By 1844, Salomon Mayer Rothschild had purchased the Wítkovice Coal Mines and Iron Works which became a top ten global industrial concern.

Benjamin Disraeli – who would subsequently twice become British Prime Minister – published *Coningsby,* in which Nathan Mayer Rothschild was referred to as being "the Lord and Master of the money markets of the world, and of course virtually Lord and Master of everything else. He literally held the revenues of Southern Italy in pawn, and Monarchs and Ministers of all countries courted his advice and were guided by his suggestions."

In 1845, former President Andrew Jackson – who unlike recent treacherous American leaders was an American patriot – died. When asked before his death what he regarded as his greatest achievement in office, he unhesitatingly replied in reference to the Rothschilds: "I killed the bank." In the meantime Baron James de Rothschild won the contract to build the first major railway line across France called the Chemin De Fer Du Nord which initially ran from Paris to Valenciennes and then joined with the Austrian rail network built by his brother Salomon Mayer Rothschild.

In 1847 Lionel De Rothschild was elected to the parliamentary seat for the City of London but left his seat vacant for eleven years because as a Jew he was unable to take an oath in the true faith of a Christian so as to enter parliament; Three years later Construction began on Mentmore in England and Ferrières in France, with many other Rothschild manor houses filled with fine works of art being established throughout the world; in 1852 N.M. Rothschild & Sons began refining gold and silver for the Royal Mint, the Bank of England, and other international clients; in 1853 Nathaniel de Rothschild purchased Château Brane Mouton, the Bordeaux vineyard which he renamed Château Mouton Rothschild; Amschel Mayer Rothschild, Salomon Mayer Rothschild, and Kalmann (Carl) Mayer Rothschild died in 1855; and in 1858 inclusion of new oaths finally enabled Lionel De Rothschild to take his seat in the British parliament and become its first ever Jewish member.

Abraham Lincoln – 16th President of the U.S. from 1860 until his assassination in 1865 – approached Rothschild influenced banks in 1861 for loans to finance the ongoing American Civil War. They agreed on condition that Lincoln renewed the Rothschild Charter for another U.S. central bank and was prepared to pay 24 to 36 percent interest on the loans. Such a high rate of interest, however, outraged Lincoln who took the decision to print his own debt free money and informed the public that it was legal tender for both public and private debts. By April the following year, $449,338,902 worth of Lincoln's debt free money had been printed and distributed which led to his comment that "we gave the people of this republic the greatest blessing they ever had, their own paper money to pay their own debts." Sometime later that year *The Times* of London published an article – no doubt Rothschild instigated – that in part stated:

> *"If that mischievous financial policy, which had its origin in the North American Republic, should become indurated down to a fixture, then that government will furnish its own money without cost. It will pay off debts and be without a debt. It will have all the money necessary to carry on its commerce.*
>
> *"It will become prosperous beyond precedent in the history of civilised governments of the world. The brains and the wealth of all countries will go to North America. That government must be destroyed or it will destroy every monarchy on the globe."*

Following the unification of Italy in 1863, the Rothschild banking house in Naples closed and the Rothschilds used one of their American agents of influence, John D. Rockefeller, to establish the Standard Oil company which eventually took over all its competitors.

Persistent and problematic Rothschild attempts to set up a central bank in Russia were of concern for Tsar Alexander II – who being sympathetic with Abraham Lincoln's similar problem with the Rothschilds – agreed to Lincoln's request for assistance in the American Civil War by dispatching some of his fleet to anchor off New York and California with a warning to the British, French, and Spanish that in the event of any attack against either side, Russia would support President Lincoln.

Much to the annoyance of Rothschild agent August Belmont – who by then was the Democratic Party's National Chairman – President Abraham Lincoln defeated General George McClellan, the Democratic nominee, in the 1864 presidential election; and in 1865 President Lincoln informed

Congress that he had "two great enemies, the Southern Army in front of me, and the financial institution in the rear. Of the two, the one in my rear is my greatest foe." Later that year Lincoln was assassinated.

That same year, following a short training period in the Rothschild's London Bank, eighteen year-old Jacob Schiff – born in the Rothschild's house in Frankfurt – arrived in America with the necessary finance and sole purpose of investment in a banking house that would eventually facilitate gaining control of America's money system through the establishment of a central bank; find suitable men, who could be bribed into being Rothschild stooges holding important positions within the federal government, the Congress, Supreme Court, and other federal agencies; engender social conflict amongst minority groups throughout the nation and especially between Whites and Blacks; and establish a movement to undermine religion in America with Christianity being the main target.

Jacob Mayer Rothschild in 1868 bought Château Lafite, one of the Premier Grand Cru estates of France, but dies shortly afterwards; Nathaniel de Rothschild passed away in 1870; and the Rothschild-Illuminati conspiracy was boosted in 1871 when Freemason Guissepe Mazzini lured into membership the prominent American Freemason, General Albert Pike – the only Confederate military officer or figure to be honoured with a statue in Washington, D.C. – who had supposedly completed his blueprint for bringing about the One World Order by means of three world wars and various revolutions throughout the globe.

The first world war was to be for the destruction – as had been promised by Nathan Mayer Rothschild in 1815 – of Russia's Tsar who would be replaced with communism which in turn was to be used for attacks on religions, especially Christianity, and to exploit differences between the British and German empires with a view to instigating a war.

The second world war was to be used to further inflame the dissension between Fascism and political Zionism with the slaughter of Germany's Jews being a vital factor in promoting hatred against the German people. The objective was the destruction of fascism (a Rothschild creation) and empowerment of political Zionism. An additional objective was an increase in Communism's power to counterbalance that of Christianity.

The third world war – whose occurrence was currently being pursued with a fair degree of success – was to be the result of animosity stirred between the Islamic world and Zionism which would force other nations with their Zionist induced Islamophobia to become involved and thereby deplete their resources and descend into social chaos.

Prior to his death in 1872, Guiseppe Mazzini chose as his successor Adrian Lemmy, another revolutionary who would subsequently be succeeded by Lenin, Trotsky, and Stalin who all had their revolutionary activities financed by the Rothschilds. The following year the loss making Rio Tinto copper mines in Spain – representing Europe's largest source of copper – were purchased by a consortium of foreign financiers including the Rothschilds.

In 1875, Jacob Schiff, by then Solomon Loeb's son-in-law, took control of Kuhn, Loeb & Co. and goes on with Rothschild money to finance John D. Rockefeller's Standard Oil, Edward R. Harriman's Railroad Empire, and Andrew Carnegie's Steel Empire; N M Rothschild & Sons launch a share issue to raise capital for the first channel tunnel project between France and England with half of the capital coming from the Rothschild owned Company du Chemin de Fer du Nord; Lionel De Rothschild secretly arranged Rothschild finance for Prime Minister Benjamin Disraeli's British government to acquire a major stake in the Suez Canal; and in 1876 conservative Prussian statesman Otto von Bismarck stated:

"The division of the United States into two federations of equal force was decided long before the civil war by the high financial power of Europe. These bankers were afraid that the United States, if they remained in one block and as one nation, would attain economical and financial independence, which would upset their financial domination over the world.

"The voice of the Rothschilds predominated. They foresaw the tremendous booty if they could substitute two feeble democracies, indebted to the financiers, to the vigorous Republic, confident and self-providing.

"Therefore they started their emissaries in order to exploit the question of slavery and thus dig an abyss between the two parts of the Republic."

In 1881, President James A. Garfield – 20th President of the U.S for only a hundred Days – stated two weeks before his assassination that "whoever controls the volume of money in our country is absolute master of all industry and commerce … and when you realise that the entire system is very easily controlled, one way or another, by a few powerful men at the top, you will not have to be told how periods of inflation and depression originate."

After six thousand feet of tunnel excavations under the English Channel (*la Manche*), the British government in 1883 abandoned the project citing the possible threat to Britain's security; two years later, Nathaniel, son of Lionel De Rothschild, became the first ever Jewish peer and assumed the title of Lord Rothschild; and in 1886 the French Rothschild bank acquired a substantial share of Russian oil fields and formed the Caspian and Black Sea Petroleum Company which rapidly became the second largest producer in the world.

The Rothschilds then moved their attention to Southern Africa in 1887 by financing the despicable Freemason and avowed racist Cecil Rhodes – supporter of the notorious South African Masters and Servants Act which was facetiously nicknamed the "Every Man to Wallop his Own Nigger Bill" – for the amalgamation of South Africa's Kimberley diamond mines into the De Beers company which subsequently contracted to sell its entire diamond production to a London diamond syndicate consisting of ten Jewish firms interconnected either through marriage or family ties.

The complete domination of diamond distribution by Jewish companies had been a reality for hundreds of years because the cutting and polishing of diamonds, was one of the few crafts in which medieval European guilds had allowed Jewish participation. So for the majority of Jews there were few vocational options other than gem-polishing or money lending which also involved dealing with diamonds.

Conrad was surprised to learn that up until the early 1700s the world's entire supply of diamonds had been sourced from India by caravan traders who crossed Arabia and exchanged their precious stones for gold and silver from Jewish traders in Aden and Cairo, who in turn sold them on to fellow Jewish merchants in Frankfurt, Lithuania, and Venice. Dealing in diamonds consequently became a hallmark for Jewish traders scattered across central Europe – who also maintained trading centres in the Ottoman Empire through which all Indian diamonds passed – where as moneylenders they were by necessity involved in the assessment, repair, and sale of precious stones that had been tendered as collateral for loans.

When the Portuguese eventually discovered different maritime routes including one to India, the camel caravan routes were gradually replaced by ships and Portugal's mainly Sephardic Jews arranged for ships' officers to buy diamonds directly from the Indian miners in Goa so that Lisbon became Europe's main entry point for the precious stones. Jewish entrepreneurs then established cutting factories in Lisbon and in Antwerp where they employed and exploited the poorer Ashkenazi Jews from Eastern Europe to do the cutting and polishing.

Diamonds also proved to be an invaluable asset for the Jews during the Inquisition because unlike most other assets, they could be easily concealed and were readily redeemable for cash in other European countries. For the Jewish people, whose self-imposed "separatism" from the goyim in ghettos and eruvs – designated areas within which observant Jews could carry or push objects on the Sabbath – had resulted in centuries of fear and uncertainty over being expelled so that diamonds became the most favoured investment option for their wealth.

When forced to relocate by the Inquisition, diamond industry Jews fled from Lisbon and Antwerp with their portable diamond cutting tools to resettle in Amsterdam which they quickly established as Europe's diamond centre. They were also instrumental in financing the Dutch East India Company which established its own trade route to India with a stopover at the *Kaap die Goeie Hoop* (the Cape of Good hope) in South Africa where Dutch settlements were established leading to the eventual Afrikaner Great Trek of 1836 – to escape British domination and anglicisation of their culture – by more than 12,000 Boers who migrated northwards in separate groups to establish independent republics. The Trek had been regarded as similar to that of the children of Israel who as the chosen people had determined to pursue their own destiny.

As the diamond yielding mines in India began to run dry, an alternative source was sought in Brazil before the eventual first recorded South African discovery of diamonds on 13 October 1867. Fearing that the market would be flooded with South African diamonds, the ten leading London Jewish merchants immediately set up a syndicate to buy all South African diamonds so as to control the market. Some of these merchants had also acquired substantial stock holdings in Cecil Rhodes' De Beers company which led to one of them, Dunkelsbuhler, to hire Ernest Oppenheimer, a sixteen year old apprentice from Friedberg in Germany, who after proving himself in London, was dispatched in 1902 to run the Kimberly office in South Africa.

Twenty-five years later, in 1927, Ernest Oppenheimer took control of De Beers before going on to found the Anglo American Corporation and thereby consolidate his monopoly over the world's diamond industry. When Oppenheimer converted from Judaism to Anglicanism in the late 1930s, some observers suggested that the conversion was intended to remove a possible obstacle to the continued sale of industrial diamonds to Hitler's Germany. Oppenheimer's involvement in other controversies included price fixing, antitrust behaviour, and an allegation of not releasing industrial diamonds for the U.S. war effort.

Conrad's assumption that the diamond trade was still dominated by Jewish corporations received timely confirmation by media reports that Tiffany & Co had sourced Blood Diamonds from the Octea Diamond Group, a Beny Steinmetz Group Resources (BSGR) in Sierra Leone where Beny Steinmetz – the Israeli tycoon who dominated the gemstone market – was facing a raft of corruption allegations in one of Africa's poorest countries. The BSGR group of companies had a unique corporate structure and was controlled by a trust fund, the Steinmetz Foundation, of which the Steinmetz family was the beneficiary. Revenue from BSGR companies was being channelled via the Steinmetz Foundation to the Israeli military which stood accused of war crimes and possible crimes against humanity by the UN Human Rights Council. The Foundation had "adopted" a Unit of the Givati Brigade of the Israeli military for which it purchased equipment and provided support during the Israeli assault on the defenceless, besieged residents of Gaza in the winter of 2008/2009 during Operation Cast Lead.

In 1891 Elijah Grant, the British Labour Leader referred to the Rothschilds as "this blood-sucking crew has been the cause of untold mischief and misery in Europe during the present century, and has piled up its prodigious wealth chiefly through fomenting wars between States which ought never to have quarrelled. Whenever there is trouble in Europe, wherever rumours of war circulate and men's minds are distraught with fear of change and calamity you may be sure that a hook-nosed Rothschild is at his games somewhere near the region of the disturbance." Such comments were of concern to the Rothschilds who by the end of the 1800's had purchased news agencies such as Reuters in London, Havas in France, and Wolf in Germany so as to exert control over what was reported to the general public.

Edmond James de Rothschild visited Palestine in 1895 and financed the first Jewish colonies to initiate the long term objective of creating a Jewish state to serve Rothschild interests. Two years later in 1897 the Rothschilds founded the Zionist Congress with its first meeting being scheduled in Munich, but local Jewish opposition forced a change of venue to Basle in Switzerland. Theodor Herzl was elected President of the Zionist Organisation which adopted the Rothschild logo that 51 years later appeared on the flag of Israel as the "Star of David" …

Foggy Bottom Neighbourhood, Washington, D.C.

When the inadequately disguised Republican Senator Edward Wright with upturned cashmere coat collar and pulled down felt Fedora hat partly covering his face arrived at Sally Berkley's Watergate South apartment in the heart of Washington DC's Foggy Bottom neighbourhood – one of the earliest settlements in what is now the District of Columbia – he was expecting to be greeted by the same vivacious brunette with whom he had become sensually acquainted on his previous visit. The door was instead opened by two characters whose sly demeanours and predacious eyes were reminiscent of shyster lawyers or hyaenas circling their prey before closing in and tearing it to pieces.

"Good evening, Senator, we've been expecting you," the shorter of the two shysters said.

Wright was completely taken aback as he stood transfixed while trying to comprehend the unexpected turn of events that now rendered him devoid of his usual composure and confidence. His initial instinct for self-preservation was to make some lame "wrong apartment" excuse and then show a clean pair of heels. But the opinion he had of himself and the presumed dignity of his political position prescribed otherwise. So he stood his ground and feigned a cavalier bravado which failed to impress either of the antagonists now confronting him.

"You'd better come in," the taller of the two commanded firmly as he turned and lead the way into the sitting room.

Wright had, or so he thought, fortuitously met the brunette Sally Berkley some weeks earlier at one of Washington's politico-social routine parties that served as Machiavellian friendship zones where political favours could be discussed and traded. The occasion was a birthday celebration for White House regular Brad Pearlman who was Chairman of the Defence Policy Board – a federal advisory committee to the U.S. Department of Defence – and also a stalwart of the Jewish Institutes involved in national security affairs whose stated aims as Washington D.C.-based pro-Israel think tanks included engaging "the American defence community about the role Israel can and does play in securing Western democratic interests in the Middle East and Mediterranean regions."

Sally's intoxicating charm and magnetic sensuality had captivated Wright who as a subscriber to the adage of "procrastination is opportunity's assassin," had wasted no time in discreetly getting her contact details and subsequently arranging to meet her. Unfortunately for Wright, in

Washington's dog-eat-dog political environment there was no such thing as either a free lunch or a free extramarital leg-over so that the final settling of accounts invariably required something more substantial than the mere swipe of a prestige credit card. He had undoubtedly been extremely naive in not thoroughly questioning the authenticity of what with hindsight was clearly an orchestrated *chance* meeting; naive in not questioning Sally's well concocted alleged career in public relations; and naive in not questioning Sally's ability to afford a relatively expensive apartment with balconies offering a stunning view of the Potomac River. Regrettably the intuitive perceptiveness that had so far enabled Wright to safely navigate hazardous political waters had been – where Sally was concerned – swept aside by the tidal wave desire of his peripatetic but maritally spoken for pecker.

Wright was invited to sit on the couch in front of the ornate glass top coffee table which on this occasion was host to an open laptop and CD instead of chilled champagne, Waterford Crystal flutes, and antique cigarette box. The shorter of the two shysters, with exaggerated theatrical precision, then inserted the CD into the laptop's player and stepped back to join his partner as they both with judgemental smirks relished the discomfort that Wright was obviously experiencing. After watching several minutes of what was obviously going to be full length feature with every kiss, lick, and libidinous thrust recorded by a hidden camera, a furious Wright, realising that he had been honey trapped, indicated with a dismissive wave of his hand that he had seen enough.

Arranging a honey trap did not simply involve the actual act of seduction because prior to the nude frolics, extensive research and meticulous planning had to be carried out in selecting the target who would invariably have had to fit one of two main psychological profiles. The first profile type consisted of those who lacked self-confidence and a sense of security; those possessing some perceived grievance; and those who longed desperately for a degree of attention and affection. The second profile type consisted of dominant egotistic characters who because of an innate belief in their own ability to deal with perilous situations, regarded rules of conduct as being inapplicable to themselves. While the former grouping may appear to be the obvious profile type to recruit and exploit, the latter of more self-assured candidates such as Wright were equally susceptible to sexual bait as indeed was the case with President John F. Kennedy who allegedly slept with several spies including a suspected Nazi sympathiser and an East German agent.

Sally Berkley was neither of these, but a Jewish American who while on a sponsored Birthright trip to Israel for young Jews in 2010 had been spotted by a Mossad recruiter as having potential for training as one of its agents. As an exponent of the dubious premise that the "State of Israel has been, and remains, under daily, tangible threats," Mossad was constantly on the lookout for accomplished young people who wanted to serve the Jewish cause and were prepared to do so by serving Israel. As to the virtue of such service, it was Oliver Cromwell, the seventeenth century English military and political leader, who once noted that, "there are great occasions in which some men are called to great services, in the doing of which they are excused from the common rule of morality."

In other words, recruits would have to abandon the basic moral standards that most people in society adhered to and instead accept the use of methods that violated all that was decent and honourable so as to ensure the success of any given mission even if it meant having sex with the target. While discussing the subject of women agents in particular, one former director-general of Mossad had observed that, "A woman has skills a man simply does not have … "

After informing Sally who he was and for whom he

worked, the recruiter plied Sally with the spiel that once accepted as a part of the Mossad family, she would be nurtured and protected for her willingness to serve in any capacity as and when required. On agreeing to make such a commitment, Sally was then told of the necessity for some preliminary oral and written assessments which she subsequently took during a period of three months in various safe Mossad locations in Tel Aviv. Sally's physical attractiveness, obvious intelligence, social graces, and American background had made her an ideal candidate for full training to which she acquiesced after first being given a chance to change her mind without there being any repercussions.

Sally's eventual espionage skills as an agent had been fine-tuned during a two-year training period at the agency's school outside Tel Aviv where she had been versed in the entire espionage-related gamut from shadowing a target to becoming an accomplished seducer of men which included being interrogated about her own sexual experiences and her willingness to sleep with a stranger if the situation required it. On completion of her training, Sally had been sent to Paris – passing herself off as an American tourist – where Mossad was particularly active because of all the Muslim populations in the European Union countries, France led the way with some 5 million, followed by Germany at 3.3 million, and Britain with 1.6 million. Keeping France's Muslims in check and ensuring that they did not propagate any sympathy for the Palestinian cause had therefore been – and was even more so now – of vital importance to Israel. After spending a year in Paris, Sally was sent to Washington where her skills were more urgently required to infiltrate the social scene for loose talk and potential sources of useful political information which if necessary she would extract with sexual favours. While by no means quite in the same league as the legendary Frisian exotic dancer and courtesan, Mata Hari – who was in due course executed by firing squad for her sins – Sally nonetheless could hold her own against any woman when it came down to exuding the sexual attraction required to capture the attention of powerful government officials. It was no coincidence that the most successful and dangerous female spies in history had been women of exceptional beauty. After all, no self-respecting man of prominence was going to be lured by the possibility of a poke with a swamp donkey.

Wright had by now realised that at the undoubted instigation of Mossad, some elaborate arrangements had been made to have him honey trapped, an action which he regarded as a betrayal by those to whom he had sold both his soul and his country's much-vaunted democracy. His feeling of betrayal was perhaps a touch ironic for someone whose political career – like that of countless others in the bicameral Congress – had been mostly spent in betraying the Pledge of Allegiance to the Flag which is made to open daily sessions of both the House and the Senate:

"I pledge allegiance to the Flag of the United States of America, and to the Republic for which it stands, one Nation under God, indivisible, with liberty and justice for all."

That raised the question of whether the United States was a republic or a democracy? Strictly speaking a democracy is a form of governance in which the people directly decided policy matters through town hall meetings, registered voter ballot initiatives, or referendums. Alternatively, a republic, is a system wherein the people elect representatives who are given the responsibility of making policy decisions on their behalf. It is also apparent that the Framers of the Constitution were profoundly suspicious of democracy in its purest form with *Federalist No. 10* – an essay written by James Madison as the tenth in a series of The Federalist Papers that argued for the ratification of the United States Constitution – stating the following:

> *"Democracies have ever been spectacles of turbulence and contention; have ever been found incompatible with personal security or the rights of property; and have in general been as short in their lives as they have been violent in their deaths – Theoretic politicians, who have patronised this species of government, have erroneously supposed that by reducing mankind to a perfect equality in their political rights, they would at the same time be perfectly equalised and assimilated in their possessions, their opinions, and their passions."*

With constant usage over time, however, the word "democracy" had come to mean a system of governance in which the government's power is derived from the people to whom it is accountable in the use of that power. On that basis therefore, the United States could be called a democracy – a democracy, however, whose concept was at odds with that of the "pure democracy" availed by many states in allowing for policy decisions to be made directly by the people's vote on ballot initiatives or referendums. The fact that the Constitution does not provide for either national ballot initiatives or referendums confirms the Framers' suspicion of, and opposition to any such truly democratic procedures.

In writing on the merits of a republican or representative system of governance, Madison noted that one of the most important differences between a democracy and a republic was "the delegation of the government [in a republic] to a small number of citizens elected by the rest," the main effect of which was to "… refine and enlarge the public views by passing them through the medium of a chosen body of citizens whose wisdom may best discern the true interest of their country and whose patriotism and love of justice will be least likely to sacrifice it to temporary or partial considerations. Under such a regulation it may well happen that the public voice, pronounced by the representatives of the people, will be more consonant to the public good than if pronounced by the people themselves, convened for the same purpose." The problem with governance by "a chosen body of citizens," is that the "chosen citizens" are susceptible to bribery and corruption.

Strictly speaking, the system of governance established by the Constitution was never intended to be a "democracy." This is not only evident from the wording of the Pledge of Allegiance, but also the Constitution itself which declares that "the United States shall guarantee to every State in this Union a Republican Form of Government." Furthermore, the system of representation and the procedures for selecting representatives established by the Constitution were clearly designed for producing a republic, and not a democracy. Madison was also perceptive and perhaps even prophetic in making the following observation:

"Knowledge will forever govern ignorance; and a people who mean to be their own governors must arm themselves with the power which knowledge gives."

While the lines may now be blurred between America's former republican roots and its current facade of democracy, the question nonetheless remained as to whether or not the American people are today sufficiently knowledgeable and suitably equipped with the necessary wisdom and prudence to carry out their responsibilities as citizens of a country that claims to be a beacon of democracy and freedom. The answer unfortunately is an indisputable and most emphatic "no!"

Like most legislators on Capitol Hill, Wright had long ago signed AIPAC's required pledge to support any policies or legislation that favoured Israel which if refused would have resulted in a termination of campaign contributions from

AIPAC's Political Action Committees (PACs) and the start of a media crusade of demonisation. Apart from the reward of campaign contributions, he had also enjoyed free junkets to Israel and other discreet fringe benefits which any official investigation would undoubtedly have adjudged as being blatant bribery and corruption.

As Chairman of the United States Senate Committee on Foreign Relations, Wright had influence over decisions relating to the supervision and funding of foreign aid programs including the funding of arms sales and training for national allies. The committee also held confirmation hearings – and could consequently block appointment of those regarded as not being sufficiently pro-Israel – for high-level positions in the Department of State (equivalent to the foreign ministries of other countries) which is responsible for U.S. international relations including U.S. diplomatic missions abroad, and the implementation of U.S. global diplomacy and foreign policy. Coincidentally, the Department was located a few blocks away from the White House in the Foggy Bottom neighbourhood.

"What happened here last week was private and confidential," the shorter shyster said in an almost bored monotone, "and there's no reason why it shouldn't stay that way … It's just that in certain quarters there is some concern about the nuclear negotiations with Iran … It's felt that Congressional approval of any agreement would not be in the best interests of the United States … Strong opposition to such an agreement is therefore essential and would be appreciated."

"It's felt that a nuclear deal with Iran based on the current framework would threaten Israel's survival," the taller shyster added with an emphatic ejection from the laptop of the CD which he offered to Wright, "you can have this, Senator, we've got copies," he added with the unuttered menace of a seasoned blackmailer.

Wright was almost speechless with rage as he stood up.

"Stick it," was all he could muster as he stormed out leaving behind two gloating shyster Zionist henchmen who exchanged high fives in celebration of a mission accomplished with the powerful Chairman of the United States Senate Committee on Foreign Relations having been well and truly screwed.

11

Saturday, 19 December

British Airways flight to Tel Aviv, Israel

Conrad and Freya spent most of their time on the flight reading with Freya concentrating on her Jerusalem guidebook and Conrad revising the research notes which he had uploaded on iCloud. It was apparent that while European monarchs had instigated anti-Jewish pogroms and expulsions of Jews, Ottoman Muslim rulers had by comparison exercised religious tolerance; protected both Christian and Jewish holy sites; permitted pilgrims of both faiths to visit Jerusalem; graciously welcomed Jewish victims of the Spanish Inquisition expelled from Spain in 1492; and even encouraged Jewish settlement throughout their empire.

It was also evident that Jews had never actually completely disappeared from Palestine because at least 5,000 were part of a 300,000 population in 1517 with Ottoman taxation registers in 1553 listing 1,958 Jews in Jerusalem alone. Jewish numbers gradually increased over time and following a surge in East European and Yemenite Jewish immigration, the Jewish population in 1895 had risen to 47,000 (8%) out of 522,000. So even before Theodor Herzl published his book *Der Judenstaat (The Jewish State)* which effectively launched the Zionist movement in 1896, there was already a significant number of Jews in Palestine living peacefully amongst Christian and Muslim Palestinians.

When the first Zionist Congress was held in Basel, Switzerland in 1897 under the chairmanship of Theodore Herzl, the Congress outlined Zionism's intention to establish for the Jewish people a publicly and legally assured home in Palestine which was to be attained by the promotion of the settlement of Jewish agriculturists, artisans, and tradesmen in Palestine; the federation of all Jews into local or general groups, according to the laws of the various countries; the strengthening of the Jewish feeling and consciousness; and preparation for the attainment of those governmental grants which were necessary for the achievement of the Zionist purpose.

Zionist plans for such an "assured home" were focussed on Britain when towards the end of the First World War it became apparent that as one of the Allied Powers, Britain, would end up in control of Palestine. The Zionist leaders then not only asked the British Government to make a declaration of support for their aims, but also proposed the draft which formed the basis for the now infamous Balfour Declaration.

Edwin Montagu – the only Jewish British Cabinet member, who strongly opposed Zionism – suggested that the "reconstitution of Palestine as the national home of the Jewish people" implied that Muslims and Christians were to make way for the Jews; that Jews would be put in all positions of preference; that the Muslims would be regarded as foreigners in Palestine; and that Jews would be treated as foreigners in every country except Palestine which was why he described Zionism as being anti-Semitic. Montagu's views obviously influenced the final version of the Balfour Declaration which – by highlighting the rights of the non-Jewish inhabitants of Palestine, and the rights of Jews outside Palestine – gave less support than had been hoped for by the Zionists:

Foreign Office
November 2nd, 1917

Dear Lord Rothschild,
I have much pleasure in conveying to you, on behalf of His Majesty's Government, the following declaration of sympathy with Jewish Zionist

aspirations which has been submitted to, and approved by, the Cabinet.

His Majesty's Government view with favour the establishment in Palestine of a national home for the Jewish people, and will use their best endeavours to facilitate the achievement of this object, it being clearly understood that nothing shall be done which may prejudice the civil and religious rights of existing non-Jewish communities in Palestine, or the rights and political status enjoyed by Jews in any other country.

I should be grateful if you would bring this declaration to the knowledge of the Zionist Federation.

Yours sincerely,
Arthur James Balfour

The rights of the existing non-Jewish inhabitants of Palestine were further recognised two years later in 1919 when U.S. President Woodrow Wilson dispatched the King-Crane Commission to areas of the former Ottoman Empire to seek opinions about their future governance. In the section concerning Palestine and Zionism the report explicitly stated the following:

"If the strict terms of the Balfour Statement are adhered to it can hardly be doubted that the extreme Zionist Program must be greatly modified. For a "national home for the Jewish people" is not equivalent to making Palestine into a Jewish State; nor can the erection of such a Jewish State be accomplished without the gravest trespass upon the "civil and religious rights of existing non-Jewish communities in Palestine." The fact came out repeatedly in the Commission's conference with Jewish representatives, that the Zionists looked forward to a practically complete dispossession of the present non-Jewish inhabitants of Palestine, by various forms of purchase.

"The non-Jewish population of Palestine, nearly nine-tenths of the whole, are emphatically against the entire Zionist program. To subject

a people so minded to unlimited Jewish immigration, and to steady financial and social pressure to surrender the land, would be a gross violation of the peoples' rights. No British officer, consulted by the Commissioners, believed that the Zionist program could be carried out except by force of arms … Decisions, requiring armies to carry out, are sometimes necessary, but they are surely not gratuitously to be taken in the interests of a serious injustice. The initial claim, often submitted by Zionist representatives, that they have a "right" to Palestine, based on an occupation of two thousand years ago, can hardly be seriously considered.

"In view of all these considerations, and with a deep sense of sympathy for the Jewish cause, the Commissioners feel bound to recommend that only a greatly reduced Zionist program be attempted, and even that, only very gradually initiated. This would have to mean that Jewish immigration should be definitely limited, and that the project for making Palestine distinctly a Jewish commonwealth should be given up."

Zionism with its usual disregard for anyone or anything that did not share and support its objectives, scornfully ignored such views while pursuing its fundamental policy – still assiduously pursued to this day – of aggressively promoting the concept of "return" so that for many Jews "next year in Jerusalem" became the mantra of a concept that Conrad regarded as having been fostered on the basis of a fallacious religious narrative and exploited by a Jewish population of whom – according to an Israeli study – 15 percent were atheists and 37 percent were agnostic. Therefore justification and support for a Jewish state stemmed not from belief in the Biblical narrative, but from an irreligious Zionist nationalism intent on displacing the Palestinian people and taking their land under the somewhat questionable pretext that the establishment of a Jewish state would guarantee prevention of a second Holocaust.

Zionists and the irreligious nonetheless required and

hypocritically clung to the Biblical narrative which impelled Israeli politics and conveniently provided divine entitlement of "return" which as far as Conrad was concerned, constituted a dishonest political euphemism for *illegally enforced Jewish settlement of Palestinian land.* So while Palestinians refugees with title deeds to their land had for decades been unable to "return" to their homeland, Jewish American college students could visit what used to be Palestine – with all expenses paid by the non-profit "educational" project *Birthright Israel,* with the conviction that it was their right to do so as Jews. The purpose for such sponsorship of students from America and other countries was not due to any altruistic inclination or desire to educate them: the the purpose was simply to brainwash them into believing that they were indeed conceived with a God-given right to "return" to the land that God "promised" Abraham so as to encourage them to immigrate to Israel.

Conrad felt that though Zionism had fully exploited the "birthright" narrative of how horrendous expulsions and widespread dispersals of the Jewish people forced them to suffer in exile for many centuries, the historical reality was quite different because Jews were already widely dispersed in both the Roman (27 BCE – 476 CE) and Parthian (247 BCE – 224 CE) empires with many of them having been born and raised outside of Judaea and perhaps even married to Gentiles. It was also more than likely that Jewish merchants were active in Ethiopia, southern Arabia, India, and by the seventh century, Jews were to be found as far afield as China.

Even the current assertion – that European Jews were mostly descended from people who left Israel and the Middle East some 2000 years ago – had also been contradicted by more recent DNA studies including one that underscored an emerging scholarly research consensus that itinerant Jewish men, from the Near East, established a mosaic of small Jewish communities that started in Italy and then scattered throughout

Europe, often taking on local gentile wives and raising their children as Jews. All of which, as far as Conrad was concerned, debunked the central tenet of Zionist Israel's "Law of Return" which not only gave Jewish people around the world the right to settle in Israel, but also supported their exclusive territorial claims even though many Arabs, including Palestinians, had a far more legitimate genetic "right of return."

In the 1920s – due to European anti-Semitism mainly in Poland; alarmist Zionist propaganda promoting Jewish settlement in Palestine; and exclusionary U.S. immigration laws, Palestine's Jewish population of eight to nine percent began to increase to about 20 percent. The increase had been preceded by the 1916 secret Sykes–Picot Agreement (Asia Minor Agreement) between the United Kingdom and France with the assent of the Russian Tsarist government defining proposed Middle East spheres of influence in the event of the Triple Entente defeating the Ottoman Empire. Following the October 1917 Russian Bolshevik Revolution, on finding a copy of the agreement in the Romanov palace, an outraged Vladimir Lenin exposed the agreement by having it published.

Following the Balfour Declaration Zionists proceeded to buy agricultural land from the profiteering Grand Mufti al-Huseini and other Muslim aristocrats thereby causing resentment – possibly stoked by Zionists – amongst the mostly poor and landless Muslims. When in early 1929 al-Huseini accused the Jews of seizing Muslim holy places on Temple Mount, Arab mobs responded with attacks on Jews that resulted in conflict and death on both sides. By 1931, the British had restored order in Palestine with an official census showing 759,952 Muslims, 90,607 Christians of mostly Arab descent, and 175,006 Jews who constituted seventeen percent of the population.

The Great Depression of the 1930s coupled with Adolf Hitler's coming to power in Germany served to intensify hostility in Germany, Poland and Romania towards Jews for whom Palestine then appeared to be beckoning as the only refuge. Consequently by 1940 the Jewish population in the British Mandate of Palestine had almost doubled to thirty percent and remained that way until the state of Israel was fraudulently and forcibly established in 1948. There could be no denying the well-documented fact that in seeking to establish *their* state, the Zionists resorted to committing crimes against humanity by terrorising some 750,000 Palestinian Arabs into fleeing their homes in fear for their lives. There was no doubt in Conrad's mind that the Palestinian Nakba, or "Catastrophe," was a cold, calculated, case of barbaric ethnic cleansing.

Furthermore, as far as Conrad could discern – though it was Britain that gave Zionism a very spurious degree of legitimacy with the Balfour Declaration – if there had been no Holocaust perpetrated by the Nazis, then it was extremely unlikely that Israel would have been established as a state because without Adolf Hitler and his Nazis effectively acting as its recruitment agents, Zionism would undoubtedly have failed to obtain the necessary financial, moral, political, and sympathetic global support to not only subject the Palestinian people to crimes against humanity, but also to do so with the arrogant impunity that had become the hallmark of the Jewish occupiers.

In the 1947 UN General Assembly partition plan for Palestine, Jerusalem had been designated as a "Separate Body" to be administered internationally – and contrary to Zionist propaganda of how they accepted the UN partition plan – the reality was that they ignored the plan and instead forcibly took possession of Palestinian territory that now included all of Jerusalem which had not been awarded to them. So despite the UN General Assembly Resolution 194 (December 11, 1948) recognising the "right of return" to their homes of those Palestinians forced to flee and equally the right of their descendants, the Israelis had to date rejected any such right because a return of Palestinians would alter the demographics and threaten the Jewish character of the state – a state which was incidentally established and continues to expand by means of illegal settlement, wanton persecution, barbaric dispossession, and ethnic cleansing of the indigenous population. Though Conrad was determined to retain his impartiality as a journalist, it was nonetheless difficult for him to honestly ignore the inhumanity with which Israel treated the Palestinian people while the rest of the world stood by silently doing nothing. It was Ethiopia's Emperor Haile Selassie I who said that "throughout history, it has been the inaction of those who could have acted; the indifference of those who should have known better; the silence of the voice of justice when it mattered most; that has made it possible for evil to triumph."

Ben Gurion International Airport, Tel Aviv

Conrad and Freya had to some extent prepared themselves for their visit to Israel by both sanitising their laptops – in case Israeli officials demanded their passwords to search through their inboxes – and by ensuring that their social media accounts contained no mention of "Palestine," "Palestinian," "solidarity," "West Bank," or other words the Israelis could construe as being subversive. Conrad had also forewarned Freya that the Israelis would probably try to provoke them by being aggressive, by being inordinately rude, and by asking accusatory questions to make them feel as though they were guilty of committing some crime. Some of the questions asked were "what is the reason for your visit?"; "Where Will you be staying?"; "What will you be doing in Jerusalem?"; "Do you know anyone in Israel?"; and "Will you be visiting the West Bank or Gaza?"

"Welcome to the only democracy in the Middle East," Freya said with a deliberately sarcastic tone to Conrad who responded by putting his forefinger over his lips.

Any doubts about their not being welcome in Israel were very quickly dispelled as they were detained for almost four hours while being processed through customs, passport control, and security screening that included being humiliated, insulted, aggressively questioned, strip-searched, and having their luggage and equipment rigorously examined as if they were dangerous criminals or terrorists. But then they should have known that as foreign journalists, they would be automatically regarded as potential enemies who might possibly report the true facts that would portray and confirm the true nature of Israel. Though a few of the security staff had feigned a barely palpable degree of civility, there was no disguising the underlying presence of suspicious hate and hostility. *These are a people in conflict with themselves and the rest of the world,* Conrad thought as he and Freya were eventually allowed to repack their equipment.

Once they were finally settled in a cab headed for Jerusalem, Freya, who was on her first ever visit to the Holy Land gazed out of the window with disbelief at a passing landscape that was breathtaking yet scarred with wire fencing, high separation walls, manned watchtowers, and checkpoints. Conrad had already explained that despite the Oslo Accords in the early 1990s – aimed at achieving a peace-treaty based on UN Security Council Resolutions 242 and 338 which were supposed to fulfil the "right of the Palestinian people to self-determination," recognition of Palestinian autonomy by Israel, and the Palestinian right of return – Israel had as usual reneged on the agreements to ensure no permanent resolution with the interim situation still being in effect.

Since 1967, Israel had then implemented a range of different strategies for restricting Palestinian access to land and resources in the occupied territories with the division of the West Bank into Areas A, B, and C with different levels of Israeli and Palestinian control. Area A was theoretically under full control of the Palestinian Authority and consisted primarily of urban Palestinian areas; *Area B* was *supposedly* under Palestinian civil control and shared Palestinian-Israeli security and included the vast majority of the Palestinian rural areas; and *Area C* was under full Israeli control with Palestinian agencies being responsible for education and healthcare.

Under the current system Palestinians had neither influence over the division of the land within Area C, nor control of the zoning of their communities or the granting of permits for construction. While greatly limiting Palestinian construction, Israeli authorities had approved plans for almost all Israeli settlements on the West Bank – ruled to be unlawful in 2004 by the International Court of Justice – where now (not counting brazenly illegal outposts) over 500,000 Jewish settlers were living. By denying Palestinians any access to the planning process while allowing full participation to the settlers, Israel had deliberately expanded settlements in violation of international law.

Because of Israel's prevention of investment in infrastructure – such as repairing roads, improving the electrical grid, or laying pipes for connection to water supplies – Palestinians in Area C which comprised 60 percent of the West Bank, could either build illegally and risk demolition, or leave their homes and move to Area A or B, where Palestinian agencies administered building permits. This deliberate Israeli strategy ensured the seemingly innocuous "silent transfer" of Palestinians from Area C as was reaffirmed by a reprehensible Israeli cabinet minister calling for its annexation: "If someone asks about Areas A and B, then their time will come. When, we will see. For now, lets agree on Area C," adding that the world should forget about there being "two states for two peoples," because it will never happen. In reporting his remarks, the *Times of Israel,* avoided the term "ethnic cleansing," and instead opted for "remove" and "evacuate." Conrad had no doubt that anyone suggesting that such comments were no different to those uttered by the Nazis about Jews, would no doubt be immediately branded as a Jew-hating anti-Semite.

As Freya continued to gaze out of the window, she began to understand the true nature of Apartheid – an Afrikaans word meaning "the state of being apart," or literally "apart-hood" – that the colonial settler Jews were imposing on the indigenous Palestinians.

"Are you okay," Conrad asked when he noticed her shaking her head in disbelief at seeing yet another separation wall.

"It's unbelievable," she said, "they've created ghettos to divide and control."

"And displace," he added, taking hold of her hand and squeezing it reassuringly before returning to his notes on the Rothschild Banking Dynasty.

It was apparently a group of Rothschild backed Zionist Jews in 1905 who along with Georgi Apollonovich Gapon – a Russian Orthodox priest and working class leader – attempted to overthrow Tsar Nicholas II of Russia in a Communist Coup known as the Bloody Sunday incident which proved unsuccessful and they were forced to flee Russia for refuge in Europe.

Consequently as a result of increased instability and competition in the region, the Rothschilds decided in 1906 to sell the Caspian and Black Sea Petroleum Company to Royal Dutch and Shell with some commentators hypothesising that this was just a Rothschild ploy to conceal the true extent of their actual wealth. The following year the head of bankers Kuhn, Loeb and Co., Jacob Schiff – the foremost American Jewish leader from 1880 to 1920 – informed the New York Chamber of Commerce that "Unless we have a Central Bank with adequate control of credit resources, this country is going to undergo the most severe and far reaching money panic in its history." This warning was followed by another Rothschild orchestrated financial crisis – a string of bank runs and national panic – that plunged numerous people throughout America into poverty while enhancing the Rothschild fortune by billions.

In order to incite Black Americans to riot, loot, and cause general mayhem that would create a rift between Black and White communities, Jacob Schiff in 1909 founded the National Advancement for the Association of the Coloured People (NAACP) which was basically run by Ashkenazi Jews so that it was not until 11 years later in 1920 that James Weldon Johnson became its first black president. In those days there were still some politicians who were prepared to speak out and in 1911, John F. Hylan, the Mayor of New York believed that "the real menace of our republic is the invisible government which, like a giant octopus, sprawls its slimy length over our city, state and nation. At the head is a small group of banking houses, generally referred to as 'international bankers.'" Conrad noted with a wry smile that 21st century New York mayors were not so forthright and instead bent over backwards to please Jews and their influential lobbies. In his book *The Jews and Modern Capitalism,* Werner Sombart asserted that from 1820 on, it was the "age of the Rothschild … only one power in Europe, and that is Rothschild."

George R. Conroy in the December 1912 issue of *Truth* magazine, asserted that "Mr Schiff is head of the great private banking house of Kuhn, Loeb and Co, which represents the Rothschild interests on this side of the Atlantic. He has been described as a financial strategist and has been for years the financial minister of the great impersonal power known as Standard Oil. He was hand in glove with the Harrimans, the Goulds, and the Rockefellers in all their railroad enterprises and has become the dominant power in the railroad and financial power of America."

In March 1913, Woodrow Wilson became the 28th President of the United States and shortly after his inauguration he was visited in the White House by Ashkenazi Jew, Samuel Untermyer, of law firm, Guggenheim, Untermyer, and Marshall. Untermyer tried to blackmail Wilson for $40,000 with regards to an affair Wilson had with a fellow professor's wife at Princeton University. As Wilson did not have the money, Untermyer offered to pay the $40,000 himself to the woman in question on condition that Wilson promised to appoint a nominee recommended by Untermyer to the first available vacancy on the United States Supreme Court. Wilson agreed and became yet another in the a long list of U.S. politicians susceptible to Jewish bribery.

Rothschild agent Jacob Schiff established the Anti Defamation League (ADL) in the U.S. to harass and slander as "anti-Semitic" – a task the ADL is still performing to this day – anyone daring to either question or challenge the Rothschild led Jewish global elite. Coincidentally that same year the Rothschilds set up the central bank in America that to this day is known as the Federal Reserve. Congressman Charles Lindbergh – who opposed both America's entry into World War One and the Federal Reserve Act – asserted that "the Act establishes the most gigantic trust on earth. When the President signs this Bill, the invisible government of the monetary power will be legalised … The greatest crime of the ages is perpetrated by this banking and currency bill." The Federal Reserve was and still is a private company that is neither Federal nor in possession of a Reserve. It has never in its history published accounts and conservative estimates place its annual profits at over $150 billion.

Being in control of the three major European news agencies, enabled the Rothschilds to covertly use Wolff in Germany to incite the fervour for war which broke out July 1914 with the German Rothschilds lending money to the Germans, the British Rothschilds lending money to the British, and the French Rothschilds lending money to the French. Two years later, President Woodrow Wilson kept his promise to the despicable blackmailer Untermyer and appointed Ashkenazi Jew, Louis Dembitz Brandeis to the Supreme Court of the United States. Justice Brandeis was also leader of the Executive Committee for Zionist Affairs, a position he held from 1914.

Though the Germans were apparently winning the war, they nonetheless made peace overtures with no requirement of reparations to Britain. But the Rothschilds, who were hoping to make even more money from the conflict, had their agent Louis Brandeis send a Zionist delegation from the U.S. to Britain with the promise of bringing America into the war on Britain's side, provided the British agreed to give Palestine to the Rothschilds. Having Palestine would eventually provide the Rothschilds with a "Jewish" state with its own military force that could be used to implement the Rothschild agenda.

President Woodrow Wilson won reelection with the slogan "Re-Elect The Man Who Will Keep Your Sons Out Of The War." But despite his promise to the American people, Wilson – under instructions from the American Zionist leader and Supreme Court Justice, Louis Dembitz Brandeis – took America into the First World War in April 1917. In keeping with their previously discussed arrangement, the Rothschilds wanted Britain's assurance of its intention to keep its side of the bargain with regards to Palestine. Consequently British Foreign Secretary, Arthur James Balfour – without bothering to ask or consult with the indigenous Palestinians – responded in that infamous letter which came to be known as the "Balfour Declaration" which proved to be the first step in eventually depriving the Palestine people of their homeland, their heritage, their history and their human rights.

In an act of revenge against the dead Tsar Alexander II (died 1881) who sided with President Abraham Lincoln in 1864, the Rothschilds in 1918 had the Russian Bolsheviks they controlled execute – despite his having already abdicated – Tsar

Nicholas II and his entire family. This venting of the vindictive Rothschild spleen was to serve as warning to anyone who dared to upset or oppose the family. In January of the following year, Ashkenazi Jews, Karl Liebknecht and Rosa Luxemburg, were killed in Berlin while in the process of leading yet another Rothschild funded Communist coup.

U.S. Congressman Oscar Callaway informed Congress that J. P. Morgan was a Rothschild front and had taken control of the American media industry:

"In March, 1915, the J.P. Morgan interests, the steel, shipbuilding, and powder interest, and their subsidiary organisations, got together 12 men high up in the newspaper world and employed them to select the most influential newspapers in the United States and sufficient number of them to control generally the policy of the daily press ... They found it was only necessary to purchase the control of 25 of the greatest papers ... An agreement was reached. The policy of the papers was bought, to be paid for by the month, an editor was furnished for each paper to properly supervise and edit information regarding the questions of preparedness, militarism, financial policies, and other things of national and international nature considered vital to the interests of the purchasers."

In 1919 Baron Edmond de Rothschild hosted the end of war Paris Peace Conference (Treaty of Versailles) to decide on reparations to be paid by Germany and to confirm the establishment of a Jewish state in Palestine – whose Jewish population was then an estimated five percent – with Britain in the meantime maintaining control. The conference was attended by a delegation of 117 Zionists headed up by Ashkenazi Jew, Bernard Baruch, whose function was to lobby for a Jewish state in Palestine. Consequently the Germans finally realised that it was the Rothschilds who turned America against them and quite rightly had felt betrayed by the Zionists. This was because when the Rothschilds had made their deal with Britain for Palestine in exchange for bringing America into the war, Germany was the most friendly and tolerant country in the world towards the Jews with the German Emancipation Edict of 1822 guaranteeing Jews in Germany the same civil rights enjoyed by non-Jew Germans.

Germany was also the only country in Europe which did not place restrictions on Jews, even providing them with refuge when they had to flee from Russia after their first attempted Communist coup in 1905 failed. In keeping their side of the bargain to get Palestine, the Rothschilds had no qualms over the fact that the achievement of their goal would come at the cost of the millions of innocents who had died in the war. Confirmation of Palestine as a future Jewish homeland under the temporary control of Britain was therefore secured by the Rothschilds who in any case controlled Britain.

The Paris Peace Conference was also part of the Rothschilds ploy to set up a world government under the pretext of ending all wars – which in most cases were of their own creation – by persuading their stooge U.S. President Wilson to initiate establishment of the "League of Nations" which as the predecessor of the United Nations failed to prevent World War Two, and did not survive for long due to a lack of interest from many nations including the United States.

The Times of London reported that "one of the curious features of the Bolshevist movement is the high percentage of non Russian elements among its leaders. Of the twenty or thirty commissaries, or leaders, who provided the central machinery of the Bolshevist movement, not less than 75% were Jews." It was alleged that the Rothschilds were angry with the Russians because of their refusal to permit a Rothschild central bank in Russia. Consequently groups of Jewish spies were sent and embedded throughout Russia to incite riots leading to a revolution. They were – in the Ashkenazi tradition of deception – given Russian names with one original name of Lev Davidovich Bronstein being changed to Leon Trotsky. It was also suspected that Vladimir Lenin had Jewish roots.

Those Jewish Rothschild funded Bolsheviks went on to slaughter 60 million Christians and Non-Jews in Soviet controlled territory. In his work *Gulag Archipelago, Vol 2,* Aleksandr Solzhenitsyn – the 1970 winner of the Nobel Prize for Literature – confirmed that Zionist Jews created and administered the organised Soviet concentration camp system in which those tens of millions of Christians and Non-Jews perished.

Conrad was not particularly surprised by this information because he recalled reading an article by his father, Mark, in which it was revealed that Stalin's death machine had been operated by Jews such as Genrikh Yagoda and Lazar Kaganovich, and that In 1934, at the peak of Stalin's purge, 38.5 percent of those holding the most senior posts in the Soviet security apparatuses were of Jewish origin. The article had mentioned two other genocides involving Jews with the first being the fact that at least a quarter of the International Brigade that fought General Franco – and was instrumental in the destruction of Catholic Spain in that bloody war – was Jewish with the Brigade's Lingua Franca being Yiddish.

The second and more recent genocide was in Rwanda where the Hutu majority-led government – with weapons imported mostly from Israel – perpetrated the mass slaughter of Tutsi and moderate Hutu people of whom an estimated 800,000 were killed. A recent Freedom of Information request to have documents – relating to the extent of Israeli "defence" exports to Rwanda 1994 –was summarily refused by Israel's Defence Ministry which stated that the information "was not to be divulged." A subsequent appeal had also been unanimously rejected by the the Supreme Court which found "that under the circumstances the disclosure of the information sought does not advance the public interest claimed by the appellants to the extent that it takes preference and precedence over the claims of harm to state security and international relations."

Suppression of such unpalatable facts about Israel was to be repeated when the U.S, Supreme Court – citing potential damage to Israel's foreign relations – rejected a petition calling for the release of details relating to Israel's arms sales involvement in the Bosnian Genocide.

Mark's article which was titled *Hypocrisy, Double Standards, And The Politicisation Of Genocide,* had highlighted the fact that while U.S. wars – including the deliberate targeting in the first Gulf War of soft civilian targets such as water treatment and sanitation facilities; electricity generating plants; roads and railways; hospitals and clinics; and the subsequent sanctions that prevented the repair of infrastructure essential to the survival of the Iraqi people – had resulted in the eventual death of millions of Iraqis, but virtually no one had dared to label the U.S. actions as "genocide." By contrast there was no hesitation in applying the '"genocide" label to the killing of 4,000 in Kosovo, 33,000 Bosnia, 300,000 in Darfur, and 800,000 in Rwanda.

Mark had also noted that the only country in the world where more civilians were murdered by the U.S. and allied forces in Iraq, was in the Democratic Republic of the Congo (DRC) where an estimated seven million civilians were killed during that country's ongoing hostilities. As was the case with Iraq, the DRC atrocities were never labelled as "genocide" because the U.S. and its allies – in their rapacious quest for the rare minerals in the DRC – were responsible for the bulk of those killings. But due to the fact that the Western Alliance controls the political discourse, such killings would never be regarded as genocide.

In spite of existing and justified suspicions of their global interference and subversive political intrigues, the Rothschilds were nonetheless awarded the permanent right to fix – fix being the operative word – the world's daily gold price, a task which they discharged each morning in their City of London offices until 2004.

In an article in the *Illustrated Sunday Herald* in 1920, Winston Churchill wrote that "from the days of Illuminati leader Weishaupt, through those of Karl Marx, to those of Trotsky, this worldwide conspiracy has been steadily growing. And now at last this band of extraordinary personalities from the underworld of the great cities of Europe and America, have gripped the Russian people by the hair of their heads and become the undisputed masters of that enormous empire."

Before his death the previous year in 1920, Jacob Schiff – who had helped finance Japanese military efforts against Tsarist Russia in the 1904 Russo-Japanese War – ordered Ashkenazi Jews, Bernard Baruch and Colonel Edward Mandell House to found the Council on Foreign Relations (CFR) so as to have an organisation that groomed and selected politicians to do the Rothschild's bidding. One of the CFR's first jobs was control of the press with John D. Rockefeller being chosen to set up a number of national news magazines such as *Life,* and *Time.* He also financed both Samuel Newhouse to purchase and establish a chain of newspapers across the country, and Eugene Meyer who bought up many publications including *The Washington Post, Newsweek,* and *The Weekly Magazine.* Control of radio, television and the motion picture industry was divided amongst the international bankers Kuhn Loeb, Goldman Sachs, the Warburgs, and the Lehmanns.

In 1933 an organisation of German Zionists came to an agreement with Nazi Germany – that was for the longterm benefit of Zionism rather than Jews – to salvage all German Jewish assets and the voluntary emigration of German Jews to Palestine before the Third Reich implemented its expulsion and subsequent extermination of Jews. This Transfer Agreement which had been induced by a sweeping, worldwide economic boycott of Germany by Jews, was instrumental between 1933 and 1939 in the emigration of 60,000 German Jews to Palestine where at the time very few Jews lived. The event was documented in 1984 by author Edwin Black in his book *The Transfer Agreement: The Dramatic Story of the Pact Between the Third Reich and Jewish Palestine.*

Swiss banking secrecy laws were reformed in 1934 to make it an offence punishable with imprisonment for any bank employee to violate bank secrecy. This was part of the Rothschild's preparations for orchestrating the Second World War wherein as was their custom they would fund both sides. I.G. Farben – the leading chemicals producer in the world and Germany's largest producer of steel – in 1939 dramatically stepped up production that was mostly used for arming Germany. Farben was under Rothschild control and would subsequently use Jews and others as slave labour in the concentration camps.

In his 1939 book *Inside The Gestapo,* author Hansjurgen Koehler reveals that Maria Anna Schicklgruber, Adolf Hitler's grandmother, "a little servant girl … came to Vienna and became a domestic servant … at the Rothschild mansion … and Hitler's unknown grandfather must be probably looked for in this magnificent house." This was substantiated in Walter Langer's 1972 book *The Mind Of Hitler* in which he states:

> *"Adolf's father, Alois Hitler, was the illegitimate son of Maria Anna Schicklgruber … Maria Anna Schicklgruber was living in Vienna at the time she conceived. At that time she was employed as a servant in the home of Baron Rothschild. As soon as the family discovered her pregnancy she was sent back home … where Alois was born."*

President Roosevelt took America into the Second World War in 1941 by discontinuing the sale to Japan of any more steel scrap or oil which Japan was totally reliant upon for continuation of its war against China. Roosevelt was aware that his decision would provoke Japan into attacking America, which it subsequently did at Pearl Harbour. A year later, Prescott Bush, the father and grandfather of two future American Presidents, had his Union Banking Corporation seized under the, "Trading With The Enemy," Act. The investment bank was operating as a clearing house for many assets and enterprises held by German steel magnate Fritz Thyssen who was helping Nazi Germany's war effort against the Allies.

Izaak Greenbaum, the Zionist head of the Jewish Agency Rescue Committee, informs the Zionist Executive Council in 1943 that "If I am asked, could you give from the UJA (United Jewish Appeal) monies to rescue Jews, I say, no and I say again no!" He further added that "one cow in Palestine is worth more than all the Jews in Poland!" Such sentiments were of course in keeping with Zionism's support for the slaughter of innocent Jews so as to scare the survivors into believing that their only hope of avoiding persecution and/or another genocide was a Jewish homeland in Palestine.

In ruthless pursuit of that Jewish homeland, the Jewish Stern Gang terrorist group led by future Israeli Prime Minister, Yitzhak Shamir, in 1944 assassinated Lord Moyne, British Minister Resident in the Middle East in Cairo; attempted to assassinate the High Commissioner of the British Mandate of Palestine, Harold MacMichael; and assassinated Count Folke Bernadotte, the United Nations representative in the Middle East, who – despite having secured the release of 21,000 prisoners including thousands of Jews from German concentration camps during World War Two – was regarded as an anti-Zionist; and in Bretton Woods, New Hampshire, the Rothschilds orchestrated the creation of the International Monetary Fund (IMF) and the World Bank.

On July 22, 1946, with the approval of future Israeli Prime Minister David Ben-Gurion, the Zionist paramilitary organisation, Irgun – commanded by another Ashkenazi Jew and future Israeli Prime Minister, Menachem Begin – carried out a terrorist attack on the King David Hotel in Jerusalem which at the time served as the Secretariat of the Government of Palestine and the Headquarters of the British Armed Forces in Palestine and Transjordan. The attack, part of the effort to drive out the British, killed 91 and wounded 45 mostly civilian people. This was just another terrorist act by ruthless Judaeo-Fascist terrorists with a "God-chosen" supremacist mindset …

12

Saturday, 19 December

The Corniche, Beirut, Lebanon

Winter in Beirut was relatively mild with a temperature average of around 58 degrees Fahrenheit and Mark Banner had as usual, rain or shine, taken his morning stroll along the palm tree-lined seaside promenade. Corniche Beirut, formerly a continuation of the Avenue des Français which was built during the time of the French Mandate of Syria and Lebanon (1923-1946) following the defeat and dissolution of the Ottoman Empire. Mark's breakfast of scrambled eggs and spicy basturma – an air-dried beef highly seasoned with crushed cumin, fenugreek, garlic, and hot paprika – was now part of a Saturday ritual to which he had been introduced by Nadine, his late Lebanese girlfriend who was murdered in London in December 2008 in what was undoubtedly a vengeful Mossad hit in response to Mark's syndicated columns with their implacable criticism of Israeli crimes in the Occupied Palestinian Territories.

Apart from being endlessly defamed as an anti-Semite and Holocaust denier, Mark had also to contend with having anything he wrote being subjected to a point-by-point refutation and ridicule by Judaeo-Zionist bloggers who in the manner of Marx and Engels – as noted by Ludwig von Mises in his *Socialism: An Economic and Sociological Analysis* – "never tried to refute their opponents with argument. They insulted, ridiculed, derided, slandered, and traduced them, and in the use of these methods their followers are not less expert. Their polemic is directed never against the argument of the opponent, but always against his person."

Apartheid Israel's disingenuous and cynical ploy of accusing others of the very crimes it was itself committing was reaffirmed by the Israeli Prime Minister when he posted an incendiary video in which he argued that any future dismantlement of Jewish settlements in the West Bank would amount to "ethnic cleansing." He further suggested that support for the uprooting of Israeli settlements – as part of an agreement with the Palestinians – by Western nations would amount to complicity in the cleansing of Jews. And this was from a man who while claiming to be speaking for "all Jews," conveniently and dishonestly overlooked the irrefutable reality that Israel was founded and continues to exist and expand – despite the Fourth Geneva Convention (article 49) which clearly states that "the Occupying Power shall not deport or transfer parts of its own civilian population into the territory it occupies" – by means of the ethnic cleansing of indigenous Palestinians. Apart from shifting the blame, the video was clearly designed to place yet another obstacle for the creation of a Palestinian state.

Rather than consider the possibility Mark was actually pro-human rights rather than anti-Semitic, his Judaeo-Zionist detractors were only concerned with silencing and demonising anything or anyone critical of Israel's criminal conduct. They were not interested in whether or not he was anti-Semitic; not interested in honestly and impartially judging his books and articles simply on merit; and were not interested in using factual evidence to refute what he wrote. Mark felt that his Jewish detractors – who were adept at using the "Jewish victim card" – should instead honestly ask themselves whether the concept of anti-Semitism was a consequence of an inherent and unreasonable hate for Jews by non-Jews, or whether it was an understandable reaction to a "Jewish separateness" inspired by a traditional mindset that promulgated Jewish supremacy over, hate for, and exploitation of non-Jews.

Another part of Mark's Saturday ritual was to visit Beirut's main Christian cemetery to pay his respects and lay fresh flowers on Nadine's grave. Losing her had shattered his life as he initially experienced shock, disbelief, numbness, sadness, anger and then finally, an aching loneliness that was still with him to this day. But life had to go on, and as always before visiting the cemetery, he would proofread what he had written – which this week was a the first of a two-part article – before emailing it to both Conrad and his London news agency for syndication.

The Zionisation And Decline of American Democracy

Part 1 of 2

Mark Banner
Sunday, 20 December

Such Zionisation has included the corruption and takeover of the bicameral Congress; the legislated denial of a citizen's right to support the Palestinian Boycott, Divestment, Sanctions Movement (BDS) which is a lawful exercise of freedom of expression; the influence over the U.S. economy through the Federal Reserve Bank which is a consortium of Jewish-owned banks; the censorship of public discourse by mostly Jewish-owned or operated media outlets such as the *New York Times* whose pro-Israel bias is a grotesque distortion of Israel's illegal occupation of Palestine; and the unashamed subservient betrayal of the American people by successive presidents to the all powerful Jewish lobby.

Despite President Truman's awareness of, and resentment over Zionist pressure back in November 1947, he nonetheless proved to be an indecisive and perhaps even detached observer whose presidential decisions were ultimately taken to satisfy the undemocratic influences of Zionism and the American Jewish population whose support was required for reelection. Truman's lackadaisical decisions served not only to cause cracks within the foundation stone of American democracy, but also to establish a precedent for American acquiescence to subsequent Zionist/Israeli demands throughout the rest of the 20th Century and into the 21st. This abysmal surrender of national interests had since become well-entrenched because of the wilful ignorance of most American people who without question accept the American media's false, ludicrous, and unstinting contention that as America's staunchest ally, Israel, was a moral nation incapable of any amoral, dishonest, or illegal behaviour.

Truman's dereliction of presidential duty may have stemmed from the fact that America was one of the original settler colonies where the colonisers often brutally displaced the indigenous inhabitants to eventually establish their own nation where the history of the atrocities they had ignominiously committed was quickly buried and forgotten. Consequently it was not difficult for Zionists to insinuate the idea that Zionist settlers in Palestine were no different from the original American "puritan" settler "pilgrims" and "pioneers" with the Palestinians now being the American native equivalent. The lie that Palestine was a "land without people for a people without land," was an echo of the U.S. settler view that America was an uninhabited land just ripe for picking.

While displacement of indigenous North American Indians was reconciled within the Christian conscience by such questionable pearls of wisdom as "the only good Indians I ever saw were dead" – attributed to General Phil Sheridan – Israel's current ethnic cleansing of Palestinians was dismissed by a "God chosen people" logic that fostered beliefs such as "to me, they are like animals, they aren't human." Though many apologists tend to blame Israel's criminality on a Zionist ideology that has nothing to do with Jews, the fact remains that Israel could not perpetrate its blatant crimes against humanity without toleration and/or support of both diaspora Jews and the all-powerful Jewish lobbies who have a devious and decisive influence over so-called Western democracies who in unison obligingly parrot the refrain that that "Israel has a right to defend itself": a hypocritical Western euphemism for Israel's ethnic cleansing.

One of the main factors that has enabled Israel to distract attention from its own crimes against humanity was and still remains the playing of the "Jewish Victim Card": a ploy which in 1958 was aided by the publication of the historically inaccurate novel *Exodus* by Leon Uris about the founding of Israel. Apart from becoming an international bestseller that was translated into over 50 languages; apart from being produced and directed as a film (with Paul Newman in the lead role) by Otto Preminger (a Jew); *Exodus* also exercised an immense sociopolitical influence in persuading the majority of American Jews – who up till then had mostly regarded the Jewish state with unease and suspicion – into becoming ardent Zionists.

Exodus was also instrumental in gaining support for Israel not only from America's political leaders, but also from the American people who to this day have maintained their blinkered allegiance to a brutal Apartheid state. There is no doubt that Uris had set out to deliberately exploit *Exodus* as an instrument for winning support, especially in the U.S., for Israel. Subsequent to the book's publication, Uris told the New York Post "I set out to tell a story of Israel. I am definitely biased. I am definitely pro-Jewish." *Exodus* can consequently be justifiably regarded without fear of contradiction as "Zionist propaganda." This was a fact acknowledged at the time by Israel's then prime minister, David Ben-Gurion, who said that "as a literary work, it isn't much. But as a piece of propaganda, it's the greatest thing ever written about Israel."

The single most effective achievement of Israel and its overseas diplomatic Jewish lobbying and secret service operations, however, has not been the global toleration of its forced expulsion of indigenous Palestinians with more than seven million of them – about one third of all refugees worldwide – constituting the most protracted and largest of all refugee problems in the world; has not been its military blockade and persecution of millions of unarmed others; but its ideological triumph in the U.S. where the doctrine of "Judaeo Israeli superiority" has secured widespread acceptance.

Advocates of Jewish Supremacism usually drum roll the fact that while Jews represent less than 0.2% of the world population, they have nonetheless provided a disproportionate 24% of the US Nobel prize winners; over 30% of Ivy League professors and students; the majority of major U.S. film, stage, and TV producers; as well as leading doctors, lawyers, and scientists like Albert Einstein. They do, however, omit to mention that many of these supremely talented Jewish individuals had in fact freed themselves from the shackles of Judaic life with its close rabbinical supervision and claustrophobic Jewish separateness and traditions.

Those same Jewish Supremacists also have the audacity to claim "ethnic credit" even for successful individuals who

– despite having openly rejected and abandoned Judaism and the concept of Israel as their spiritual homeland – have managed as a result of their global renown to escape being labelled as apostates or "self-hating Jews." Albert Einstein, the often cited example of "Jewish genius," denounced Israel's war crimes such as those in 1948 at Deir Yassin and when asked for assistance by a Zionist organisation, made it very clear that he did not want to see "anybody associated with those misled and criminal people."

The downside of the Jewish Supremacist doctrine has been the creation of a disproportionate block of educated Jews who now embrace an "ethno-religious" supremacist dogma that binds them to a ruthless Apartheid, militarist state with an ideology lacking in any conscience and quite prepared to drag the world into a global and possibly nuclear conflict. With Jewish lobby orchestration, the U.S. is now suffused with Islamophobia and minority discrimination that are a combined affront to the values of a much acclaimed and supposedly pluralistic society that purports – at least in theory – to represent fairness, justice, and human rights for all humanity. The U.S. was a nation built by immigrants and on the principle of offering refuge to the homeless, weary and oppressed as is inscribed on the interior wall of the pedestal of the Statue of Liberty:

"Not like the brazen giant of Greek fame, with conquering limbs astride from land to land; Here at our sea-washed, sunset gates shall stand a mighty woman with a torch, whose flame is the imprisoned lightning, and her name Mother of Exiles. From her beacon-hand glows world-wide welcome; her mild eyes command the air-bridged harbour that twin cities frame, 'Keep, ancient lands, your storied pomp!' cries she with silent lips. 'Give me your tired, your poor, Your huddled masses yearning to breathe free, The wretched refuse of your teeming

shore, Send these, the homeless, tempest-tost to me, I lift my
lamp beside the golden door!'"

Instead of adhering to such noble sentiments, the U.S. has instead allowed itself to become the driving force behind endless wars that have plunged the Muslim world into a profound jihadi-ridden chaos of failed Arab states careering beyond the point of safe return. Consequently the region will in due course become so inundated with maniacal terrorists and hapless refugees, that the current Western people's reluctance for having their armed forces intervene with "boots on the ground," will be swept aside by government induced fear and mainstream media orchestrated outrage. Then, the West – led by an AIPAC-controlled U.S. with its insatiable Military Industrial Complex – will finally have the required mandate to totally and permanently colonise the Greater Middle East for the ultimate benefit of America's "staunchest ally," the Apartheid state of Israel; the energy industry which is the third largest industry in the U.S.; and the Military Industrial Complex which is the recipient of over $600 billion annually.

> *"In the councils of government, we must guard against the acquisition of unwarranted influence, whether sought or unsought, by the military-industrial complex. The potential for the disastrous rise of misplaced power exists and will persist."*
> **President Dwight D. Eisenhower in his Farewell Address in 1961.**

Israel – with its pro-Israel lobby and neocon influence over U.S. foreign policy – has always been able to pursue its Middle East strategy of "divide and conquer" which in the early 1980s the Israeli diplomat and journalist Oded Yinon outlined – in what came to be known as the "Yinon Plan" – a proposal for the "dissolution" of "the entire Arab world including Egypt, Syria, Iraq and the Arabian peninsula." The target countries were to be made to "fall apart along sectarian and ethnic lines" with the resulting fragmentation causing each one to be "hostile" to its "neighbours." In Yinon's implausible opinion "this state of affairs will be the guarantee for peace and security in the area in the long run." The reconfiguration of the Middle East's geo-political environment through the balkanisation of neighbouring Arab nations into smaller, weaker states was to be achieved by fomenting discord and war amongst the Arabs: "Every kind of inter-Arab confrontation will assist us in the short run and will shorten the way to the more important aim of breaking up Iraq into denominations as in Syria and in Lebanon."

Israel's conniving use of the U.S. to promote and maintain Inter-Arab confrontations was motivated by the Israeli belief that so long as such endless confrontations caused the Arabs to bleed and haemorrhage amongst themselves, then they could never be a serious threat to Zionism's grand design for a "Greater Israel." In other words, Israel prefers being surrounded by jihadi terrorists who with Israel's direct involvement and materiel support unleash horrific civil wars on Muslim civilians, to having as single stable Arab Muslim neighbour state that was not compliant and subject to the will of Israel and the United States.

A 1996 "divide and conquer" strategy document produced for the Israeli government by a neocon study group – headed by future Bush administration Iraq War architects – was described as "a strategy based on balance of power." This involved allying with some chosen Muslim powers such as Jordan, Turkey, and Saudi Arabia to undermine and eventually overthrow others starting with a regime change in Iraq so as to destabilise Syria.

Destabilisation of both Syria and Iran was primarily aimed at countering the potential opposition those countries posed to Israel's machinations in Lebanon including its covetous desire for the waters of the Litani River which originated and flowed entirely within Lebanon's borders.

Israel consequently embarked on a series of invasions of Lebanon including Operation Litani In 1978; the Lebanon War in 1982; Operation Accountability in 1993; Operation Grapes of Wrath in 1996; and another Lebanon War – a conflict in Lebanon, northern Israel and the Golan Heights – in 2006. Whenever confronted by massive popular resistance to its occupation of South Lebanon, Israel employed an "Iron Fist" response with raids on villages, mass arrests of civilians, wide-scale destruction of homes and property, and assassinations with the full knowledge such actions would serve to alienate the population and fuel further savage internecine warfare between the different religious factions.

Israel's "divide and conquer" policy has since been confirmed by a Wikileaks archive of former U.S. Secretary of State Clinton, in which an email shows that in 2012 the Israeli intelligence service regarded a potential Sunni-Shiite war in Syria as a favourable development for the Jewish State and the West. In the email sent to then Secretary of State Clinton by Sidney Blumenthal – an American journalist, activist, writer, former aide to President Bill Clinton, and long-time confidant to Hillary – he quotes an Israeli security source as saying that "if the Assad regime topples, Iran would lose its only ally in the Middle East and would be isolated. At the same time, the fall of the House of Assad could well ignite a sectarian ·
between the Shiites and the majority Sunnis of the
drawing in Iran, which, in the view of Israeli c·
would not be a bad thing for Israel and its We·

Blumenthal also quoted an alternative and more reasonable view which showed less enthusiasm for conflict escalation in Syria: "Israeli security officials believe that Prime Minister Benjamin Netanyahu is convinced that these developments (expanding Arab civil war) will leave them [Israelis] vulnerable, with only enemies on their borders." This would suggest that there was a political debate taking place as to whether the Syrian people should be destroyed as a means of weakening Iran, or simply to destroy Iran just for the sake of it. More recently, in an email she sent to an unknown account, Clinton wrote that "the best way to help Israel deal with Iran's growing nuclear capability is to help the people of Syria overthrow the regime of Bashar Assad." A nuclear capability, incidentally, which like Iraq's is nonexistent.

With continual inter-Arab confrontations creating a more dangerous Middle East, Israel can rely on both U.S. government ambivalence over efforts for a fair and just peace agreement with the Palestinians, and the American people's toleration of Israel's brutal criminality so long as chaos prevails in the neighbouring Arab states. Consequently as far as Israel is concerned, the best solution to any Arab conflict such as the Syrian civil war, was to have no solution – irrespective of the horrific human cost – so as to maintain the status quo with the combatants gradually destroying each other courtesy of weapons supplied by the U.S. and Israel.

nity, Israel's racist and supremacist
ith the fallacy of an "American
itains the U.S. is qualitatively
erior – to all other nations. This
persists despite the reality that
$600 billion on the military –
all federal annual discretionary

spending – in a "superpower" country where more than 50 million Americans live below the poverty line; where 48 million of them receive food stamps; where more than one in five children is on food stamps and living in poverty; where an astounding 15% of senior citizens live in poverty; where ethnic poverty rates were 28% for Blacks, 24% for Hispanics, 10.5% for Asians, and 10% for Whites; where being Black lowers one's credit score by 71 Points; where a new AFL-CIO study on last year's corporate salaries found that CEOs made 335 times more than the average employee who earned $36,875 while the the big company CEOs got approximately $12,400,000; where according to a Forbes survey 56% of Americans have less than $1,000 in their combined cheque and savings bank accounts; and where an observation once made in April 4, 1967 by Martin Luther King Jr. is fast becoming a reality: "A nation that continues year after year to spend more money on military defence than on programs of social uplift is approaching spiritual doom."

In the meantime, and according to the Institute for Policy Studies, the 20 wealthiest people in the U.S (the 0.000006 Percent) now own more wealth than the bottom half of the U.S. population combined which totals 152 million people in 57 million households. As a good deal of that wealth is secreted in offshore tax haven bank accounts, the reality is probably far worse. The Forbes 400 richest Americans now own about as much wealth as the nation's entire African-American population and more than a third of the Latino population combined; more wealth combined than the bottom 61 percent of the U.S. population which is equivalent to an estimated 194 million people or 70 million households. Furthermore much of that wealth is Jewish money that controls most of what Americans read, hear, and watch. The perils of such control had been recognised some time ago in a report by the Commission On Freedom Of The Press which stated that "protection against government is now not enough to guarantee that a man who has something to say shall have a chance to say it. The owners and managers of the press determine which person, which facts, which version of the facts, and which ideas shall reach the public."

While belief in American "exceptionalism," may have encouraged patriotic pride, it has also served to blinker the American people to the realities of a U.S. which routinely violates international laws and treaties with no repercussions from international organisations including the ICC and the UN which it bullies into rubber stamping illegal U.S. interventions and wars that have undermined democracy and destroyed numerous countries refusing to capitulate to U.S. demands; a U.S. which in Latin America alone has intervened more than 50 times while often overthrowing democratically elected leaders as was the case in Guatemala in the early fifties with U.S.-backed dictators and death squads killing 200,000 Guatemalans; a U.S. that subsequently perpetrated other bloody interventions in the Dominican Republic and Chile; a U.S. that officially maintains an estimated 800 military bases around the world spanning 63 countries with 179 of those bases being in Germany alone; a U.S. that had in less than a year clocked up $33 billion in Arms Sales from Middle East wars that served Israel's purpose; and a U.S. where a poll had revealed that an astonishing 49.2 percent of Americans believed that Palestinians occupied Israeli land rather than the other way around.

Of the forthcoming year's 1.1 trillion of U.S. tax dollars allocated for discretionary spending, 54% or $599 billion will go on military expenditure with only a pathetic 6% for education and 6% for healthcare. Furthermore, the U.S. only unleashes its military might to protect its power and wealth by using it as a battering ram to further its economic policies and protect a transnational corporate capitalist power structure that prioritises profit over the welfare of the planet and its people through extortion, subjugation, and Rothschild influenced/ controlled organisations such as the International Monetary Fund (IMF) and the World bank (WB) who together have helped to create new forms of debt slavery and colonialism.

The emergence of a challenge to such geopolitical dominance by U.S.-based financial and diplomatic control has recently gathered pace as a consequence of efforts for independence by other nations being led by China and Russia – who by investing in neighbouring economies on terms that advance Eurasian integration through financing in their own currencies – were helping to entrench trade and investment in their own currencies instead of dollars. This has resulted in the creation of both the Shanghai Cooperation Organisation (SCO) – an alternative military alliance to NATO – and the Asian Infrastructure Investment Bank (AIIB) which pauses a threat to the IMF and World Bank duopoly over which the U.S. wields its will with a restrictive power of veto. Following the U.S. threat to undermine Russia's banking connections by cutting it off from the SWIFT interbank clearing system, China accelerated its creation of both the alternative China International Payments System (CIPS), and its own credit card system so as to protect Eurasian economies from such unilateralist U.S. threats. By using trade and credit linkages to support their diplomacy, Russia and China are simply doing what the U.S. has been doing all along to keep global financial control anchored in Washington at the IMF and World Bank offices. Any attempt to shift that centre of power, will be resisted with all the means the U.S. has at its disposal.

As the leading international monetary agency, the IMF's supposed function is to maintain the stability of the global financial system with loan conditions designed to boost economic recovery and growth. In reality, however, IMF policies are dictated by the U.S. and West European states whose objectives are to further the interests of their leading multi-national corporations and financial institutions by dominating expansion and profits. This U.S.-West European collusion is perpetrated with a division of powers so that the executive directors of the IMF are European, and their counterparts in the WB are American. Both sets of executive directors closely consult with their respective governments' Treasury Departments before deciding on policy priorities including the countries that are to receive loans, the amount of the loans, and the terms under which the loans are to be provided.

Such decisions as set by the IMF are then methodically dovetailed with the private banking sector and serve as sanction for the multinational banks to lend to, invest in, and generally exploit the resources of debtor countries. After setting the ground rules for the major banks, the IMF then takes on the responsibility of enforcement through interventions which include usurping the sovereignty of debtor countries; demanding privatisations; reducing social expenditures, salaries, wages and pensions; ensuring the priority of debt payments; and acting as the smokescreen behind which the major banks hide from political criticism and social unrest.

In their pursuit of acquiring lucrative loan deals with developing countries, the banks employ what can only be described as "economic hit men" who persuade governments of developing countries that borrowing large amounts of money to help finance development projects will raise the country's living standards. The borrower is assured that the project would increase Gross Domestic Product and tax revenues which would in turn facilitate repayment of the loans. After accepting the over-estimated merits of such loans – as a result of naivety, bribery, or threats – indebted countries soon discover they are unable to repay both the principal and the interest.

It is then at that point that the IMF appears on the scene with the promise to save the credit ratings of the indebted countries by providing the loans with which to repay their creditors. This serves to replace the country's indebtedness to banks with indebtedness to the IMF which then imposes austerity plans that include cuts in employment, wages, social pensions, social services, and the selling of national assets to private investors so as to meet repayments to the IMF. Such deals include the coercion of debtor countries into agreeing to vote with the U.S. at the UN and to accept U.S. military bases. Any leader of a loan seeking country who refuses such terms and conditions, quickly becomes subject to removal by an engineered coup d'état or assassination. Bank plundering activities – once restricted to developing countries – are now also to be found in the West with Greece, Ireland, Italy, Portugal, Spain, and even the U.S. itself being some of the more recent victims.

In view of the fact that the IMF is the instrument by which debtor countries have their sovereign rights violated, their people impoverished, and their democratic institutions eroded, it is not surprising that its list of past and present executive directors reads like a rogues gallery including a rapist; one who as a tax evader hid 27 million euros in 70 overseas banks while swindling thousands of small investors whom he persuaded to put their money in a Spanish bank that subsequently went bankrupt; and another who was accused of "negligence by a person in a position of public authority" over the award of a government payment of a more than €400 million – to a controversial tycoon who supported former president Nicolas Sarkozy – while she was Finance Minister: a crime of which she will undoubtedly be found guilty, but for which she will she will not serve any time in jail.

In the opinion of the International Consortium of Investigative Journalists (ICIJ) – a global network of some 185 reporters in more than 65 countries who collaborate on in-depth investigations – "Over the last decade, projects funded by the World Bank have physically or economically displaced an estimated 3.4 million people, forcing them from their homes, taking their land or damaging their livelihoods. The bank has also failed regularly to live up to its own policies for protecting people harmed by projects it finances. Furthermore, its private-sector lending arm, the International Finance Corporation, has financed governments and companies accused of human rights violations such as rape, murder and torture. In some cases the lenders have continued to bankroll these borrowers after evidence of abuses had emerged."

Apart from its Rothschild-instigated financial shenanigans, the U.S also appears to have no problem with hypocritically reconciling the irrefutable reality of its global criminal subversion of human rights – including a carte blanche for Israel's boundless criminality – with its official position on the subject as declared by the U.S. Department of State:

> *The protection of fundamental human rights was a foundation stone in the establishment of the United States over 200 years ago. Since then, a central goal of U.S. foreign policy has been the promotion of respect for human rights, as embodied in the Universal Declaration of Human Rights. The United States*

understands that the existence of human rights helps secure the peace, deter aggression, promote the rule of law, combat crime and corruption, strengthen democracies, and prevent humanitarian crises. Because the promotion of human rights is an important national interest, the United States seeks to:

- *Hold governments accountable to their obligations under universal human rights norms and international human rights instruments;*
- *Promote greater respect for human rights, including freedom from torture, freedom of expression, press freedom, women's rights, children's rights, and the protection of minorities;*
- *Promote the rule of law, seek accountability, and change cultures of impunity;*
- *Assist efforts to reform and strengthen the institutional capacity of the Office of the UN High Commissioner for Human Rights and the UN Commission on Human Rights; and*
- *Coordinate human rights activities with important allies, including the EU, and regional organisations.*

Such unabashed superpower hypocrisy which overlooks Israeli violations is equally evident in the U.S. Department of State's high-minded pronouncement on "Democracy" which asserts the following:

Democracy and respect for human rights have long been central components of U.S. foreign policy. Supporting democracy not only promotes such fundamental American values as religious freedom and worker rights, but also helps create a more secure, stable, and prosperous global arena in which the United States can advance its national interests. In addition, democracy is the one national interest that helps to secure all the others. Democratically governed nations are more likely to secure the peace, deter aggression, expand open markets, promote economic development, protect American citizens, combat international terrorism and crime, uphold human and worker rights, avoid humanitarian crises and refugee flows, improve the global environment, and protect human health. With these goals in mind, the United States seeks to:

- *Promote democracy as a means to achieve security, stability, and prosperity for the entire world;*
- *Assist newly formed democracies in implementing democratic principles;*
- *Assist democracy advocates around the world to establish vibrant democracies in their own countries; and*
- *Identify and denounce regimes that deny their citizens the right to choose their leaders in elections that are free, fair, and transparent.*

The Bureau of Democracy, Human Rights, and Labor (DRL) is committed to supporting and promoting democracy programs throughout the world. As the nation's primary democracy advocate, DRL is responsible for overseeing the Human Rights and Democracy Fund (HRDF), which was established in 1998 to address human rights and democratisation emergencies. DRL uses resources from the HRDF, as well as those allocated to Regional Democracy Funds, to support democratisation programs such as election monitoring and parliamentary development.

Over the past quarter-century, a large number of nations have made a successful transition to democracy. Many more are at various stages of the transition. When historians write about U.S. foreign policy at the end of the 20th century, they will identify the growth of democracy – from 30 countries in 1974 to 117 today – as one of the United States' greatest legacies.

The United States remains committed to expanding upon this legacy until all the citizens of the world have the fundamental right to choose those who govern them through an ongoing civil process that includes free, fair, and transparent elections.

Despite espousing such high-principled commitments to democracy, the U.S is itself undeniably a plutocracy – a government run by the rich, for the rich – where a monied, oligarchic elite calls the shots in Washington and the mainstream media, while the militarised police and surveillance sector keep the masses under control. In a constitutional law case, Citizens United v. Federal Election Commission, the U.S. Supreme Court allowed the corporate role in politics to be increased by ending 100 years of law protecting citizen democracy from the influence of large corporate donations. By removing all limits on the amount of money that corporations, multi millionaires, and billionaires could donate in order to unfairly influence elections and buy political power, the U.S Supreme Court effectively hammered another nail into the coffin of democracy in the U.S. where breathtaking "superpower" hypocrisy reigns supreme.

The pernicious effect of unlimited political contributions was illustrated this summer after a historic nuclear accord with Iran was finally signed with Iran pledging to eliminate its stockpile of medium-enriched uranium, decrease its stockpile of low-enriched uranium by 98%, and reduce approximately two-thirds the total number of gas centrifuges for 13 years. Despite the merits of the agreement including an obvious victory for diplomacy over military conflict and the promise of improved relations, Israel remained obstinate in its opposition with the AIPAC-led pro-Israel lobby unleashing its attack dogs on the U.S. government by paying off Republican Senators in Congress to oppose the deal. One Arkansas Republican

Senator alone – who had kowtowed to the Israel lobby in the past – received almost $1 million ($960,250) for his campaign from the Emergency Committee for Israel, a U.S.-based rightwing political advocacy organisation. Shortly afterwards this Senator led the writing of an open-letter, signed by 47 Republicans, stating that a GOP (Republican/Grand Old Party) White House would not adhere to any accords with Iran. So if you want to identify the criminals stealing democracy from the American people, just follow the money.

Even though the U.S. professes – with delusional and hypocritical regularity – to oppose Israel's settlement building on Palestinian land which is illegal under international law, it has nonetheless between 2009 and 2013 allowed some 50 American organisations to raise $281 million in tax-deductible donations of which $224 million was transferred directly to Israeli settlements for property purchase, home amenities, and in some cases even to support families of convicted Jewish terrorists. The donation's tax-deductible status meant that the U.S. government was incentivising and effectively supporting a monstrous and illegitimate Israeli settlement policy.

Apart from such brazen conduct and double standards, the U.S. has also developed a far more sophisticated "doublespeak" than the "doublethink" envisioned in George Orwell's *Nineteen Eighty-Four* book. The unacceptable systematic "torture" of detainees; the "toppling" of foreign governments; and – with Israeli propaganda assistance – the ethnic cleansing of the Palestinian people have all been euphemistically transformed into the more acceptable "enhanced interrogation techniques"; "regime change"; and "Israel's right to defend itself."

Doublethink – which as part of newspeak is also related to hypocrisy and neutrality – is the act of ordinary people simultaneously accepting two mutually contradictory beliefs as being correct without them being aware of any conflict or contradiction. This allows the government to pursue morally contentious narratives and policies that go largely unquestioned by the mainstream media and the general public. The general public's laissez-faire attitude in this regard constitutes collaboration in the government's control of the population and enables the government through the mainstream media to selectively focus on its enemies' transgressions while overlooking those committed by itself and its allies including Apartheid Israel.

Implementing population control in the U.S. requires not only doublethink but also National Security Agency (NSA) spying that is perpetrated without any legal, constitutional, or "national security" justification; requires complete abdication of responsibility to the United States Bill of Rights by Congress, the White House, and the Judiciary; and requires the establishment of a police/warfare state that was further entrenched and justified – following the September 11, 2001 coordinated terrorist attacks allegedly carried out by the Islamic terrorist group al-Qaeda – as necessary protection against "terrorists" in the monumental hoax known as the "War on Terror."

> " … in America, we have achieved the Orwellian prediction – enslaved, the people have been programmed to love their bondage and are left to clutch only mirage-like images of freedom, its fables and fictions. The new slaves are linked together by vast electronic chains of television that imprison not their bodies but their minds. Their desires are programmed, their tastes manipulated, their values set for them."
> **Gerry Spence, From Freedom to Slavery: The Rebirth of Tyranny in America.**

In spite of its strident and frequently professed dedication to democracy and human rights for everyone, the U.S. is – unfortunately for humanity – in reality seriously misguided in its interpretation and adherence to both concepts. It has for example a long and iniquitous history of staunchly supporting right-wing dictators; of consorting with absolute monarchies in Arab countries where political activity or dissent is severely dealt with by a judicial system that lacks jury trials and observes few human rights formalities; of funding certain candidates or parties and disrupting countless elections throughout the world; and of overthrowing numerous democratically elected foreign governments – regime changes – which in the Middle East primarily serve the interests of an Apartheid Jewish state..

> *"Americans cannot escape a certain responsibility for what is done in our name around the world. In a democracy, even one as corrupted as ours, ultimate authority rests with the people. We empower the government with our votes, finance it with our taxes, bolster it with our silent acquiescence. If we are passive in the face of America's official actions overseas, we in effect endorse them."*
> **Mark Hertzgaard, author and independent journalist.**

Mamilla, West Jerusalem

After finally reaching West Jerusalem, checking into their hotel, unpacking, showering, and having an early dinner, Conrad and Freya returned to their room for some much needed rest following their encounter with Israeli hospitality at Tel Aviv's airport which had drained them of any romantic inclinations that they might of otherwise had. Instead they propped themselves against their pillows as they lay in bed and settled for some reading. Though Conrad had been fascinated by the information he had acquired on the subject of his intended documentary, he had also been deeply disturbed by some of the revelations concerning the establishment of Israel as a state and the extent to which the Rothschild family had managed to covertly spread its poisonous tentacles to even include the Orient.

When on October 1, 1949, Mao Zedong in Beijing's Tiananmen Square announced the establishment of the People's Republic of China, it was due to Zedong having been financed by Rothschild's Russian Communism as facilitated by the following Rothschild agents: Solomon Adler, a former United States Treasury official and confirmed Soviet Spy who returned to China where he became involved with translating Zedong's works into English; Israel Epstein, who as a Polish born Jew became a naturalised Chinese journalist and author who was one of the few foreign-born Chinese citizens of non-Chinese origin to become a member of the Chinese Communist party, and whose father was a Jewish Bolshevik imprisoned by the Tsar in Russia for trying to incite a revolution; and Virginius Frank Coe, a U.S. government official identified as an underground member of the of the communist party – and member of the Soviet spy group known as the Silvermaster ring – who served as a technical secretary for the Bretton woods Conference before becoming Secretary of the Rothschild influenced International Monetary Fund.

The following July, Israel passed the Law of Return and on April 1, 1951, Mossad, the Israeli Secret Intelligence Agency came into being with a motto that some would say epitomised the base instincts and mentality of a nation bereft of any morality and whose creation had been justified by contrived biblical narratives: "By Way Of Deception, Thou Shalt Do War."

On October 14, 1953, Unit 101, led by future Prime Minister Ariel Sharon – a virulent anti-Arab racist with a long and bloody history of murder and repression against the

Palestinian people – attacked Qibya, a small, undefended village inside the West Bank, and massacred 69 people of whom many were burned alive inside their homes. Unit 101 suffered no casualties with the atrocity having been sanctioned at the very top and carried out for political ends.

The next few years had witnessed the "Lavon Affair" Israeli false flag operation; the discovery of a hidden microphone planted by the Israelis in the Office of the U.S. Ambassador in Tel Aviv; the Compagnie Financiere, was set up in Paris by Edmond de Rothschild; and listening devices connected to several telephones in the residence of the U.S. military attaché in Tel Aviv, were discovered.

Announcement of James de Rothschild's death in 1957 was accompanied by Rothschild owned media reports that he had bequeathed a very substantial amount of money for the building of Israel's Knesset which he felt should be "a symbol, in the eyes of all men, of the permanence of the State of Israel" – a permanence that would first necessitate the calculated and merciless obliteration of an entire people and culture. Conrad could not help asking himself whether *Israel's plan to destroy an entire people and culture would, unlike Hitler's, prove successful and go unpunished.*

The Editor of Burke's Peerage, L.G. Pine, in his book *Tales of the British Aristocracy,* stated the following about the Jews:

> *"They have made themselves so closely connected with the British peerage that the two classes are unlikely to suffer loss which is not mutual. So closely linked are the Jews and the lords that a blow against the Jews in this country would not be possible without injuring the aristocracy also."*

In 1962 the de Rothschild Frères set up an umbrella company for all their mineral mining interests which was in line with the assertion in Frederic Morton's book, *The Rothschilds,* that:

"Though they control scores of industrial, commercial, mining and tourist corporations, not one bears the name Rothschild. Being private partnerships, the family houses never need to, and never do, publish a single public balance sheet, or any other report of their financial condition."

During 1962-63 Senator William J. Fulbright, the Foreign Relations Committee Chairman, convened hearings which uncovered evidence that the Jewish Agency – a predecessor to the state of Israel – had operated a massive network of financial "conduits" that funnelled funds to Israel lobby groups which raised the question of ever-growing Zionist influence on U.S. policy decisions. In April 1973, on CBS *Face the Nation,* Fulbright stated that:

"Israel controls the U.S. Senate. The Senate is subservient, much too much; we should be more concerned about U.S. interests rather than doing the bidding of Israel. The great majority of the Senate of the U.S. – somewhere around 80% – is completely in support of Israel; anything Israel wants; Israel gets. This has been demonstrated time and and again, and this has made [foreign policy] difficult for our Government."

In June 1963 President John F. Kennedy signed Executive Order 11110 which re-established the U.S. government's authority to issue currency without having to go through the Rothschild controlled Federal Reserve Bank. Consequently more than $4 billion in United States Notes were brought into circulation in $2 and $5 denominations. Kennedy's assassination less than six months later removed the requirement for the main Zionist lobbying group to register as a foreign agent; resulted in Executive Order 11110 being set aside with all the "United States" notes being gradually withdrawn; and ended the U.S. government's strong opposition to Israel's desire for possession of nuclear weapons.

In his book *They Dare to Speak Out,* Paul Findley stated that during Kennedy's campaign for president in 1960 he had a meeting with some prominent Jews. Kennedy was very insulted when one of the Jews said they knew Kennedy's campaign was in financial difficulty and that he and his Jewish friends would "help and help significantly" John Kennedy's campaign if, as president, Kennedy "would allow them to set the course of Middle East policy over the next four years. It was as a consequence of this meeting that Kennedy decided to work for a law that would have had the U.S. Treasury pay a set and equal amount to all politicians running for president who secured a to be determined percentage of signatures from people supporting their campaign.

In his 1991 book *The Samson Option: Israel's Nuclear Arsenal and American Foreign Policy,* Seymour Hersh stated:

"He saw this as the only way to prevent the nightmare of today, which has not only the President, but the overwhelming majority of people in Congress bought and paid for by the very powerful Israeli lobby."

More recently – as Conrad had learnt from one of his father's newspaper articles – in April 2014, the U.S. Supreme Court struck down limits on individual campaign contributions, ruling that federal caps on combined donations to candidates, parties and political action committees are an unconstitutional infringement on free speech. In other words, the very rich could go shopping for political candidates over whom they would subsequently have complete control. Of the nine Supreme Court Justices three were Jewish while none were Christian Protestant (the largest religious group in the US) or Muslim (Muslim-Americans are about equal in number to Jewish-Americans) which would again confirm that money can buy disproportionate representation.

In 1965, the U.S. Nuclear Materials and Equipment

Corporation illegally supplied enriched uranium to Israel which is believed to now be in possession of as many as 400 nuclear weapons.

Though unprovoked, in 1967 Israel suddenly attacked its Arab neighbours to gain control of the Sinai including Gaza, the West Bank, and the Jordan River. On June 8, the USS Liberty was attacked by Israeli aircraft and motor torpedo boats in an Israeli false flag operation intended to blame Egypt and bring the U.S. into the war. On the following day, Israel illegally occupied the Golan Heights in Syria – which subsequently provided Israel with one third of its fresh water – from where 130,000 Arab inhabitants were expelled.

It was now obvious to Conrad that the Golan Heights example served as yet one more reminder that Israel's Middle East conflicts were very different from the *hasbara* story that Israel presented to the world. Such conflicts were not simply about an ongoing battle between Western and Muslim worlds; they were not clashes between cultures, religions, or values; and Israel's illegal occupation of Palestinian territories was not a necessary security measure to protect Israel from "terrorists." It was instead all about an Apartheid racist Jewish state that unilaterally privileged Jewish interests and rights while treating the interests and rights of the indigenous non-Jews with contemptuous disregard and merciless inhumanity.

During 1970, while working for Senator Henry "Scoop" Jackson on the Senate Armed Services Committee, Zionist Ashkenazi Jew Richard Perle was caught on an FBI wiretap passing classified information to someone at the Israeli Embassy. No action was taken against the treacherous Perle who went on to become much involved with the Reagan Administration, served as an assistant Secretary of Defence, and worked on the Defence Policy Board Advisory Committee (1987-2004), and was its Chairman in 2001 under the Bush administration when with other Jewish neocons and Israeli biased think tanks such as the Institute for Advanced Strategic & Political Studies, blatant lies were used to justify an illegal Iraqi war whose catastrophic consequences were still ongoing to this day.

That same year, British Prime Minister Edward Heath made Lord Victor Rothschild the head of his policy unit during which time Britain became a member of the European Community which was just one more step towards a World government with a common political authority for all of humanity subject to Rothschild control and influence. That influence was subsequently discussed in Gary Allen's *None Dare Call It Conspiracy* in which it was stated that "one major reason for the historical blackout on the role of the international bankers in political history is the Rothschilds were Jewish ... The Jewish members of the conspiracy have used an organisation called The Anti-Defamation League (ADL) as an instrument to try and convince everyone that any mention of the Rothschilds and their allies is an attack on all Jews. In this way they have stifled almost all honest scholarship on international bankers and made the subject taboo within universities."

In his 1976 confidential and controversial interview, Harold Wallace Rosenthal – a Jewish administrative assistant to one of America's ranking senators, Jacob Javits R-NY – after admitting Jewish dominance in all significant national programs, said "it is a marvel that the American people do not rise up and drive every Jew out of this country." Rosenthal added that "we Jews continue to be amazed with the ease by which Christian Americans have fallen into our hands. While the naive Americans wait for Khrushchev to bury them, we have taught them to submit to our every demand."

When asked how a nation could be taken over without their knowing it, Rosenthal attributed success to the absolute control of the media. He boasted of Jewish control of all news with any newspaper refusing to submit to Jewish control of news being brought to its knees by withdrawal of advertising. Failing that,

"It's a very simple matter," the Jews would stop the supply of newsprint and ink.

As to the question of men in high political office, Rosenthal replied that no one since 1976 had achieved any political power without Jewish approval. "Americans have not had a presidential choice since 1932. Roosevelt was our man; every president since Roosevelt has been our man."

An Ashkenazi Jew Senate Foreign Relations Committee staffer, Stephen Bryen, in 1978 offered confidential documents to top Israeli military officials in a Washington D.C. hotel. Though the matter was headed for the grand jury with lawyer Nathan Lewin representing Bryen, the case was suddenly and mysteriously dropped with Bryen subsequently going on to work for that other traitor, Richard Perle.

The 1979 Egyptian-Israeli peace treaty was underwritten by naive U.S. taxpayer dollars to the tune of $3 billion to Israel which showed its customary gratitude by having Shin Bet, the Israeli internal security agency, attempting to gain access to the U.S. Consulate General in Jerusalem by honey trapping a clerical employee who was having an affair with a Jerusalem girl. And the following year the Rothschilds initiated the global craze of privatisation which would help them to gain control of more publicly owned global assets.

In 1982, Ariel Sharon – who as a war criminal, terrorist, mass murderer, and torturer epitomised the pure, unmitigated evil of Zionism – orchestrated the invasion of Lebanon and deliberately facilitated the Sabra and Shatila massacres during which time he vented his Ashkenazi spleen in a Hebrew-language interview with Israeli writer Amos Oz as follows:

"Even today I volunteer to do the dirty work for Israel, to kill as many Arabs as necessary, to deport them, to expel and burn them, to have everyone hate us, to pull the rug out from underneath the feet of the Diaspora Jews, so that they will be forced to run to us crying. Even if

it means blowing up a few synagogues, I don't care. And I don't mind if after the job is done you put me in front of a Nuremberg Trial and then jail me for life. Hang me if you want, as a war criminal ... What your kind doesn't understand is that the dirty work of Zionism is not finished yet, far from it."

Following a four-month investigation into the Sabra and Shatila massacres, the Kahan Commission on February 8, 1983 submitted its report which concluded that direct responsibility rested with the Gemayel Phalangists and though no Israelis were deemed directly responsible, Israel was held to be indirectly responsible with Defence Minister Ariel Sharon bearing personal responsibility. So once again an Israeli war criminal escaped punishment and went on to become prime Minister from 2001 to 2006.

In 1985, *The New York Times* reported that the Federal Bureau of Investigations (FBI) was aware of at least a dozen incidents in which American officials transferred classified information to the Israelis, but that the Justice Department did not prosecute; Richard Kelly Smyth was indicted on charges of exporting nuclear timing devices to Israel through the full-fledged operative for Israel's top-secret intelligence agency, Arnon Milchan, whose activities included "buying components to build and maintain Israel's nuclear arsenal" and supervising "government-backed accounts and front companies that financed the special needs of Israel's entire intelligence operations outside the country." Milchan was and still is a successful film producer whose films included *Pretty Woman, 12 Years a Slave, L.A. Confidential, JFK, Heat, Fight Club, Mr. and Mrs. Smith,* and many others.

Despite Israel's official position of never confirming or denying its possession of nuclear weapons, such possession was an open secret with U.S. and European intelligence services being fully aware that Israeli nuclear bombs were being covertly built – with one actually being tested in 1979 of the coast of then Afrikaner friendly Apartheid South Africa – using technology and materials provided by conniving powers or stolen by clandestine agent networks.

It finally took a brave former technician at Israel's Dimona nuclear installation, Mordechai Vanunu, to reveal information about Israel's nuclear programme – including secretly taken photographs at the Dimona site – to *The Sunday Times* in London. Having been previously duped and embarrassed by the Hitler Diaries Hoax, *The Sunday Times* was understandably cautious and took some time investigating Vanunu's claims which were eventually verified by experts. In the meantime a frustrated Vanunu had approached the *Sunday Mirror* whose owner was Robert Maxwell, a shyster and Mossad agent who was plundering his own employees' pension fund in an effort to save his crumbling business empire. Maxwell's Mossad connection was subsequently revealed before his death by a former Mossad officer, Ari Ben-Menashe, who claimed that Maxwell had alerted the Israeli Embassy in London about Vanunu's intentions. In a further effort to save his empire, Maxwell tried to put the squeeze on Israel for a financial bailout by threatening to expose what he knew, and Mossad without the slightest compunction had him assassinated (Gordon Thomas & Martin Dillon, *The Assassination of Robert Maxwell: Israel's Super Spy,* Robson Books Ltd, 2003).

After his approach to the *Sunday Mirror,* Vanunu became a Mossad priority so that one of its agents from America, Cheryl Bentov, was flown to London where she joined a team of nine Katsa Israeli field intelligence officers. Bentov wasted no time in using her seduction skills to "come alongside" Vanunu in Leicester Square and to quickly develop an amorous relationship with him. When Vanunu suggested spending the night together, Bentov agreed with the suggestion that they should go to Rome and "enjoy a few romantic days in the city of love." Five other members of the Mossad team were also on the flight to Rome where in the old quarter of the city, Bentov led Vanunu to an apartment which she claimed belonged to her sister. Israeli agents waiting in the apartment overpowered Vanunu, injected him with a paralysing drug, and then transported him by freighter to Israel.

Vanunu was subsequently tried in secret on espionage and treason charges for which in 1988 he received an eighteen-year prison sentence eleven of which he spent in near total isolation. Amnesty International called his treatment by Israel as being cruel, inhuman or degrading such as that prohibited by international law. Every year from 1988 to 2004 Vanunu was nominated for the Nobel Peace Prize amongst many other nominations and awards.

Though in April 2004 Vanunu was finally released conditionally, he remained defiant under interrogation by Israel's internal security service. In recordings of the interrogation made public he was heard to say "I am neither a traitor nor a spy, I only wanted the world to know what is happening … We don't need a Jewish state. There needs to be a Palestinian state. Jews can, and have lived anywhere, so a Jewish state is not necessary."

Vanunu had to date been continually harassed, rearrested and imprisoned for violating the terms of his release which included not being allowed to have contact with citizens from other countries; not to use phones or own cellular phones; not to have access to the internet; not to approach embassies or consulates of other countries; not to come within five hundred metres of any international border crossing; not to visit any port of entry or airport; and not to leave the state of Israel. *And this,* Conrad thought, *is the only democracy in the Middle East.*

Confirmation that the decades-old U.S policy of silence on Israel's nuclear weapons would persist came from the President during his first White House press conference in 2009 when journalist Helen Thomas – who once said "You cannot criticise Israel in this country [USA] and survive" – asked if he knew of any nations in the Middle East with nuclear arms. By replying that "with respect to nuclear weapons, you know, I don't want to speculate," Obama was suggesting that Israel's irrefutable possession of nuclear weapons was only a matter of rumour and conjecture.

Edmund de Rothschild, in 1987, created the World Conservation Bank – and with chicanery sneaked it into the UN system – which was designed to provide debt transfer and loan facilities for third world countries who in return would give mineral rich land to the bank. This gave the Rothschilds control of land in third world countries which represented 30% of the Earth's land surface. By also obtaining large tracts of farmland in developing countries and by having the crops transported back to the home countries, the bank was leaving the already starving third world populations with even fewer crops resulting increased food prices.

Following the Lebanese magazine *Ash-Shiraa's* revelation in November 1986 that senior U.S. administration officials had secretly facilitated the sale of U.S. arms to embargoed Iran by first supplying them to Israel which then sold them on to Iran – so as to facilitate securing the release of several American hostages and funding the Contras in Nicaragua – *The Wall Street Journal* reported the following April that Israel's role in the Iran-Contra Scandal would not be subject to detailed examination by investigators.

The Anti Defamation League (ADL) in 1988 initiated a nationwide competition for law students to draft anti-hate legislation for minority groups. The winner's thesis proposed that not only should hate motivated violence be banned, but that any words encouraging suspicion, friction, hate, and possible violence, should also be criminalised. It also suggested that state-agencies should monitor and restrict free speech in general; should censor all films that criticise identifiable groups; and even if accused persons can justify their statements – for example criticism of homosexuality by Christians because the bible expressly forbids it – that such mitigation would not constitute a defence in court. All that would be necessary for a conviction of hate speech would be that something was said, and that a minority group or one of its members had felt emotionally damaged as a consequence of the criticism. Such laws – thanks to covert Rothschilds lobbying – were now in place in most so-called democratic countries and served to protect the Rothschilds against any criticism which could be discredited as being anti-Semitic and subject to possible imprisonment.

When Mikhail S. Gorbachev had stepped onto the world stage in March 1985 as the new leader of the Union of Soviet Socialist Republics (USSR), it had become immediately apparent that he would be different from his older predecessors. As a 54 year-old, Gorbachev was significantly younger than other members who had in the past led the Communist superpower and his being from a younger generation meant a new approach to the challenges that faced the country.

Gorbachev immediately hallmarked his time in office by launching his nation on a new dramatic course with the dual program of "perestroika" ("restructuring") and "glasnost" ("openness") which resulted in profound changes with regards to the economy, internal affairs, and international relations. Within five years, Gorbachev's revolution had swept communist governments throughout Eastern Europe from power; brought an end to the Cold War (1945-91); virtually ended political and economic rivalry between the Soviet Union and the United States; and eased the tensions between the Eastern and Western alliances that had emerged following World War Two. Gorbachev's groundbreaking policies had fortuitously initiated the eventual collapse of the Soviet Union in 1991 which dissolved into 15 individual republics.

Gorbachev's successor and first President of Russia was the vodka-guzzling Boris Yeltsin whose reign from 1991 to 1998 was marked by widespread corruption resulting in persistent low oil and commodity prices, inflation, economic collapse, and calamitous political and social problems that also affected the other former states of the USSR.

Yeltsin's endeavour to transform Russia's socialist economy into a capitalist market economy – with the implementation of economic shock therapy, price liberalisation and nationwide privatisation – led to a perilous economic shift with the majority of the national property and wealth falling into the hands of a small number of mostly Jewish oligarchs such as Roman Abramovich, Mikhail Fridman, Valery Kagan, Alexander Mashkevitch, Ihor Kolomoyskyi, Viatcheslav Kantor, and Vladimir Gusinsky who were Zionist supremacists with dual Israeli-Russian citizenships.

The collapse of Communism in Russia saw the start of a mass exodus of some 700,000 Jews from the former Soviet Union to Israel: a land from which 750,000 indigenous Palestinians had previously been terrorised, driven out, and denied a legally justified "right of return" which was otherwise granted to Jews with no legal claim or connection to Palestine whatsoever.

N. M. Rothschild announced establishment of a new subsidiary, Rothschild GmbH, in Frankfurt, Germany, which claimed to offer its customers "wealth management services in the field of asset management and financial planning with a high level of personal service."

Subsequent to Iraq's invasion of Kuwait in August 1990, the U.S. and Britain decided in February 1991 to subject Iraq to an aerial bombing campaign with fuel air bombs that slaughtered 150,000 Iraqi troops who were fleeing on an overcrowded highway from Kuwait to Basra. U.S. aircraft and ground troops – on President George H.W. Bush's order – killed the surrendering soldiers and bulldozed them, even those who were still alive, into mass unmarked graves in the desert. This by any standard was a heinous war crime committed by a barely literate politician who along with his neocon henchmen was fulfilling the wishes of his Zionist puppet masters at AIPAC.

At the annual June closed session of the Bilderberg Conference attended by some 120 to 150 political leaders and experts from industry, finance, academia and the media in Baden-Baden, Germany, Rothschild agent David Rockefeller made the following statement,

"We are grateful to the Washington Post, the New York Times, Time Magazine, and other great publications whose directors have attended our meetings and respected their promises of discretion for almost 40 years. It would have been impossible for us to develop our plan for the world, if we had been subjected to the lights of publicity during those years. But the world is now more sophisticated and prepared to march towards a world government. The super-national sovereignty of an intellectual elite and world bankers is surely preferable to the national auto-determination practised in past centuries."

That same year N. M. Rothschild & Sons advised the British government on the privatisation of British Gas and subsequently also counselled on virtually all other privatisations of state owned assets including British Steel, British Coal, all British regional electricity boards, and all British regional water boards. Norman Lamont – a former Rothschild banker, a British Member of Parliament, and a future Chancellor of the Exchequer – was very much involved in those privatisations. Deep Rothschild involvement in, or control of the central banks of most nations had resulted in those central banks deliberately impoverishing their host nations so as to justify economic and legal adjustments that facilitated financial fleecing by foreign interests. Recently, for example, nations such as Greece, Ireland, and Italy have forfeited their national sovereignty to the European Central Bank (ECB) which has exploited loans and liquidity as a means of fleecing European nations.

In another Rothschild "revolving door" scenario, former U.S. Federal Reserve Board Chairman, Paul A. Volker, became Chairman of the European banking firm, J. Rothschild, Wolfensohn and Co. in March, 1992.

Stephen Bryen, who was caught offering confidential documents to Israel in 1978, joined the board of the pro-Israeli Jewish Institute for National Security Affairs while amazingly remaining as a paid consultant – with security clearance – on exports of sensitive U.S. technology.

In his book *The Samson Option,* Seymour M. Hersh stated the following:

> *"Illicitly obtained intelligence was flying so voluminously from LAKAM (a secret Israeli intelligence unit, a Hebrew acronym for Scientific Liaison Bureau) into Israeli intelligence that a special code name, JUMBO, was added to the security markings already on the documents. There were strict orders, Ari Ben-Menashe recalled, 'Anything marked JUMBO was not supposed to be discussed with your American counterparts.'"*

The Wall Street Journal reported another Israeli spy scandal involving the theft of Recon Optical Inc's top-secret airborne spy-camera system. One of the spies cooperating with the FBI investigation, casually dismissed the spying by claiming that such spying was harmless, because Israel and the United States were very good friends.

On September 16th Britain's pound collapsed when currency speculators led by Rothschild agent, Ashkenazi Jew, George Soros, borrowed pounds sterling and sold them for Deutsche Marks, in the expectation of being able to repay the loan in devalued currency and to pocket the difference. This resulted in the British Chancellor of the Exchequer, Norman Lamont, – a former Rothschild banker – announcing a 5% rise in interest rates in one day which drove Britain into a recession lasting for many years and caused numerous businesses to fail along with the crashing of the housing market. The Rothschilds – who having privatised Britain's state owned assets during the 1980's – then boosted share prices before collapsing the markets to facilitate their buying the shares for pennies rather than pounds. This was a repeat of Nathan Mayer Rothschild's ploy of 1812. Having achieved the collapse of the British economy to profit the Rothschilds, Norman Lamont left the British government the following year and returned to N. M. Rothschild and Sons as a director.

As a follow-'on to his first book *They to Dare Speak Out: People and Institutions Confront Israel's Lobby,* former Congressman Paul Findley's *Deliberate Deceptions: Facing the Facts About The U.S.- Israeli Relationship was* published in 1993 as an antidote to the mainstream media's disinformation pandemic that was, and still is, creating an American mindset that regarded Palestinians as terrorists rather than a brutally oppressed and occupied people outraged at the world's silent tolerance of their unjust and inhumane treatment by Israel.

The book's "fact" and "fallacy" format, addressed the events of 1948 and 1967 which were responsible for creating the Palestinian refugee crisis, and cited insider accounts of how Israel's lobbyists and supporters had established an unassailable bicameral congress and media blackout that prevented informed debate on U.S. Middle East policy. *Deliberate Deceptions* devoted a separate chapter to each basic fallacy and analysed the separate components of the historical misrepresentations with assiduous documentation and footnoted statements of fact.

In the first chapter, British Zionist author Israel Zangwill's 1987 description of Palestine as "the land without people for the people without a land," was refuted with the point being made that even at the time of the 1917 Balfour Declaration – and following the initial two major waves of Zionist immigration, there were only 60,000 Jews living in Palestine among 600,000 Palestinian Arabs.

The second fallacy dealt with concerned a 1975 statement by then-Israeli Prime Minister Golda Meir who claimed that when Israel was established in 1948, "we were, of course, totally unprepared for war." Meir's assertion was clearly another blatant Zionist lie because just two weeks after the May 15, 1948 proclamation of the state of Israel, Israeli forces had seized 400 square miles of the territory allotted to the Palestinians by the U.N. partition plan. Furthermore, according to a June 1 Israeli government communique, "the territory of the State of Israel is entirely free of invaders."

The third fallacy related to Israel's first prime minister, David Ben-Gurion's 1949 statement that "there are no refugees–there are fighters who sought to destroy us, root and branch," which was refuted by United Nations documentation that same year. A UN report in late 1949 had stated that well over half of the Palestinians, 726,000 of the total population of 1.2 million, had been uprooted from their homes and turned into refugees, with a further 25,000 "borderline" cases not included in the count.

Arab sources had maintained the true figure to be closer to one million with even former Israeli Foreign Ministry Director General Rafael Eytan reporting that "the real number was close to 800,000." Such figures belied Ben-Gurion's claim because the almost two-thirds of Palestine's total population who were driven out of their homes and not allowed to return were certainly not "fighters." Similar fallacies were refuted regarding the additional 323,000 Palestinians driven from their homes in 1967, of whom 113,000 were second-time refugees, having lost their original homes inside Israel's "Green Line" in 1948 before being driven out again in 1967 after Israeli forces occupied the remaining areas of Palestine.

The frequently heard mendacious propaganda that all of Israel's wars – including the 1956 Suez war – were forced upon it, is also refuted with a quote from President Dwight Eisenhower who on learning of Israel's sneak attack on Egypt with support from France and Britain, instructed Secretary of State John Foster Dulles thus: "Foster, you tell 'em … we're going to apply sanctions, we're going to the United Nations, we're going to do everything that there is so we can stop this thing."

In his biography of Eisenhower, Stephen E. Ambrose wrote that "Eisenhower's insistence on the primacy of the UN, of treaty obligations, and of the rights of all nations gave the United States a standing in world opinion it had never before achieved … The introduction of the American [cease-fire] resolution to the UN was, indeed, one of the great moments in UN history."

Deliberate Deceptions also highlighted the stark contrast between Eisenhower's stand and that of President Lyndon Johnson who after the 1967 war – and despite Israel's deliberate attack on the USS Liberty – did not apply any U.S. pressure to force Israel to "surrender its gains." Former Israeli Ambassador Abba Eban's statement to the UN that "Arab governments … methodically prepared and mounted an aggressive assault designed to bring about Israel's immediate and total destruction," is also disproved as was the then U.S. Ambassador to Israel Walworth Barbour's statement that the Israeli government "has no, repeat no, intention of taking advantage of the situation to enlarge its territory."

Just a few more Israeli lies and as Paul Findley pointed out, "the captured territory increased Israel's control of land from the original 5,900 square miles awarded it in the 1947 UN Partition Plan to 20,870 square miles. Despite Israel's initial promise in 1967 that it sought no territory, it immediately moved to expel Palestinians and establish Jewish settlements in the occupied territories, including Arab East Jerusalem." And was still doing so with impunity to this very day.

Conrad also learnt that in 1993, the San Francisco District Attorney released 700 pages of documents implicating the Anti-Defamation League (ADL) – an organisation claiming to be defending civil rights – in a vast spying operation directed against American citizens opposed to the apartheid policies of the Israeli and South African governments to whom it passed on the information. Among the ADL's targets were the San Francisco Labor Council, ILWU Local 10, Oakland Educational Association, NAACP, Irish Northern Aid, International Indian Treaty Council, the Asian Law Caucus, the San Francisco Police, and thousands of Arab-Americans. Following the inevitable pressure from Jewish organisations and the spending of millions of ADL dollars for the subversion of the judicial system including costly appeals, the criminal case was dropped, but the ADL was subsequently obliged in a a civil lawsuit to make an undisclosed cash settlement.

This raised the question for Conrad as to what the outcome of the criminal case would have been had such activities been conducted by Arab-American or Muslim organisations. On delving deeper into the extent of Jewish-American support for Israel, he soon realised that apart from influential Pro-Israel millionaire and billionaire Jewish Individuals who "bought" U.S. politicians, no other ethnic group in the U.S. could match – either in number or financial support – the hundreds of pro-Israel Jewish organisations that operated at every level in the United States with most Americans being none the wiser.

Such organisations included the Aaron and Marie Blackman Foundation which with net assets of over $7 million provided grants to both Israeli organisations and organisations in relationships with Israel; the American Friends of Ateret

Cohanim which is a Jerusalem based non-profit organisation – with an office in New York – involved in the urban renewal of Jerusalem through Jewish gentrification including the introduction of a Jewish presence in the Christian and Muslim quarters of the Old City which it claims as belonging to every single Jew despite the fact that Israel's occupation of East Jerusalem is still not recognised under international law; the Amcha Initiative aims to protect Jewish students from anti-Semitism which it broadly defines as being virtually any criticism of Israel and its human rights violations, and regards organisations such as BDS as being examples of anti-Semitism; the American Israel Education Foundation (AIEF) with an annual budget of $26 million which takes Congressional Representatives on all-expense-paid trips to Israel; the American Jewish Committee (AJC) which was established in 1906 and is San Francisco based – with assets of $135 million and an annual income of about $50 million – advocates the right of Israel as an exclusionary Jewish State; and the American Israel Public Affairs Committee (AIPAC) with a £100 million endowment and annual revenues of over $60 million with which to completely control the U.S. Congress ...

The America's Voices in Israel (AVI) which strives to "strengthen American understanding of, and support for Israel by inviting U.S.-based radio talk show hosts to visit Israel and broadcast their programs live from Jerusalem"; the AMIT which has numerous chapters throughout the U.S. – with annual expenses of over $8 million and net assets of some $12,000,000 – is "the world's leading supporter of religious Zionist education and social services for Israel's children and youth, nurturing and educating Israeli children to become productive, contributing members of society"; the Anti-Defamation League (ADL) masquerades as a civil rights institution while in reality promoting Israeli interests and defaming anyone critical of Israel by labelling them as "anti-Semitic"; The Avi

Chai Foundation with total assets of $615,000,000 million is primarily involved in "Promoting Jewish Peoplehood and Israel"; the Birthright Israel organisation has total revenues of over $100 million to provide free ten-day holidays to Israel for young Jewish adults aged between 18 and 26 for the purpose of strengthening Jewish identities and Jewish community solidarity with, and support for Israel; the Chabad-Lubavitch – with an estimated net worth of $1 billion – is an 18th. century Hasidic movement that has grown to be the largest Jewish organisation in the world. Despite its being a religious group, its support of Israel is zealotic to the extent that some Chabad rabbis have encouraged Jewish people to kill "Arab men, women, and children." Chabad has also openly taught that "the soul of the Jew is different than the soul of the non-Jew"; and the Christians United for Israel (CUFI) which is a right-wing Evangelical Christian organisation with more than one million members nationwide advocating American support for Israel that is based mainly on Biblical prophecy …

The Conference of Presidents of Major American Jewish Organisations (CoP) consisting of some 51 Zionist organisations which advocate on behalf of Israel with annual revenues of around £3 million; the David Project is a non-profit educational program which has an annual income of $3 million for the dissemination in schools of pro-Israel propaganda that justifies Israeli actions through the Hebrew term *hasbara* which means "explaining"; the Emergency Committee for Israel (ECI) which consists of leading American conservatives who attack anyone taking an "anti-Israel" position; the Foundation for Defence of Democracies has an annual income of £2.5 million to increase support for "Jewish domestic and foreign policy priorities" and to secure a democratic Jewish state in Israel"; the Foundation for Jewish Camp has a grant of more than $8 million jointly funded by The Jim Joseph Foundation and the AVI CHAI Foundation to have its camps focus "on Zionism and the role of Israel in Jewish life"; the Friends of the Israeli Defence Forces (FIDF) which with annual revenues of some $60 million and net assets of $80 million, brings hundreds of Israeli soldiers to the U.S. every year to lecture at synagogues, universities, and schools so as to increase American support for Israeli policies; and the Friends of Aish Hatorah – "fire of the Torah" – is an Orthodox Jewish organisation involved with pro-Israel programs such as the Theodore Herzl Mission, which brings heads of state to Israel for one week each year; and the Hasbara Fellowship which teaches people from around the world to effectively engage in pro-Israel propaganda ...

The Hadassah (Women's Zionist Organisation of America) which has annual revenues of almost $100 million and net assets of $400 million to inspire "a passion for and commitment to its partnership with the land and people of Israel"; the Hillel, is a Jewish international student organisation that "fosters an enduring commitment to Jewish life, learning and Israel" and annually collects gifts, grants, and contributions in excess of $26 million for its "birthright" trips which promote the perception of Israel as the "homeland" for European and American Jews; the International Fellowship of Christians and Jews (also known as Stand for Israel) has annual revenues of over $100 million and purports "to promote understanding between Jews and Christians and builds broad support for Israel"; the Ir David foundation (Amutat ELAD) – with unknown but very substantial revenues – is ostensibly dedicated to the preservation and development of the Biblical "City of David" and its environs while duplicitously and ruthlessly pursuing its policy of "Judaisation of east Jerusalem" through often violent forced evictions and dubious purchases of Palestinian properties; the Israel-America Chamber of Commerce (AmCham Israel) is involved with the two-way promotion of trade and investment between Israel and the U.S.; the Israeli American Council (IAC) – funded mainly by casino magnate Sheldon Adelson –

aims to establish the Israeli expatriate community residing in the U.S. "as a 'strategic asset' for Israel in the U.S." with a view to its being "a potent political force in the future"; and the Israel Project with an $11 million annual budget helps advocates of Israel with its renowned *Global language Dictionary* which deliberately provides simplistic, diversionary, and deceitfully crafted language and talking points that favour Israel …

The Jewish Agency for Israel (known as The Jewish Agency) links "Jews around the world with Israel as the focal point" and in addition to extensive programs in Israel, it operates in some 80 countries on five continents through a network of over 450 emissaries, including hundreds of formal and informal educators. The world Jewish community participates in the Jewish Agency's decision-making process through the Assembly, its supreme governing body, and its Board of Governors, which is responsible for policy making and oversight; the Jewish Council for Public Affairs (JCPA) which has an annual funding of some $3.5 million is an umbrella for many smaller organisations who work for "the safety and security of the State of Israel"; the Jewish Day Schools which is tax exempt and consequently subsidised by U.S. taxpayers promises to "instil in our students an attachment to the state of Israel" that includes school trips to that country; the Jewish National Fund (JNF) which is an international organisation with assets of $1.2 billion that was originally founded by Theodore Herzl in 1901 at Basel in Switzerland for the purpose of purchasing land in Palestine for a future Jewish state; the Jim Joseph Foundation – with assets of some $840,000,000 – sponsors "Israel Education," with activities that include "twinning day schools with schools in Israel, integrating Israel education with learning taking place in general studies courses, and showcasing Israel's arts and culture so students and teachers are in direct contact with what is happening in Israel today"; the Leona M. and Harry B Helmsley Charitable Trust which is valued at between $4 to $8 billion and supports programmes that are primarily focussed on "the security and development of Israel"; and the Middle East Media Research Institute (MEMRI), which is a shadowy tax exempt Mossad brainchild annually receiving donations and grants totalling some $5 million to finance its propaganda which includes circulating blatantly biased translations with a view to portraying Arabs in a negative light …

The National Council of Young Israel is a group of 146 "fiercely Zionist" Orthodox Jewish congregations that offer material support to the Israeli Defence Force for its attacks on Palestinians. Its being an umbrella for over 100 individual non-profit organisations makes it difficult to ascertain the source and exact amount of its income; the National Jewish Democratic Council (NJDC) operates with an annual income of over $1.2 million; Pro-Israel Political Action Committees (PACs) – only four of which have names indicating their true agendas, such as "Allies for Israel" or "World Alliance for Israel" with the rest having innocuous labels like "National Action Committee" or "Heartland PAC" – and which constitute AIPAC's political campaign finance network; the Republican Jewish Coalition (RJC) has a Victory Fund of over $2 million and annual revenues of more than $10 million for control of a Super Pac war chest to effect the "embrace of a pro-Israel foreign policy"; the Simon Wiesenthal Centre with an annual budget of $25 million and net assets of £67 million confronts anti-Semitism, defends Jewish safety worldwide, and ensures that future generations never forget the Holocaust …

The Stand with Us which with an annual U.S. budget of $4 million and chapters in Israel, Europe, Australia, and South Africa, erects numerous pro-Israel, anti-Palestinian billboards and trains student leaders to advocate for Israel on campuses around the country; the Washington Institute for Near East Policy (WINEP) is a highly influential Israel-biased think tank with annual revenues of around $10 million and net assets of some $25 million; the World Jewish Congress (WJC) – which has an annual U.S. revenue of $6 million with unknown global finances – is an international organisation representing Jews in 100 countries with its main focus being on support for Israel; and the Zionist Organisation of America (ZOA) – which has over $8 million in assets – works to surreptitiously spread the Zionist message throughout all levels of American society while advancing the interests of Israel and Jewish people within the American legal system.

Conrad could only conclude that if you tore off the mask of "we the people" American democracy, you would find actual governance of the American people is being conducted by "them the pro-Israel" advocates whose only priority is to serve the interests of a Zionist state for Jews irrespective of the cost to the American people, the indigenous Palestinians, or for that matter, the rest of non-Jewish humanity.

In the meantime some of those U.S.-based tax-exempt organisations – who annually raise an estimated $1 billion for illegal Jewish settlements on Palestinian lands – are facing a lawsuit by pro-Palestinian plaintiffs seeking an investigation into violation of U.S. laws that prohibit mail fraud, money laundering, war crimes, and the financing of terrorism. Past requests for Internal Revenue Service investigations have, however failed to elicit any determined action, and despite the fact such funds finance wholesale violence, ethnic cleansing, theft of private property, murder, and the maiming of innocent civilians, the U.S. Treasury Department is likely to ask for a dismissal of the lawsuit.

While the U.S. led the way with hundreds of pro-Israel organisations, there were thousands more all over the world – and particularly in Europe – who are ready, willing and able to fanatically protect Israel's public image and reputation. Such organisations mostly get – to varying degrees – instructions from officials in Israel with many of them fully cooperating with the Israeli government, its parastatal organisations, and faux-NGOs including the the Mossad proxy lawfare centre Shurat HaDin. The main objective of such organisations was the spreading of propaganda to influence the public opinion in their respective countries of residence into either toeing the line as prescribed by Israel, or confusing the narrative so as to stifle debate whenever the subject of Israel's criminality was raised.

This endeavour was supported by a resolute and well organised government apparatus disgorging disinformation to confuse public opinion by obfuscating the issues relating to Israeli policies. The Prime Minister's office and the Israeli Foreign Ministry had at their disposal a corps of paid "volunteers" who monitored websites worldwide so as to counter any negative information about Israel. Such monitoring ensured that any negative story appearing in either the social or mainstream media about Israel would immediately be met with a torrent of pro-Israel comments making the same coordinated points in a barely literate manner. In some cases they are actually able to suppress negative comments by flooding the site with "Dislike" responses which results in such comments being automatically blocked or removed.

The extent of this highly organised and enormously financed global network prompted Conrad to recall what he had once read about *The Protocols of the Elders of Zion* document which was also known as *The Protocols of the Meetings of the Learned Elders of Zion.* Published in Russia in 1903 and translated into many languages for global dissemination in the early part of that century, the *Protocols* were supposedly the minutes of a late 19th-century meeting of Jewish leaders who discussed the achievement of global Jewish domination by subverting the morals of Gentiles, and by controlling the the mainstream media and global economies.

The American industrialist Henry Ford – founder of the Ford motor company – had payed for the printing of 500,000 copies for distribution throughout the U.S. in the 1920s, and Adolf Hitler had proved to be an obvious proponent of the *Protocols* which became a subject for study in German classrooms after the Nazis came to power in 1933. Since then, Cesare G. De Michelis, a scholar and professor of Russian literature at the University of Tor Vergata – amongst others – had argued that the *Protocols* were concocted in the months following the Russian Zionist congress of September 1902, and were originally a parody of Jewish idealism meant for internal circulation among anti-Semites before being edited and published as being authentic.

The second publication of the *Protocols* in 1922 was titled as the *World Conquest Through World Government* and was graphic – with a profound understanding of the human condition and mind – in its contempt for those destined to be its victims while detailing the methodology that would be used against, and with the complicity of, the world's population, in such a manner as to go unrecognised by the vast, pathetic majority. The *Protocols* included as some of its basic doctrines the use of economic wars; the methods of conquest; the replacement of religion by materialism; a description of despotism and modern progress; the techniques for takeover; the exploitation of worldwide wars; the provisional government; the preparations for attaining power; the totalitarian state; and the control of the media as per following quote:

> *"Not a single announcement will reach the public without our control. Even now this is already being attained by us inasmuch as all news items are received by a few agencies, in whose offices they are focused from all parts of the world. These agencies will then be already entirely ours and will give publicity only to what we dictate to them."*

The *Protocols'* proposed use of terror to keep Western democracies in check and tolerant of Zionist policies had since come to pass with a gradual erosion of virtually all fundamental rights and liberties – with little or no awareness amongst the the masses – with the "War on Terror" fostering an arbitrary system of justice wherein people can be treated as second-class citizens, have their assets seized, have their rights including the right to travel restricted, and be stigmatised, imprisoned, or even killed by government decrees justified by "state of emergency" powers.

"In a word, to sum up our system of keeping the governments of the goyim in Europe in check, we shall show our strength to one of them by terrorist attempts and to all, if we allow the possibility of a general rising against us, we shall respond with the guns of America or China or Japan."

Conrad felt that even if the *Protocol's* were an anti-Semitic concoction, then its authors must have had amazing prophetic powers because world events had since unfolded in accordance with the concepts of a New World Order and One World Government being facilitated by the gradual movement of nation states into larger power blocks such as the European Union (EU), the North American Free Trade Agreement (NAFTA), and a United Nations (UN) obligingly acting as a global police force under the pretext of being the benefactor and protector of all humanity. The Jews had in the meantime "returned" to Palestine where the State of Israel was established as the official "homeland" for all Jews with a right to "return" despite the fact that virtually all of them had no ethnic or other connection whatsoever with Palestine.

Conrad was in no doubt that Israel – whose perceived democratic and independent status he regarded as being morally bogus – could not have survived as a fledgling state had it not been backed by the influence and power of the worldwide network of Judaeo-Zionist organisations, and the billions of dollars that were still being annually poured into the country. He could not help sympathising with the Palestinian people whom he admired for their undying courage because despite all the odds against their survival – including betrayal by most of their own leaders and the rest of the world – they had clung tenaciously to the hope of one day achieving justice and freedom.

Even the very limited support they were getting from pro-Palestinian activist groups was under threat from a highly coordinated and well financed worldwide campaign by Israel and its supporters to criminalise any activism against, or criticism of Israel. He also felt that if more people were to speak up and actively oppose having their justified concerns and criticisms gagged by pro-Israel Jewish lobby groups; that if more people were to challenge and if necessary even defy Jewish lobby inspired legislation criminalising criticism of Israel; that if more people were to reject politically correct hypocrisy and insist that national affairs be conducted to serve justice rather than the lobbied agendas of well financed special interest groups; that if more people would honestly recognise that by idly standing by and allowing their political leaders to be blackmailed, bribed, and bullied into supporting the warmongering Apartheid state of Israel, they were forfeiting not only their own legal and human rights to live in peaceful coexistence with others, but also the legal and human rights of future generations; then, and only then, would they be able to take the first step towards the creation of a better world where racists and religious fanatics will not silence their voices, thwart their hopes, or control their destinies.

"We have to condemn publicly the very idea that some people have the right to repress others. In keeping silent about evil, in burying it so deep within us that no sign of it appears on the surface, we are implanting it, and it will rise up a thousand fold in the future. When we neither

punish nor reproach evildoers … we are ripping the foundations of justice from beneath new generations."

Aleksandr Solzhenitsyn (1918 – 2008), Russian novelist, historian, and an outspoken critic of the Soviet Union and Communism.

13

Sunday 20, December

Mamilla, West Jerusalem

After having breakfast without their usual rashers of smoked back bacon – an essential ingredient for a good English breakfast – Conrad and Freya decided that as they were not meeting with Adam Peltz and Sami Hadawi until one o'clock, they would use the time to read up on Bethlehem which they planned visiting on Christmas Eve for three-day stay. Before doing so, however, Conrad explained to Freya that on his previous visit to Jerusalem he and Sami had discussed the possibility of Sami going with them to film in Bethlehem, but after discussing the difficulties involved, the idea was dropped because strict control of Palestinian movement had been one of the features of Israel's illegal occupation of Palestinian territories since 1967. The draconian system of movement controls had become increasingly institutionalised and restrictive with a permit system being established in the early 1990s that required all Palestinians to obtain military issued permits to move between the West Bank, Gaza, and East Jerusalem, or to travel abroad. Such restrictions had since been complemented by a permanent network of roadblocks, gates, and checkpoints; by the notorious Wall; by other obstacles to movement in the West Bank and East Jerusalem; and by the blockade of those living in Gaza.

The combination of those factors had caused forced displacement; restricted Palestinian access to basic resources including land and water with over 90 percent of the water extracted from the Gaza aquifer being unsafe for human consumption because the needed filtration equipment could not be imported due to the blockade; the denial of basic services such as health care and education; and the perpetuation of an Apartheid system with legal and structural inequalities between Palestinians and Israelis.

"I thought the EU was providing aid." Freya said.

"What's the good of aid if the blockade still prevents the import of goods," Conrad said, and by way of explanation added that over the past five years, direct support to the Palestinian budget from the EU and others has fallen from around $1.3 billion a year to less than $700 million with the decline being attributed largely to frustration over money not being spent where it was intended, not being fully accounted for, or simply being stolen by Israel.

Theft of Palestinian aid money by Israel had been confirmed in a report by an Israeli economist who spent years investigating the sleight of hand economics of the occupation. The report revealed that international aid had only helped Israel to avoid responsibility for paying the cost of its decades-long occupation with at least 78 percent of that humanitarian aid for Palestinians ending up in Israeli coffers with huge sums being involved because Palestinians were among the most aid-dependent people in the world.

Furthermore, in 2013 the World Bank had very conservatively estimated that the Palestinians were losing at least $3.4 billion a year in resources plundered by Israel whose penchant for wholesale theft was apparently also facilitated by its insistence that all aid to Palestinians must go through Israel. Therefore in order to help the Palestinians, donors had no alternative but to go through Israel, thereby enabling it to subvert and divert aid intended for the victims of their brutal occupation. Aid diversion was further facilitated by Israel's total control of all movement of people and goods while also imposing unreasonable charges for transportation, for storage, and for levy "security" fees.

"The situation was made worse," Conrad explained, by the fact that as the Palestinians were a blockaded and captive market, they virtually had no access to goods or services that were not of Israeli origin. One dairy company alone with a monopoly in the West Bank had a turnover of $60 million annually."

"If you really think about it," Freya said with some disgust, "it's not the Palestinians who are the most aid-dependent people in the world, it's the Israelis."

"Talking of dependence, a recent announcement that Israel was to get increased American aid, was followed by news that more than half a million Americans will be losing their food stamp benefit."

"I just don't know how they get away with it." Freya said, and being visibly upset moved on to the subject of Bethlehem which was apparently first mentioned in the Amarna letters – an archive written on clay tablets consisting mostly of diplomatic correspondence between the Egyptian administration and its representatives in Canaan and Amurru during the New Kingdom between 1570 and 1069 BCE – which was Egypt's most prosperous period and marked the height of its power. Bethlehem also had significant mentions in the Old Testament history of the Israelites where it was referred to as Ephrat allegedly both before they entered Egypt and after the Exodus. It was supposedly in Bethlehem that Rachel, the beloved matriarch of the Jewish people and the favourite wife of Jacob, died during childbirth with her Tomb now being a place of pilgrimage for both Jews and Muslims. Other Biblical mentions of Bethlehem included Naomi and Ruth, the anointment of King David by Samuel, and the well from which David's warriors brought him water. The Bible referred to it as "Bethlehem of Judah" (belonging to the tribe of Judah), so as to distinguish it from the other Bethlehem, which lay in the north in Zebulon's territory.

According to yet another unsubstantiated claim in the Hebrew Bible – contradicted by Bethlehem's existence during the period of Egypt's New Kingdom – Bethlehem was built by the Israelite king, Rehoboam, whose father was Solomon and grandfather was David. It was also claimed that David was from Bethlehem where he was crowned King of Israel; that it was the birth place of Jesus; that it was destroyed by the Emperor Hadrian during the last of three major Jewish-Roman wars (132–135 CE); and that its rebuilding had been championed by the Empress Helena, the mother of Constantine the Great who in 327 CE commissioned the building of the Church of the Nativity – badly damaged and sacked by the Samaritans during a revolt in 529, but subsequently rebuilt a century later by Emperor Justinian I – which was still believed to be the location over the cave where Jesus of Nazareth was born.

Constantine's conversion to Christianity was probably a case of deathbed insurance rather than one of faith and came about when Christian bishops were successful in convincing him that their God would absolve him of his sins and install him in heaven. So with death approaching, Constantine decided that "the salvation which I have earnestly desired of God these many years I do now expect. It is time therefore that we should be sealed and signed in the badge of immortality." He was then duly baptised and passed away with the deluded expectation of a heavenly resurrection. Despite that conversion, his had been a "sun emperorship" under which Christianity enjoyed a degree of freedom and tolerance, but at no time during his reign (306 – 337 CE) did Christianity come close to replacing the state religion of Sol Invictus, or "Unconquered Sun," the official sun god of the later Roman Empire whose symbol was prominent on many public features including banners and coins.

Though Constantine was subsequently portrayed as the effective architect of the Christian Church, his zeal for its teachings never quite matched that of his mother who was an obsessive enthusiast. It was she who insisted that extensive searches be carried out until all holy sites were were identified and appropriately marked with some imposing shrine. Imperial subordinates no doubt eager to please Her Royal Highness had wasted no time in not only identifying the site where Jesus was crucified, known as "Calvary," but also in locating Christ's place of burial and resurrection where the Church of the Holy Sepulchre now stands in the Christian Quarter of the Old City of Jerusalem. Most impressive of all, if it is to be believed, was the discovery of the precise spot where Mary Magdalene had been standing when she received the glad tidings of Christ's resurrection, and it was Helena herself who apparently found the True Cross with its unmistakable "King of the Jews" plaque.

The city was also of importance to the Crusaders who conquered it in the year 1100, but years of fighting between the Crusaders and the Muslims had destroyed it, before it was subsequently rebuilt. It was destroyed again by the Turks in 1244, but the church somehow escaped damage, and the city was once again rebuilt. When the Crusaders were eventually driven from Palestine in 1291, the Muslim rulers exploited the holy places for political and financial gain. In 1332 Pope John XXII wrote to Edward III of England, to David II of Scotland and to the Archbishop of Canterbury, asking them to help the bishop of Bethlehem to regain his position and return to Bethlehem so that repairs could be carried out.

Centuries of subsequent historical damage, restorations, and notable events were added to in April 2002 during the Second Intifada which was the consequence of a provocative visit to Temple Mount by then Israeli right-wing opposition leader Ariel Sharon. About 50 armed Palestinians being sought by the Israel Defence Forces, had barricaded themselves in the church while holding hostage some 200 monks and other Palestinians who happened to be present for some reason or other. Because of the building's historic significance, the IDF – rather than resorting to its usual vindictive, disproportionate and destructive response – instead laid siege to the building while preventing the delivery of food. During the ensuing 39-day stand-off, some of the gunmen were shot by IDF snipers before lengthy negotiations culminated with the remaining gunmen being evacuated to Gaza, Spain, and Italy.

It was during this second uprising by the oppressed Palestinians, that the Israeli government decided to build a separation barrier around the occupied Palestinian Territories. The barrier consisted mostly of a multi-layered wire fence system and an eight-metre high concrete Apartheid Wall that deliberately deviated from the Green Line and swallowed up more Palestinian land. Though the city had come under Israeli rule following the Six-Day War, it reverted to Palestinian control in December 1995 with Israelis still having access to Rachel's tomb. Nonetheless, occasional outbreaks of violence had continued to occur between Palestinian demonstrators from Bethlehem and Israeli troops stationed outside the city's limits.

Baka, West Jerusalem

Adam Peltz lived in Baka, an idyllic neighbourhood in southern Jerusalem which after the 1948 Arab-Israeli war was left on the Israeli (western) side of the dividing line between West Jerusalem and East Jerusalem. The population of Baka (officially known as Geulim) had changed as did many other neighbourhoods on both sides of the dividing line. Consequently many of old Arab style houses had been renovated and expanded as middle class Jewish professionals began to move in. The name "Baka" was taken directly from the Arabic word for "valley" which described the area's topography. During the last decade, numerous Jewish immigrants from Europe and North America had moved in with the purchase of large houses in the area so that it was now not uncommon to hear English and French regularly spoken in public.

Peltz left home for his arranged one o'clock meeting with Conrad and Freya just before 12.30 p.m. which would give him plenty of time to get to their hotel on King Solomon Street with its views of the Old City walls, the Tower of David, and the Jaffa Gate. Peltz had become an Israeli human rights activist following his national service with Israeli Defence Force towards the end of which he had taken part in the 2008-9 Operation Cast Lead in Gaza. The experience had forced him to subsequently question not only his own humanity, but also that of a country established as a homeland apparently promised to the Jewish people by the God who chose them. Apart from his archaeology related activism, Peltz was also associated with "Breaking the Silence," the Israeli NGO in West Jerusalem established by Israeli IDF soldiers and veterans to provide a platform from which they could confidentially testify about their experiences in the Israeli-occupied territories. Israel was now trying to force the group to reveal the identities of the soldiers who testified to it about alleged military misconduct during the 2014 Gaza war, a move which the group claimed would effectively put it out of business.

Peltz had witnessed the unnecessary and wanton destruction of homes, schools, hospitals, and public utilities; the uprooting and burning of crops, the slaughter of unarmed innocents with women and children killed in cold blood; the use of illegal weapons, white phosphorous munitions, and shrapnel spreading fragmentation bombs; the free-fire orders to shoot and kill anything or anyone that moved, and the cowardly use of civilians as human shields including young children who would have rifles place on their shoulders and made to advance as shields in front of IDF soldiers. Peltz had felt ashamed and sickened by the operation's reign of terror which was a direct consequence of the IDF's rules of engagement including the sanction of a shoot to kill policy with no questions asked.

While the U.S. Jewish establishment, Israel, and some other Zionist lackey countries accused non-Jewish critics of Israel of being "anti-Semitic" in an effort to stifle discussion and debate, Jewish human rights activists and critics like Peltz were accused of being "self-hating Jews." One of the many Jews branded as such, was Sir Gerald Kaufman – a Labor member of the British Parliament since 1970 – who in a January 17 speech during Israel's Operation Cast Lead in Gaza, explicitly identified Israel with Nazi Germany: "My grandmother was ill in bed when the Nazis came to her hometown of Staszów [in Poland]. A German soldier shot her dead in her bed. Madam Deputy Speaker, my grandmother did not die to provide cover for Israeli soldiers murdering Palestinian grandmothers in Gaza. The present Israeli government ruthlessly and cynically exploits the continuing guilt among Gentiles over the slaughter of Jews in the Holocaust as justification for their murder of Palestinians. The implication is that Jewish lives are precious, but the lives of Palestinians do not count. On Sky News a few days ago, the spokeswoman for the Israeli Army Major Livovich was asked about the Israeli killing of, at that time, eight hundred Palestinians. The total is now a thousand. She replied instantly, 'Five hundred of them were militants.' That was the reply of a Nazi. I suppose the Jews fighting for their lives in the Warsaw Ghetto could have been dismissed as militants."

Another fearless parliamentarian, Irish Senator David Norris, in an videotaped speech to the Seanad Éireann – available on YouTube – had the following to say on the genocide In Palestine:

> "People ask: "What for? What can Seanad Éireann do?" The answer in the international context is "Nothing," because nobody will pay that much attention to what Ireland does. I remember being in Palestine some years ago in an area that was heavily controlled by the Israelis, and I said to my Palestinian hosts, "You know there is nothing I can do, I

will have no effect," and they said, "But at least you will be a witness, you will be a record to our suffering, and we will not go unnoticed," It is for that reason I called for the recall of the Seanad.

I am very sad. I am not anti-Israeli; I am not anti-Semitic. I supported the State of Israel. However, in the 40 years that I have known the State of Israel and sometimes had a home there, I have seen it completely change. It changed from a left wing, socially directed country to an extreme right-wing regime that is behaving in the most criminal fashion, defying the world and unscrupulously using the Holocaust to justify what they are doing. It is time that rag was torn away from them.

Israel is afraid of Palestinian unity. That is what all of this is about. It has nothing to do with the appalling murder of those three Israeli kids. The Israeli police knew that Hamas had nothing to do with it before this war started. Israel created Hamas in order to split Fatah, so it is responsible for Hamas. I had this confirmed at the highest level in the foreign ministry in Jerusalem some years ago. It is astonishing to me that those in the West prate about democracy, yet every time an Islamic government crops up around the Mediterranean, they refuse to deal with it, they subvert it and they destroy it. Where is the democracy in that? We may not like it. They may be antagonistic. My Jewish friends and Israeli friends sometimes say to me, "How would you fare, as a gay man, in any of these?" I know exactly how I would fare, but it does not mean it is correct to deny people the right to choose their own government. What self-respecting or sane people would allow their enemies to choose their government for them? Can anyone imagine it happening in this country? I certainly cannot.

America has a shameful role to play in this. Israel could not get away with these disgraceful acts of international piracy and brigandage if it was not for the protecting shadow of the United States of America. I condemn President Obama for his utter inaction. I have to say I was a bit taken aback when I saw Ukraine had been added to the statements as it is irrelevant. It is a bit of "whataboutery." What about Syria? What about the Congo? What about Iraq? What about everything?

However, the one thing it does is to show the extraordinary discrepancy here. At the instructions of the Americans we are prepared to boycott, go after the Russian banks and do this, that and the other. What do we do about Israel? We do not even mark a protest note with our vote at the United Nations Human Rights Commission.

That is shameful – absolutely shameful. I would have interjected that it had been better to be one country in the right than be with all the rest of them in the wrong.

There are no words to describe what happened yesterday in Jebalyia where there were six attacks on schools. They are deliberate, I have no doubt, because 3,300 people were sheltered there. They had been directed there by Israel. The co-ordinates were given 17 times. How could anybody claim that they did not know what they were doing? Israel's policy is shoot first and weep afterwards saying, "Oh, did we hit children? What a terrible tragedy." Nobody believes Israel anymore. It is doing this to exert pressure on Hamas. It will not resolve this problem until, as we did in this country, it involves both of the participants.

There is no point in having any kind of an alleged truce when it only has one side. It was laughable the rubbish produced by the Israelis, Americans and the Egyptians. They did not consult Hamas, which is madness. Tony Blair was involved. My God, that man is shameless.

He should keep his face out of the Middle East after what he and George W. Bush have done to the region.

On the other side, three moth-balled schools were used to store weapons. That was discovered by the UN and reported by it, not by the Israelis.

Entire families have been obliterated and in one case, 20 members of the same family were slaughtered. Also, a disproportionate amount of women and children have been killed in this situation, which is a violation of all the spiritual beauty that Judaism stands for – the respect for life and the fact that if one saves one life then one has saved the universe. All of that is blown out of the window and done so, as I saw, by the arrival of 1,200,000 extreme right-wing former citizens of the Soviet Union.

It is time people told the truth about what is being said in Israel. For example, the interior Minister, Eli Yishai, stated in 2012 that Israel would send Gaza back to the Middle Ages. Defence deputy Minister Matan Vilnai stated that it would visit the Holocaust on the Palestinians. That is Nazi talk. I am not saying that he is a Nazi but what he is saying makes him sound like a Nazi.

What should we do? First, we must remove the embargo. Then there is the Euro-Med agreement, to which human rights protocols attach. Time after time on the foreign affairs committee, I have asked for the situation to be monitored. People will not even monitor the human rights agreements. What human rights are there when thousands of women and children are being killed and injured?

Israeli goods, particularly those from the settlements, should be boycotted and there should be an expulsion of the Israeli ambassador. I delayed in saying this, but he always has his fingers in his ears and just repeats slogans from Jerusalem.

I have received a considerable volume of correspondence, 90% of it in support of the Israeli side. I respect all of my correspondents but it is clearly an organised campaign. They all thank Ireland for voting the way we did at the UN. That tells the story. The Israeli spokesmen, all with South African, English or American accents, referring to the land of Palestine, also congratulated us.

The UN should accept full and permanent responsibility for the welfare of the people of Gaza. If that means the deployment of an international force, fine. This country should explore the possibility of using our civilian services, for example, the ESB, to rebuild the only power station in Gaza. Cutting off electricity to people who are being squeezed into an appalling punishment camp, only to then cut back on food imports and claim – this is where I say "Nazi" – that Israel is placing the people of Palestine on a diet shows contempt for human beings.

We should stand against that contempt and in favour of human rights. I am in favour of human rights, whether one is Israeli, gay, a woman or black. I am not changing my position. I am not anti-Israel or anti-Semitic, but I am pro-human rights for every human being."

As a Jerusalem-born Israeli Jew, Peltz was familiar with the city's history which was said to have begun way back in time with recurrent water gushes – *giha* in Hebrew and much later to be named "Gihon" – from between the rocks of a spring in the heart of a mountain with one legend stretching the imagination with visions of a dragon resting in the heart of the mountain and periodically spewing out the water it had swallowed. The discovery of ceramics and flint artefacts dating back from 6000 to 7000 years suggested that from time to time shepherds used to set up camp with their flocks close to the stream at the bottom of the slopes with their down flow of water.

Centuries later, permanent homes began to appear so that by about 3000 BCE the area had developed into a small village whose residents used to bury their dead in the mountainside caves. The area where Jerusalem was later to be built was initially isolated because of the spring's undesirable location on a steep slope surrounded by barren hills; because it was off the beaten track from the routes that served the the Judaean Hills and Samaria; and because it was encircled by barren valleys bordering a desert that could not support much life. The village consequently went through a cycle of human settlement and abandonment with only a few shepherd families remaining.

But sometime after 1800 BCE, the Canaanites – a sophisticated agricultural and urban people whose name was derived from *Canaan* meaning the "Land of Purple" because a purple dye that used to be extracted from a murex shellfish (a medium-sized species of sea snail) found near the shores of Palestine – channelled the spring water to help establish the foundations for an emerging mountain kingdom. The Canaanites – who had already absorbed and assimilated the attributes of numerous other cultures from the ancient Near East over a period of some 500 years before the Israelites entered their domain – were the people believed to have invented the form of writing that became the alphabet, which, passing through the Greeks and Romans, was to eventually influence the alphabets of many Western cultures.

The two Canaanite alphabet branches were sub-divisible into several secondary branches with the first, Early Hebrew having three secondary branches – Moabite, Edomite, and Ammonite – and two offshoots including the script of Jewish coins and the Samaritan script still being used today but only for liturgical purposes. The second sub-division of Phoenician can itself be divided into Phoenician proper and "colonial" Phoenician. It was from the latter that the Punic and neo-Punic scripts developed along with the probable development of the Libyan and Iberian scripts.

The term Early Hebrew was used to distinguish this branch from the subsequent so-called Square Hebrew. Early Hebrew had already begun acquiring its distinctive character by the 11th century BCE and was officially used until the 6th century BCE but hung on for several more centuries while its stylised form was used on Jewish coins from between 135 BCE and 135 CE. The most ancient example of Early Hebrew writing was that of the Gezer Calendar – a small inscribed limestone tablet discovered in 1908 in the ancient Canaanite city of Gezer, 20 miles west of Jerusalem – which having not been excavated in a "secure archaeological context," had been variously dated from 10,000 to 1,000 BCE with scholarly division over whether the language was Phoenician or Hebrew; and whether the script was Phoenician, Proto-Canaanite, or paleo-Hebrew.

The importance of the Phoenician (North Semitic) alphabet in the history of writing should not be underestimated with the earliest clearly readable inscription being the inscription on the Ahiram sarcophagus – discovered in 1923 in tomb V of the royal necropolis of Byblos – which probably dated from the 11th century BCE. It is equally certain, however, that the Phoenician use of the North Semitic alphabet went even further back and because of its adoption and subsequent adaptation by the Greeks, this North Semitic/Phoenician alphabet directly influenced all Western alphabets. Numerous Phoenician inscriptions have been found in Cyprus, Greece, Malta, Marseille, North Africa, Sardinia, Sicily, and Spain.

The Canaanite religion was centred around agriculture with pronounced fertility motifs with gods named the Baalim (Lords) and their consorts the Baalot (Ladies), or Asherah (singular), but usually referred to by the personal plural name Ashtoret. The God of the city of Shechem, which was peacefully assimilated by the Israelites under Joshua, was known as Baal-berith (Lord of the Covenant) or El-berith (God of the Covenant). Shechem became the first cultic centre of the religious tribal confederacy – the equivalent of a Greek amphictyony, or association of neighbouring states formed around a religious centre – of the Israelites during the period of the judges. Excavation of Shechem at the start of 1960s, resulted in the temple of Baal-berith being partially reconstructed with the sacred pillar – phallic symbol or representation of the Ashera, the female fertility symbol – was placed in its original position before the entrance of the temple.

The Canaanite religion held a strong attraction for the less sophisticated and nomadic-oriented Israelite tribes with numerous Israelites succumbing to the allurements of its fertility-laden rituals and practices which offered something new and different from the Yahwistic religion whose rigorous faith and ethic lacked the attraction of sexually orientated worship. As a consequence of closer contact between Canaanite and Israelite cultures, the Israelite religion began absorbing elements of the Canaanite religion with some Israelites even naming their children after the Baalim and one of the judges, Gideon, becoming known as Jerubbaal – "Let Baal Contend."

Meanwhile, villages started emerging throughout the land in the plains and in the hills with mounds being fortified, water systems being dug, shrines being built, and a network of satellite settlements being established around the main cities. Jerusalem became a part of this development with the building of stone fortifications and the control and channeling of spring water through pools and tunnels to secured sites. Villages mushroomed on the outskirts of the walled city to form an integrated system that provided labour and agricultural produce for the city which in turn offered the the surrounding area security and political power.

It is conceivable that the appropriation of nature's spring-water with the power of its vital importance was supplemented by having a hilltop temple where priests – acting as intermediaries between God and man – could please the gods with blood sacrifices and the burning of incense. whether such a temple – as has been discovered in many Canaanite cities – actually existed, cannot be ascertained with certainty because all that has survived is the legendary sanctity of the much abused hilltop.

Despite the evident decline in Jerusalem's relative prosperity and stature during Egyptian rule in Canaan (1500 to 1200 BCE), it had nonetheless established some lasting links that would influence the city's future history: a link between the netherworld (the spring) and the celestial (the hilltop); a link between the settled land and the barren desert; and a link between those that had died and those who were living. Endeavouring to maintain a peaceful balance between such links had since been the hallmark of Jerusalem's historical existence.

Archeological remains suggest that for the first 250 years of the kingdoms of Israel and Judea, Jerusalem was a relatively small bastion for a ruling elite with the existence of a few villages on its outskirts. While folklore has it that the city expanded northwards to Temple Mount, there is no actual physical evidence to support such an assumption. It was only after

750 BCE that ancient Jerusalem went beyond the Canaanite hill limits with expansion toward the north and west. It was during this time that the city witnessed concerted activity with construction and fortification of the hill; with development of administrative and economic regulations using inscriptions, seals, and weights; with control of the water source from the Shiloah Tunnel; and with construction of a necropolis initially on the slope of the Kidron – today's Old Silwan – and subsequently on all sides of the residential city.

By the latter days of the Judaean Kingdom, Jerusalem was a large city with the southeast hill accounting for quarter of its size. Townhouses were built to the north of the hill which overlooked the poorer neighbourhoods below. The city's expansion resulted in social tensions with substantial gaps in earnings and resentful resistance to the ruling elite. In the lower parts of the city many houses were eventually abandoned so that by the time of its destruction, the city was sparsely populated. Consequently when the Babylonians took the city in 586/7 BCE, only the elite northern quarter was worth sacking thereby sparing the physical destruction of the abandoned parts of the city.

Not much was known about Jerusalem under Babylonian and Persian rule (580–330 BCE) while sparse remains and a handful of graves testify to the abandonment of the eastern slope of the hill during Hellenistic and Hasmonean rule which ended around 63 BCE. Under the Romans, Jerusalem once again became prosperous with the southeast hill being rebuilt; with its streets being paved; with water collection and drainage channels being built; and with the erection of imposing structures. Such urban renewal may have been primarily intended to serve the requirements of Herod's temple on the Temple Mount.

As far as Adam Peltz was concerned, today's Jerusalem – falsely referred to by an Apartheid Israeli government as its eternal, undivided capital – had serious ethnically oriented political, religious, and social divisions which made it one of the most dangerous cities in the world. Following Israel's unprovoked 1967 military conquest of East Jerusalem and the West Bank – both under Jordanian administration at the time – the city's municipal boundaries were accordingly expanded so that some 37 per cent of its residents were Palestinians who did not enjoy or share the same social facilities or citizen rights as their colonial masters who now used overhead camera equipped drones to maintain surveillance over them. These pilotless aircraft had also become Israel's weapon of choice in its attacks on the Gaza Strip with 37 percent of the known 2131 Palestinians killed during the last summer's Operation Protective Edge having died in such cowardly drone attacks.

Though Jerusalem's Palestinian residents have the right to apply for Israeli citizenship, they are, however, required to first have a reasonable familiarity with Hebrew and to renounce their Jordanian or other citizenship while swearing allegiance to Israel. More than 95 per cent have so far refused because doing so could be seen as an acquiescence that legitimised Israel's occupation. Since the city's occupation in 1967, some 15,000 Palestinians have had their residency revoked and though permanent resident Palestinians are entitled to vote in municipal elections – but not Israeli national elections – more than 99 per cent boycott such elections.

Despite having to pay taxes as do all Jerusalem residents, the percentage of the municipal budget allocated to about 300,000 Palestinians from a city population of 815,000 is less than 10 per cent with the provision of services being flagrantly unequal. In the East, there are five benefit offices compared to 18 in the West; four health centres for mothers and babies compared to 25 in the West; and 11 mail carriers compared 133 in the West. Most roads in the East were in a state of disrepair and in many cases too narrow for garbage trucks, thereby forcing Palestinians to burn rubbish outside their homes while the shortage of sewage pipes necessitated the use of septic tanks that often overflowed. Palestinian students were crammed into overcrowded classrooms or converted apartments with at least over 2200 additional classrooms being required. More than 75 percent of the city's Palestinians were living below the poverty line.

Since 1967 no new Palestinian neighbourhoods were established in the city; Jewish settlements surrounding existing Palestinian areas had continued to mushroom; restrictive zoning regulations had prevented Palestinians from building legally; Israel had designated 52 per cent of land in East Jerusalem as being unavailable for development; a further 35 per cent was occupied by Jewish settlements; Palestinians got what was left and already built on so that growing families were left with the options of either building illegally or leaving the city; and as a consequence of those deciding to build, some 95,000 of them were living under the ever-present threat of being made homeless – as part of a deliberate displacement policy – by Israel's powerful D9 bulldozers which were supplied by a U.S.-based heavy-equipment company with full knowledge of their intended use for house demolitions.

But that was to be expected from a nation where corporate hypocrisy was part of internal and external political, economic, and military policies that were divorced from anything to do with democracy, human rights, or justice; and where everything was about deceit, exploitation, hegemony, and control of the majority by the few. Former President John F. Kennedy's hope for America's future will never come to pass: "I look forward to a great future for America – a future in which our country will match its military strength with our moral restraint, its wealth with our wisdom, its power with our purpose."

Mamilla Mall, West Jerusalem

When Adam Peltz finally entered the hotel after parking his car in the underground 1,600 vehicle multi-story parking facility, he found Conrad and Freya were already sitting in the hotel lobby. Also sitting nearby was Yakov Katzir, inconspicuous and feigning preoccupation with his newspaper. Nestled in the shoulder holster under Katzir's left armpit was an Israeli made Jericho 9mm combat handgun. As far as he was concerned, the Jericho was better than any Beretta, Glock, SIG Sauer, or Smith and Wesson.

After the initial exchange of greetings, the three of them were discussing the Israeli provoked rioting and violence that was currently occurring on Temple Mount when Conrad received a call on his mobile phone. It was Sam Hadawi letting him know that he was waiting outside because the doorman, an overbearing Jewish American immigrant, was refusing to let him into the hotel. On their way out, a clearly annoyed Conrad made a point of curtly reprimanding the churlish doorman for making his friend wait outside. Sami, however, was full of cheerful exuberance which Freya found endearing and she wondered how these people, with all the discrimination, hardships, and injustice they were forced to endure on a daily basis, could still keep smiling and be so generous of spirit.

They were closely shadowed by Katzir as they walked to the upmarket open-air Mamilla Mall – a 610 metre pedestrian promenade boasting the Old City Walls for a background and lined with 140 cafés, restaurants and stores – which was part of the Arlov Mamilla Quarter, a $400 million mixed-but-not-for-Palestinian-use development. When they entered the café restaurant which Conrad had frequented during his previous visit to Jerusalem, Sami was suspiciously scrutinised by the Jewish waiting staff who were unaccustomed to seeing Palestinians in their establishment. Despite the staff's obvious hostility, they were shown to a table with grudging reluctance and given menus which they examined while making small talk. But once the formality of having their orders taken by an aloof and clearly racist waitress was over, their mood became more serious. In the meantime they had not noticed Yaakov Katzir walk in and sit at a nearby table.

"The situation was bad in September," Sami said to Conrad and Freya in reference to the prevailing unrest, "but it is much worse now." He then recalled that his grandfather, who had since passed away, had told him how there was a time when Palestinians and Sephardic Jews used to peacefully coexist in Palestine. But the arrival of Ashkenazi Russian emigrants had changed all that. They had brought with them extreme right-wing attitudes that fuelled the rise of pro-settler, xenophobic and anti-democratic agendas which sidelined Israel's left and diminished prospects for peace with the Palestinians. Such aggressive and uncompromising colonialist tendencies – selfishly opposed to the division of the land with the Palestinians – were epitomised by the Russian-born Minister of Foreign Affairs Avigdor Lieberman who headed a party founded by Soviet immigrants, Yisrael Beiteinu, which advocated an ultranationalist platform including the expulsion of Israel's Arab citizens.

"They want to take it all and leave us with nothing." an impassioned Sami said, adding that the Israelis treated the Palestinian people with contempt and had not honoured the original agreement that East Jerusalem would remain as part of Palestine. Because they had no respect for international law or other people, they consequently also had no self-respect. They just used force to plunder whatever they wanted whether it was houses, land, water, or Palestinian blood. He cited the case of a Likud member of the Knesset who had claimed that if the day came and he had the opportunity to lead the country as prime minister, he would build the temple on Temple Mount. When asked how he would demolish the Al-Aqsa mosque and Dome of the Rock in order to make way for a Jewish temple, he had replied that it would be irresponsible for him to comment on how that would be done at the present time, but that he would now reiterate loud and clear that when the opportunity presented itself, he would do it. He had also confidently predicted that demolishing Islam's third holiest site would not incite a violent blowback or elicit a significant international reaction or condemnation.

"Sami's right. They're targeting Temple Mount with various archaeological projects to encircle the compound and have nearly finished isolating it from East Jerusalem's Palestinian neighbourhoods," Peltz said and with the added explanation that despite the existence of unwritten understandings that were supposed to ensure the religious administration of the compound remained solely with the Waqf Islamic authority – while Israel controlled the policing of the area – the Israelis had reneged on such understandings. While Jews were permitted to visit the mosque area and had been doing so in ever increasing numbers escorted by armed Israeli police, they were prohibited from actually praying there. By focussing on this fact, Israel was drawing attention away from its activities outside the compound which were restricting access and prayer rights for Muslims, and completely changing the atmosphere and nature of East Jerusalem in general and the Old City in particular. The Israeli government and the settlers were conniving to create the impression that the Old City was at the very core of Jewish identity and history and must therefore be subject to Israeli sovereignty.

"They stop Palestinians going to the Al-Aqsa during the morning hours because Jews are visiting." Sami said. "In October they stopped 500 Muslim children who study there from entering the compound. Army and police barriers and checkpoints also stop Gaza and West Bank Christian and Muslim Palestinians from coming to Jerusalem to visit the holy sites." He added that even the Palestinians who lived in Jerusalem as well as those from Israel's large minority of 1.6

million Palestinian citizens were subject to entry restrictions.

Peltz agreed that such arbitrary and unreasonable actions were responsible for provoking the current Palestinian unrest, and in particular those Israeli activities which sought to cut off the Al-Aqsa compound from its Palestinian surroundings with changes that included the extension of secretive excavations and tunnelling around the compound to create an "underground Jewish city" on the western and northern flanks of the Haram al-Sharif; the transfer of an archaeological park on the western and southern walls of Al-Aqsa to an extremist Jewish settler organisation; and the enforced closure of a historic but active Muslim cemetery, the length of the eastern side of the compound, denying Palestinian families access under the pretext that it falls within an Israeli national park. The object of such changes was to emphasise the Jewish nature – both above and below ground – of Al-Aqsa's surrounding area. Even though the UN Educational, Scientific and Cultural Organisation approved a resolution condemning Israel for limiting freedom of worship for Muslims and for its management of holy sites under its control, the Israeli government had as usual insisted that the current unrest in Jerusalem and in the West Bank was due to "incitement" by Palestinian leaders.

"Last month that cursed bitch, the deputy foreign minister said on TV that her dream was for the Israeli flag to fly over the Temple Mount because it is the holiest place for the Jews, and that 'the creator of the world' took the land from the Palestinians 'and gave it to us.'" Sami said with heartfelt indignation. "Other government ministers say they want to build a third temple in place of al-Aqsa, and a Likud member said the Al-Aqsa Mosque compound was 'the centre of Israeli sovereignty, the capital of Israel.' Fanatical Jewish extremists just want to blow it up."

"Unfortunately that's all true," Peltz said nodding his head. "This is not just inflammatory talk by a few ultra-nationalists, but an organised and concerted campaign involving Israel's political mainstream, archaeologists, and Jewish religious authorities." He further explained that the government, the Israel Antiquities Authority, and the Western Wall Heritage Fund were all working covertly on extensive excavations next to the mosque compound with the intention of creating a network of secret underground tunnels and chambers the precise purpose of which, though not yet known, was nonetheless creating the suspicion that they would extend under the mosque and possibly damage its foundations.

"We know they don't want us in Jerusalem," Sami echoed, "even the Sephardic Chief Rabbi has said that non-Jews should not live in the Land of Israel and should be sent to Saudi Arabia if they did not accept and live by the set of seven laws mandated by Judaism." This same Chief Rabbi had also stressed that the only reason non-Jews were still allowed to live in the Jewish state was the fact that the Messiah had yet to arrive. He had explained that if the Jewish hand had been firmer, and they had the power to rule, then that's what would have happened to non-Jews. But their hand was not yet firm enough because they were still waiting for the Messiah. He added that gentiles who agreed to take on the Noahide Laws – a basic moral code that included prohibitions on denying the existence of God, blasphemy, murder, illicit sexual relations, theft, and eating from a live animal, as well as a requirement to establish a legal system – would be allowed to remain in the land and fulfil the roles reserved for gentiles in the service of Jews.

"He actually said that?" Freya asked incredulously.

"He did." Sami said. "How can a religious leader think in this way? Where's the humanity? Where is the love of God?"

"It's outrages." Freya agreed.

"Even in Silwan there's a lot of digging going on under our homes which could be damaged or taken over for more Jewish settlers. They're also giving control of the archaeological park and the Davidson Centre to Elad," Sami added in reference to the settler organisation already controlling many parts the Silwan neighbourhood.

Peltz felt the need to explain to Freya that the Davidson Centre in the Jerusalem Archaeological Park, was located on the western and southern flanks of the al-Aqsa compound. The Centre offered guided tours and included as one of its highlights a three-dimensional virtual reconstruction of the Temple, based on ancient writings and excavations, and was produced by a team from the Department of Urban Simulation at the University of California, Los Angeles (UCLA). Apparently, pictures generated every 41 millionths of a second gave participants the uncanny feeling that they were actually walking up the staircase to the Temple, through its towering colonnades, and standing before the grandeur of the Holy of Holies.

Peltz emphasised that Elad's intention was to connect its Silwan complex with the Davidson Centre so as to reinforce an exclusive Jewish narrative about ancient Jerusalem. Elad also planned to build a 16,000 square metre complex in the village of Silwan and intended to bury – in the Centre's basement – the remains of the most important archaeological excavation recently discovered at the site. The complex would include a parking lot, shops, offices, a museum and a visitors centre similar to the nearby "City of David" national park. This was being achieved with unprecedented political pressure being applied by the government on the planning and building professionals responsible for evaluating the plan. Israel's National Parks Authority had also sealed off Bab al-Rahmeh – an ancient Islamic cemetery on the mosque's eastern side – with barbed wire to prevent access or burials for Palestinians – which he regarded as the conclusion of the long struggle between Palestinians and settlers over control of the eastern wall of Jerusalem's Holy Esplanade. Right-wing political leaders and groups had also called for Israel to exercise greater control over the Al-Aqsa Mosque compound in response to the ongoing Palestinian unrest which was in any case the result of harsh and unjust measures by the Israelis.

Despite the Israeli Prime Minister's repeated claims that his government had no intention of changing the "status quo" at the Al-Aqsa Mosque compound with claims to the contrary by Palestinians being either mistaken, or acts of calculated deception, the irrefutable fact remained that the Israeli government and the Jerusalem municipality funded radical Jewish groups – supported by many Israeli politicians – who were actively dedicated to the ultimate goal of building a "Third Temple" after the Al-Aqsa Mosque's physical destruction. The change of "status quo" was confirmed by official Israeli police data that showed the instances of access restrictions to Al-Aqsa Mosque compound for Muslim worshippers had dramatically increased in 2014. In the meantime, the number of Jews visiting Al-Aqsa Mosque compound had gradually risen to more than double the number in 2009.

"It's the Israeli police, not the Waqf, who decide who can go to the Al-Aqsa and they stop Palestinian religious leaders and politicians from going in," Sami said, "they keep invading the holy site, the Al-Aqsa Mosque, and they fire tear gas and stun grenades at the protesters barricaded inside."

Peltz was concerned over the fact that the violence had since reverberated across the city and beyond. Israeli authorities had also severely tightened control on Palestinian access to al-Wad Street in the Old City's Muslim quarter which Jewish settlers had long been targeting for takeover because it is connected to the Western Wall. Palestinians suspected that Israel wanted to either physically divide the compound to create a separate prayer area for Jews or to insist on separate prayer times for Jews as had been the arrangement imposed by Israel on Hebron's Ibrahimi mosque since the 1990s.

It had also been reported that the recently formed New Israeli movement, Save Jewish Jerusalem, had called for the building of a wall encircling 28 Palestinian villages in East Jerusalem so as to preserve the city's Jewish identity. The manifesto's authors had explained that by removing about 200,000 Palestinians from the municipal boundaries of Jerusalem, the city's Jews would constitute more than 80 percent of its residents while less than 20 percent would be Palestinian instead of the current 40 percent. After the villages' separation from Jerusalem, the IDF and other security agencies would then control and operate within them in the same manner they did in the rest of the West Bank.

The conversation soon switched to Conrad and Freya's intended visit to the Al-Aqsa compound which Jews and tourists could only access after passing through a strict security screening in the Jewish Quarter that led to the wooden bridge along which people could walk above the Western Wall to the Mughrabi Gate and up to the compound. But before doing so they would visit the Western Wall Plaza which as Conrad knew had been nicknamed "The Wailing Wall" due to the sound of Jews crying and praying by the side of the Wall. Jews believed that since the Temple's destruction, God's presence, though hidden from mankind, was lurking in the background and still to be very much felt. This was symbolised in the Songs of Songs as if He were hiding behind a wall: "My beloved is like a gazelle or a young hart; behold, he standeth behind our wall, he looketh in through the windows, he peereth through the lattice" (Song of Songs 2, 8).

The Sages interpreted the wall mentioned in this verse to be the Western Wall. While there was disagreement over whether this referred to what today was known as the Western Wall – which was the western wall of the Temple Mount – or to the western wall of the Temple itself, the message was nonetheless clear: God was very close but with a wall separating Him from the people who poured their prayers and tears near Wall in the hope that He would soon reveal His presence to them and all of mankind. There was a Jewish tradition wherein prayers were written on pieces of paper and stuffed in cracks in the wall. Every few days, a caretaker then collected all the prayers and buried them on the Mount of Olives in a 2,000-year-old cemetery where every one of them became an "eternal prayer."

It was, however, decided that initially Sami would meet them the next day at the Damascus Gate and guide them through the Muslim Quarter which would enable them to photograph and film before they walked from the end of El-Wad Street through the tunnel leading to the Orthodox and ultra-Orthodox Jewish Western Wall Plaza from where the wooden bridge could be accessed.

The food finally arrived and the waitress made a point of deliberately slamming Sami's plate down in front of him as she gave him a disapproving and contemptuous glare which he countered with a "thank you very much" and the sardonic smile which he flashed whenever rudely belittled by his racist immigrant occupiers. Sami had ordered the salmon fillet which had been seared to such perfection that the first mouthful of its succulent texture startled his taste buds. He almost choked as he instinctively thought of his family and was overwhelmed by a sudden sense of profound guilt with a slight hint of moisture welling up in his eyes. He could not recall the last time he had shared a meal of fresh fish with his wife Miriam and their two young children.

14

Monday 21, December

Prime Minister's Office, 10 Downing Street, London

10 Downing Street with its three overlapping functions – official residence of the British Prime Minister; Office of the Prime Minister; and the venue for entertaining royalty and visiting world leaders – vied with the White House as being the world's most important political building in the modern times and had been the residence of British prime ministers since 1735 with many decisions of vital importance being taken behind its black door over a period of more than 280 years. In the 21st century alone decisions had been taken for military involvement in the Sierra Leone Civil War (2000); the War in Afghanistan (2001-14); the Iraq War (2003-11); the Libyan Civil War (2011); and the still ongoing Military intervention allegedly against ISIS in Syria (2014).

Today the Prime Minister and his advisors were discussing a report from the Intelligence and Security Committee of Parliament (ISC) which apart from overseeing the operational activity of the three main intelligence and security Agencies, also provided oversight of Defence Intelligence in the Ministry of Defence and the Office for Security and Counter-Terrorism in the Home Office. The report, based on intelligence provided by Mossad, was of the opinion that fighting terrorism in Yemen was in the interests of the international community, and required the root of the problem to be tackled through the establishment of long-term stability. The implication was that the country had become a foothold for highly adaptive, transnational terrorist networks with Al-Qaeda – still retaining affiliates in Somalia, Syria, Yemen, North Africa, and South Asia – remaining as a serious threat to Western interests worldwide. The armed men who attacked the French magazine *Charlie Hebdo* in France had for example been trained in the Yemeni region of Hadramout. The probability of Israeli involvement in such training was, however, not mentioned.

Though one of the advisor's cautioned against accepting Mossad's assessment without bearing in mind that Mossad had been ultimately responsible for much of the false "intelligence" about Iraq's possession of WMDs which led to the Iraq War, the Prime Minister – who had previously pledged his "unbreakable" support for Israel – chose to ignore the warning. So apart from its direct involvement in wars, Britain had also on the basis of Israeli influenced "intelligence" become indirectly associated with other questionable conflicts including the Saudi instigated civil wars in Syria and Yemen on Israel's behalf.

Evidence of Israeli-Saudi collusion had surfaced during the summer when Some 20 Israeli Mossad officers and 63 Saudi military men and officials were killed and many others taken captive when Yemen's Shia Houthi Ansarullah movement, backed by the Yemeni army, attacked Amir Khalid airbase in Southern Saudi Arabia. Britain's indirect involvement in this particular conflict had been highlighted days earlier in a legal opinion – obtained by Amnesty International and other human rights groups – stating that UK arms sales to Saudi Arabia were fuelling the civil war in Yemen and were breaching domestic, European and international law obligations.

The UK government had been aware for months that the weapons systems it was supplying to Saudi forces were being used against civilian targets including hospitals, schools, markets, grain warehouses, ports and a displaced persons camp resulting in a huge humanitarian crisis. Since the conflict's escalation in mid-March, some 6,000 people had been killed, tens of thousands wounded, and 2.5 million forced to flee their homes. More than 80% of the country's population of 21 million were currently in need of humanitarian aid with 2 million children at risk of malnutrition.

The legal opinion had stressed that by continuing to authorise transfers of weapons and related equipment to Saudi Arabia, Britain was breaching obligations under the UK's consolidated criteria on arms exports; obligations to the EU common position on arms exports; and obligations to the arms trade treaty. But with the UK's House of Commons already in recess for Christmas, the government was hoping the report would be buried and forgotten during the season of goodwill and cheers to all when the Prime Minister would send his best wishes – with commendable concern for refugees apart from those seven million Palestinians forcibly displaced by his Israeli political masters – to everyone celebrating Christmas in the UK and around the world in what could only be described as the best of British Prime Ministerial codswallop and hypocrisy:

"If there is one thing people want at Christmas, it's the security of having their family around them and a home that is safe. But not everyone has that. Millions of families are spending this winter in refugee camps or makeshift shelters across Syria and the Middle East, driven from their homes by Daesh and Assad. Christians from Africa to Asia will go to church on Christmas morning full of joy, but many in fear of persecution. Throughout the United Kingdom, some will spend the festive period ill, homeless or alone.

"We must pay tribute to the thousands of doctors, nurses, carers and volunteers who give up their Christmas to help the vulnerable – and to those who are spending this season even further from home. Right now, our brave armed forces are doing their duty, around the world: in the skies of Iraq and Syria, targeting the terrorists that threaten those

countries and our security at home; on the seas of the Mediterranean, saving those who attempt the perilous crossing to Europe; and on the ground, helping to bring stability to countries from Afghanistan to South Sudan.

"It is because they face danger that we have peace. And that is what we mark today as we celebrate the birth of God's only son, Jesus Christ – the Prince of Peace. As a Christian country, we must remember what his birth represents: peace, mercy, goodwill and, above all, hope. I believe that we should also reflect on the fact that it is because of these important religious roots and Christian values that Britain has been such a successful home to people of all faiths and none.

"So, as we come together with our loved ones, in safety and security, let's think of those who cannot do the same. Let's give thanks to those who are helping the vulnerable at home and protecting our freedoms abroad. And let me wish everyone in Britain and around the world a very happy and peaceful Christmas."

Paris, France

Malek Bennabi bought a newspaper to read during his Metro journey to the Saint-Paul station on the Rue de Rivoli where he would be meeting Aziz Gharbi and his brother Rachid to go over their plans for one final time. The only piece of news that was of interest to Malek was the fact that a UN study had found that 70 percent of Syrian refugees in Lebanon were living in "extreme poverty" that forced them to borrow – putting nearly 90 percent of them in debt – just to cover the most basic needs of food, rent, and healthcare. The situation was so desperate that parents were taking their children out of school and putting them to work so that only five percent of 15-17 year olds were attending school with many of them working in agricultural fields for as little as $4 a day.

As an intelligent person, Malek was only too aware that by instigating the flood of refugees from the Middle East, Israel was fulfilling its agenda for the creation of a Greater Israel (Eretz Israel) stretching from the Nile to the Euphrates as supposedly promised to the Israelites by God himself. Malek understood that in order to achieve its goal, Israel was overcoming indigenous Semite (Arab) resistance to its colonisation plans by using groups such as ISIS and Al Qaeda to terrorise native Muslim populations and force them to flee the region; by exploiting Jewish influence over EU immigration policies to incentivise such an Arab exodus; By creating real and imagined scenarios – a Second Holocaust – in which European Jews appear to be persecuted by Arabs and other "anti-Semites" so as to encourage those terror-stricken Jews to emigrate to Israel; by using the mainstream media to publicise ISIS atrocities in the Western world so as to make it appear that military intervention in the region was the only solution; by fuelling the "clash of civilisations" concept in Europe where the influx of Arab refugees could be exploited to persuade Europeans to favour the civilised Jews and disapprove of the primitive Muslims; and by employing multiculturalism to undermine and eventually weaken Europe through forced assimilation while simultaneously criminalising and isolating pro-Palestinian activism – such as the BDS campaign – which posed the greatest threat to Israel's hegemonic plans.

Malek decided he would use the topic of Arab refugees in his final pep talk to the Gharbi brothers who were already waiting for him at the café on the Rue de Rivoli. As they drank their coffees they talked in hushed tones with Malek showing them the news item about Syrian refugees while assertively stressing Israel's responsibility for the problem. The plans for the attack were then gone over with meticulous attention to detail and after another round of coffees during their 45-minute discussion, they left the café for a "dry run" walk along the route the brothers would be taking right up to where the getaway van would be parked and waiting for them. Though outwardly calm, the brothers were nevertheless quietly seething with excitement at the prospect of unleashing murderous mayhem on the streets of Paris.

Damascus Gate, East Jerusalem

When Conrad and Freya left their hotel and started walking towards the Old City, they were unaware that Yaakov Katzir – dressed in washed denim jeans, shirt and jacket with the brim of a New York Yankees baseball cap pulled down and covering the upper part of his face – was on the opposite side of the road following them. On arriving at the Damascus Gate, which was the most ornate and busiest of the entrances to the Old City, they found Sami already waiting for them at the top of the Roman stadium style semi-circular set of stairs that led down to the gatehouse. Because of the current unrest, the presence of heavily armed police and Israeli Occupation Force (IOF) soldiers was conspicuously evident with access being cordoned off with metal crowd control barriers. Snipers equipped with Dan .338 sniper rifles were positioned on nearby rooftops and additional surveillance cameras had been installed with nearby trees having either been trimmed or uprooted to provide a clear view for the cameras.

Identity checks were being carried out and only residents of the Old City itself and others with business or justifiable reasons being allowed access. Palestinians were questioned, searched, manhandled, and deliberately humiliated in a manner that had become the hallmark – and a source of sadistic amusement and pleasure – for Israeli security forces. Sami was eventually cleared in his capacity as companion and guide to Conrad and Freya who, laden with the more than the average amount of tourist photographic equipment, were looked over suspiciously and warned to stay clear of, and avoid filming any trouble. The warning was not out of concern for their safety, but rather for the Israeli benefit of not having videotaped recordings of IOF and police brutality.

Located on the Old City's northern wall, Damascus Gate was the entrance most used by Palestinians. After a short walk beyond the entrance, the street divided in two directions with Khan al-Zeit veering slightly to the right and continuing towards the Jewish Quarter, while Al-Wad Street continued a shade to the left and down towards the Western Wall plaza. The gate and these two streets leading from it were built by the Romans in the 2nd Century, and had since become the central arteries in the Old City. Khan al-Zeit Street intersected with David Street – which started at the Jaffa Gate and separated the Christian Quarter from the Armenian – and led to Chain Street. Both Streets were fashioned on Roman-era urban planning – with the city then being known as *Aelia Capitolina* – and today they served as the streets most frequented by tourists.

Al-Wad Street – with several alleyways leading to the gates of the Dome of the Rock – also meant that for Muslim worshipers it was the best route for reaching the Haram Al-Sharif/Temple Mount. The compound's eastern and southern gates had been blocked for centuries with the seven gates still open to the public being located on Al-Wad or on Via Dolorosa. Because it was the the main artery serving worshipers from all religions and particularly the Muslims, Al-Wad Street was also where the Ateret Cohanim organisation – founded in 1978 and originally known as Atara Leyoshna (returning the former glory) – began Judaising the Muslim Quarter by establishing a Yeshiva in the 1980s at the crossroads of Via Dolorosa and al-Wad with the latter being the location on which Ariel Sharon in an act of deliberate provocation purchased a house. Ateret Cohanim had also made a point of purchasing some apartments on the street. One of the small alleys that branched off al-Wad led to the Iron

Gate (Bab al-Hadid) of the Al-Aqsa compound next to which was an area known as the "Little Western Wall" – considered to be the closest prayer site to the Holy of Holies, outside the Temple Mount compound – where the ultra-Orthodox and other groups organised by Ateret Cohanim were encouraged to pray.

As they passed through the Damascus Gate, Conrad and Freya noted the high level of police and military presence and despite the Israeli lockdown with many shops remaining closed, they still sensed the tension and anger amongst a people who for decades had been dehumanised, labeled as savages, and denied their very existence. Sami informed them that the Muslim Quarter was first settled at the end of the Second Temple period (70 CE) and was included within the second city wall built by Herod the Great whose insanity drove him to commit vile crimes – including the murder of his own family and numerous rabbis – so as to gratify his unbounded ambition. Jews and Arabs then joined forces to fight against the Crusaders, but were by the end of the 12th century evicted to be replaced by Syrian Christian Jacobites. Arabs, however, returned to the quarter after Saladin's 1187 conquest of Jerusalem. They were later joined by Jews from the ancient Galilean city of Safed (Tsefat) in the 1800's so that by the late 1800's Jews outnumbered the Arabs. The two groups managed to coexist peacefully until 1929 when a long-running dispute between them over access to the Western Wall escalated into Arab violence against Jews who consequently fled the Old City.

Sami then took Conrad and Freya down El-Wad street before turning left into the Via Dolorosa – Way of Grief/Sorrows/ Suffering – where on their left stood the Austrian Hospice which in 1863 opened as the first national pilgrims' guesthouse in the Holy Land. On their right was the location of the Fourth Station of the Cross where according to tradition the Virgin Mary stood – while observing the sufferings of her son carrying the cross on his way to be crucified – at the ancient street level underneath the Armenian Catholic Church of our Lady of the Spasm, built in 1881. Former Byzantine archaeological remains on the site, included a 5th century CE mosaic floor depicting a pair of sandals which later tradition mentioned as symbolising the place where Mary stood weeping and hence the word "spasm" in the church's name being a reference to that occasion of extreme anguish and desolation. The church was one of several Christian establishments in the Muslim Quarter.

The Via Dolorosa connected to Mujahidin Street which led to the Lion's (St Stephen's) Gate with a view of the Mount of Olives rising to a height of some 2,800 feet (850 metres). Separated from the Eastern Hill's Temple Mount by the Kidron Valley, the Mount of Olives had always been a prominent feature of Jerusalem's landscape. Since the 3rd millennium BCE until the present, the mount had served as a one of the city's main burial grounds with its two-mile (3.2 kilometre) long ridge boasting three summits on each of which a tower had been built. Following Saladin's conquest, the Church of the Holy Ascension – traditionally regarded as the site from which Jesus ascended into heaven – was converted into a mosque which had remained to this day. Another feature of the mount which lay at the bottom of its slope was the Garden of Gethsemane where a Byzantine, a Crusader, and a modern church were successively built with the belief that it was the site from which Jesus some hours prior to his crucifixion prayed to God the Father.

From the Lion's Gate the trio doubled back and Sami mentioned that Israeli excavations had been ongoing all the time with the Elad foundation having dug from the Pool of Siloam to the Givati Parking Lot and all the way to the Mughrabi Bridge. As far as Elad was concerned, Silwan was the "City of David" and it was doing everything possible to legitimise that assertion both above and below ground. The digging was constant with tunnels from the Western Wall reaching all the way to the Via

Dolorosa. Sami stressed that virtually all of the excavations were not only under entirely Muslim strata, but also under Mameluke structures dating from the 14th and 15th centuries. Sami believed that the ultimate objective of such tunnelling was to create a Jewish-Israeli Jerusalem by digging under the Palestinian reality, and reinforcing the Israeli national narrative. Tunnelling had become the means with which to prevent a political two state solution in both the Historic Basin area and the adjacent Haram al-Sharif /Temple Mount.

As they walked towards the intersection, they turned left into El-Wad Street and walked southwards instead of continuing eastwards along via Dolorosa whose route had changed several times over the centuries. Though various routes were still being used according to varying Christian denominational opinions, the main route being currently followed with its 14 Stations of the Cross was that of the early Byzantine pilgrims who had set off from the Monastery of the Flagellation near the Lion's Gate and finished at the Church of the Holy Sepulchre in the Christian Quarter. Sami explained that for Israel and settler organisations, creating a Jewish identity and presence on the access roads to the Western Wall, was an essential part of their strategy. Palestinians, on the other hand, regarded such presence as a dangerous and provocative intrusion. It was therefore understandable that out of desperate frustration at not being able to get any degree of justice or international recognition of their persistent persecution, that some Palestinians – with the certain knowledge that they would end up being killed – had resorted to knife attacks against Israelis. Sami asked Conrad and Freya the rhetorical question of whether those attackers were to be regarded as homicidal assassins or heroic martyrs sacrificing themselves for the right to exist as human beings and a people in their own right.

The plan was for Sami to take them to Al-Qattanin Street and show them around the indoor Cotton Merchants' Market

– built in the 14th century by the Mameluke Emir Tankiz with a rectangular design incorporating an arched ceiling with a barrel-shaped vault divided into a series of 30 arched sections – at the end of which a flight of stairs manned by the IOF soldiers led to the gate which provided the closest access to the Al Haram Al-Sharif for Muslims wishing to visit or worship. They would then return to El-Wad Street, turn left and continue towards the Western Wall Plaza where Sami would leave them as they continued to the wooden bridge leading to the Mughrabi Gate where non-Muslims and tourists could access the Al Haram Al-Sharif/Twmple Mount between 12:30pm – 1:30pm.

As they approached Al-Qattanin Street, however, they came upon an incensed Palestinian Muslim crowd who were being denied access through the market to the Al-Aqsa compound as apparently was the case at all other entry points. As the Palestinian crowd tried to surge forward towards the entrance with angry shouts, they were pushed and beaten back by the Israelis using their rifle butts and pepper spray that caused an immediate closure of the eyes, difficulty in breathing, runny noses, and coughing that could last for up to 45 minutes, with diminished effects lasting for hours. The restrictions had been imposed as part of alleged Israeli attempt to establish a daily schedule for Jewish prayer during which time Muslim worshipers would be denied access. Meanwhile, the groups of right-wing Jews touring the compound were being escorted by a substantial number of Israeli police officers.

While some Palestinians in the crowd where recording the unrest on their mobile phones, it was Conrad and Freya's obviously more professional equipment that the Israelis noticed and focussed on with one soldier smashing Conrad on the forehead with his rifle butt and another pushing Freya and grabbing her expensive digital SLR camera which with its padded black neoprene strap was slung around her neck. As Sami went to her aid and tried to intervene, Yaakov Katzir appeared from nowhere, drew a handgun from his shoulder holster and shot Sami in the back. The impact caused Sami's body to arch backwards before falling face down on the ground. As the crowd screamed and shied away forming a circle around Sami's body, Katzir stood over him and fired two more shots into the back of his head which tore through hair, flesh, and muscle before smashing into and shattering several of the eight cranial bones intended for the protection of the brain causing it to immediately cease functioning so that Sami was dead within a fraction of a second. Katzir re-holstered the gun and as he knelt down on one knee to check the lifeless body, he brushed its side with his left hand within which was concealed a small knife; raised the hand holding the knife to triumphantly display it for everyone as justification for the killing; and then stood up before dropping the knife by Sami's lifeless body. Planting knives by the bodies of extrajudicially killed Palestinians was a ploy that had become a ritual for their Israeli executioners.

Though Conrad and Freya had been aware of and seen YouTube video clips of Israel's extrajudicial murder of Palestinians, actually being involved in one – especially of someone personally known to them to be a decent, law abiding and most certainly unarmed individual – resulted in an initial state of unspeakable shock followed by an eruption of mixed and outraged emotions. Such unethical extrajudicial killings that bypassed due process had during decades of callous occupation become symbolic of Israel's culture of impunity and blatant disregard for international law. Had such killings been committed by anyone else other than Israeli Jews, they would have rightly been globally condemned as coldblooded murder, but when committed by "God's chosen people" they were unashamedly and universally excused by a mealy-mouthed mainstream media as being "self defence" by the world's "perennial victims" who appeared to revel in being hated.

For some reason, Jews derived a depraved satisfaction from being supposedly disliked and condemned globally. It has affirmed their belief throughout the ages that all the world's nations hate them because they are special and superior to the rest of humanity. While always tenaciously holding on to such a belief, they have never paused to consider the possibility that such "hate" was a consequence of their own behaviour, rather than the unadulterated anti-Semitism of others.

At least half a dozen menacing Israeli police and military personnel surrounded the by now highly distraught and outraged Conrad and Freya who had their cameras and iPhones confiscated, were handcuffed with plastic nylon zip locks, and led to the Jaffa Gate from where a police van took them to the nearby Zion Police Station where they were detained in separate rather dirty cells to be strip searched down to their underwear. After being kept waiting to sweat it out for at least two infuriating and despairing hours without being allowed to phone or otherwise communicate with anyone, they were aggressively interrogated at intervals for a further two and a half hours by security officers whose intelligence quotients had been seriously stymied by years supremacist indoctrination.

They were, however spared what was termed in newspeak as "enhanced interrogation techniques" – otherwise more appropriately known as torture – that Shin Bet routinely used on Palestinian adults and children which involved the use of direct physical violence including sleep deprivation induced by the use of shouting, loud music, or bright lights; "dry" beatings which alternated between slaps and punches to kicks to the body; very tight handcuffing that caused intense pain and stopped the flow of blood to the palms of the hand; the sudden jerking of the body while the detainees' hands were cuffed behind them and connected to a loop on the seat of the chair, so that any sudden movement caused intense pain to the hands, arms, and joints; the sudden twisting of the head with the interrogator either grabbing the detainee's head and twisting it sharply to one side, or forcing the head back with a punch to the chin; the "frog" crouch with detainees being forced on their toes continually for several minutes during which time they were pushed or struck so as to cause the loss of balance; the "banana" position which required detainees to arch their backs over the seat of the chair with the backrest to the side so that their hands and ankles could be shackled underneath the chair; and last but not least, the sexual abuse – particularly of children – by a people whose conduct could be easily construed as being amongst the most morally perverted in the world as in their manic rush to grab more and more Palestinian land, they stampeded like wild animals over every one of their God-given commandments … A people with little or no time to pause and consider the immorality of their actions in accordance with the Talmud's two components: the Mishnah (c. 200 CE), a written compendium of Rabbinic Judaism's Oral Torah (Talmud translates literally as "instruction" in Hebrew); and the Gemara (c. 500 CE), an elucidation of the Mishnah and related Tannaitic writings that often ventured onto other subjects while expounding broadly on the Hebrew Bible.

To begin with there was the Talmudic conception that mankind was one of unity acquiring its character from a common origin and destiny. The basic components of this doctrine were set out in the Bible which traced the origins of the human race to a single person who was formed in God's own image. It was in the Talmud that this doctrine was further developed with the question of "why did the Creator form all life from a single ancestor?" To which the reply was "that the families of mankind shall not lord one over the other with the claim of being sprung from superior stock … that all men, saints and sinners alike, may recognise their common kinship in the collective human family."

While human behaviour may vary infinitely, the underlying nature of humans was essentially the same. Man as an earthly creature was at the same time a child of God infused with a divine spirit. The appraisal of moral categories suggests that all people were endowed with tendencies to view in their own persons the ultimate conclusion of their seeking transcendence towards which they were but contributing instruments. From these two tendencies flowed good and evil which in varying degrees existed within every individual as part of his or her inherent means for life. Furthermore, the Talmud advised that one will discover that "even the greatest of sinners" abounds in good deeds as does a pomegranate abound in seeds. Alternatively, even the greatest saints have their share of moral imperfections because all human beings are cut from the same cloth and there are no distinctions between them.

The sanctity of life was intrinsic to the individual irrespective of national origin, religious affiliation, or social status, and as one Talmudist commented: "Heaven and earth I call to witness, whether it be an Israelite or pagan, man or woman, slave or maidservant, according to the work of every human being doth the Holy Spirit rest upon him." It followed therefore that non-Jews living in Jewish communities were to enjoy all the same benefits as their Jewish counterparts. While Jews were, according to the rabbis, ordained to support their needy, visit their sick, and bury their dead, they were equally "obligated to feed non-Jews residing among us even as we feed Jews; we are obligated to visit their sick even as we visit the Jewish sick; we are obligated to attend to the burial of their dead, even as we attend to the burial of Jewish dead." This rabbinic requirement was based on the premise that those were "the ways of peace."

From this it followed that the supreme sanctity of all human life was pertinent to man's place in the universe: "He who destroys one person has dealt a blow at the entire universe, and similarly, he who makes life livable for one person has sustained the whole world." All law, civil and religious, has as its purpose the promotion of human life, and when it ceases to serve that end it becomes obsolete and is superseded. These were teachings that Conrad had encountered while doing his research and as he now faced his insufferable inquisitors, he wondered whether all Jewish people should perhaps honestly consider the possibility that Zionism had superseded Judaism which had become obsolete.

After hours of questioning, Conrad and Freya's interrogators – despite their low level blinkered and racist IQs – finally realised that their two British "suspects" had nothing incriminating to divulge and consequently released them at around seven o'clock without apology and the customary lack of Israeli civility. Once outside the police station, the first thing they did was to check their cameras and were not surprised to find that the recordings of that afternoon's events had been deleted. They also had no doubt that their iPhones had been trawled for any contact numbers of pro-Palestinian activists in Israel, the Occupied Territories, or even in the UK. As they were still shaken and traumatised by Sami's murder and their own violent brush with Israeli security, they were uncertain about their next course of action but finally decided to phone Adam Peltz who listened to Conrad's account of what had occurred in shocked silence.

"Does Sami's wife know?" He asked.

"I've no idea."

"Probably not," Peltz guessed, "informing the family won't be one of their priorities. Do you have Sami's address Silwan?"

"I've got it saved on iCloud."

"Good. Where are you now?"

Conrad looked around for a street sign. "On Heleni Ha-Malka."

"Okay. Just walk southwards on the Jaffa Road, it will take you to your hotel. It's not far. I'll pick you up there and we'll go to see his wife."

"I dread having to break … " Conrad began to say but was interrupted.

"Don't worry, I know enough Arabic to break the sad news …"

Washington D.C.

Abe Goldman's hotel on Maryland Avenue, SW, was within walking distance of AIPAC headquarters on H Street Northwest by way of Independence Avenue, past the Smithsonian's National Air and Space Museum, past the curvilinear National Museum of the American Indian, and northwards along 3rd Street NW where he was scheduled to meet Steve Appelman, a friend, a fellow Mason, and head of AIPAC's Political Development Section. Seventy-two-year-old Appelman's gaunt, aquiline features – with a wrinkled forehead merging into a shiny, bald pate fringed by short greying hair at the back and sides – belied the fact that he was a shrewd, calculating puppet master within the Washington corridors of power.

The seeds of AIPAC'S creation had been sowed soon after Israel's establishment as a state in 1948 when it became apparent that in order to cope with the influx of some 700,000 Jewish immigrants – space for whom had been created by the depopulation and destruction of more than 500 Palestinian villages and the forcible expulsion of an estimated 750,000 Palestinian civilian men, women, and children – Israel would require a lot more financial assistance than the American Jewish money already being raised under the disingenuous and cynical name of American Friends of the Fighters for Freedom of Israel who were in fact the brutal Jewish Terrorist groups that included the Lohamei Herut Yisrael also known as the LEHI or Stern Gang after its founder Avraham Stern.

Prior to the UN Partition of Palestine and the creation of

Israel in May 1948, a Mr. Shepard Rifkin, had tried to solicit Albert Einstein's help in raising money for the "Fighters for Freedom" who were in the process of creating a Jewish state. On the day after the infamous April 9, 1948 massacre of Arabs at Deir Yassin, Einstein's reply was curt and to the point: "When a real and final catastrophe should befall us in Palestine the first responsible for it would be the British and the second responsible for it the Terrorist organisations built up from our own ranks. I am not willing to see anybody associated with those misled and criminal people."

Though Jewish Americans subsequently responded with unprecedented generosity, by 1950, it nonetheless became apparent to U.S. Jewish leaders that much more financial aid was required and accordingly they devised a four-point strategy which included increasing donations from Jewish individuals; encouraging U.S. corporate investment in Israel; promoting the sale of Israeli bonds; and requesting that Israel become a recipient of assistance from the U.S. aid program for underdeveloped countries. Despite such efforts, the demand of Israel's economic and military requirements could not be met by Jewish diaspora handouts alone. Consequently in 1951 the American Zionist Council (AZC) was established to promote a pro-Israel lobbying campaign that would concentrate on influencing Congress for American taxpayer dollars.

As it had been established as a tax-exempt entity, the AZC was not legally permitted to Lobby in the U.S. on Israel's behalf and in 1954 was faced with a possible investigation for its violations. Therefore to avoid any official scrutiny of its illegal activities, the AZC rebranded itself as the non-tax-exempt American Zionist Committee for Public Affairs. Over a period of time, however, it was realised that Zionism's actual objectives may not be to the liking of some of the American Jews whose support was required, so the Committee shrewdly once again rebranded itself by substituting the word *Israel* for the word *Zionist* to become the American Israel Public Affairs Committee.

During 1962-63 Senator William J. Fulbright, the Foreign Relations Committee Chairman, convened hearings which uncovered evidence that the Jewish Agency – the predecessor to the state of Israel – had operated a massive network of financial "conduits" that funnelled funds to Zionist Israeli lobby groups whose increasing influence over U.S. policy decisions had become a cause for alarm. In April 1973, on CBS *Face the Nation,* Fulbright stated that "Israel controls the U.S. Senate. The Senate is subservient, much too much; we should be more concerned about U.S. interests rather than doing the bidding of Israel. The great majority of the Senate of the U.S. – somewhere around 80% – is completely in support of Israel; anything Israel wants; Israel gets. This has been demonstrated time and again, and this has made [foreign policy] difficult for our Government."

The probability of Mossad's involvement in JFK's assassination was in 1994 clearly substantiated by author Michael Collins Piper who in his incisive book, *Final Judgment: The Missing link in the JFK Assassination Conspiracy,* asserted that Israel's motive for the assassination was JFK's opposition to Israel's nuclear ambitions which outraged Ben-Gurion who commanded the Mossad to become involved. Piper concluded that "Israel's Mossad was a primary (and critical) behind the scenes player in the conspiracy that ended the life of JFK. Through its own vast resources and through its international contacts in the intelligence community and in organised crime, Israel had the means, it had the opportunity, and it had the motive to play a major frontline role in the crime of the century – and it did."

In March 1992, former Rep. Paul Findley (R-Ill.), stated in the *Washington Report on Middle East Affairs,* "It is interesting – but not surprising – to note that in all the words written and uttered about the Kennedy assassination, Israel's intelligence agency, the Mossad, has never been mentioned. And yet a Mossad motive is obvious. On this question, as on almost all others, American reporters and commentators cannot bring themselves to cast Israel in an unfavourable light – despite the obvious fact that Mossad complicity is as plausible as any of the other theories." JFK's assassination served the dual purpose of eliminating both the threat to Israel's nuclear aspirations and the need for the main Zionist lobbying group to register as a foreign agent.

Approximately one-third of AIPAC's Washington staff were administrative and clerical with the remainder specialising in areas of strategic importance including communications and leading-edge weapons technology. AIPAC was structured to effectively maximise its lobbying efforts by concentrating on the Executive Branch, Legislation, Research, and political development. Influencing the Executive Branch that was not elected but appointed and accountable only to the President was of vital importance when dealing with issues – such as the ongoing charade of the Middle East peace process – that were initiated in the Oval Office rather than by the bicameral Congress. By ensuring the presence of Jews within the ranks of the Executive Branch, AIPAC, rather than having to react to U.S. Middle East policy decisions, was instead able to exert influence during their formulation.

AIPAC enforced a U.S lawmakers' allegiance to Israel – that far surpassed loyalty to the U.S. itself – by requiring from every candidate a "signed pledge" to support Israel which if refused resulted in a cutoff from AIPAC's financial support and a campaign of demonisation. Candidates who complied would then join the AIPAC gravy train with constituency rewards and free junkets to Israel. AIPAC's organisational skills through its regional offices also ensured that while the core Jewish population was only some 6.75 million – 2.2 percent of the U.S. population – Jews nonetheless had the highest ethnic group percentage of actual voters (90 percent) with an estimated 89 percent of them living in the 12 key electoral college states. Furthermore, despite comprising of only 1.8 percent of the college age population in the U.S., Jews – to their credit – totalled an astonishing 25 percent of Harvard and Ivy League college enrolment which would subsequently see them holding key positions of influence over U.S. policy decisions.

AIPAC also contributed to, and participated in the global Jewish lobby's efforts to advance Zionist Israeli interests with a comprehensive multi-point plan that included placing agents of influence and sayanim (helpers) in positions of importance within political parties, non-government organisations, and both overt (e.g. Rotary) and covert (e.g. Masonic) clubs and societies; endeavouring to appoint puppet leaders who were susceptible to blackmail and could consequently be coerced into taking decisions that favoured Israel; resorting to extortion, paying hush money, and using threats to achieve Zionist goals; controlling the mainstream media through full or part ownership, through watchdog organisations, or simply through intimidation; using such control of the media for Zionist propaganda including *hasbara;* pushing for legislation that curtailed and criminalised criticism of Israeli policies; subverting education by means of disinformation and restriction of intellectual debate in schools, colleges, and universities; rewriting history – particularly that of Palestine – to suit the Jewish/Israeli/Zionist narrative; fomenting conflicts between non-Jewish races, religions and social classes; and exploiting successful, socially prominent people by appealing to their egos and holding out for them the promise of further material advancement.

The responsibilities of AIPAC's Political Development Section included grassroots lobbying, fundraising, and development of constituent participation in local and national politics; providing information to Congressional incumbents and aspirants on Israeli issues; running pro-Israel political leadership development programmes on colleges campuses throughout the U.S. with a view to getting students involved in pro-Israel activities with regional field organisers arranging workshops and conferences to recruit and train students as activists who were encouraged to prepare reports on faculty members, other students or college organisations that were either critical of Israel or supportive of the Palestinian cause. Such information was then used to publish the AIPAC College Guide which exposed the *miscreants* who were subsequently subjected to harassment, suspension, or in some cases, even dismissal.

In a constant fight to justify the legitimacy of both its existence and its questionable conduct to Jewish Americans, Israel – through AIPAC – resorted to disinformation, miseducation, dishonesty, and unashamed manipulation of the Holocaust which had become a hundred million dollar a year industry in its own right. While AIPAC did not directly donate to political campaigns, it oversaw a carefully monitored campaign finance network of some 30 Pro-Israel Political Action Committees (PACs).

AIPAC'S control of the White House and the bicameral U.S. Congress – the most powerful and longest running political scam ever perpetrated on a Western democracy – was financed by some $6 billion that served to totally corrupt the democratic process and not only disenfranchise some 220 million Americans eligible to vote, but also to negatively impact on the lives of billions of other people around the world. Israel's selfish, self-serving machinations for absolute control of U.S. global foreign policy – particularly with regards to Europe and the Middle East – was a worldwide threat to both human and civil rights with the former including the right to life, education, free expression, protection from torture, and a fair trial; and the latter covering those rights that an individual enjoys by virtue of citizenship in a particular nation or state. The attack on such rights could ultimately lead to a nuclear war with appalling consequences for all humanity.

By ruthlessly promoting on behalf of Israel the destabilisation and destruction of Arab countries in the Middle East, AIPAC was also assisting the U.S. defence industry which this year alone would be spending over $56 million – down from a 2013 all-time high of $78 million – lobbying the federal government. Apart from the U.S. defence industry and Israel, other defence-related industries – such as those involved with healthcare, computer technology, and oil – were also in cahoots in coercing the White House and Congress to wage more illegal and unnecessary wars. Of the defence industry's almost 380 lobbyists, approximately 66 percent were "revolvers" – former defence industry employees – whose insider knowledge and connections were useful in exerting influence.

The defence industry's expenditure on lobbying was surpassed by the oil and gas industry's $97 million with over 760 lobbyists being involved. Leaked secret memos had linked oil companies directly with the invasion of Iraq. Even after the "departure" of many U.S. troops from the country, the oil industry remained behind with BP and Royal Dutch Shell earning billions – and still doing so today – from lucrative Middle East contracts. The current Syrian civil war with its consequent refugee crisis was also fuelled by competing gas pipelines as disclosed by Wikileaks revelations of U.S. State Department leaks outlining plans to destabilise Syria and overthrow the Syrian government as far back as 2006. It was clear from those leaks that the plans were given to the U.S. directly from the Israeli government and were to be formalised through instigation of civil strife and sectarianism in partnership with nations such as Qatar, Turkey, Saudi Arabia, and possibly Egypt to destroy Syria's power structure so as to weaken Iran as a potential regional power and counter Hezbollah – the Party of God – the powerful political and military organisation in Lebanon consisting mainly of Shia Muslims. AIPAC, in the meantime with assistance from major donors had formed a special advocacy group with other Zionist organisations, Citizens Against a Nuclear Iran, just to reinforce its hitherto unsuccessful attempt to sink the nuclear deal with Iran.

Following the customary Jewish greetings between two long-time friends, Goldman – a grey-haired 76-year-old with a slight stoop and still somewhat breathless from what was for him a longer than usual daily walk – settled gratefully in the chair across the desk from Appelman whose calm, confident bearing and demeanour where in stark contrast to the bombastic arrogance that had become the trademark of Israeli Jewish government officials and leaders of Israeli lobby organisations. Real power and authority did not have to be boastfully flaunted to be effective. Appelman was confident in the knowledge that with a single phone call he could within minutes have virtually any lawmaker on Capitol Hill scurrying around and loudly extolling the virtues of Israel as a democracy; as the staunchest ally of the U.S.; and as a partner in the war on terror which incidentally, the U.S. and Israel had created as justification for endless conflicts resulting in untold death and destruction. Appelman wasted no time on small talk and opened the discussion by venturing the opinion that the Third Temple was "under siege like never before." It was a reference to both the state of Israel and plans for the building of a Jewish Temple on the site of the Islamic Dome of the Rock.

"Not for the first time, and wont be the last," Goldman said in his still unmistakable vowel shifting South African accent, "but now we are a force that can't be pushed around anymore." His tone was aggressive and determined.

Appelman nodded his head in acknowledgement of that

fact, "that may be, but the complaints and reports of discontent now reaching us are from the Jewish community," he said, adding that if such growing discontent was not nipped in the bud, then AIPAC'S funding could gradually dry up because as the current major "Zionaire" donors – of whom the richest were well advanced in years – passed on, they would not be easily replaced from a newer generation of potential donors that was disillusioned with Israel.

Goldman peered over his spectacles. "Do you really think that will be a problem?"

"It already is … Generating support for Israel amongst the Jewish community, and the young in particular, is becoming far more difficult if not virtually impossible," Appelman said and backed up his assertion by pointing out that the negative trend amongst the young had also been noticed by the Birthright organisation – with its renowned travel-program-cum-dating-service – which was considering a decision to no longer offer trips to Israel for young Jewish people because given the rightward and patently racist reality in Israel, they could no longer conduct trips that would present the country in the most flattering and positive light. Birthright had definitely established that many young Jewish Americans – after years of exposure to Jewish educational programs – had a better opinion of Israel prior to their visits which only served to put them off once they saw what it was really like. Birthright had therefore concluded that in order to build support for Israel, it would be best to leave it to young people's imagination with U.S.-based programs that offered participants an immersive exploration of Israeli history, politics and culture through screenings of the films like *Exodus* and *You Don't Mess with the Zohan*. Even those Jews who had been brainwashed into unconditionally supporting Israel, were starting to have openly expressed misgivings over the Israeli government which was becoming an embarrassment to American Jews who were showing increasing reluctance to continue lending their support to a Jewish state with a ruthless rightwing Zionist Apartheid Ideology.

"So, we've had some setbacks recently but … "

"But nothing," Appelman interrupted, "a report by a leading polling agency has just revealed that support for Palestinians is growing among young, progressive Americans. Between 2006 and July 2014 the number of those expressing support for the Palestinians has risen from nine percent to 20 percent with more than one-quarter, 27 percent, currently supporting the Palestinians."

"Okay, but I still have faith in our network of Zionist organisations with their effective control of the media. The tide can still be turned in our favour."

"Which brings us to two other concerns of mine," Appelman said and proceeded to point out that with regards to the Zionist network support, some prominent American Zionist organisation leaders had already openly expressed disillusion with one in particular stating that Israel had failed in every important way with the Zionist dream having curdled into Jewish selfishness. As a lifelong supporter of Israel, that leader now believed that Israel had since its foundation spiralled into a society of occupation and Jewish particularism where the concept of *"Tikkun olam"* or "world repair" – connoting social action and the pursuit of social justice with the phrase having its origin in classical rabbinic literature and in Lurianic Kabbalah, a major strand of Jewish mysticism originating with the work of the 16th-century Kabbalist Isaac Luria – had deteriorated into political, spiritual and religious failure with Israel having discarded the rational, the universal and the visionary. He felt that such values had been replaced by a brutal and iron-fisted occupation, unconditional materialism, and severe inequalities exceeding the worst to be found in the Western world. Furthermore, the original vision had been distorted by a fanaticism, obscurantism, and religious fundamentalism that encouraged the worst possible behaviour instead of the best.

"I understand where you're coming from," Goldman conceded, "a few weeks ago I lunched with a board member of the the Jewish People Policy Institute. They're completing a study to be published next summer which more or less confirms what you're saying." According to Goldman the main points established by the study were that a majority of diaspora Jews doubted Israel's sincerity in wishing to reach a peace settlement with the Palestinians; that only a few believed Israel was serious in its attempts to achieve peace; that many were unconvinced Israel was doing enough to avoid military conflicts and substantial civilian casualties; that diaspora Jews were generally finding it more difficult to continue supporting Israel when faced with accusations that Israel was using unreasonable and disproportionate force; that there was a feeling that Israel's conduct, which they wanted stopped, was reflecting badly on Jews; and that in return for their support, they wanted to have a greater say in how Israel conducted its affairs.

"I'll take that as confirmation of my first concern," Appelman said. "The second is that time is fast approaching when Israel, its lobby groups, and supporters will find it increasingly difficult to control the mainstream's political discourse." He went on to remind Goldman that as the older generation aged and passed away – that is the generation that grew up without the benefit of computers and the internet and instead relied primarily on the mainstream media for its news – it would be replaced by a younger generation accustomed to getting information and news from the internet and social media. That was a significant factor because according to recent surveys, 70 percent of Americans disagreed with the statement that the media "tries to report the news without bias." It had also been established that trust in the media had dropped by 17 percentage points since the previous year, and by 22 percentage points since 2013. Confidence in the media was lowest – just

7 percent– among those aged 18 to 29. Appleton stressed that in the not too distant future those listening to, and reading the mainstream media propaganda would be outnumbered by those using the internet. Such distrust could also take root in Israel and encourage human rights activists, the Israeli peace groups, and joint Israeli-Palestinian peace organisations.

"We're aware of that, and that's why a bill in the Knesset targeting groups who campaign for Palestinian human rights has just passed its first hurdle in the process of becoming law." Goldman said by way of reassurance, adding that the proposed legislation would compel non-governmental organisations (NGOs) to officially declare any funding from overseas including donations by EU countries. The legislation would only apply to leftwing Israeli organisations and not rightwing NGOs, which were supported by private donations from wealthy supporters of Israel. Despite opposition from some MPs who described the politically sectarian nature of the legislation as "political persecution" that would erode Israeli democracy, Israel's rightwing justice minister claimed that it would boost transparency as the government sought to prevent foreign interference and attempts to delegitimise the state of Israel.

Furthermore, according to Goldman, a coordinated campaign – involving the government, Knesset members, the police, various semiautonomous right-wing groups, and the media – was now behind politically driven harassment, illegal and violent arrests, denial of legal support during interrogations, malicious incitements, smear campaigns, and even death threats issued by proxy against members of such pro-Palestinian activist organisations which the Israeli right had always regarded as treasonous. While in the past such sinister and ruthless tactics had been restricted for use against Palestinians, they would now also be employed against Jewish members of the Israeli left so as to create a palpable sense of danger that would discourage activism and impede freedom of action. An initial clause in the bill requiring representatives of left-wing organisations that received foreign funding to wear identity badges whenever they entered the Knesset or other public places was, however, quashed because of the obvious similarity to the badges that Jews were forced to wear in public by the Nazis.

The two main organisations being targeted by this government led McCarthyist campaign were B'Tselem, which was most prominent and effective in advocating human rights, and Breaking the Silence, which specialised in documenting soldiers' firsthand testimony about what they had done and witnessed in Gaza and the occupied territories. The government's invective and threats had also extended into the shadowy world of clandestine operations with right-wing spies and moles infiltrating human rights and peace organisations with a view to discovering incriminating documents. The governments campaign would in effect transform the human rights and peace activists from simply being protestors – theoretically protected by law – into being dissidents with subversive views whom the government could legitimately prevent from supporting the principles of democracy.

"That's another concern," an increasingly exasperated Appelman said, "and this kind of government descent into unmasked, right wing extremism is not helping any. You now have cabinet ministers calling for the death of Palestinian mothers because they give birth to 'little snakes' and the prime minister claiming that there will never be a Palestinian state while he's around. He has become a rabid dog that must be muzzled."

"But it's what most Israelis want to hear," Goldman said almost apologetically.

"That may be," Appelman paused with a shake of the head before continuing. "We used to be perceived as the 'good guys' but now we're inviting censure by lashing out and being mad at everyone." He added that in the last few months alone Israel had quarrelled with Spain over arrest warrants issued for the Israeli Prime Minister and six other Israeli officials for the 2010 attack on the Gaza Freedom Flotilla; had attacked college campus student groups supporting the BDS movement; had vilified academic associations for issuing calls for academic boycotts of Israeli universities; had remonstrated with Brazil over its refusal to recognise an Israeli ambassador who hailed from the right-wing Israeli settler movement; had suspended contact with European Union bodies because of EU requirements for the labelling of products from Israeli settlements; had accused the UN Secretary General of stoking Palestinian terrorism over his criticism of the illegal settlement building; and was continuing to condemn Sweden over comments by its foreign minister – by accusing her of "ignorance and arrogance" with the suggestion that she might meet a violent end – who had called for an investigation into the extrajudicial Israeli executions of Palestinians.

"I'll admit there's been some bad press." Goldman said.

"Bad press!" Appleman exclaimed with astonishment, "we claim to be the civilised peacemakers not the murderous savages. For decades we've played for time with the pretence of peace talks leading to a two state solution and then suddenly this fascist cretin tells the whole world there isn't going to be one. How in hell are you going to get back the support of those Jews who have been alienated by what they are currently hearing, reading, and seeing?"

Goldman's lips took the form of an artful sneer. "No problem at all," he said dismissively, "we just have to make sure Jews everywhere feel victimised and threatened. We have to make them believe that only in Israel will they be safe."

"But that's what you've been doing from the start."

"And must continue doing at all costs," Goldman said with

the added explanation that while the gradual appropriation of more Palestinian land was essential for a Greater Israel, such land would be of little use without an influx of more Jewish immigrants to populate and possess it. Though he acknowledged that the concept of "making Aliyah" by moving to the Land of Israel – one of Zionism's most basic tenets – was being aggressively promoted by the Jewish Agency for Israel with the country's Law of Return making it easy for American and European Jews to regard Israel as their "homeland," Goldman nonetheless felt much more had to be done.

"Like what?" Appelman asked.

Goldman replied that while pro-Israel efforts in America were much appreciated such as for example the Jewish gambling magnate holding a meeting at his Las Vegas casino with fellow pro-Israel billionaires and activists to discuss combatting the growing university campus movement here and in Europe to boycott Israel; and AIPAC's push for legislation that penalised international participation in the BDS campaign; he nonetheless felt any problems Israel may have could easily be countered with more "Islamic" attacks in the West so as to focus the public's attention on Islamic terrorism.

"False flags?"

"That and continued pressure for legislation to oppose BDS like in Britain where we've secured the current government's full commitment to improving and protecting its ties with Israel." Goldman added that apart from reneging on its long-held policy positions on illegal Israeli settlements and the two-state solution, and quashing criticism of Israel while working to undermine the effectiveness of the BDS campaign against Israeli organisations and products considered complicit in the occupation, Britain had also increased levels of technological and scientific cooperation with investment and trade amounting to $7 billion annually.

"And in Israel?" Appleton asked.

Goldman replied that the government was stepping up its efforts to censor criticism of Israel by having the internet and social media "policed" by Zionist watchdog organisations including the Zionist Federation of Australia; the Britain Israel Communications and Research Centre (BICOM); the Centre for Israel and Jewish Affairs (CIJA) in Canada; the Conseil Representatif des Institutions Juives de France (CRIF) in France; and the Zionist Federation of New Zealand.

"Good," Appelman said, "they must also call on European governments to enact legislation that while appearing to be for the purpose of protecting Jews from anti-Semitism, is actually for protecting Israel from criticism."

"Exactly. France already has legislation protecting Jews by using hate crime laws to limit the French people's ability to criticise Israel." Goldman said with a beaming smile and added that a French court had recently ruled that a peaceful protest promoting the BDS campaign against Israel was illegal.

"Our Canadian friends have also had some success," Appelman said with the explanation that despite the fact Canada was imposing sanctions on 22 other countries for violations that included human rights, the Canadian Parliament by a vote of 229-51 had overwhelmingly favoured a motion stating that given Canada and Israel had shared a long history of friendship as well as economic and diplomatic relations, the House rejected the Boycott, Divestment and Sanctions (BDS) movement, which promoted the demonisation and delegitimisation of the State of Israel, and called upon the government to condemn any and all attempts by Canadian organisations, groups or individuals to promote the BDS movement, both at home and abroad. He stressed that support of this nature had to be sought from so-called democracies worldwide irrespective of any claims that freedom of speech and conscientious objections to buying products from countries contravening international law are the core values of free and democratic societies.

Goldman nodded but pointed out that the sanctions tactic that succeeded against Apartheid South Africa, would fail where Israel was concerned because Zionist parastatal organisations and faux-NGOs would continue to exploit lawfare, the illegitimate use of domestic or international law to discredit and criminalise pro-Palestinian individuals or organisations. The ploy was forcing many countries to embrace the Israeli narrative while stifling any public debate over Israeli policies.

"But will that be enough?" Appelman asked.

"Probably not. That's why we need more false flag operations." Goldman said with the added explanation that such operations were necessary to both spread and entrench Islamophobia. We have to target leading EU countries like Germany and France ... And of course Brussels. Europeans have to be riled up and filled with fear so that their governments are forced to respond to concerns about security and immigration. We also need to put the fear of God into European Jews so that when they visit their kosher restaurants or supermarkets they will fear being attacked and start believing Europe is no longer safe for them."

Appleton nodded with the reply that apart from false flag ops, Western Zionist journalists and ideologues had to persuade more of the major U.S. and European political institutions and media outlets that the Islamic terrorism was on the rise and a danger to all democracies.

"What democracies?" Goldman asked mockingly, "they tremble at the sound of our voices and obey our demands. We have replaced their democracies with our Ziocracies."

Though somewhat taken aback by Goldman's fervid triumphalism, Appelman nonetheless maintained his customary equanimity and acknowledged the achievements of wealthy Zionist individuals and organisations who had worked tirelessly to create political and social environments wherein it was virtually impossible for anyone to safely criticise Israel for its actions with most people either completely shutting up or self-censoring their comments about Israel's blockade and occupation of Palestinian territories.

Goldman leaned forward in his chair. "Even when confronted with our recent assault on Gaza, the world was easily forced to look the other way and move on." He supposed that this was because all Jewish organisations overseas had worked in unison to ensure that business, professional, and university group members frowned upon and demanded dismissal of colleagues who supported free speech and assembly by critics of Israel. The flames of anti-Muslim and anti-Arab rhetoric had been stoked to such an extent that criticism of Islam had become mandatory within the mainstream media whose journalists were leashed and muzzled with regards to commenting on Israel.

"The main problem now," Appelman said, "is not our anti-Semitic enemies but those Jews with troubled consciences."

"Maybe, but we're always going to have our fair share of Jewish bleeding-heart liberal dreamers who think a Jewish state should hold the moral high ground," Goldman said, but then pointed out that the the Jewish moral high ground was an illusion because Israel, like any other settler-colonial state, was guilty of crimes against humanity that were about as immoral as you could get. He thought that the apparent rise in diaspora Jewish concern was a load of bullshit because Israel's conduct hadn't just recently gotten worse. It had been consistently brutal from day one because throughout history the success of any settler-colonialism had always been dependent on suppression and displacement of indigenous populations. This was a fact that liberal diaspora Jews had either been blissfully unaware of, or had deliberately remained in denial about so as to avoid facing the reality of Israel not being a shining God chosen democracy, but rather a rapacious, racist state universally reviled for its treatment of Palestinians. Being reviled was an essential asset, because without it, Israel would be deprived of its ultimate and most terrifying deterrent to criticism: the ability to label such revulsion as being anti-Semitic.

This was not entirely what Appelman hoped to hear and he was momentarily lost for words. The best he could muster was to ask, "so what are you saying, exactly?"

"I'm saying that most Jews in diaspora have been duped about Israel's true nature, and even those that had not, had learnt that awkward realities about Israel can be neutralised by reminders of the Holocaust. Even the dumbest amongst us knows that the idea of 'a land without a people, for a people without a land,' was nonsense because of Palestinian presence in Palestine. Despite that Zionism had still managed to create Jewish state where Jews as a people, and Judaism as a religion, were incidental but essential pawns for the success of Zionism."

Though recognising that most of what Goldman had said was true, Appelman was still plagued with doubt and reiterated his concern. "I'm still worried that this new trend amongst diaspora Jews with a conscience will cause a split between them and Israel ... You must understand there is difference between the ordinary diaspora Jews and those Jews who actually hold all the financial and political power." He elaborated by adding that while Israel's treatment of the Palestinians – whose land had from the beginning been forcibly appropriated – was reprehensible in the eyes of many, a well-organised *hasbara* had so far managed to deflect criticism and implant the idea that Palestinians/Arabs/Muslims were all terrorists intent on destroying the legitimately established and peace-seeking democratic state of Israel. The perception of Jews being the "innocent" victims was no longer being blindly accepted because of Israel's highhanded arrogance and contemptuous conduct in international affairs which was drawing unwelcome attention to the channels of Jewish political influence and financial power that impelled major world governments to support and act as mere puppets on the jewish state's behalf. Israeli Jews had to be mindful of this fact and recognise the importance of not allowing their inherent supremacist arrogance to highlight the criminality of the occupation with its policy of ethnic cleansing.

"I hear what you are saying," Goldman said.

It was also Appelman's belief that while the average diaspora Jew was not necessarily being directly affected by a closer global scrutiny of Israel's brazen conduct, financially and politically powerful Jews with global agendas regarded such conduct as a threat to both themselves and the empires they had built by virtue of having hijacked control of most world economies. Jewish possession of such covert control was now being threatened by closer public scrutiny as a result of recent Israeli actions and conduct. Consequently a daring and dramatic response was necessary – apart from combatting, controlling, and criminalising criticism of Israel whether in public forums, the media, or on the internet – to preserve the established status quo.

"That's being done already," Goldman said because Israel would soon be starting to escalate its campaign to unprecedented levels with $26 million being allocated to attack and sabotage global human rights movements including BDS. A number of Israeli tech companies would be unleashing a worldwide wave of cyber-attacks with sly algorithms to restrict the activists' online circle of influence. This would also include forensic intelligence gathering with detection of digital or semantic signatures buried in activists' coding so that their online activity could be tracked and restricted. Such acts of sabotage would be accompanied by a torrent of material promoting a more positive perception of Israel. The non-profit organisation Firewall Israel – which encouraged activists and thinkers to join cyber and technology experts to build a network and design tech tools to combat the delegitimisation of Israel – would be sponsored by the government-linked Reut Institute, a think tank whose objective was to build an online platform to assist pro-Israel activists around the world to inform about anti-Israel activism in their communities. On another front, efforts were also being increased to heighten the global paranoia over terrorism by having Israeli agents at the UN supplying misleading intelligence reports for the forthcoming "Nuclear Terrorism" Summit. The reports – as had been the case with the doctored intelligence about Iraq's weapons of mass destruction – would suggest that terrorists had the means, knowledge and information to create a nuclear bomb.

"But that still doesn't address the fact that past achievements have led to a swaggering sense of invincibility that must be avoided because it is costing us friends and influence. Israel's agenda has to be deployed quietly, without bravado, without chutzpah. Our prolonging peace negotiations for a two-state solution to gain time for more settlement construction will no longer be effective if we have Israeli leaders boasting that there will never be a Palestinian state."

"Good point. I'll report back with that."

"The real danger is not just a split between diaspora Jews and Israel, but the potential isolation of Israel." Appleton said, adding that despite EU and U.S. support – including billions of dollars in aid; political protection against sanctions; and high levels of academic, cultural, economic, and military cooperation – boycott campaigns led by the BDS movement were causing Israel to become more isolated at the grassroots level with its support increasingly coming from ultra-right, anti-immigrant, overtly racist, and Islamophobic movements and governments. AIPAC's push for Congressional legislation targeting boycotts would be passed in due course. But in the meantime all the stops had to be pulled out to influence countries like France to portray BDS as anti-Semitic and illegal; to persuade the British government to undermine BDS support within its trade unions, local government councils, university campuses, and non-governmental organisations and institutions. The entire Jewish lobby and world Zionist network had to use the lawfare crusade to discredit BDS and apply pressure to have it silenced and criminalised.

"We're already on it," Goldman said, "but right now there is Knesset concern about the Iran nuclear negotiations and it's an agreement that has to be prevented at any cost."

Appelman responded by assuring his friend that everything was being done to prevent such an agreement with an all-out, multi-pronged effort that involved not only AIPAC'S 100,000 members, but also AIPAC and the Republican Jewish Committee which were preparing to spend over $40 million on advertising designed to kill any possibility of an Iran deal. The advertisements would target the home districts of Congressmen whose votes could be a key in overriding a presidential veto of a legislative effort to scuttle the agreement. Appelman added that the AIPAC-backed nonprofit Citizens for a Nuclear Free Iran had so far raised some $30 million for advertisements in 40 states; that calls would be made and emails sent by activists to their congressional representatives; that Israel's Ambassador to Washington would be briefing and urging conservative Republicans and leading Democrats to kill any possibility of an agreement; that steps had already been taken to keep the Chairman of the Senate Foreign Relations Committee onside: that a pledge had been obtained from the Republican House speaker to do whatever he could do stop a deal; that even if a deal were reached, some of AIPAC's most dedicated members would descend on Washington to protest against congressional approval; that plans for next summer were already being made to take all members of Congress, apart from a few freshman, to Israel; and that by next spring a $100 million war chest would be available to fight congressional approval of any agreement.

"The real danger of an agreement," Goldman said, "is that apart from easing the tensions with Iranians and depriving us of an excuse to bomb the hell out of them, to push for regime change, and to demand more American aid, is that people everywhere will start thinking that diplomacy in the Middle East can be an alternative to war."

"I agree. The last thing we need right now is regional peace and harmony between Islam's Sunnis and Shiites. It would compromise our strategy of constant Middle East conflict as a distraction from our building of more Jewish settlements."

After having discussed the Iran nuclear negotiations, it was a logical progression for Appelman and Goldman to address Israel's covert alliance of shared interests with Saudi Arabia which had recently intensified as a consequence of their mutual distrust of, and opposition to Iran becoming a dominant regional power. Saudi Arabia which – with its strategic location, religious significance and oil riches – could have burgeoned into one of the world's more notable powers, had instead become preoccupied with preventing the democratisation of its Arab neighbours which it rightly regarded as a threat to its own autocratic system of governance.

Despite many years of sanctions, Iran – which in recent history had never invaded a neighbouring country – was militarily superior, more sophisticated strategically, and fast becoming more influential across the region. Saudi Arabia on the other hand, had suffered a series of setbacks including the U.S. President's determination – despite bitter and strident Israeli and Saudi Arabian opposition – to sign a nuclear deal with Iran; its request for assistance in the Yemen war being refused by a vote in Pakistan's parliament; and Russia's escalated involvement in Syria where after almost collapsing against a Sunni coalition, the Alawite Syrian regime was now being backed by a powerful nuclear power. Consequently as Saudi Arabia became more isolated with fewer friends and political policy options, its only port of refuge was Israel.

During the past half century, Saudi Arabia with its vast oil wealth had endeavoured – through expensive law firms and public relations experts – to establish a lobby in the U.S. that could compete with that of Israel. But despite that, and their exploitation of personal connections to powerful families like the Bushes, the Saudis failed to even come close to establishing the level of organised political influence that Israel and its American supporters enjoyed in Washington. American legislators, academic institutions, and non-governmental organisations who did accept the Saudi riyal were inevitably attacked as Arab surrogates by the already powerful Israel Lobby which made the political cost of benefitting from Saudi generosity too high a risk for most people and organisations.

The Saudis, however, soon realised that Israel could provide an alternative route to buying influence in the U.S. and had accordingly over the past few years funnelled some $16 billion through a third party Arab country into an Israeli "development" account in Europe to assist finance Israeli infrastructure projects and the building of settlements in the West Bank. For the Saudis it was a case of if you can't beat them, buy them, so that Israel played the leading role in enlisting U.S. Congressional opposition – something Israel would have done anyway – to an international nuclear agreement with the Iran.

By being allied with the U.S. and Saudi Arabia in the real "axis of Evil" – with assistance from Turkey whose increasingly authoritarian Sunni Islamist government was still brutally suppressing Kurdish aspirations for self-determination – Israel was not only getting its two allies to help achieve its goals, but was also charging them exorbitantly for the privilege. If the Israelis and Saudis were successful in wrecking the negotiations with Iran, then the door would be open to various possibilities including more punitive sanctions against the Iranians; the granting of Saudi permission for Israeli fighter aircraft to overfly Saudi airspace for bombing raids on Iran; and persuading the war addicted and seriously psychotic U.S. to take part in inflicting even more destruction on the Iranians.

Appelman and Goldman were agreed that if despite all efforts to sabotage the Iran nuclear negotiations, an agreement was reached and signed, then AIPAC would have to assist in ensuring the U.S. would compensate Israel by substantially increasing its annual financial aid by at least a billion dollars; would accept responsibility to finance further development of Israel's Iron Dome anti-missile system; and to replenish Israel's supply of missiles which had been seriously depleted during the summer's military assault on the Gaza. Goldman also emphasised that in the current political climate, Israel had to wage war on all fronts with every means at its disposal including false flag terrorist operations that would fan the flames Islamophobia in the West. He finished off by assuring Appelman with a mischievous wink, "don't worry my friend … and I tell you this in the strictest confidence, come New Year, there's gonna be some fireworks in Europe."

15

Tuesday, 22 December

UNHCR, Geneva, Switzerland

The United Nations High Commissioner for Refugees June *Global Trends Report*: *World at War,* had stated that wars, conflict and persecution had forced the most people ever since records began to flee their homes to seek refuge and safety elsewhere with worldwide forcible displacement at a staggering 59.5 million for 2014 compared to 51.2 million a year earlier and 37.5 million a decade ago. Syria was the world's biggest producer of both internally displaced people (7.6 million) and refugees (3.88 million), but most alarmingly, half of all refugees were children of whom 50 percent were out of school. Conflict in Ukraine, a record 219,000 Mediterranean crossings, and the large number of Syrian refugees in Turkey – which in 2014 became the world's top refugee-hosting nation with 1.59 million Syrian refugees at year's end – brought increased public attention, both positive and negative, as to what to do with refugees and highlighted the failure of the world's most powerful political and religious leaders to end wars.

The UNHCR was currently in the process of collating information for its next report – based on data from governments, partner agencies and UNHCR's own tracking of forced displacement – confirming that by the end of 2015 more than 65 million people will have been displaced. If measured against the world's population of 7.4 billion people, this would mean that one in every 113 people globally is now either an asylum-seeker, internally displaced or a refugee at a risk level for which UNHCR had known no precedent. One of the most visible consequences of the world's conflicts and the horrendous hardships they imposed on people had been the dramatic increase in the number of refugees seeking safety through hazardous sea journeys across the Mediterranean with the hope of reaching Europe where those who make it – without capsizing and drowning – were dealt with like criminals who would invariably be fingerprinted; numbered on their wrists or arms with permanent marker pens; and detained in accordance with EU laws that allow refugees to be locked up for 18 months without a criminal conviction.

According to some reports, ISIS was planning to instigate a flood of 500,000 migrants into Europe as a form of psychological warfare. They also wanted to use the movement of peoples to bring several thousand of their followers into Europe's communities. Whether or not such reports were accurate, was irrelevant because the possibility of ISIS entering Europe along with the thousands of migrants who were mostly Muslim had come to be regarded as a real threat and had both encouraged fever pitch xenophobic attitudes amongst Europeans, and boosted support for far-right political parties and nationalist movements which suited Israel's purpose of gaining European toleration of its treatment of Palestinians through the spread of Islamophobia.

Apart from UNHCR reports, several articles – of the type that the freedom-of-speech-loving and journalistic-standards-upholding mainstream media avoids like the plague – by reputable writers had also appeared that addressed Zionist Israeli efforts to redraw the Middle East to suit its Colonisation of Palestinian territories. According to *The Washington Report on Middle East Affairs,* for example, the American Zionist Council had between 1978 and 2014 paid a total of $56.73 million to ensure the selection of its approved congressional candidates

– who were more interested in luxury holidays in Israel rather than in American freedom, justice, civil rights and the public they were supposed to represent – in order that the House of Representatives and the Senate would support Israel's Zionist agenda including the illegal colonisation of the Occupied West Bank.

Such illegal colonisation was and still is a basic Zionist objective to eradicate Palestine from the map – with pressure on Google Maps to do so – both as a political entity and as a basis for nationality so that today more than half of Palestinians were in effect considered as being stateless persons. Furthermore, institutional discrimination against Palestinian refugees in Arab countries had devastated the lives and well-being of entire Palestinian communities whose legal status, residency and civil rights have become increasingly uncertain, particularly in Lebanon and Egypt where they are denied rights to secure residency, employment, property, communal interaction and family unification. Procedures to allow non-residents to apply for naturalisation in Lebanon, Egypt and Saudi Arabia do not apply to stateless Palestinians. Palestinian refugees in Jordan – the largest community in any of the host countries – have Jordanian nationality but are denied equal political participation while being subjected to not so subtle forms of discrimination. Jordanian authorities have refused to offer naturalisation to those Palestinians who at the time of their displacement in 1967 did not hold Jordanian passports with most of them being denied any civil rights and confined to refugee camps.

The right to having a nationality is a fundamental human right with Article 15 of the Universal Declaration of Human Rights of 1948 declaring that "everyone has the right to a nationality" from which other rights and entitlements follow including education, medical care, work, property ownership, travel, and state protection: all of which means full participation in a world composed of nation states. Consequently changing the status of people to non-citizens or threatening the security of their residency status without due regard for the rule of law generates insecurity with devastating long-term social and psychological effects.

Stateless persons are the first to be in the line of fire whenever political uncertainty and chaos occur in the countries in which they happen to be. Without access to education or employment, stateless people become vulnerable to political manipulation, exploitation and poverty. The costly effect on host countries, the region and the world is monumental with impoverished and marginalised and stateless refugees – especially the Palestinians – constituting a major destabilising factor. Being stateless without the right to return to their country has been at the very core of the Palestinian refugee problem and it could be justifiably argued that the fact of being stateless was more deleterious than being a refugee. Earl Warren, who served as chief justice on the US supreme court, regarded statelessness as being "the total destruction of an individual's status in organised society." It should be remembered that even in East Jerusalem, the Palestinian people are stateless.

Mamilla, West Jerusalem

Conrad and Freya had spent the previous night in bed anxiously tossing and turning before eventually dozing fitfully until this morning. Despite a room service breakfast with lots of black coffee for their hangovers, they were both still numbed by the trauma of witnessing Sami's coldblooded murder; the ordeal of their arrest and interrogation by the Israeli police; and the subsequent tribulation of going with Adam Peltz to Silwan to break the tragic news to Sami's family. It had all been a rather harrowing experience from which they would require time to recover. To begin with there had been the difficulty of finding Sami's house which was located near one of the Jewish enclaves

– taken over by Israeli settlers accompanied by police who had attacked, pepper sprayed, and forcibly evicted at least a dozen Palestinian residents – which was part of the Judaisation of East Jerusalem by right-wing Israeli settler organisations such as the Ir David Foundation, Ateret Cohanim, and the Israeli Land Fund. Part of that Judaisation included eviction orders by Israeli courts against Palestinian families; the refusal of building permits for Palestinians while permitting Jewish construction for settlement expansion; and the Israel Land Fund's mission to enable all Jews – even those who are not Israeli citizens – to own a part of Israel so that "Jewish land" could once again be reclaimed and in Jewish hands. The denial of land or property sales to Palestinians had also been justified on religious grounds by invoking the Torah wherein it is apparently written that Jews cannot sell property to non-Jews.

Conrad and Freya had felt a helpless outrage at what was a deliberate execution justified by what must have been the subsequent staged planting of the knife next to Sami's body. They were positive the knife had been planted because Sami had been thoroughly searched at the Damascus Gate and had then remained with them constantly without having any opportunity to get hold of any kind of weapon. Apart from that, they were certain that he was not the kind of person who would resort to such desperate measures while knowing full well that his incarceration or death would leave his family destitute.

Being witness to the outpouring of grief from Miriam Hadawi and her children over Sami's violent death, had been particularly painful for them because understandably they – being the reason for Sami's presence in Al-Qattanin Street – felt somehow responsible. They had spent several hours with the grieving family in their hour of need by consoling them with repeated assurances that they would do everything to help and would come to see them again on their return after Christmas from Bethlehem where they had already made and paid for a hotel reservation. Initially Miriam had refused to accept the 700 shekels in cash which the three of them happened to have on them – perhaps regarding the offer as being "blood money" – but was eventually persuaded to take the cash for the sake of the children who would now more than ever require looking after.

While it was natural for Miriam to want to view Sami's body and make arrangements for his burial, it was agreed that Peltz would make enquiries on the family's behalf because it was a well known fact that Israel – as part of its punitive measures to make life as difficult as possible for Palestinians – invariably refused to release bodies of Palestinians killed with some families not being able to bury their dead for periods of up to a year or more.

One of Miriam's main concerns, however, was that the Israelis would use the lie – of Sami being a potential attacker armed with a knife – as an excuse to demolish their home. It was a standard procedure for Israeli forces to carry out demolitions – declared legal by Israeli courts despite international criticism – of homes belonging to the families of those whom the state suspected of terrorist activities. The arbitrary nature of this wanton vandalism dated back to the 1945 British Mandate emergency regulation in pre-state Palestine that permitted the British military to confiscate and destroy any home used to discharge a weapon, or any home used by someone who violated military law.

Peltz had assured Miriam that he would contact both the Jerusalem Human Rights Legal Aid and the Israelis Against House Demolitions organisation with the latter having been established to resist the destruction of Palestinian Homes in the Occupied Territories by Israel whose punitive demolitions had become one of the hallmarks of its punishments for Palestinians. The organisation had stressed that such attacks were not only a pointless lashing out against defenceless civilian families, but also positively counterproductive. Since its unprovoked attack and land grab in 1967, Israel had demolished some 50,000 Palestinian homes in the Occupied Palestinian Territories either as "collateral damage" during military operations, or because of Israel's racist refusal to grant building permits to Palestinians, who then being forced to build "illegally," inevitably faced having their buildings demolished. In virtually all of the cases involved, "security" was not the reason for demolition as confirmed by the fact that none of the owners were ever arrested or charged.

After reluctantly leaving the heartbroken Hadawis with the promise of further contact the following day, they had returned to the hotel where Peltz joined them for some much required alcohol induced solace in the hotel bar. As they had thankfully sank back in the comfort of their armchairs with their drinks, the topic of conversation inevitably focused on Israel's recent run of unrestrained indulgence in extrajudicial killings.

While with naked chutzpah and unashamed hypocrisy Israel had repeatedly proclaimed itself a democracy, the irrefutable reality was – for anyone bothering to refer to historical facts and scholarly commentary beyond the misleading mainstream media headlines – far different with daily occurrences of Palestinians being arbitrarily detained or extrajudicially killed. Furthermore the concept a two-state solution leading to Palestinian self-determination was fast becoming an impossibility because of Israel's creeping annexation of Palestinian land by means of a barbarous occupation that entrenched Apartheid as part of the hard-right Zionist vision of Israel – firmly embedded within the ranks of a rightwing government pandering to the whims of an Ultra-Nationalist Settler Movement – which viewed the occupied Palestinian West Bank as the biblical Judea and Samaria.

The arbitrary demolitions of Palestinian homes in occupied East Jerusalem; the expropriation of large tracts of land in the

Jordan valley; the repeated destruction of Palestinian Bedouin villages; the rampant expansion of illegal Jewish settlements; and the revocation of residence permits of Jerusalem Palestinians, were all part of a much larger game plan to displace Palestinians and disrupt neighbouring countries in keeping with the Yinon Plan:

> "The plan operates on two essential premises. To survive, Israel must 1) become an imperial regional power, and 2) must effect the division of the whole area into small states by the dissolution of all existing Arab states. Small here will depend on the ethnic or sectarian composition of each state. Consequently, the Zionist hope is that sectarian-based states become Israel's satellites and, ironically, its source of moral legitimation … This is not a new idea, nor does it surface for the first time in Zionist strategic thinking. Indeed, fragmenting all Arab states into smaller units has been a recurrent theme."

As the three friends – numbed by the tragedy of Sami's murder – sipped their drinks and discussed the situation, they agreed that Israel's realisation of its plans could not have been possible without the amoral indifference of the U.S. and the EU who while constantly espousing the merits of democracy for all humanity, had with timorous regularity tolerated Israel's extensive violations of international law with arrogant impunity.

"The the illegality of the killings is bad enough," Peltz said with genuine concern, but what really disturbed him was that a recent Democracy Institute survey had found that 53 percent of Israelis supported the on the spot extrajudicial killings of alleged Palestinian attackers even after they had been arrested and posed no threat whatsoever. State involvement in such murders had been confirmed some years earlier by an Israeli journalist – subsequently arrested – who during her military service had copied secret documents showing that undercover Israeli agents were conducting targeted assassinations of non-combatant

Palestinian political opponents. They would plan the killings months ahead and then pass them off as "accidents" during "bungled" operations to arrest them.

"I remember reading about that," Conrad said, "another journalist who covered the story had to go into self-imposed exile to avoid being questioned by Shin Bet."

"That's right. He fled to London. And as for our claim to having a vibrant national discourse and a free press, an Israeli court ordered the media not to publish or broadcast anything about the allegations."

"Who was it that said truth is the enemy of the state?" Freya asked.

"It's attributed to Goebbels," Conrad obliged, "but whoever said it, it's still very true of Israel."

"And whenever faced with unpleasant truth," Peltz confirmed, "they denounce the source as being anti-Semitic. Or as in my case, a self-hating Jew and a traitor."

"Just as they're doing now to the Swedish Foreign Minister," Freya added, "all she said was that Israel's extrajudicial killings should be investigated."

"Seems to me," Conrad said, "that Israel was established with a persecution complex belief that all non-Jews want to delegitimise and destroy it."

Peltz nodded in agreement. "And unfortunately that complex has become the excuse for undermining democracy, imposing Apartheid, and committing appalling crimes against the Palestinians."

Mention of the appalling crimes led to Freya asking why the West and its leaders continually failed to condemn Israel's atrocities, while showing no hesitation in condemning much lesser crimes committed by other regimes. Peltz explained that the problem was substantially more complex than was appreciated by either the casual observer or the better informed political aficionado. While it was true that Western governments led by the U.S. were reluctant to pressurise Israel into ending its defiance of international law and crimes against humanity because of certain entrenched fears – they feared loss of election campaign funding, feared losing the Jewish swing vote, and feared being deluged with wild and unfounded accusations of anti-Semitism – the main reason was perhaps their subliminal fear that if the Israelis with their nuclear weapons were pushed to a point that was unacceptable to their Zionist ideology of a Greater Israel for Jews only, then its deluded, psychotic, and Hitleresque leaders would resort to using nuclear weapons.

"Are they really that mad?" A dismayed Freya asked.

"Afraid so." Peltz said with a hint of regret and shame that obliged him to elaborate on his laconic reply. He began with the fact that following the start of the October 6, 1973 Yom Kippur War when the Israelis were suffering the worst defeat in their history, Prime Minister Golda Meir and her top aides took the decision to place eight nuclear armed F-14s at Tel Nof Airbase on 24-hour alert and to make operational as many nuclear missile launchers as possible at the Sodot Mikha Airbase. While that nuclear alert was intended as a precaution to be activated if necessary, it also served to pressure the Soviet Union into restraining the Arab offensive and to blackmail U.S. President "Tricky Dick" Nixon into initiating Operation Nickel Grass which included 567 missions to airlift 22,000 tons of munitions with a further 90,000 tons being delivered by sea thereby enhancing Israel's ability to stem enemy advances.

Peltz pointed out that Israel's first mention of an official policy on the use of nuclear weapons occurred in 1966 and was based on four "line in the sand" situations that could provoke an Israeli nuclear response including a successful military penetration into populated areas within Israel's post-1949 (pre1967) borders; the destruction of the Israeli Air Force; the exposure of Israeli cities to massive and devastating air attacks, or to possible chemical or biological attacks; and the use of nuclear weapons against Israeli territory. This policy was reinforced by the Menachem Begin doctrine – regarding their potential enemies' capability to possess weapons of mass destruction – following Israel's preemptive Operation Opera attack on Iraq's Osirak nuclear reactor in June 1981.

While the concept of Mutual Assured Destruction (MAD) – a theory of deterrence in which the full-scale use of nuclear weapons by two or more opposing sides would annihilate both the attackers and the defenders – had so far prevented superpower nuclear wars because the incentive to initiate a conflict or to disarm had been removed, such means of deterrence would not be applicable in the Middle East because Israel – while possessing some 400 nuclear weapons and refusing to sign the Nuclear Non-Proliferation Treaty (NPT) – had steadfastly either alone or with others used diplomatic, military, and covert action initiatives to prevent other Middle East nations from acquiring nuclear weapons as had been the case with its false weapons of mass destruction alarmism regarding Iraq and Iran.

For Conrad this raised the hypothetical question of the Islamic world's reaction in the event of Israel's destruction and takeover of Haram al-Sharif/Temple Mount for construction of the Third Temple. He noted that the political leaderships of virtually all Islamic countries including the Arab ones had so far offered no more than meaningless mealy-mouthed expressions of feigned disapproval over Israel's treatment of the Palestinian people; that at the forefront of such indifference were the oil rich Gulf monarchal states such as Saudi Arabia; and that such indifference had been aided and abetted by treacherous military dictatorships as was the case in Egypt which for decades had on behalf of Israel been bought off by the U.S. with substantial annual military aid packages that AIPAC with its control of Congress always ensured Egypt received. "But what if," he asked, the majority of Muslim people themselves – with a worldwide population of some 2.1 billion – who despite their invariably corrupt governments' reluctance to act, took to the streets in their millions and insisted on the Islamic holy sites being protected in defiance of Israel's acquisitive intentions? Would Israel, in the face of such determined and overwhelming Islamic odds, use nuclear weapons to retain possession of its ill-gotten gains?

Freya, who like Conrad, had already just witnessed the murderous insanity of one Israeli had "no doubt about it," and said so emphatically.

"I wish I could say you're wrong, but I can't. Not only would our government use them, they would also have the support of most Israelis." Peltz said and cited the example of historian Benny Morris who some years earlier in an ill-considered op-ed entitled "Using Bombs to Stave Off War" in *The New York Times,* had suggested an Israeli nuclear attack on Iran was inevitable.

Conrad recalled that Morris was also "the guy who said that the only mistake the Israeli leadership made in 1948 was to not go all the way with the expulsion of the Palestinians." Morris had also expressed his belief that "something like a cage should be built for them and though it sounded terrible and was really cruel, there was no other alternative … There was a wild animal there that had to be locked up in one way or another."

Freya shook her head in disbelief. "Where does that kind of thinking come from?" She asked. "Adam, you're an Israeli. Can you please explain it to me. Is it some kind of warped and misplaced patriotism?"

A noticeably troubled Peltz considered her question carefully before answering with heartfelt emotion. "No amount of blind 'my country, right or wrong' patriotism can ever override my sense of humanity and concern for fellow human beings irrespective of their colour, ethnic origin, or religion. We Jews, wherever we are, cannot and must not ignore what is being done to the Palestinian people by simply blaming Zionism because," he paused to catch his breath, "the suppression of the Palestinian people is being committed by a Jewish state claiming to speak for and represent all Jews. If some of us don't agree with that claim, then we have a duty do everything possible to deny it. If we don't, then our silence will amount to complicity. We Jews, we cannot on the one hand accept and recognise the existence of a Jewish state, and then on the other deny involvement in its crimes. We can't have it both ways … "

Silwan, East Jerusalem

Though still feeling somewhat the worse for wear, Conrad and Freya had by about 10:30 a.m. recovered sufficiently to buy a basket of mixed fruit for Sami's family before catching a cab to Silwan. The driver agreed to wait for them during their half an hour visit to the inconsolable family for whom the stark reality of Sami's coldblooded killing was still incomprehensible. There was nothing they could say or do to alleviate the family's utter despair and when they eventually parted company for the short ride to the Dung Gate, they did so with hearts that ached over an injustice about which they could do absolutely nothing.

They arrived at, and entered through the Dung Gate shortly before midday and had to queue for half an hour to go through security for access to the wooden walkway that led to the Mughrabi Gate and Haram al-Sharif/Temple Mount. Though the walkway was littered with some discarded riot shields as evidence of the current volatile situation, it nonetheless provided them with an excellent view of the plaza below – known to Muslims as the Buraq Plaza – with its Jews praying at the Wailing Wall.

After they finished filming the animated scene and continued along the walkway, Conrad mentioned it was generally regarded as inevitable that during the coming year the Executive Committee of the United Nations Educational, Scientific and Cultural Organisation (UNESCO) would pass a resolution refusing to accept the Jewish people's connection to the Haram al-Sharif/ Temple Mount and the Western Wall; would condemn Israel for its actions in the disputed Eastern part of Jerusalem, the West Bank, Gaza Strip; would accuse it of planting fake Jewish graves inside centuries-old Muslim graveyards; would charge it with fraudulently converting many of Islamic and Roman remains into old Jewish places for praying; and would criticise its illegal measures against the freedom of worship at the Muslim religious sites of worship at the Al-Aqsa Mosque complex.

They continued along the walkway, passed through the Mughrabi Gate where the previous day some 170 extremist Israeli settlers escorted and closely protected by Israeli police and armed occupation forces – had stormed the Mosque courtyards and attacked the Palestinian worshipers who tried to protect their holy site.

Thankfully the situation was calmer today and they were met by a smiling Palestinian boy who offered – for ten shekels – to take them to a window with a view of the interior of the Al-Aqsa Mosque which of course they were not otherwise allowed to enter. It was too good an opportunity to miss and while photographing and filming the Mosque's magnificent interior, they were interrupted by one of the Al-Aqsa Mosque guards – often the subject of harassment, arrest, and kidnapping by Israeli soldiers – who sternly reprimanded them and led them away towards the steps leading up to the iconic Dome of the Rock which had so far stood in defiance of all attempts at Judaisation.

As part of that Judaisation, the Batan al-Hawa neighborhood, in the heart of Silwan, was due to be he next target for the most extensive expulsion in East Jerusalem for many years with eviction claims having been filed against more than 80 Palestinian families that have been living there for decades. Ever since Israel annexed East Jerusalem, Israeli authorities have employed discriminatory policies against the city's Palestinian residents; have employed different ploys for decreasing the number Palestinians while increasing the number of Jewish residents; and have done so with a view to achieving demographic and geographic conditions that would obstruct any future attempts to question Israeli sovereignty over East Jerusalem.

Adam Peltz had already informed them that the organisation to which he belonged intended submitting a petition to the Jerusalem District Court demanding that the Israeli state reveal the names of archaeologists who excavate in antiquities sites in the West Bank and other locations of archaeological finds, as was expected of the Israel Antiquities Authority within Israeli borders. The reason for the secrecy was that the State feared an academic boycott that would prove detrimental to the archaeologists and make it difficult for Israeli research to be continued in the Occupied Territories including excavations under Haram al-Sharif/Temple Mount.

Peltz had also mentioned a forthcoming report from the Israel State Comptroller criticising the state's management of the Old City's Historic Basin and warning of the state authorities surrendering land, antiquities, and educational responsibility to the Elad Foundation, while abandoning their functions and responsibilities by acting against the public whom they were supposed to represent and serve. Having been witness to what Israel was doing at the heart of East Jerusalem, Conrad had to agree with the assertion in one of his father's articles: *Temple Mount: A Detonator For World War III.*

800 Second Avenue, New York

The Permanent Mission of Israel to the United Nations was staffed by Israel's recently appointed Permanent Representative (the de facto Israel Ambassador to the UN), diplomats from

317

the Ministry of Foreign Affairs, civil servants, and intelligence officers from Mossad working under diplomatic cover and immunity. While ostensibly representing the State of Israel, its citizens and the Jewish people on the international stage of the UN, the Permanent Mission was also responsible for mustering support for Israel while constantly endeavouring to limit any UN criticism of Israel's repeated inhumane violations of international law. This was achieved by employing the same tactics – blackmail, bribery, and bullying – as were originally used on UN member states to effect the controversial establishment of the state of Israel. Apart from relying on U.S. vetoes of UN resolutions condemning Israel, the Permanent Mission also pressured and coerced the UN staff and delegates of other countries into expurgating, delaying publication of, or completely abandoning reports that were condemnatory of Israel's conduct in the Occupied Palestinian territories (OPT).

Reports had already revealed that Israel's deliberate disabling of the Palestinian educational process had increased with 53,998 Palestinian male and female students and 3,840 Palestinian male and female teachers, as well as a number of the staff of the Palestinian Ministry of Education and its institutions, had been subjected to attacks by the Israeli occupation forces (IOF) during the last year; and that such attacks included killing, wounding, arrests and detentions, as well as house arrests, restriction of movement at checkpoints and denial of safe access to schools.

This morning's meeting chaired by the Ambassador was concerned with just acquired information that a forthcoming report from the Office of the Special Representative of the Secretary-General for Children and Armed Conflict would be very critical of Israel's occupation and its effect on Palestinian children throughout the OPT who according to numerous children's charities and organisations have continued to face disproportionate physical violence, restricted access to education, and psychological trauma at the hands of Israeli forces and Jewish settlers with accountability for shootings by Israeli forces or attacks by settlers being virtually unheard of.

The report would apparently reveal that the situation was marked by heightened tensions translating into widespread violence, especially in the West Bank, including East Jerusalem; that the detrimental impact of grave violations and an increasingly violent and oppressive environment continued to mark the lives of Palestinian children; that the year's killing and injuring of over 1,735 Palestinian children had been carried out by both Israeli forces and settlers; that there were concerns regarding the excessive use of lethal force even when the children posed no imminent or immediate threat to life; that an increased number of Palestinian children were arrested and detained by Israeli forces and prosecuted by juvenile military courts in the West Bank; that in East Jerusalem, 860 Palestinian children were arrested, including 136 between 7 and 11 years of age, which was under the age of criminal responsibility; that a worrisome development was the recommencement of administrative detention of children, which had not been used in East Jerusalem since 2000 and elsewhere in the West Bank since 2011; that in the West Bank, attacks on schools and protected personnel, and a pervasive environment of violence, harassment and intimidation, continued to have an impact on children's access to education; and that the UN had documented 283 incidents relating to education, including 96 cases of schools coming under fire during military-led operations and clashes, 46 attacks and threats of violence against students and teachers by Israeli security forces and settlers, and 62 instances of interference with education owing to the closure of schools or the arrest and detention of staff and students. Yet despite all efforts by Israel to disrupt and prevent the education of Palestinian children, Palestinians still had the highest ratio of PhDs per capita in the world.

Furthermore, the Israeli Government in 2015 had deliberately restricted the rights of Palestinians including children with the Knesset passing temporary amendments to the Penal Code that increased the maximum sentence for stone-throwing to 20 years with the accused in the meantime being detained until the end of legal proceedings.

The report would also highlight the fact that Israel had continually failed – despite being urged to do so in the previous report – to take concrete and immediate steps to protect children, schools and hospitals, in particular by ensuring accountability for alleged violations. Of the 190 cases of alleged violations of international humanitarian law during the hostilities in Gaza in 2014 referred to the Israeli Defence Forces Fact-Finding Assessments Mechanism, the Israeli Military Advocate General has indicted three soldiers for looting and theft. Investigations into numerous incidents, including the killing of four children on a beach in Gaza City in July 2014, had been closed without criminal or disciplinary proceedings. The report would also reiterate its concerns regarding the practice of punitive demolitions of the homes of Palestinians accused of attacking Israelis, which had rendered their families and neighbours, including children, homeless.

The Ambassador – new to the job and still trying hard to justify his appointment – was insistent that everything possible should be done to discredit the report including such customary public denunciations that the UN was biased against Israel with disproportionate resolutions and condemnations that were tantamount to anti-Semitism; that Israel was being discriminated against in UN activities and forums; and that Israel was doing more than any other country in the blood-soaked Middle East to promote and protect human rights and liberal values. Persuading other member state governments to side with Israel was also made easier by the fact that many of them were reliant on Israel's weapons and security technology for the control and/or suppression of their own people for which in return they refrained from condemning Israeli violations.

Suppressing the facts about the reality of Israel's odious conduct – Israel remains in defiance of more than 70 United Nations Security Council Resolutions – was a full-time global enterprise with the Israeli Ministry of Foreign Affairs employing some half dozen public relations firms in the U.S. alone to promote a "positive image" of Israel amongst the American public. This had also included joining with Aish HaTorah ("Fire of the Torah") in 2001 to establish the Hasbara Fellowships which had so far taken over 2,000 students from some 220 North American campuses to Israel to be trained as effective pro-Israel activists on college campuses. The policy was in keeping with the Nazi belief that to get people on your side you need to get them on your side when they are young because younger people are far easier to influence than when they are adults. To this end 97 percent of German teachers joined the Nazi teachers organisation and attended a 6-week course to learn the Nazi way of teaching and brainwashing children. The other three percent of the teachers were sacked and sent to re-education camps.

Brainwashing the young has also been an important feature of Israel's education system with a special report – referred to in *Washington Report on Middle East Affairs* – having revealed that according to recent academic studies and surveys, Israeli school textbooks as well as children's storybooks, portray Palestinians and Arabs as "murderers," "rioters," "suspicious," and generally backward and unproductive. Direct delegitimisation and negative stereotyping of Palestinians and Arabs in Israeli schoolbooks was the rule rather than the exception … But then that was to be expected from a fascist state whose monstrous Apartheid racism is unashamedly overt.

"Monsters exist, but they are too few in number to be truly dangerous. More dangerous are the common men, the functionaries ready to believe and to act without asking questions."
Primo Levi, Holocaust survivor

Dirksen Senate Office Building, Washington, D.C.

Senator Edward Wright had not planned on being in his office today, but with the U.S. Congress unlikely to block the Iran nuclear deal, and thanks to his recent intimate encounter with the honey trapping Sally Berkley – if that was her real name – he was now obliged to put in some extra effort and hours canvassing support for legislation in Congress that would pave the way for new sanctions on Iran, even if some existing ones were ended by the nuclear accord. Up until very recently Wright had seen nothing wrong – and in fact was quite comfortable with – accepting Jewish lobby campaign contributions, free junkets to Israel, and other persuasive fringe benefits that obliged his support for Israel. But all that was before he had been confronted with the taped recording of his sexual shenanigans. What had previously been acceptable subtle bribery which his conscience could live with, had now become undisguised blackmail that was akin to the Sword of Damocles hanging over his head for as long as he held a position of influence in the U.S. government.

While Wright and many other congressional leaders were endeavouring to persuade top Republicans to do their utmost to scrap the President's nuclear deal with Iran, AIPAC was preparing for an all-out campaign to pressure other more cautious congresspeople into rejecting the agreement. With the opening of a 60-day review of the deal in Congress, the Republican U.S. House of Representatives Speaker had informed the House Press Gallery's gaggle of presstitutes that "because a bad deal threatens the security of the American people, we're going to do everything possible to stop it."

Wright had already been asked to make a strong condemnatory statement on the website of AIPAC's recently launched advocacy group to oppose the Iran nuclear deal. Known as the Citizens for a Nuclear Free Iran, the group was dedicated to informing the public "about the dangers of the proposed Iran deal." The group's advisory board included five former Democratic members of Congress amongst whom former Jewish Senator Joe Lieberman of Connecticut was adamant that "this Iran deal is dangerous for America, for Israel and for the world … Iran has violated over 20 international agreements, is the number one sponsor of terrorism in the world, and has been working to acquire nuclear weapons for years. Unfortunately, this agreement won't stop them." Mister Lieberman said that with a straight face despite the fact that it was Israel rather than Iran that came close to fitting his description.

The fact that Wright felt he had been unnecessarily betrayed by AIPAC, had hurt his feelings and weakened his commitment to a people to whom he had been unstinting with his loyalty and devotion. Their apparent lack of trust in him, had finally forced him to consider the morality of what had been, and still was, being done to the American people by their government. Americans were allowing themselves to be led to the abyss while stubbornly refusing to open their eyes to the reality that Israel had expelled three quarters of a million Palestinians from their land in 1948 while continually denying full rights and privileges to Palestinians living in Israel; that Israel's 1967 seizure of what was now termed as the Occupied Palestinian Territory (OPT) was an illegal act of war subsequently condemned by the UN in Resolution 242 which emphasised "the inadmissibility of the acquisition of territory by war and the need to work for a just and lasting peace in which every state in the area can live in security"; that Israel had consistently violated human rights with arrogant impunity while refusing visits to the OPT by human rights inspectors; that Israel's occupation was the only continuous colonisation campaign in the world with Illegal confiscation of land, demolition of homes, and the construction of illegal settlements that were all part of a systematic and unending agenda to inflict misery, hardship, and death upon a captive indigenous Palestinian population; that the occupation was inflicting a gradual death toll with a stranglehold that enforced an illegal embargo, destroyed the infrastructure, siphoned off resources – such as electricity, water, and Gaza's offshore natural Gas – and created unacceptable levels of unemployment; that Israel was deliberately targeting children with a UNESCO report unequivocally stating that student deaths during the conflict constituted more than a quarter – or 27.4 percent – of total civilian deaths incurred in Palestine; that since 2000 Israel had arrested and imprisoned over 7,000 children; that numerous organisations, religious groups, and individuals including civic leaders and artists had opposed the illegal occupation by supporting BDS against Israel; and that the U.S. was due to soon be annually sending Israel almost $4 billion taxpayer dollars of direct, unrestricted military aid.

Having in his opinion been betrayed by those on whose behalf he had betrayed his family, friends, and country – not to mention the loss of his irreplaceable dignity and integrity – Wright began tackling the task of drumming up opposition to the Iranian nuclear accord with a refreshing impartiality that recognised the prevailing and dishonest double standard that made no mention whatsoever – either in Congress or the media – about Israel's own nuclear arsenal. As Chairman of the Senate Committee on Foreign Relations, Wright had from time to time been privy to intelligence reports on Israel's nuclear program which had been initiated by Israel's first Prime Minister, David Ben-Gurion shortly after the establishment of Israel. The country's Scientific community had been instructed to create what was then termed "the bomb in the basement" which was to serve as a last-resort option to thwart a cataclysmic defeat by Arab forces, or at least make the cost of victory for them unacceptably high. Consequently part of the finance that had been raised abroad for the State of Israel – including contributions from diaspora Jews – was funnelled to the project with Israeli scientists and intelligence officials being directed to acquire from foreign sources the necessary equipment and knowledge for building a nuclear bomb.

Acquisition of what was required initially came mostly from France with whom the establishment of a close relationship had given Israeli scientists access to French nuclear research sites. This eventually led to the purchase of the Dimona reactor complex so that during the late 1950s over 2,500 French technical experts worked at the reactor site behind a wall of secrecy so extreme that they were forbidden to correspond directly with their families so as not to disclose their whereabouts. Whenever questioned by the Americans and British about Dimona, the Israelis glibly passed it off variously as a grasslands research institute or a manganese processing plant. Though the Franco-Israeli nuclear alliance had started to cool by the time Charles de Gaulle became President in 1959, Israel had nonetheless acquired sufficient contraband components, purloined technology, and scientific competence to begin its own fully-fledged, independent weapons program.

The independence of Israel's nuclear program would not have been possible without its breaking of treaties banning nuclear tests along with numerous national and international laws restricting the traffic in nuclear materials and technology. Such customary Israeli disregard for international law was assisted by more than a few nations – including committed campaigners against proliferation such as Britain, France, Germany, the U.S., and even Norway – who either turned a blind eye to the violations, or covertly sold Israel whatever was necessary to produce a nuclear weapon. Israel's nuclear plans, however, came under threat when John F. Kennedy (JFK) was inaugurated as U.S. President in January 1961 and made clear his desire to prevent a nuclear arms race in the Middle which was one of several reasons for his assassination.

On realising that JFK would not budge on the issue, Ben-Gurion – who earnestly believed that possession of nuclear weapons was essential for Israel's survival – then decided to join forces with Communist China. As both countries were bent on creating nuclear programs, they began secretly developing their own nuclear capability through intermediary and "richest Jew in the world" Shaul Eisenberg who was a close friend of the duplicitous Henry Kissinger and a partner of Mossad gun-runner Tibor Rosenbaum. In his book *Seeds of Fire: China and the Story Behind the Attack on America*, author Gordon Thomas exposed how Mossad and the CSIS (Chinese secret service) frequently conspired to not only steal American military secrets, but to also doctor U.S. intelligence programs.

Another colourful Israeli agent – and member of a spy ring called Lakam (Hebrew acronym for a harmless sounding Science Liaison Bureau) – was Arnon Milchan, the billionaire Hollywood producer behind some 50 films including *Once Upon a Time in America, Pretty Woman,* and L.A. *Confidential.* Milchan was an acknowledged Israeli intelligence agent for Mossad and successful arms dealer; was a business associate of News Corporation's Rupert Murdoch; was listed by *Forbes* as the 240th richest in the world; was a staunch supporter of Israel and personal friend of Israeli President Shimon Peres who had recruited him as a spy; and was himself a recruiter of other Hollywood A-listers such as Sydney Pollack. Milchan at one time operated thirty companies in seventeen countries on behalf of Israel. He also underwrote the Israeli Network which transmitted Israeli television programs to Canada and the U.S. via cable and satellite television.

Israel's nuclear duplicity, however, did not fool JFK and 50 declassified documents from the early 1960s by the U.S. National Security Archive – including papers from the White House, the State Department, the Atomic Energy Commission, and U.S. intelligence agencies – confirm that the Americans had concluded that the Israelis were providing "untruthful cover" about their intentions to build a nuclear bomb. The bottom line was that "in 1961 the CIA already knew or understood that the way Israel referred to Dimona, whether through Ben-Gurion or through its scientists, was an untruthful cover."

JFK consequently had no doubts that while Israel was masquerading as a friend and ally of the U.S., it was simultaneously lying repeatedly about its nuclear weapons development program. In June 1963, in the last of a series of insistent letters to Israeli Prime Minister David Ben-Gurion, JFK stressed that as a professed ally of the U.S., Israel should prove "beyond a reasonable doubt" that as the Middle East's Zionist enclave it was not developing nuclear weapons. The letter had been cabled to Tel Aviv but before it could be physically delivered by the U.S. ambassador, David Ben-Gurion abruptly resigned for undisclosed personal reasons. Since then it had become apparent that in his final days as Prime Minister, Ben-Gurion commanded the Mossad to become involved in a plot for the American President's assassination in which Tibor Rosenbaum played a pivotal role.

The probability of Mossad's involvement in JFK's assassination was in 1994 clearly substantiated by author Michael Collins Piper who in his incisive book, *Final Judgment: The Missing link in the JFK Assassination Conspiracy,* asserted that Israel's motive for the assassination was JFK's opposition to Israel's nuclear ambitions which outraged Ben-Gurion who commanded the Mossad to become involved. Piper concluded that "Israel's Mossad was a primary (and critical) behind the scenes player in the conspiracy that ended the life of JFK. Through its own vast resources and through its international contacts in the intelligence community and in organised crime, Israel had the means, it had the opportunity, and it had the motive to play a major frontline role in the crime of the century – and it did."

JFK's assassination served the dual purpose of eliminating not only the threat to Israel's nuclear ambitions, but also the need for the American Zionist Council (AZC) – whom Attorney General Robert F. Kennedy (RFK) had ordered to openly register and disclose its foreign funded lobbying activity in the U.S. – to register as a foreign agent. So when Vice President Lyndon Johnson (LBJ) was sworn in as JFK's successor, he wasted no time in increasing Israel's arms budget and turning a blind eye to its nuclear arms development program. A further blow to the integrity and independence of the U.S. government occurred in November 1963, when Nicholas Katzenbach replaced RFK as Attorney General with the result that the AZC evaded registration and calculatingly morphed into the American Israel Public Affairs Committee (AIPAC) which has since continued to buy influence over U.S. government legislators who ensure that come hell or high water, the U.S. would unconditionally support and steadfastly remain allied to Israel irrespective of its numerous flagrant violations of international law..

Israel's intense dislike for the Kennedy clan reared its ugly head again on June 6, 1968 when RFK during his presidential campaign was assassinated by Mossad's Palestinian "patsy" Sirhan Bishara Sirhan who to this day has maintained that after having coffee with a woman, the next thing his conscious memory can remember was his being choked and unable to breathe moments after the Kennedy shooting. Then on July 16, 1999, John Fitzgerald Kennedy Jr. – an American lawyer, journalist, magazine publisher, and only surviving son of former President John F. Kennedy – who was about to reveal some new allegations about his father's assassination, died in mysterious circumstances in a plane crash over the Atlantic Ocean.

Wright who had been a prolific reader of books on U.S. history, now wondered how many of his fellow countrymen were sufficiently literate to revisit their history and familiarise themselves with President George Washington's 1796 Farewell Address to the Nation which contained the following uncannily prophetic warning regarding the cost and pernicious consequences of having preferred alliances such as that with Israel:

" … *So likewise, a passionate attachment of one nation for another produces a variety of evils. Sympathy for the favourite nation, facilitating the illusion of an imaginary common interest in cases where no real common interest exists, and infusing into one the enmities of the other, betrays the former into a participation in the quarrels and wars of the latter without adequate inducement or justification. It leads also to concessions to the favourite nation of privileges denied to others which is apt doubly to injure the nation making the concessions; by unnecessarily parting with what ought to have been retained, and by exciting jealousy, ill-will, and a disposition to retaliate, in the parties from whom equal privileges are withheld. And it gives to ambitious, corrupted, or deluded citizens (who devote themselves to the favourite nation), facility to betray or sacrifice the interests of their own country, without odium, sometimes even with popularity; gilding, with the appearances of a virtuous sense of obligation, a commendable deference for public opinion, or a laudable zeal for public good, the base or foolish compliances of ambition, corruption, or infatuation.*

As avenues to foreign influence in innumerable ways, such attachments are particularly alarming to the truly enlightened and independent patriot. How many opportunities do they afford to tamper with domestic factions, to practice the arts of seduction, to mislead public opinion, to influence or awe the public councils. Such an attachment of a small or weak towards a great and powerful nation dooms the former to be the satellite of the latter.

Against the insidious wiles of foreign influence (I conjure you to believe me, fellow-citizens) the jealousy of a free people ought to be constantly awake, since history and experience prove that foreign influence is one of the most baneful foes of republican government. But that jealousy to be useful must be impartial; else it becomes the instrument of the very influence to be avoided, instead of a defence against it. Excessive partiality for one foreign nation and excessive dislike of another cause those whom they actuate to see danger only on one side, and serve to veil and even second the arts of influence on the other. Real patriots who may resist the intrigues of the favourite are liable to become suspected and odious, while its tools and dupes usurp the applause and confidence of the people, to surrender their interests."

16

Thursday, 24 December

Bethlehem, West Bank

After checking out of their Jerusalem hotel at about 9:00 a.m., Conrad and Freya, instead of taking a cab to Bethlehem, decided on walking to the Arab East Jerusalem Central Bus Station on Sultan Suleiman Street across from the Damascus Gate where they caught a bus for the half hour journey to the biblical city which was located some six miles (ten kilometres) away within the West Bank's "Area A" zone under Palestinian Authority administration. The bus travelled directly to the heavily militarised Bethlehem Checkpoint with its full-body turnstiles and what resembled caged cattle chute passageways from where it was only a short walk to their virtually empty hotel on Manger Street just off Manger Square.

"Where's everybody?" Conrad asked the hotel receptionist.

"I thought it would be packed this time of year." Freya added.

"Usually it is. But now things are not normal," the receptionist replied, smiling politely but with evident regret over the hotel's current low occupancy rate. Apparently though Bethlehem was traditionally host to spectacular markets, festivals, parades, and church services during the Christmas festive season with Christians from all over the world coming to the city where it was believed Jesus was born – the Church of the Nativity, one of the oldest Christian churches in the world, had been built on the presumed site of the manger where Mary took refuge – this year it was relatively quite with most celebrations having been scaled down or completely cancelled due to the prevailing powder keg situation. The tourist slump had begun in October as a result of a wave of political violence that had spread from Jerusalem to the West Bank and Gaza with stabbings, shootings, car ramming attacks, and the to be expected disproportionate Israeli response with a high Palestinian death toll as compared to the number of Israelis injured or killed.

After being shown to their room, they discussed the sequence of their intended visits for the rest of the day as they unpacked. "What do you want to do first?" Freya asked.

Conrad walked up behind her, put his arms around her waist, kissed the back of her head, and pressed hard against her. "Mmmmmm … " was all he said.

"That's not on the agenda 'til tonight."

"Pity," he said, still holding her tightly. "We could start off with the Nativity Church, grab some lunch, and then, as you are the expert, you can decide the next move."

She turned around, held his head in both hands and kissed him affectionately. Witnessing Sami's murder along with what they had endured together during the past few days had somehow strengthened their commitment and love for each other.

While it had been agreed that Conrad would concentrate on researching Jerusalem's history for his documentary, Freya had undertaken to read up on Bethlehem which the New Testament Gospels of Matthew and Luke Identified as the birthplace of Jesus – though some researchers dispute this claim, asserting instead that it was a town of the same name in Galilee, Christian tradition had for over two thousand years sanctified the town in Judea as the holy birthplace – Bethlehem was also claimed as the birthplace of David where he was years later also anointed as king by Samuel, one of the foremost leaders in the history of ancient Israel and Judea who according to the first of the Books of Samuel in the Hebrew Bible was the last of the Hebrew judges, a seer, a prophet, a priest, a warrior, a national unifier, and a kingmaker.

While the Gospel of Matthew – generally believed to have been composed between 80 and 90 CE – implied that Mary and Joseph were from Bethlehem and later moved to Nazareth because of Herod's decree, the Gospel of Luke indicated that Mary and Joseph were from Nazareth, and Jesus was born in Bethlehem while they were in town for a special census. With both irreconcilable versions being thought to have been written around 80 and 90 CE, scholars have been inclined to favour Matthew over Luke because of the historical problems with the latter's version. Both accounts, however are agreed that Jesus was born in Bethlehem and raised in Nazareth. According to Luke 2:7 Mary "laid him in a manger because there was no room for them in the inn" without there being any gospel mentions of a cave until a century later when both Justin Martyr and the Protoevangelium of James said that Jesus was born in a cave.

The cave narrative had come about as part of Christianity's concerted effort to supplant the more prominent pagan religions in the Roman Empire such as Mithraism. Apart from Mithraism, there was also the monotheistic sun-worshipping cult of Sol Invictus, or "Invincible Sun," whose doctrinal belief that its god possessed the attributes of all the other gods precluded the need for competition with its rivals. It was therefore to the relative success of this cult that Mithraism attached itself by various means including depictions that had Mithras sharing the banquet with Sol after the former had sacrificed the bull.

As state recognition and political power were nonetheless urgent priorities which Christianity was prepared to acquire by any means even if it meant temporarily playing down the role of Jesus who had after all been a Jewish Zealot agitator – a fact from which Christianity wished to distance itself – whose condemnation and crucifixion resulted from his outspoken criticism of social injustice which the Roman authorities regarded as subversive political activity. Consequently in 321 as part of the "shedding" of its Jewish heritage, Christianity switched its sacred day of observance from Saturday, the Jewish Sabbath, to Sunday, the state's sacred and "venerable day of the sun." Further changes included "borrowing" the aureole of light that crowned the sun god's head to create the Christian halo and Christ's birthday was changed from January 6 to December 25 in keeping with the sun's rebirth celebration.

Other changes that were incorporated so as to facilitate the supplanting of Mithras – variously known as "Invictus Mithras," "Deus Invictus Mithras," or by the full title of "Deus Sol Invictus Mithras" – by Jesus Christ included similarities that showed both were born in a cave; both were part of a trinity; both were mediators between God and man; both committed a sacrifice for the benefit of mankind – though in different ways – wherein blood was the symbol of regeneration; and both celebrated a "last supper" with their respective twelve followers who in Mithras' case represented the twelve signs of the zodiac. Christianity's seven sacraments were a follow-on from the seven degrees of initiation in Mithraism; both religions promulgated concepts concerning man and the immortality of his soul; and both had mysteries from which the lower ranks were excluded.

Christianity's quest to be recognised as the official state religion was then pursued with an impressive ruthlessness and included the seizure of Mithras' temple on Vatican Hill in 376 CE – the temple over which St. Peter's Basilica was built and is still accessible to this day – and persistent efforts by Bishop Ambrose of Milan to persuade the initially tolerant Roman Emperor Theodosius I (392 – 395) to prohibit pagan sacrifices and destroy pagan temples so that Christianity could by the default become the state religion.

In the meantime during the Roman and Byzantine periods, Bethlehem was destroyed by the Emperor Hadrian during the Bar Kokhba revolt (c. 132 – 136 CE), but was rebuilt at the instigation of the Empress Helena, mother of Constantine the Great who in 327 CE commissioned the octagonal Church of the Nativity to be built over the supposed site of the cave which could now be viewed through a wide hole encircled with a railing. Though the ensuing Samaritan revolt of 529 resulted in Bethlehem being sacked, its walls being destroyed, and the Church of the Nativity being severely damaged, it was rebuilt a century later by Emperor Justinian I who built the much larger church that remained to this day.

The Church was then spared by the Persians during their 614 invasion because, according to legend, they were impressed by a representation of the Magi – who were not three kings but priests from ancient Persia who came to be known as the Magi – that decorated the building. Initially the Magi were not priests in the strictest sense of the word, but shamans of a distinct tribal caste from Media which lay south of the Caspian Sea. The Medes like the Elamites from the nearby Kingdom of Elam, were aboriginal and in no way connected to either the Aryans or Semites who at that time shared most of Western Asia between them. As Shamans they did not subscribe to any established or organised form of religion and instead preached that the world was inhabited by both good and evil spirits which only they could control. Their rituals included both fire and animal sacrifices that were invariably accompanied by drunken shouting and dancing after liberal consumption of an intoxicating drink made from the fermented juice of the haoma plant.

Apart from being avid practitioners of consanguineous marriage – related to or descended from the same ancestors – which they rated highly for its accumulative benefits, the Median shamans also claimed expertise in the occult, practiced divination, foretold the future, interpreted dreams, transmitted and received omens, read signs in the flight of birds and the movement of the stars, and preached that they were the only seers capable of recognising the coming of the Messiah's star which would correctly identify the Divine Child on the occasion of his birth. Consequently those scribes responsible for writing the biblical birth narrative no doubt felt that having some of the Magi visit the infant Jesus shortly after his birth, would serve to legitimise the claim that he was the Son of God.

Following the Muslim conquest in 637, Bethlehem – Bayt Lahm meaning "House of Meat" in Arabic, and Bet Lehem meaning "House of Bread" in Hebrew – became part of Jund Filastin, a military district of Palestine, and remained under Muslim rule until its conquest during the First Crusade (1096–1099) by the Christian Crusaders who replaced the town's Greek Orthodox clergy with a Latin one from Rome. In the mid-13th century the Mamluks destroyed its walls which were subsequently rebuilt by the Ottomans in the early 16th century. Control then passed from the Ottomans to the British at the end of the First World War; to the Jordanians during the 1948 Arab-Israeli War; and finally to the Israelis following their rapacious land-grabbing 1967 Six-Day War.

Since the 1995 Oslo Accords, Bethlehem had been supposedly administered by the Palestinian Authority, but In reality, the Israelis were in complete control of the area with the city being surrounded on three sides by Israel's eight-metre-high concrete wall and more than 20 illegal Israeli settlements including Nokdim with its notorious "hilltop youth" and Avigdor Lieberman, who as Israel's far-right foreign minister was the only foreign minister in the world not living within the boundaries of his own country. In fact More than half a million Israelis lived in more than 150 Jewish-only settlements across the West Bank, as well as in several enclaves within East Jerusalem's Palestinian neighbourhoods. So despite the charade of Palestinian Authority administration, Christ's biblical birthplace had been subject to Israeli confiscation of large chunks of its land while its colonised tourism-dependent economy had been severely affected so that in the West Bank Palestinians had an unemployment rate of 25 percent, and a level of poverty at 22 percent.

As a consequence of these deliberately engineered Israeli hardships, Palestinian Christians had continued to emigrate so that their proportion of Bethlehem's population had decreased in recent decades from 95 percent to about 30 percent. In 1948, Christians in Palestine accounted for approximately 18 percent of the Arab population, but today they made up less than 2 per cent of the population in the Occupied Palestinian Territory. While Christians the world over condemn the persecution of Christians in the Middle East and Africa, they never express concern for, or solidarity with those in Palestine. Perhaps part of the explanation for that glaring double standard was Israel's disingenuous assertion that the decline of the Palestinian Christian population was due to the intolerance of militant Muslim groups such as Hamas and Islamic Jihad. Unfortunately – yet again– the facts do not fit the Israeli narrative which has conveniently overlooked the reality that of the 1948 forced displacement of hundreds of thousands of Palestinians, some 50,000 were Christians. And this was long before the existence of either Hamas or other Islamic militant group. Israel's ploy of "divide and conquer" had required pitting Palestinian Christians against Palestinian Muslims by blaming the latter for the persecution and emigration of the former.

Despite now having a Muslim Majority, Bethlehem was still host to a substantial Palestinian Christian community which contributed significantly towards the provision of services for the tourists who were city's main source of income. While Christians from all over the world had been making their pilgrimage mainly to the Church of the Nativity for over

2000 years, other tourist destinations included the Milk Grotto where the Holy Family took refuge during the Slaughter of the Innocents by Herod's soldiers; the Greek Orthodox Mar Saba Monastery in the middle of a desert, east of Bethlehem; Banksy's Art on the Israeli West Bank barrier including an image of a Christmas tree surrounded by a wall; Herodium, the more than 2000 years old volcano-like hill with a truncated cone where Herod the Great supposedly built a fortress and palace; the Old City of Bethlehem with its ancient narrow streets including Star Street which Joseph and the Virgin Mary followed on their way to the Grotto of the Nativity; Beit Sahour's Shepherd's Fields which since ancient times had been identified with the shepherds who saw the Star of Nativity and followed it to Bethlehem; and the small Cremisan vineyard that produced wine from the luscious grapes grown on the slopes of a hillside whose picturesque location had also faced the threat of encroachment from Israel's separation wall.

Conrad and Freya's hotel was just a short walk across Manger Square to the Church of the Nativity where they entered through the Door of Humility, the small rectangular entrance created in Ottoman times to prevent carts being driven through and to force even VIPs to dismount from their horses so as to enter the holy place. The doorway had been reduced from an earlier Crusader doorway, the pointed arch of which could still be seen above the current door with the outline of the Justinian square door also being visible.

The church's nave from Justinian's time was still intact with a 15th century roof that had undergone 19th century restoration. Thirty of the nave's 44 polished pink limestone columns were decorated with now faded Crusader paintings of saints and the Madonna holding her child. The church's focal point, however, was the Grotto of the Nativity with a silver star set in the floor over the spot where Christ was allegedly born. It was in Bethlehem that Saint Jerome – born in Stribo near

Venice (c. 342 – 420) – who after travelling widely, eventually settled in Bethlehem and founded a monastery. Inspired by the Pope's suggestion that a single book should replace the numerous different texts in circulation, Saint Jerome completed a new version of the Bible that appeared around the year 404 and subsequently came to be known as the Vulgate. Tradition now placed Jerome's study and tomb next to the Grotto of the Nativity.

Despite some of the church's interior being obscured by scaffolding for the renovations that had started two years earlier, Conrad and Freya got a sense of the church's former glory when a tarpaulin covering a wall was removed for their benefit to reveal an elaborate mosaic with its colours dulled to sepia and brown by centuries of candle smoke and moisture from a leaking roof that had once again just been renovated. Along the top of the churches nave, a procession of Byzantine angels in flowing white garments had also been restored to their original magnificence in glass, mother of pearl, stone, and gold leaf. The angels faced towards the grotto as a signpost to the pilgrims who had been travelling to the site for many centuries.

Yet amidst all this religious splendour and tradition, violence had been known to periodically erupt due to perceived encroachment on jurisdictional boundaries within the church between the rival Christian denominations – Greek Orthodox, Roman Catholic, Armenian Apostolic, and Syriac Orthodox – that shared responsibility for the church. One recent conflict had started when a clergyman of one of the orders accidentally pushed his broom into space managed by another group. The ensuing battle had involved about 100 priests and monks clad in traditional robes who flung fists, brandished brooms, and exchanged irreverent insults with peace being eventually restored only after the intervention of baton-wielding Palestinian police. It seemed strange but not surprising to Conrad and Freya that despite God's commandant of "Love your neighbour as yourself" (Mark 12:31), different religious denominations consistently failed to do so. They felt that such dissension did not bode well for Christian unity in opposing human repression and doing the work of Jesus who is reported to have told his disciples:

> *"If anyone would come after me, let him deny himself and take up his cross and follow me. For whoever would save his life will lose it, but whoever loses his life for my sake will find it. For what will it profit a man if he gains the whole world and forfeits his soul? Or what shall a man give in return for his soul?"*
> **Matthew 16:24-26**

After spending several hours in the Church of the Nativity and the adjoining St. Catherine's Church taking photographs and filming, they lunched in Manger Square where the café owner shared his belief that if Jesus were to visit Bethlehem tomorrow he would find it closed; that Mary and Joseph would require Israeli permission to get in; that even if they had permission they would still have to spend hours waiting at one of the more than 30 physical Israeli barriers restricting Palestinian movement including checkpoints, roadblocks, dirt mounds, and gates. Despite the owner's rather gloomy speculations, he served up a more than adequate lunch consisting of a local chicken and rice speciality which – though not *Michelin Guide* rated – was sufficiently satisfying to refuel their energies for the rest of the afternoon's tour of the old town before returning to their hotel. That evening they would revisit Manger Square for the Christmas Eve midnight mass.

Jewish Quarter, Occupied East Jerusalem

Apart from being a dedicated member of the Hiramic Brotherhood of the Third Temple, Yaakov Katzir had also naturally followed with interest the activities of the Temple Institute whose international director believed that a pure red heifer could be used as part of a ritual to bring about the Biblical prophecy of a new Jewish temple on the site of the Al-Aqsa Mosque. The director was imbued with a combination of a 2,000-year-old Judaic tradition and the latest in American cattle-breeding technology. His holy grail was to genetically engineer the perfect red heifer which if successful, he believed would pave the way for the destruction of the Al-Aqsa Mosque and in turn facilitate its replacement by a Jewish temple. In his promotional video which was available on YouTube, he described efforts to raise a herd of red cows as an "unprecedented historical project … For 2,000 years, we've been mourning the destruction of the holy temple, but the future is in our hands … The challenge is to raise a perfect red heifer according to the exact Biblical requirements here in the land of Israel. It's time to stop waiting and start doing." In order to help fulfil this biblical temple building prophesy, a crowdfunding appeal was launched during the summer.

The idea therefore was to implant red-cow embryos in the wombs of surrogate mother cows who would be meticulously monitored and cared for during nine months of gestation prior to giving birth. In the eventuality of one of the calfs being a totally red heifer, it would be declared the first authentic red heifer since the days of the Second Temple. Then after becoming two years old, the heifer would be slaughtered, burned, and its ashes mixed with water so that finally, after 2,000 years, Jewish believers could be purified from the ritual impurities associated with coming into contact with the dead, and will then be free to ascend to all parts of the Temple Mount. Obtaining a truly kosher red heifer was of vital importance because the lack of red heifer ashes is one of the most serious halakhic – the collective body of Jewish religious laws – obstacles to building the third Temple on the Temple Mount. Jewish law asserts every Jew is currently ritually impure from having been near a dead body or gravesite. Such impurity can only be overcome by water mixed with the ashes of a truly red heifer.

Consequently Jews subscribing to this belief have for decades been searching for the miraculous red cow, known in Hebrew as the para aduma. It was not until some years ago, that Temple Institute researchers discovered a farm in Texas with a breed of red cows called Red Angus with reputedly very high-quality meat. A delegation from the Institute flew to Texas and purchased some frozen Red Angus embryos that met the criteria set by Jewish law. A farm was subsequently found in the south of Israel that specialised in raising cows to host the surrogacy process. The surrogate mothers and their offspring at this farm are now subject to closed-circuit surveillance while receiving extra special treatment and protection to ensure that all halakhic criteria are met.

Though initially regarded as an extremist group on the fringe of lunacy, the Institute had since gained increasing support not only from Jewish settlers and American Christian Zionists, but also from Israeli politicians – with government ministers parroting its call for a third temple – and education ministry funding annually helping to expose tens of thousands of pupils to its dangerously provocative agenda. The project's eventual success is entirely dependent on breeding a totally red heifer without any white or black hairs because according to the Book of Numbers, God instructed Moses to "speak unto the children of Israel, that they bring thee a red heifer without spot, wherein is no blemish, and upon which never came yoke." The animal was to be ritually sacrificed and its ashes mixed with cedar wood and hyssop so that the high priest could then bathe in the mixture for the "purification of sin."

Jewish scholars subsequently extended this cleansing ritual to the priestly caste that served in both the legendary temple built by King Solomon and in the Second Temple where a pure red heifer was last seen. Jewish religious teaching maintained that from the time of Moses until the destruction of the Second Temple, only nine perfect red heifers were discovered. According to the Jewish philosopher Maimonides, the tenth will herald the coming of the messiah.

Apart from the Temple Institute there were other fringe organisations such as the religious group known as the "Women for the Temple" whose members are hard at work preparing themselves for the temple's numerous requirements when it becomes a reality. They spend their time poring over Sacred Texts that provide instructions for the preparation of sacrificial offerings. They learn how to bake the sourdough bread required for the rites; how to cultivate the so-called crimson worm with which the priests' vestments are dyed; and possibly most important of all, they are studying how to make the *parochet* – the great curtain in ancient times that separated the Temple's main hall from the Holy of Holies which supposedly contained the Ark of the Covenant – which now covered the Torah ark in synagogues.

Groups such as the "Women of the Temple" are supportive of The Temple Institute's efforts and tagline – "It's time to build" – for the organisation's controversial mission to rally Jews for the construction of a "Third Temple" by using internet tools including Facebook to spread its message among the masses. Jewish claims to the Haram al-Sharif/Temple Mount basically stem from biblical narratives which according to the rabbinic sages – whose debates produced the Talmud – this was the site from which the world expanded into its present form and from where the Abrahamic God gathered the dust used to create Adam, the first man. Therefore on the basis of the Genesis creation narrative, all of these amazing events occurred during a relatively short period of time somewhere between 5,700 and 10,000 years ago.

The problem with using Biblical myths to justify or

legitimise religious or political claims of the present, is that such myths are easily debunked by irrefutable scientific evidence. Scientific consensus, for example, with backing from a 2006 statement by sixty-eight national and international academies, asserted that evidence-based fact derived from observations and experiments in multiple scientific disciplines show that the universe existed almost 14 billion years ago in an extremely hot and dense state. It was about that time, according to the Big Bang theory, that the universe then began to cool and expand towards its present dispersed state with the earth being formed 4.5 billion years ago and life first appearing no less than 2.5 billion years ago. That self-induced expansion was still ongoing to this day without any influence or input from some God or Supreme Being.

As for the idea of Adam being created on Haram al-Sharif/ Temple Mount, it is now an established fact that the evolution of human beings – Homo sapiens – first began in Africa (either East or South) where archaeological evidence of our ancestral Y chromosome and mtDNA (mitochondrial DNA) has been discovered. It must therefore be very disconcerting for white supremacists and others of their ilk to learn that geneticists have identified groups of chromosomes called haplogroups – "genetic fingerprints" which define populations – that trace their ancestral origins to the "subhuman" races of Africa. The ethnocentric concepts of a God Chosen People, a Master Race, or the feasibility of producing perfect "Racial Purity" as was the case in the Nazi Lebensborn breeding programme are therefore unadulterated racist nonsense.

Historically for Jews who lived among Christian populations in Eastern Europe and Russia, Christmas Eve was a time to keep off the streets for fear of violent confrontations with Christian celebrants. That situation, however, had been reversed and now in occupied East Jerusalem it was the goyim who had to watch out. Apart from the increased Israeli police and IDF presence to quell the current tensions, Yaakov Katzir gathered with hundreds of other Temple activists in the Western Wall Plaza in a show of provocative defiance. The mass gathering was similar to that of the *Ta'anit Ester* (Fast of Esther), which was first decreed by Ester 2500 years ago when the Jews in the Persian Empire were in danger of extinction at the hands of the evil Haman.

The activists faced the Haram al-Sharif/Temple Mount to plead with God for compassion and deliverance from the evil schemes of those seeking to destroy Israel. As was the custom, the plea was accompanied by the blasts of silver trumpets that had been specifically made for use in the yet to be built Third Temple. In his code of law – the Mishne Torah – Maimonides had stated that it was a positive Torah commandment to cry out and sound the trumpets "against an enemy who oppresses you, you shall sound short blasts of the trumpets." (Numbers 10:9). It would seem to have escaped the attention of those God chosen supremacists who were gathered with rapacious intent that the Palestinian people were also seeking a little heavenly compassion and some long overdue divine deliverance from their barbaric oppressors.

17

Friday, 25 December

Bethlehem, Occupied West Bank

Because Bethlehem had been one of the focal points for clashes between Israeli troops and Palestinian protesters during the months-long wave of violence, hundreds of Palestinian policemen and security officers were deployed in and around Bethlehem as part of an unprecedented security operation to maintain law and order during the Christmas celebrations which apart from hymns, "national songs," and music played by marching bands and scout troops, would include the lighting of the Manger Square Christmas tree which had been decorated with the red, black, white, and green colours of the Palestinian flag.

As the current troubles had halved the number of pilgrims and tourists usually expected at this time of year, Conrad and Freya had no trouble pre-booking their places for the Midnight Mass which – despite their not being particularly religious – was at least metaphysically inspiring. The Mass in the Church of St. Catherine, in the Basilica of the Nativity, was attended by – in the eyes of many Palestinians – the inconsequential President (a Sunni Muslim) of the Palestinian National Authority and presided over by the Latin Patriarch who had led a procession from his Jerusalem headquarters to Bethlehem through Israel's concrete separation barrier: a separation barrier that Palestinians regarded as being part of a land grab that had also stifled Bethlehem's economy.

Before Mass, the Patriarch had opened the Holy Door of the Church of St. Catherine for the Extraordinary Jubilee Holy Year of Mercy. Also referred to as Holy Years, jubilees usually occurred every 25 years with special celebrations and pilgrimages, calls for conversion and repentance, and the offer of special opportunities to experience God's grace through the sacraments, especially confession. This Year of Mercy had been unexpectedly announced by Pope Francis during a penitential service at St. Peter's Basilica in March. It began on the 8th of December's Solemnity of the Immaculate Conception and would end in 2016 on the 20th of November's Solemnity of Christ the King. Its motto was "Compassionate like the Father." Extraordinary holy years, such as the Holy Year of Mercy, were less frequent but offered the same opportunities. The last extraordinary jubilee was called by St. John Paul II in 1983 to mark the 1,950 years after the death of Jesus. John Paul had also led the last holy year, known as the "Great Jubilee," in 2000.

Following the three hour-long proceedings, as Conrad and Freya walked back to their hotel, they discussed the actual usefulness of such meaningless pomp and circumstance when the true value of humanity – to respect the rights of every individual, and to understand and accept our own value and cherish our own right to life; to protect the intrinsic value and potential of every individual without discrimination so that everyone – could live with respect from others; and to show one's concern through heartfelt actions that delivered warmth and practical assistance to the needy so as to establish a mutually caring culture – was being ignominiously ignored by most religions which had so far tended to rationalise hatred and prejudice and allow religious doctrines to be used as justification for oppressive actions and destructive wars.

While religions had usually been started on the supposed existence of people such as Buddha, Jesus, and Zoroaster whose professed aims were to help humanity understand and achieve higher levels of spirituality so as to make the world a better place, such noble intentions were eventually abandoned by power hungry religious leaders who formalised the original teachings into a sets of doctrines that helped establish religious institutions with seats of power facilitating the corrupt control of people and the devious deprivation of their human rights.

As civilisation progressed from Neolithic farming villages through to the first towns, cities, states, nations, and eventually to the current economic governance by transnational communities and treaties such as the EU and the Trans-Pacific Partnership (TPP), the harmonious coexistence that religion espoused within such transnational borders had been more than offset by the animosity that rival religions – Christianity, Judaism, and Islam – had deliberately instigated without due consideration for the welfare of humanity as a whole.

As a result of their research for this trip, Conrad and Freya had learnt that the concept of "religion" – a word derived from the two latin words "re" and "ligare" meaning "to reconnect" – was a relatively recent phenomenon considering its general assertion that the universe, the earth, and life on earth were the direct acts of the Abrahamic God during a relatively short period of between 5,700 and 10,000 years ago. Abrahamic religions were the monotheistic faiths of Judaism, Christianity, Islam, and Bahá'i – with the latter being founded in nineteenth-century Persia by Bahá'ulláh – that either emphasised and traced their common origin to Abraham, or recognised the spiritual tradition identified with him.

Conrad and Freya regarded all religions – with their gods, punishments, and rewards in the afterlife – as mere man-made contrivances exploited by the ruling classes for domination and control of the masses whose susceptibility to superstitions and mumbo jumbo rituals spawned a tribal fealty that generated suspicion and animosity towards heretics and infidel outsiders.

The concept of an afterlife with heaven or hell had been an ancient Egyptian innovation motivated by the elite's desire to retain absolute power. Immortality was initially a privilege which only the Pharaohs enjoyed after death, embalmment, and reunification with their ancestors. A Pharaoh, however, could in his capacity as a god extend the privilege to high priests and favoured officials by allowing them to build their tombs within the confines of the royal necropolis, and to use secret formulae to facilitate their journey to the afterlife.

The Ancient Egyptian ruling elite, in their never-ending quest to retain their privileged positions, however, soon realised that the concept of immortality was a potentially powerful weapon with which to control an ever-growing and increasingly disaffected population. So as the advantages of retaining the privilege of afterlife for themselves began to be outweighed by the benefits of making the afterlife an entitlement for everyone, the necessary theological adjustments were made so that by the onset of the Middle Kingdom (c. 1550 – 1650 BCE) the notion of the soul's immortality became universal. The concept of accountability and possible damnation in the afterlife for one's actions on earth was thus established, and its potential as a means of controlling the actions of the common people had since been fully exploited by all major religions. The Greek historian, Polibius (c. 200 – c.118 BCE), an author of books on the history of the Roman Republic and renowned for his ideas on the separation of powers in government which were later to be consulted for the drafting of the United States Constitution, had this to say on the subject:

> *"The most important difference for the better, which the Roman Commonwealth appears to me to display, in their religious beliefs, for I conceive that what in other nations is looked upon as a reproach, I mean a scrupulous fear for the gods, is the very thing that keeps the Roman Commonwealth together. To such an extraordinary height is this*

carried among them in private and public business, that nothing could exceed it. Many people think this unaccountable, but in my opinion their object is to use it as a check upon the common people. Where it possible to form a state wholly of philosophers, such a custom would be unnecessary. But seeing that every multitude is fickle and full of lawless desires, unreasoning anger and violent passion, the only resource is to keep them in check by the mysterious terrors and scenic effects of this sort. Wherefore to my mind the ancients were not acting without purpose or at random when they brought in among the vulgar these opinions about the gods and the punishments of Hades."

The Arab Quarter, Paris

For most Parisians Christmas was *"le plus merveilleux"* time of the year when the city glittered with colourful seasonal lighting in splendid locations such as Faubourg Saint-Honoré, Place Vendôme, Avenue Montaigne, Bercy Village, Forum des Halles, Viaduc des Arts, and the Champs Elysées with its 150,000 Christmas lights. It was also the season for indulgence with caviar, fresh oysters, scallops, lobster, foie gras, truffles, all kinds of wild fowl, roast turkey with chestnut stuffing, and of course champagne. Apart from the cotillon chocolat French Christmas cake, patisserie counters were also laden with the usual tempting tarte tatins, éclairs, multicoloured macarons, mille-feuilles, Paris-Brests, and the traditional Gâteau St. Honoré. For Malek Bennabi, however, this was not a day for *joie de vivre,* and rather than celebrating the joys of life, he was instead intent on making preparations for its violent disruption.

He had met with Pierre yesterday for the usual covert exchange of holdalls so that he was now in possession of 120 rounds of 7.62 x 39 mm calibre ammunition and all the components required for making the explosive device including three kilograms of plastic explosive. The first plastic explosive had been invented in 1875 by the Swedish chemist

Alfred Nobel – he of the Nobel Peace Prize – who was also the inventor of dynamite and owner of Bofors whose original role as an iron and steel producer he transformed into a major manufacturer of cannon and other armaments.

Nobel's invention was developed further during the Second World War when when special task units required a high performance, easy to shape, safe to manipulate explosive that was resistant to high temperatures and water. This was originally achieved by mixing a crystalline high explosive with oil, vaseline or natural rubber. This procedure for producing the plastic properties of explosives, however, was gradually improved upon with the use of synthetic binders and plasticisers leading to the development in the late 1950s of Semtex with large scale production being launched in the 1960s. This led to other similar types of explosives – also known as plastic bonded explosives or PBX– being produced in the U.S., the UK, France; Poland; Germany; Yugoslavia; Slovakia; Austria; and Sweden.

The explosive supplied to Malek was C4 (composition 4) plastic explosive with which he was already familiar and had previously used during his time in Beirut. C4 with its plastic coating binder was relatively safe to handle because of its reduced sensitivity which prevented detonation by heat, physical shocks, gunshots, exposure to fire, or microwave radiation. The inclusion of a plasticiser also made it more malleable so that it could be moulded into different shapes for controlling the direction of the explosion.

Antiterrorism laws in most countries required the tagging of explosives which involved adding a detection taggant – such as the volatile organic compound 2,3-dimethyl-2,3-dinitrobutane, otherwise known as DMDNB or DMNB, which can be detected by dogs or special detection machines – to facilitate the detection of explosives before detonation. Identification taggants were also intended to serve the purpose of tracing explosive materials to their source after detonation. Without such detection additives, plastic explosives would be difficult to detect, and consequently the plastic explosive provided by Pierre had been specially produced in Israel without any detection taggants.

Malek placed all the necessary components on the table, unrolled the small polyester toolkit, and began by removing the outer casing of the untraceable cellphone. He then plugged in the soldering iron and soldered the wires of an instantaneous electrical detonator (IED) to the phone's ringer so that when that phone's number was called, the ringer would generate an electric current and activate the detonator. The task of finally inserting the detonator into the C4 explosive would be carried out on the morning of the attack. Malek had no doubt that the detonation of his "little package" would contribute to the successful completion of the operation's objectives.

Vatican City, Italy

In his traditional Christmas Day "Urbi et Orbi" – a Papal address and Apostolic Blessing given to the city of Rome and to the entire world from the central balcony of St. Peter's Basilica – the Pope urged the world to unite in ending the atrocities committed by Islamist militants that were causing immense suffering in numerous countries. Amid tight security – with counter-terrorist police discreetly patrolling the area in unmarked vans with darkened windows – tens of thousands of people had their bags checked and were required to pass through airport-style screening before being allowed to enter St. Peter's Square.

After calling for an end to the civil wars in Syria and Libya, the Pope hoped that "the attention of the international community be unanimously directed to ending the atrocities which in those countries, as well as in Iraq, Libya, Yemen and sub-Saharan Africa, even now reap numerous victims, cause immense suffering and do not even spare the historical and cultural patrimony of entire peoples." The Pope was clearly referring to Islamic State militants who had carried out numerous attacks in those countries and destroyed many cultural heritage sites such as the blowing up of the Arch of Triumph, a jewel in the exquisite collection of ruins in the Syrian oasis city of Palmyra. His Holiness was obviously unaware that most of the Islamic state terrorist groups to which he was referring had in fact been created and were still being supported by Israeli and/or the United States.

His Holiness also believed that "only God's mercy can free humanity from the many forms of evil, at times monstrous evil, which selfishness spawns in our midst ... The grace of God can convert hearts and offer mankind a way out of humanly insoluble situations ... Where peace is born, there is no longer room for hatred and for war. Yet precisely where the incarnate Son of God came into the world, tensions and violence persist, and peace remains a gift to be implored and built." All of which unfortunately failed to explain why a God capable of converting hearts and offering mankind out of humanely insoluble situations had supposedly chosen a people who were the root cause of the current problems.

While calling for peace between Israelis and Palestinians in the area where Jesus Christ was born, the Pope also asked God to bring consolation and strength to Christians who were being persecuted around the world, and called for peace in the Democratic Republic of Congo, Burundi, South Sudan and Ukraine.

The Pope's seemingly sanctimonious but possibly well-intentioned expressions, however, ran contrary to the policies of a Roman Catholic Church whose strident opposition to birth control and pregnancy termination – out of an alleged respect for the "sanctity of human life" – had inflicted untold hardships and inhumane suffering on hundreds of millions of people. By wishing for peace between Israelis and Palestinians without recognising Israel's brutal occupation and ethnic cleansing of Palestinian people, the Holy Father was aligning himself with the audacious hypocrisy of other religious and political leaders in the West who apart from tolerating Israeli crimes which invited a retaliatory Islamic hatred, were also responsible for the instigation, the financing, and the supply of weapons to Islamic terror groups so as to perpetuate financially lucrative conflicts. The "Sanctity of Human Life" – backed by the Universal Declaration of Human Rights – to which the Vatican was so attached, appears to be inapplicable to the victims of both Israel's crimes against humanity and the West's phoney global War on Terrorism.

It was evident that while for most Westerners the almost seven decades of inordinate suffering by the Palestinian people was an inconvenient conscience pricking reminder of Israeli atrocities, they nonetheless managed to reconcile their consciences by regarding the legal and human rights of Palestinians as an irrelevance when compared with the ever-playing soundbite of "Israel has a right to exist": an existence which incidentally Israel had without question enforced with blatant discrimination and ethnic cleansing. The extent of such pathological pro-Israel bigotry had for example obliged presumptive presidential nominees – vying for Jewish lobby votes and financial support – to accuse human rights organisations of being anti-Semitic without fear of challenge or recrimination. The front-running, broom-riding political virago for the Democrats had unwittingly revealed her own anti-Palestinian bigotry while brown nosing the Jewish lobby by equating BDS supporters with anti-Semites, rather than with supporters of human rights:

"Many of the young people here today [at AIPAC] are on the front lines of the battle to oppose the alarming boycott, divestment and

sanctions movement known as BDS ... Particularly at a time when anti-Semitism is on the rise across the world, especially in Europe, we must repudiate all efforts to malign, isolate and undermine Israel and the Jewish people ... I've been sounding the alarm for a while now. As I wrote last year in a letter to the heads of major American Jewish organisations, we have to be united in fighting back against BDS. Many of its proponents have demonised Israeli scientists and intellectuals, even students ... to all the college students who may have encountered this on campus, I hope you stay strong. Keep speaking out. Don't let anyone silence you, bully you or try to shut down debate, especially in places of learning like colleges and universities ... Anti-Semitism has no place in any civilised society, not in America, not in Europe, not anywhere."

In fairness to the "lady," in her biased diatribe she did manage to highlight Western double standards and hypocrisy when she told people to "keep speaking out. Don't let anyone silence you, bully you or try to shut down debate, especially in places of learning like colleges and universities," while in the same breath denying those same people the right to choose and boycott Israel as it was once the right thing to do against Apartheid in South Africa. She also raised the point that "anti-Semitism has no place in any civilised society, not in America, not in Europe, not anywhere," without realising that a great many people in the world today do not regard America as being even remotely civilised, but rather as the greatest threat to peace on earth for all humanity.

The White House, Washington, D.C.

In his weekly address the President was joined by the First lady in wishing Americans a tongue-in-cheek Merry Christmas.

PRESIDENT: Merry Christmas, everybody! This is one of our favourite times of the year in our household, filled with family and friends, warmth and good cheer. That's even true when I spend all night chasing Bo and Sunny away from the cookies we leave for Santa. It's also my favourite weekly address of the year, because I'm joined by a special holiday guest star: my wife.

FIRST LADY: Merry Christmas, everyone. Here at the White House, we've spent the past month helping everyone get into the holiday spirit. Our theme this year is "A Timeless Tradition," and the decorations in each room reflect some of our country's most cherished pastimes – from saluting our troops and their families to helping children dream big dreams for their future. And we've invited thousands of families here to the White House to enjoy the festivities – because there's no holiday tradition more timeless than opening our doors to others.

PRESIDENT: Today, like millions of Americans and Christians around the world, our family celebrates the birth of Jesus and the values He lived in his own life. Treating one another with love and compassion. Caring for those on society's margins: the sick and the hungry, the poor and the persecuted, the stranger in need of shelter – or simply an act of kindness. That's the spirit that binds us together – not just as Christians, but as Americans of all faiths. It's what the holidays are about: coming together as one American family to celebrate our blessings and the values we hold dear. During this season, we also honour all who defend those values in our country's uniform. Every day, the brave men and women of our military serve to keep us safe – and so do their families.

FIRST LADY: So as we sing carols and open presents, as we win snowball fights …

PRESIDENT: Or lose snowball fights …

FIRST LADY: Let's also take time to pay tribute to those who have given our country so much. Go to JoiningForces.gov to see how you can serve the troops, veterans, and military families in your community. And together, we can show them just how grateful we are for their sacrifice. That's a tradition we all can embrace – today and every day.

PRESIDENT: So on behalf of all of us here at the White House – Merry Christmas. May God bless our troops and their families. And may God bless you all with peace and joy in the year ahead.

While the President and First Lady may have "invited thousands of families here to the White House to enjoy the festivities," it is certain that none of the invited where from the estimated 60,000 homeless veterans who in the past had made personal sacrifices to keep America safe. In keeping with other American traditions of seasonal goodwill, the U.S. promised to increase military aid to Israel in support of that Apartheid country's ethnic cleansing of Palestinians, and American forces on this Christmas day continued keeping "Americans safe" by carrying out 17 airstrikes in Syria and Iraq with all U.S. aircraft and their extremely brave crews returning safely. So after some 15 years since 9/11 and the global war on terror initiated by such war criminals as George Bush and Dick Cheney, the U.S. was continuing to carry out assassinations, covert operations, drone strikes, attacks by special forces, and combat missions by American ground forces in Afghanistan and Iraq where headway and victory had remained obstinately elusive to the benefit of the military industrial complex on whose weapons almost two trillion dollars were being spent annually. The pitfalls of continual warfare had been recognised over 220 years earlier by James Madison, the fourth President of the U.S., who was hailed as the "Father of the Constitution" for his significant role in drafting and advancing the U.S. Constitution and the Bill of Rights.

"Of all the enemies to public liberty war is, perhaps, the most to be dreaded because it comprises and develops the germ of every other. War

is the parent of armies; from these proceed debts and taxes ... known
instruments for bringing the many under the domination of the few ...
No nation could preserve its freedom in the midst of continual warfare."
James Madison, *Political Observations,* **1795.**

18

Sunday, 27 December

Malmilla, West Jerusalem

The most notable aspect of Conrad and Freya's return bus journey to Jerusalem on Boxing day was at the checkpoint where they and other tourists were allowed to remain on the bus, while all Palestinians had to disembark for permit, electromagnetic ID card, and biometric fingerprint checks by obnoxious Israeli soldiers. Such restrictions on the freedom of movement for Palestinians in the West Bank – designed to humiliate and make life as difficult as possible – were enforced by a system of fixed checkpoints, surprise flying checkpoints, physical obstructions and roadblocks, roads for Jews only, and gates along the Separation Barrier – all of which enabled Israel to serve its own selfish interests while denying Palestinians their rights. Prolonged checks and searches at most checkpoints, humiliating treatment by soldiers, and long lines deterred Palestinian drivers from using those few roads still open for their use. Consequently Palestinians avoided travelling on many of the main roads in the West Bank which were used almost exclusively by settlers. There were apparently some 96 fixed checkpoints in and around the West Bank including 57 located well within the the area.

After they had checked into their hotel in Mamilla at 12:30 p.m., they phoned the grieving Miriam and her children who were still waiting to be officially informed of Sami's death and the whereabouts of his body. Peltz had made enquiries on the family's behalf, but because Israeli authorities were always deliberately uncooperative and hostile if not downright obstructive where Palestinians were concerned, he had been unable to obtain any information. Conrad and Freya had then taken a cab to Silwan and spent several hours with Sami's family before going to film and photograph a nearby house where another family had been forced to evacuate their home due to its becoming totally unsafe because of serious damage caused to its walls and foundation by underground Israeli excavations. They were told that many other Palestinian homes and buildings in Silwan had also suffered similar gaping cracks in walls and floors that endangered the lives of dozens of residents who even if they had the financial resources, would still be unable to find alternative accommodation.

One of the young Palestinian men volunteered to give them a brief tour of the beleaguered village with its fortified and well guarded enclaves of Jewish settlers after which Conrad and Freya left to visit the nearby City of David Archaeological Park where the main narrative told to the hundreds of thousands who visited the park annually, was that they were visiting the site of ancient Jerusalem from the time of David, Solomon and the kings of Judah. The veracity of such claims had been disputed by scholars and the controversy over the evidence found at the site was still raging with archaeological research and findings neither confirming nor refuting the biblical narrative.

Conrad was already aware from his research that this obsessive compulsion to substantiate the past existence of the "City of David" was not a recent phenomenon because in 1913, Baron Rothschild purchased some 30 dunams of land on the eastern slope of the "City David" and sought the services of French-Jewish archaeologist Raymond Weill, who excavated the site from 1913 – 1914 and from 1923 – 1924. Weill was considered to be the first Jewish archaeologist to have worked in Jerusalem with his excavations being carried specifically with the aim of validating the descriptions of Charles Clermont-Ganneau (1846 – 1923) – the noted French orientalist and archaeologist – regarding the location of the tombs of the Kings of Judah on the Eastern slope of the ancient city.

As they entered the park, Conrad recalled that in *The Bible in History: How Writers Create a Past,* a book his father Mark had lent him, the author Thomas L. Thompson had stated the following:

> *"There is no evidence of a United Monarchy, no evidence of a capital in Jerusalem or of any coherent, unified political force that dominated western Palestine, let alone an empire of the size the legends describe. We do not have evidence for the existence of kings named Saul, David or Solomon; nor do we have evidence for any temple at Jerusalem in this early period. What we do know of Israel and Judah of the tenth century does not allow us to interpret this lack of evidence as a gap in our knowledge and information about the past, a result merely of the accidental nature of archeology. There is neither room nor context, no artefact or archive that points to such historical realities in Palestine's tenth century. One cannot speak historically of a state without a population. Nor can one speak of a capital without a town. Stories are not enough."*

After leaving the park, they walked round to the nearby Citadel – an imposing stronghold with a now dried-out and partially filled in moat – adjoining the Jaffa Gate entrance to the Old City. The present-day structure dated mainly from the Middle Ages and included additions made by Suleyman the Magnificent in 1532. Excavations had, however, revealed remains dating back to the 2nd. century BCE which hinted at the possible existence of fortifications from the Herodian period. This had led to speculation that it was the most likely site of Jesus Christ's trial and conviction. The Citadel was also known as the Tower of David with the misnomer being due, and dating back to Byzantine confusion over the city's geographical layout.

Other features of notable interest for their cameras had included the Tower of Phasael, one of three built by Herod and named for his brother Phasael, his wife Miriam, and his friend Hippicus – that were built to defend the city and Herod's palace which was presumed to have been located nearby. The top of Phasael's Tower – marked by smaller stones added during the Mamluk period – offered a spectacular 360-degree panoramic view of East and West Jerusalem.

The Hasmonean Wall was a segment of the wall that surrounded Jerusalem during the second century BCE Hasmonean period and was referred to as "the First Wall" by Josephus Flavius – a first-century Romano-Jewish scholar, historian and hagiographer, who was born in Jerusalem – because it was the first of three walls surrounding Jerusalem during the Second Temple period. In Herod's time and in the later Byzantine period, additions were made to the wall.

The Citadel's courtyard contained the remains of the Muslim Tower, a round tower which was part of a Muslim fortress that was the first to be built during the rule of the Ummayid dynasty (7th and 8th centuries CE).

They visited the mosque from the Mamluk period which – as indicated in the stone inscription located at the entrance – was renovated toward the end of the Ottoman period by Abdul Hamid II. It currently served as a gallery housing the Early Muslim Period exhibition. The hall had a mihrab – a niche directing worshippers towards Mecca – which was built during the Mamluk period. There was also a minbar, or pulpit, built towards the end of the Turkish rule during which time in 1635 an impressive minaret was added which subsequently came to be known as the Tower of David and symbolised Jerusalem. Though Conrad and Freya as they left the Citadel were conscious of the awe inspiring aura generated by its historic setting, there still was no escaping the disturbing sense of potentially explosive tension that prevailed amongst a captive indigenous population unable to escape the rapacious inhumanity of their occupiers.

Conrad and Freya had booked in advance for today's tour of the Western Wall Tunnels and as they walked from the Jaffa Gate towards the Western Wall Plaza, Conrad recounted what he had learnt during his previous visit to the tunnels, from his subsequent research, and from what Adam Peltz who had told him about the government's scheduling of a meeting in May to coincide with Jerusalem Day when plans for strengthening the city's economy and reinforcing its status as the capital of Israel would be revealed. Such revelations would include the government's intention to provide the Western Wall Heritage Foundation and the Western Wall Tunnels with 100 million shekels during the next five years.

As the most active organisation in archaeological excavations in the Old City, the Western Wall Heritage Foundation was established by the Ministry of Religious Affairs in 1988 to develop, foster, and preserve the Western Wall along with its tunnels. It was responsible for both excavations beneath the Muslim Quarter known as the "Western Wall Tunnels," and the excavations beneath the synagogue "Ohel Yitzhak," which was also in the Muslim Quarter. The Foundation had also initiated the establishment on the Western Wall Plaza of the "Beit HaLiba," a contentious three-storey facility with a large ground floor lobby leading to three classrooms and a 155-seat auditorium with a "systems room" and the "Hall of Yearning" for educating visitors about the history of the Western Wall; a top floor featuring a library, office space, a learning centre, a room for guides, a classroom, and another "systems room"; a roof serving as an observation deck; and a basement level providing access to the archaeological site and to an old Roman road leading to the Dung Gate. The Foundation was also responsible for the rebuilding of Mughrabi Bridge access to Haram al-Sharif/Temple Mount with the project being currently on hold because of existing politically charged issues between the Islamic Waqf, Jordan, and Israel.

Today the Mughrabi Bridge had been crossed by extremist Jewish settlers who then stormed the the Al-Aqsa Mosque from the Mughrabi Gate amid tight security protection from Israeli police whose increased presence around the mosque had facilitated incursions by about 100 settlers while preventing access for Muslim worshippers under the age of 35. The rabble-rousing settlers had stormed into Al-Aqsa Mosque and walked inside its courtyards. When the Al-Aqsa guards and worshipers tried to prevent settlers from performing Talmudic rituals, they had been ushered away from the mosque by police. Such provocative incursions had only served to heighten an already inflammatory situation.

Though the tunnels were not necessarily recognised as being religious or sacred, they were nonetheless covered by regulations on safeguarding the Jewish holy places including the Western Wall, the adjacent plaza, and every overpass or underground passageway with an entry point at the plaza. The fact that the entrance to the tunnels was at the Western Wall plaza meant that legally they were regarded as being sacred.

Western Wall Tunnel excavations began in 1969 and had been continuous – apart from occasional interruptions – to the present day. Such archaeological activities had increased since 2004 with excavations being conducted non-stop on land owned by Jewish organisations but under the houses of Palestinians living in the Muslim Quarter. The main significance of the Western Wall Tunnels for the Jewish people was the northward extension with its exposure of a wall built with enormous stones that formed the outer foundations of the Haram al-Sharif/Temple Mount. This foundation wall was associated with King Herod's renovation of the temple in the first century

BCE. Additional tunnels and spaces along the Western Wall – mostly from later periods – had also been excavated.

Conrad explained that there was a contradiction between the tunnel narrative presented by the Western Wall Heritage Foundation and the research findings from excavations as they appeared in scientific publications. The consensus of research opinion was that the underground spaces had been built throughout various Islamic periods with for example the suggested date of the covered "secret cave" – now serving as the main entrance to the tunnels – being in the Early Islamic Abbasid period from 8th century CE onwards. It was also the considered opinion of excavators that the main spaces of the Western Wall Tunnels belonged to later periods such as that of the Mamluks starting in the 13th century CE. The buildings and streets under the Muslim layers were dated to the Late Roman period (2nd – 4th century CE) or the Byzantine period (4th – 7th century CE). There were also remains, mostly cisterns and baths, dating to the Early Roman period. Archaeologists were in agreement that most of the remains post-date the destruction of the Second Temple.

The narrative provided by the Western Wall Tunnel guides, however, was completely different from the actual history of the archaeological discoveries with the tour dealing almost exclusively with the history of the Haram al-Sharif/Temple Mount as the holiest Jewish site. The route included several stations which portrayed the Haram al-Sharif/Temple Mount as being central to the narrative with the enormous foundation wall being identified with the original stones of the temple's foundation; with the doorways which had been blocked over the years being identified as entrances to the Temple; and with other nebulous assumptions in the same vein. The guides' narrative entirely ignored the history of Jerusalem after the Jewish temple periods with virtually no mention of either Jerusalem's pagan-Roman and Byzantine eras which formed the Old City's foundations, or the impressive remains from Islamic periods.

The guides' oral presentation of the Western Wall Tunnel history had been designed to emphasise the Judaic narrative's yearning for the Haram al-Sharif/Temple Mount while completely ignoring the non-Jewish aspects of the site's long history. Archaeological excavations from the 1970s had for example exposed buildings from different periods with the most notable being street remains dating to the Second Temple (1st century CE); facilities associated with the Tenth Legion of the Roman army; remains from the Byzantine period (4th – 7th century CE); the Umayyad period (7th or 8th century CE); as well as later Islamic Periods. The dedication of a prayer area which had hitherto served to recount the story of the Old City through archaeological evidence, provided further confirmation of the growing tendency to intentionally disregard secular historical perspectives and replace them with a strictly Jewish religious viewpoint.

Earlier that year, the Company for the Reconstruction and Development of the Jewish Quarter – run by the Ministry of Housing – which owned the Davidson Centre, had signed an agreement transferring the management of the archaeological park to the Elad Foundation. Because of the Centre's sensitive location adjoining the Haram al-Sharif/Temple Mount, it had always been managed by state authorities whose former Housing Minister was a strong advocate of the need to build the Third Temple. Elad in the meantime had avoided declarations regarding the Mount and purportedly focussed its attention on archaeological activities designed to bolster the relationship between Israelis and the Mount. One such Elad project involved sifting the debris dug up by the Islamic Waqf during its development work on Al-Aqsa between 1996 and 1999 with visitors now being allowed to become involved by sifting the dirt to uncover archaeological relics of questionable scientific value.

Managing the Davidson Centre had enabled Elad to entrench the link between Silwan and the Old City including the Western Wall plaza. Visitors to the Davidson Centre could now follow an underground archaeological route directly to Silwan, while Elad conducted tours along the drainage channel connecting the two sites. Elad had also continued to fund the digging of additional underground tunnels and routes with a view to linking the different sites under its management. Elad's Kedem Centre – a tourist centre to be established at the entrance to Silwan – would link the "City of David" National Park and the Western Wall plaza. It was certainty that Elad would invest heavily in archaeological excavations, and run the Davidson Centre with the same objective as it did the City of David, and that was to showcase a totally biased Jewish archaeological presence that would inevitably result in increased inter-religious tensions.

Conrad and Freya were left with no doubt that while at present Israel was not physically transforming the Haram al-Sharif/Temple Mount, it was, however, actively and deliberately changing the face of the surrounding area, including its foundations, in order to boost its identification with Jewish history at the expense of its Muslim identity and heritage. This strategy was evident from the ongoing archaeological activity in the tunnels that stretched underneath the Muslim Quarter; from the decision to transfer the management of the Davidson Centre from the government to the settlers; from the restrictions on burials at Bab al-Rahma cemetery east of the Old City walls; and from the process of reinforcing the Jewish-religious narrative in archaeological sites in the Old City.

It was also evident that for Muslims walking through the Old City to attend prayers at the Haram al-Sharif, the Jerusalem that was once an inseparable part of their Palestinian-Muslim society, had been drastically changed. If for example they were walking from Silwan in the south, they would pass by the

"City of David" visitors' centre and the various excavations as they continued to the Old City. Furthermore, because access through the Dung Gate – the closest entry point to the Western Wall plaza and Al-Aqsa – is closed to Muslim worshippers, they have to walk through the Jewish Quarter or proceed around the Old City walls, then enter through Lion's Gate in the east where Jewish presence and friction with them was minimal. Israel, however, was also creating tension at this location by erecting a fence around the Bab al-Rahma Cemetery.

Access from the Damascus Gate in the north entailed walking along Al-Wad Street which had become more Israeli-orientated with the purchase of homes by the settlers' group Ateret Cohanim and an increased presence of security forces. Al-Wad Street, one of the main streets used by Muslim, Christian, and Jewish worshippers wishing to access the Haram al-Sharif/Temple Mount and the Western Wall from the Damascus Gate, was now subject to conservation works by the Antiquities Authority. Such blatant Judaisation efforts had understandably created the suspicion, tension, and violence which Israel welcomed as an excuse for its brutal and disproportionate response.

On their return to the hotel, Conrad and Freya caught up on their email correspondence and then checked newspaper websites for the second part of Mark's article on America.

The Zionisation And Decline Of American Democracy

Part 2 of 2

Mark Banner
Sunday, 27 December

Back in 1944, Juan José Arévalo – a liberal with relatively moderate policies – was elected President of Guatemala following a people's revolution that toppled the U.S.-backed right-wing dictator Jorge Ubico who since 1931 had ruled the country ruthlessly while fancying himself as a 20th-century Napoleon. Ubico had given rich landowners and the United Fruit Company – a U.S. corporation that later became Chiquita – generous access to Guatemala's natural resources while using the military to violently suppress his people's attempts to organise labour dissent. The U.S., however, favoured having a right-wing puppet regime that would reinstate the privileges previously granted U.S. corporations and eventually in 1949, it backed an attempted coup which failed.

Two years later in 1951, Arévalo was succeeded by the slightly more left-wing but still moderate Jacobo Árbenz whom the U.S. subsequently claimed was close to Guatemala's communists and could therefore become an ally of the Soviet Union. Árbenz, a social democrat who actually persecuted Guatemalan communists, was only guilty of believing that the Guatemalans people themselves, and not foreign multinational corporations, should benefit from the country's resources. Consequently he pursued land reform policies that would end the control exercised over the country by rich families and the United Fruit Company. Such policies resulted in U.S. President Truman authorising a 1952 coup attempt which was abandoned when details of the operation became known. Undeterred, the CIA and U.S. State Department, under the Dulles Brothers, bombed Guatemala City in 1954 in a coup that violently toppled Guatemala's democratic government. The U.S. then put into power Carlos Castillo Armas, the first of a serious of authoritarian right-wing tyrants – who until the end of the Guatemalan Civil War in 1996 – brutally repressed left-wing dissidents and carried out a campaign of genocide against peaceful indigenous peoples.

In 1951, Mohammad Mosaddegh became the prime minister and only democratically elected leader of Iran, which was then a secular democracy. Mosaddegh was neither socialist nor communist and in fact repressed Iranian communists while pursuing progressive, social democratic policies which included nationalising the Anglo-Persian Oil Company, cancelling its oil concession, and expropriating its assets all of which in any case belonged to Iran and its people. Consequently in 1953, the CIA colluded with British intelligence to overthrow Mosaddegh in a coup led by CIA operative Kermit Roosevelt Jr., grandson of former President Theodore Roosevelt.

A U.S. backed coup d'état by some of the Brazilian Armed Forces in 1964 toppled left-wing Brazilian President João Goulart who was not viewed favourably by Washington because of his independent stand in foreign policy; his resumption of relations with socialist countries including his opposition to sanctions against Cuba; his passing of a law restricting the amount of profits multinationals could transfer out of the country; his nationalising of a subsidiary of International Telephone & Telegraph (ITT); and his promotion of economic and social reforms.

Because of its proximity to the U.S. and the activity of left-wing movements on its continent, Latin America had from 1898 to 1994, suffered at least 41 U.S interventions with numerous Latin American military dictators having been trained at the School of the Americas, a U.S. Department of Defence Institute in Fort Benning, Georgia. Recently released diplomatic cables by the whistleblowing organisation WikiLeaks showed that the U.S. is still involved in systematic campaigns with the specific intention of overthrowing left-wing Latin American governments.

Apart from its interference in Latin America, U.S. involvement in "regime change" also occurred in Syria in 1949 with the Syrian Army Chief of Staff having met with CIA operatives on at least six occasions prior to the coup; in Indonesia where in 1958 due to their anti-communist rhetoric, the rebels received arms, funding, and other covert assistance from the CIA; in Cuba where the infamous Bay of Pigs Invasion by CIA-trained Cuban anti-communist exiles and refugees failed miserably; in Iraq between 1962 and 1963 The U.S. was concerned about the growing influence of Iraqi Communist Party government officials; in the newly independent Democratic Republic of the Congo from 1960 to 1965 where the presence of communist influence and a visit by Che Guevara prompted the military support of Western nations, including the U.S., for a coup by Joseph Mobutu who became mainly renowned for looting his country's treasury to the tune of billions of U.S. dollars.

In the Dominican Republic where in 1961 the CIA supported the overthrow of President/Dictator Rafael Trujillo; in Turkey when in 1980 3,000 U.S. troops of the Rapid Deployment Force started the "Anvil Express" manoeuvre on Turkish soil one day prior to the military coup; in Poland where between 1980 and 1989 due to fears of "an imminent move by large Soviet military forces into Poland," the CIA annually transferred about $2 million in cash to the Independent Self-governing Trade Union "Solidarity"; in Nicaragua from 1981 to 1990 where apart from arming and financing the rebel Contras (Iran–Contra scandal), the CIA also created the Unilaterally Controlled Latino Assets (UCLAs) to sabotage ports, refineries, boats and bridges, and to endeavour to make it appear as the work of the contras; in Iraq during 1992 to 1996 when the CIA supported a bomb and sabotage campaign that failed to topple Saddam Hussein.

Following the end of World War II when the First Indochina War began with tension between the independence-seeking Viet Minh and the returning French in late 1946, the Viet Minh led by General Giap, retreated to remote areas to train, gather support and instigate a protracted war with the help of the Viet Cong political organisation and army in South Vietnam. The ensuing French military failures led to France attempting to undermine the Viet Minh by establishing an independent republic of Vietnam under the puppet emperor Bao Dai who was allowed to form a Vietnamese National Army (VNA) in support of the French. In 1952-53 the Viet Minh invaded French-occupied Laos which resulted in the French Far-East Expeditionary Corps being decisively defeated at the Battle of Dien Bien Phu in March to May 1954 – subsequently subject of a 1992 French film regarded as one of the more important war movies in French filmmaking history – which culminated in the signing of the 1954 Geneva Accords with the stipulations that Vietnam would be temporarily divided at the 17th. parallel and that an election would be held on July 1956 to decide the government of a reunified Vietnam.

Fearing a communist victory in the election, the U.S. – with its increasing post-war obsession of stemming the spread of communism – decided against having the election held and instead backed (with the CIA buying off or intimidating his opponents) the staunch anti-communist Ngo Dinh Diem in a fraudulent 1955 plebiscite that saw him win 600,000 votes from an electorate of 450,000 and establish a right-wing dictatorship in South Vietnam that ended in a coup and his assassination on 2 November 1963. In the meantime, the Vietnamese Nationalist Movement leader Ho Chi Minh – who had already fought against the Japanese and French colonial powers – took on the US-backed South Vietnamese forces.

It was in Vietnam that the U.S. perfected its method of bringing freedom and democracy to other countries and for the Vietnamese people such U.S. freedom-providing largesse was launched from 30,000 feet overhead in the form of carpet bombing B-52s disgorging both Dumb and Guided Bombs, Fuel Air Explosives, Napalm, and Agent Orange. By the end of the war, seven million tons of bombs had been dropped on Vietnam, Laos, and Cambodia which was more than twice the amount of bombs dropped on Europe and Asia in World War Two. The war's casualties included an estimated two million Vietnamese civilian deaths with massacres such as My Lai by U.S Forces; the U.S. herbicidal warfare programme's use of Agent Orange which killed or maimed some 400,000 and to this day is still afflicting three million as a result of birth defects – and that is without counting the millions more of their relatives who bear the brunt and hardship of looking after them; between 200,000 and 250,000 South Vietnamese soldiers killed; some 1.1 million North Vietnamese and Viet Cong fighters killed; and some 58,200 members of U.S. armed forces who died or were missing. Ultimately it was for the U.S. a costly, divisive, and increasingly unpopular war which in 1973 led to the U.S. forces withdrawing with their tails between their legs and the unification two years later of Vietnam under Communist control.

The anti-war sentiment in the U.S. had by 1967 witnessed Martin Luther King Jr. becoming not only the country's leading opponent of the Vietnam War, but also a staunch critic of overall U.S. foreign policy which he viewed as being militaristic. In his "Beyond Vietnam" speech delivered at New York's Riverside Church on April 4, 1967 – a year to the day before he was assassinated – King accused the U.S. of being "the greatest purveyor of violence in the world today." *Time* magazine's reaction was to describe the speech as "demagogic slander that sounded like a script for Radio Hanoi," while *The Washington Post* echoed that King had "diminished his usefulness to his cause, his country, his people." The following is an excerpt from King's speech:

> " ... *At this point I should make it clear that while I have tried in these last few minutes to give a voice to the voiceless on Vietnam and to understand the arguments of those who are called enemy, I am as deeply concerned about our troops there as anything else. For it occurs to me that what we are submitting them to in Vietnam is not simply the brutalising process that goes on in any war where armies face each other and seek to destroy. We are adding cynicism to the process of death, for they must know after a short period there that none of the things we claim to be fighting for are really involved. Before long they must know that their government has sent them into a struggle among Vietnamese, and the more sophisticated surely realise that we are on the side of the wealthy and the secure while we create hell for the poor ... "*

The debacle in Vietnam, however, had proved to be the rule rather than the exception because since June 5, 1944, the day before D-Day – when U.S. General George S. Patton climbed onto a makeshift platform in southern England and proudly informed thousands of American soldiers that "Americans play to win all of the time ... That's why Americans have never lost nor will ever lose a war, for the very idea of losing is hateful to an American" – U.S. forces have experienced little other than military stalemate and loss. They have not actually won a single war on the ground – not in Afghanistan, not in Iraq, not anywhere. They simply lay waste to infrastructures and destroy millions of lives before leaving despair and devastation in their wake.

Despite its humiliation in Vietnam and domestic opposition to anymore overseas intrigues or military involvements, the U.S. – through its inappropriately named and not very smart Central Intelligence Agency – maintained its obsession with communism by interfering in the affairs of other countries with special attention and resources being expended on Latin America. In 1970 Marxist leader Salvador Allende was democratically elected president of Chile despite U.S. President Nixon's order to the CIA to make Chile's "economy scream," or to "prevent Allende from coming to power or to unseat him." Immediately following Allende's election, the U.S. government provided right-wing opposition groups with material support and bribed Chile's conservative media outlets with millions of dollars. The deputy director of Central Intelligence Agency (CIA) outlined plans in a memo which stated "it is firm and continuing policy that Allende be overthrown by a coup … It is imperative that these actions be implemented clandestinely and securely so that the USG [U.S. government] and American hand be well hidden."

It was not at all surprising that the arrogant Jewish megalomaniac and war criminal, Henry Kissinger – U.S. National Security Advisor (January 20, 1969 – November 3, 1975) and U.S. Secretary of State (September 22, 1973 – January 20, 1977) – expressed the following disdainful opinion:

> *"I don't see why we need to stand by and watch a country go communist due to the irresponsibility of its people. The issues are much too important for the Chilean voters to be left to decide for themselves."*

Consequently on September 11, 1973, in a U.S.-backed violent coup, Allende's democratic government was overthrown and in an emotive speech prior to dying, Allende declared his willingness to give his life in defence of Chilean democracy and sovereignty. Such democracy and sovereignty was subsequently crushed by far-right dictator Augusto Pinochet's fascistic police state repression which resulted in tens of thousands of Chilean leftists, labour leaders, and journalists being tortured, "disappeared," or killed with hundreds of thousands more being forced into exile. During this cold war period, one of the West's propaganda myths was that the socialist system of governance relied on brute force to repress the people. Chile's example, however, had served to prove that the exact opposite was true with many impoverished and oppressed masses electing socialist governments that the U.S. and other Western allies saw fit to violently overthrow. Prior to Allende being overthrown, many South American socialists had naively believed that popular Marxist movements could achieve power through the democratic election process. After witnessing how the U.S. violently toppled Allende's elected government, however, they soon changed their minds and instead of relying on the ballot box, they resorted to alternative methods including guerrilla warfare.

The U.S. was also involved in the 1976 right-wing military coup d'état in Argentina which replaced President Isabel Perón with General Jorge Rafael Videla whose "National Reorganisation Process" junta increased political repression in a "Dirty War" that "disappeared" some 30,000 people. Amongst the disappeared were an estimated 500 children who had been kidnapped by the government or born in detention. Most of those children were given to military families who raised them as their own so as to prevent their true identities becoming known and to avoid questions as to what happened to their parents many of whom were "disappeared" by simply having them thrown from military aircraft into the Atlantic Ocean. The *Asociación Madres de Plaza de Mayo,* is an association of Argentine mothers who to this day are still trying to find their missing children and grandchildren.

Advancing democracy overseas first became an integral part of U.S. foreign policy during the early 1900s when the U.S. began playing a major role on the international stage and used the "Advancement of democracy" as an excuse with which to oppose the rival ideologies of imperialism, fascism, and finally communism. U.S. obsession with communism manifested itself in a number of undemocratic ways including the Alien Registration Act that was passed by Congress in June 1940 – and which within four months saw a total of 4,741,971 aliens being registered – with a view to mainly undermining the American Communist Party; the investigations of the Hollywood Motion Picture Industry in 1947 by the House Un-American Activities Committee; and an era of witch hunts by Senator Joseph McCarthy that led to the word "McCarthyism" becoming synonymous with the practice of making wild accusations of subversion and treason without appropriate regard for evidence or due process.

The U.S obsession with thwarting the spread of communism began to crumble when in 1986 Soviet Union President Mikhail Gorbachev initiated his new policy of *perestroika* (restructuring) which involved radical reforms that were followed by the introduction of *Glasnost* which gave the Soviet people freedoms they had never previously known including greater freedom of speech, far less press censorship, and the release of thousands of political prisoners and dissidents. Gorbachev's service to the people of the Soviet Union culminated on Christmas Day 1991, when the Soviet flag flew over the Kremlin in Moscow for the last time. Years later, Gorbachev was to observe – and correctly so – that the collapse of the Soviet Union was the worst thing that had happened to humanity, because the Soviet collapse removed the only constraint on Washington's power.

The next Latin American country in line for U.S. backed "democratisation" was Venezuela whose democratically elected and popular President Hugo Chávez was temporarily ousted in a 2002 coup d'état attempt. But due to his popularity, however, Chavez was restored to office within 47 hours by a combination of military loyalists and support from mostly poor Venezuelans. On 5 March 2013, Vice President Nicolás Maduro announced on state television that Chávez had died – apparently from a massive heart attack with his cancer being very advanced – at a military hospital in Caracas. Suggestions of American foul play with the implication that Chávez had been poisoned or somehow infected with cancer – an echo of a similar plot against Cuba's Fidel Castro – were denied as "absurd" by the disingenuous U.S. State Department. President Maduro, inherited the same U.S. meddling in Venezuelan affairs which forced him to fiercely criticise Washington for its hypocrisy, double standards and interventionism. Efforts to overthrow Maduro's government have continued to this day.

The biggest act of U.S. led terrorism, however, was the 2003 invasion of Iraq which had so far accounted for well over a million Iraqi deaths: Iraqi deaths that on a weekly basis continue to exceed the combined casualties of all terrorist attacks – probably Israeli false flag operations – in European cities such as London and Paris. As for the tragedy of September 11, 2001, that death toll of almost 3,000 people is frequently matched or surpassed every month in Iraq. And yet despite the death tolls in Iraq, Afghanistan, Libya, and Syria, the West – with its unmitigated hypocrisy and double standards – has never wrung its hands, observed moments of silence, lit up the Eiffel Tower with the colours of the victims' national flag, or displayed solidarity by singing a national anthem at London's Wembley football stadium with its landmark arch lit with a national flag. Such double standards merely confirm the reigning success of Israeli instigated Islamophobia in the West.

Since 2005 to the present time, the Zionised U.S. – egged on by continuous but unfounded and hysterical Israeli claims that Iran was "advancing towards the development of nuclear weapons" – has through the CIA carried out black operations (covert subversion) against Iran with a view to destabilising the country and its government. In 2007 for example, media reports asserted that President Bush had authorised a $400 million covert operation to create unrest among the Iranian government that was designed to pressure Iran into stopping its nuclear enrichment program.

More recently in Egypt's January 2011 revolution, dictator Hosni Mubarak – a close ally of the U.S. and Israel who had ruled Egypt with an iron fist for almost 30 years – was toppled as part of the Arab Spring that had begun with the Tunisian Revolution in December of the previous year. Following a 2012 vote – in a result that displeased both the U.S and Israel – Mohammed Morsi, became Egypt's first democratically elected president.

Needless to say Morsi did not last very long and as subsequently became apparent, his July 2013 removal by a military coup, was supported by the U.S. which once again had bankrolled opposition forces to overthrew a democratically elected government. Thanks to the U.S. perception of "democracy," Egypt now has the brutal despot Abdel Fattah el-Sisi as president who in August 2013 oversaw a slaughter of over 800 peaceful activists at Raba'a Square. Despite heinous human rights violations – the shooting of peaceful protesters and the jailing of some 40,000 political prisoners including journalists – Sisi remains a close ally of the U.S. and Israel, two nations whose own hypothetical pursuit of democracy and respect for human rights leave very much to be desired. The Israeli Defence Minister admitted in his speech at the annual AIPAC conference, the largest Zionist lobby supporting Israel in the US, that the overthrow of Mohamed Morsi and the installation of Egyptian President Abdel Fatah Al-Sisi was planned, in cooperation with generals in the Egyptian and Gulf armies and intelligence agencies. He also said that Israel's interests will always be served by having military regimes in the Arab world, especially in Egypt.

This was not the only Israeli admission of the need to keep Al-Sisi as president of Egypt in order to serve Israel's interests and there is no shortage of documented flattery and statements of unconditional support between the two governments. Morsi's removal enabled Israel to maintain its strategy of relations with selected Arab countries including cooperative projects, cultural exchanges, and bilateral economic and trade agreements. Such relations served the dual purpose of not only allowing the illegal Israeli occupation of, and Jewish settlement expansion on Palestinian territories, but also prevented the Arab countries concerned from criticising Israeli policies while instead labelling token Palestinian resistance as "terrorism."

The popular uprisings that swept across the Arab world against autocratic rulers in 2011, also inspired the Libyan people to take to the streets and demand change. Unsurprisingly, long established Libyan dictator Muammar Gaddafi was not amused and said he would call the people to "cleanse Libya house by house" unless protesters on the streets surrendered.

The protesters, however, did not surrender and Libya's security forces were uncompromising in their crackdown on demonstrations across the country. The U.S.-controlled NATO's subsequent humanitarian intervention – obligingly hailed by the Western media as Libya's "liberation" but regarded by some members of the UN Security Council as an act that overstepped its mandate of protection and was instead designed to achieve regime change – resulted in the barbaric murder of Gaddafi after his captors had sodomised him with a knife. Gaddafi did not even get to appear before a kangaroo court as was the case with Iraq's Saddam Hussein and Libya is now in a state of civil war and absolute chaos to the delight of Israel.

Various theories exist as to the true reason behind this U.S.-driven intervention including designs on Libya's oil by Western nations. But a more likely explanation, supported by emails released from Hillary Clinton's private email server, is that Gaddafi's plan to stop selling Libyan oil in U.S. dollars – demanding payment instead in gold-backed "dinars" (a single African currency made from gold) – was not welcomed by the power elite responsible for controlling the world's central banks. Gaddafi, whose regime had amassed some 150 tons of gold and silver with an estimated value of $7 billion, was also urging other African and Middle Eastern governments to follow suit. While the plan would have benefited the entire African continent as a result of economists and investors seeking to back sound money, it would have also devastated the U.S. economy, the U.S. dollar, and especially the Rothschild-led elite who controlled the system. Had Gaddafi's gold-driven monetary revolution been successful, it would have benefited both the Libyan people and the rest of the world while imperilling the position the of central bankers and their political and media power-brokers.

The discovery of Libya's plan by French intelligence officers was was apparently one of the the factors that influenced President Nicolas Sarkozy – otherwise known as Sarko the Sayan for his allegedly being a Mossad agent – to commit France for the attack on Libya. Other factors included a desire to gain a greater share of Libyan oil production; increase French influence in North Africa; improve his internal political situation in France; provide the French military with an opportunity to reassert its position on the world stage; and address the concern of his advisors over Qaddafi's long term plans to supplant France as the dominant power in Francophone Africa.

A sequence of events similar to those that occurred in Libya – involving the global monetary system with its use of the U.S. dollar as a global reserve currency supported by the trading of oil in American dollars – have also been associated with other U.S. government targets for intervention. One such target happens to be Iran which remains as one of the very few nations in the world with a state-owned central bank. It should also be noted that Iraqi dictator Saddam Hussein – armed and encouraged by the U.S. government to wage war against Iran – had also threatened to start selling oil in alternative currencies to the U.S. dollar which subsequently prompted the Bush administration's Zionist instigated neocon "regime change" policy.

The protection of American oil interests has been at the core of U.S. Middle East policy for decades and had to a sizeable extent also driven Washington's Israel policy with policymakers having to choose between protecting U.S. oil interests, and deferring to supporters of the partition of Palestine that led to establishment of a Jewish state. Ultimately the choice was not one of oil or Israel, but of oil and Israel versus radical change in the Arab world where despite the differences between them for over a thousand years, the Sunnis and Shias had for the most part managed to co-exist.

But as much of modern geopolitics is driven by hydrocarbons (oil and gas), that peaceful coexistence was shattered when the U.S and its allies supported the Sunnis against the Shias in order to wage war for oil which which was mostly located in Shia countries and in the Shia-minority sections of Sunni-majority countries. The fact that most of the Persian Gulf's fossil fuels are located beneath Shiite territory is said to be due an unusual correlation of religious history and anaerobic decomposition of plankton which is also the case in Sunni Saudi Arabia where the major oil fields are in the Eastern Province where the majority of the population is Shiite. Consequently, the nightmare scenario for the ruling House of Saud family, is that the Saudi Shiites will secede along with their oil and ally themselves with Shiite Iran.

Because of such concerns Saudi Arabia has desperately endeavoured to staunch any thought of self-determination – a core principle of international law – not only amongst Saudi Shiites but also those Shiites in neighbouring oil sheikhdoms such as Bahrain where the majority Shiites are ruled over by a Sunni monarchy that Saudi Arabia obligingly helped to crush the Bahraini version of the Arab Spring in 2011. Similar thinking was behind Saudi Arabia's friend and ally, President George Bush Sr., when in 1991 he chose to stand idly by – to the satisfaction of U.S. allies Saudi Arabia and Turkey – while Saddam Hussein used chemical weapons to quell an insurgence by Iraqi Shiites at the end of the Gulf War. All of which explains why the Sunni Gulf monarchies in Bahrain, Kuwait, Oman, Qatar, Saudi Arabia, and the United Arab Emirates have ganged up on Iran and the Shias who are squatting on most of the oil and gas resources. This clique of Sunni monarchies are doing everything within their power to provoke a Sunni-Shia war – with surreptitious Israeli incitement – throughout the Middle East and North Africa so as to justify seizing the gas and oil resources by force.

While the concept of "American exceptionalism" is open to challenge, there is no doubt that the U.S. is unique amongst the nations of the world with U.S. government insistence that its dictates and jurisprudence take precedence over the sovereignty of other nations. The power of the U.S. judicial system is imposed on foreign nationals along with claims of extra-territorial jurisdiction over foreign activities of which either the government or American interest groups disapprove. Such unilateral and arrogant disregard for the sovereignty and rights of others includes the extrajudicial seizure and detention of foreign nationals merely on the basis of U.S. concocted terrorism charges that have no concrete or verifiable evidence as was the case of detainees at Guantánamo Bay detention centre – a symbol of torture, rendition and indefinite detention without charge or trial – which after 15 years is still in existence despite the U.S. President's 2008 post-election promise to close the camp within a year.

America is now also a nation where voter apathy leaves the system open to political corruption with economic and social exploitation that denies human rights and justice to tens of millions of Americans including African Americans who are systematically hampered by a dysfunctional educational apparatus and obstacles to voter registration while also being denied economic opportunities and basic civil and human rights that result with incarceration in brutal prison-industrial-complexes by out of control racist, militarised, and often murderous police forces backed by an unjust judicial system.

Furthermore a forthcoming report from the Economic Policy Institute will reveal a stark disparity exists between the hourly pay of blacks and whites with on average whites making 26.7 percent more than blacks by earning $25.22 an hour as compared with $18.49 for blacks. Astonishingly, blacks are now earning less relative to their white counterparts than they did in 1979. So while many Americans may have the perception that racism still exists but is declining, the reality is that it was getting worse. So while race should not be a skill or characteristic with a market value in relation to wages, in reality it is.

To make matters worse for those unfortunate Americans, virtually all members of Congress and the Senate – thanks to AIPAC – owe their first allegiance to the racist Apartheid state of Israel rather than to the American people who while being deprived of their democracy and human rights, are sedated with talk of God, freedom, and a terrorist threat to America and its "staunchest ally," Israel.

Examples of unabashed treasonable subservience – to Israel and its well-financed, powerful Zionist Jewish lobby groups – by non-Jewish leaders of Western governments is repeatedly reaffirmed as was the case when on a visit to Israel, the Canadian Prime Minister, ingratiatingly extolled its imaginary virtues:

> *"Shalom. And thank you for inviting me to visit this remarkable country and especially for this opportunity to address the Knesset … Ladies and gentlemen, Canada and Israel are the greatest of friends, and the most natural of allies … But, in much of the Western world, the old hatred has been translated into more sophisticated language for use in polite society. People who would never say they hate and blame the Jews for their own*

failings or the problems of the world, instead declare their hatred
of Israel and blame the only Jewish state for the problems of the
Middle East. As once Jewish businesses were boycotted, some
civil-society leaders today call for a boycott of Israel. On some
campuses, intellectualised arguments against Israeli policies
thinly mask the underlying realities, such as the shunning of
Israeli academics and the harassment of Jewish students. Most
disgracefully of all, some openly call Israel an apartheid state ...
But this is the face of the new anti-Semitism ... I believe the
story of Israel is a great example to the world ... and therefore,
through fire and water, Canada will stand with you."

What the Canadian Prime Minister was in effect saying on
behalf of the Canadian people was that Canada – a nation
once arguably renowned for its moral integrity – would
unconditionally support Israel's contemptuous disregard for
international and human rights laws including numerous UN
resolutions that do not even include those the U.S. vetoed.

Not to be outdone by his Canadian counterpart, the British
Prime Minister while on his visit to Israel a few months later,
pledged to stand by Israel "every step of the way"; religiously
avoided criticising Israeli policies that violated international
law; offered no advice on how to restart the stalled "peace
process"; omitted to mention the inhumane air, land, and sea
blockade of the Gaza Strip; and failed to broach the subject
of Israel's occupation of the West Bank with its deliberate
program of illegal Jewish settlement building.

After almost seventy years of being paralysed into silence by the
Zionist venom – the stigma of anti-Semitism and Holocaust
denial – that prevented condemnation of incalculable cheating,
lying, stealing, murdering, and ruthless denial of the legal and
natural human rights of the Palestinian people by a nation

devoid of conscience, humanity, or any of the noble principles of the religion to which it claims to belong, the world in general and the West in particular had recently once again been witness to Israel's arrogant, barbaric, and contemptuous assault on the Universal Declaration of Human Rights.

By causing Gaza's biggest humanitarian crisis in many years; by savagely killing over 2,200 Palestinians; by deliberately causing hundreds of thousands to be left homeless; and by diabolically destroying virtually all essential infrastructure, Israel with its supremacist, "God-chosen" impunity – and knowing full well that the rest of the cowardly world would do nothing – then added insult to injury by announcing plans to expropriate four square kilometres of Palestinian land in the occupied West Bank. This outrageous expropriation in the area of Gush Etzion south of Bethlehem, including many centuries-old Palestinian olive groves, constituted the largest illegal seizure by Israel in 30 years and will facilitate the expansion of a settlement named Gevaot.

Such arrogant Israeli violations with impunity are possible because of AIPAC/U.S.-led Western hypocrisy, double standards, and the politicisation of genocide which have consistently undermined the main international institutions such as the UN and the ICC that were established for the supposed enforcement of human rights, the implementation justice, and the betterment of conditions for all humanity. Honest, self-respecting human beings – yes, including Jews – cannot on any grounds deny that Israel's callous treatment of the Palestinian people warrants unconditional universal condemnation; warrants support for the Boycott, Divestment and Sanctions (BDS) non-governmental organisation; and warrants an unencumbered opening of investigations into Israel's war crimes by the ICC. Anything less would constitute yet more contemptible criminal complicity by the West and the rest of the world.

On 17 July 1998, the international community had reached an historic milestone – that has so far proved sadly ineffective – when 120 States adopted the Rome Statute, the legal basis for establishing a permanent International Criminal Court (ICC). The Court's mandate was "to try individuals rather than States, and to hold such persons accountable for the most serious crimes of concern to the international community as a whole, namely the crime of genocide, war crimes, crimes against humanity, and the crime of aggression, when the conditions for the exercise of the Court's jurisdiction over the latter are fulfilled." Therefore on that basis and in view of the fact that Israel has for almost 70 years painstakingly ensured qualification for all four of the aforementioned criminal categories, then why has the ICC failed to initiate proceedings against those Israelis who while with impunity committing heinous crimes against humanity, arrogantly legitimise their actions by quoting both a concocted biblical narrative of having been promised Palestine by God Himself, and the transparently bogus excuse of "self-defence."

"This country exists as a fulfilment of a promise made by God Himself. It would be ridiculous to ask it to account for its legitimacy."
Golda Meir (Israeli Prime Minister 1969-74), *Le Monde***, 15 October 1971.**

The concept of legitimacy cannot be claimed on the basis of some Biblical narrative written thousands of years ago by ancient Jewish record-keeping scribes intent on inventing a Jewish people and creating a Jewish nation. Genuine legitimacy, like respect, cannot be feigned, fabricated, purchased or purloined: it has to be earned with commendable conduct and well intentioned cooperation in the affairs of all humanity.

Genuine legitimacy for a Zionist Apartheid Israeli state, therefore, cannot be established by the silencing of demands for accountability for contemptible and illegal behaviour with impunity; it cannot be established by devilish duplicity, rambunctious denial of obvious criminality, or the deprivation of human and political rights for others; it cannot be established by numerous self-serving false flag operations such as the 1954 Lavon Affair, the 1967 USS Liberty Incident, the assassinations of John F. Kennedy and his brother Robert F. Kennedy, the 9/11attacks, and even the frequent and deliberate targeting of Jewish people and organisations with a view to laying the blame on various groups ranging from radical Muslims to even harmless environmentalists; it cannot be established by a Fascist ideology based on the "supremacy" of a "chosen people" whose colonial Apartheid objectives include the savage military ethnic cleansing of the indigenous people of Palestine; it cannot be established by the continual bribing and corrupting of the elected representatives of other nations; and it cannot be established by forever committing crimes against humanity to legitimise the illegitimate because the time will certainly come – as it did for the Nazis – when there has to be a reckoning that demands justice and retribution which no doubt will once again come at a great cost to all humanity.

In view of this summer's diabolical and devastating Israeli spree – some 17,000 homes bombed and destroyed, over 2,200 civilians killed including over 500 children, and more than 500,000 people made homeless – the time for that reckoning cannot be postponed indefinitely! People everywhere, including all those Americans who are either too Zionised, politically illiterate, or simply naively oblivious to reality and the true facts, have to be resolute in deciding that goodwill towards Israel and tolerance for its crimes against humanity can no longer be tolerated because of regret over the Holocaust. Jews do not have a monopoly on suffering as is witnessed by the fact that – and that is not counting the millions of injuries and fatalities resulting from Israeli-instigated conflicts in the Middle East and elsewhere – twelve million children under the age of five die annually from preventable diseases and malnutrition. People must determine that "never again" shall be equally applicable to Palestinians as it is to Jews; that Israelis, like the Nazis, must be made accountable and punishable for their war crimes; and that collective cowardice, criminal cooperation, and culpable complicity by the West with regards to Israel are an irresponsible dereliction of duty to all humanity.

The collective cowardice resulting from the fear of being stigmatised as anti-Semites or Holocaust deniers is an irrational and amoral reaction to the well financed and carefully orchestrated Zionist campaign for the promotion of guilt-inducing reminders of the Holocaust – otherwise known as the Holocaust industry. Current and future generations cannot be held hostage in perpetuity by zionist Israel for crimes committed by past generations. Furthermore, past persecutions of the Jewish people do not grant Judaeo-Zionism the automatic right to now ethnically cleanse the Palestinian people. Shrill and constant cries of anti-Semitism to silence criticism of Apartheid Israel are now so commonplace that they are becoming monotonous, meaningless, and markedly irrelevant.

Criminal cooperation is the provision to Israel of preferential access to U.S. and European Union markets including the latter's failure to enforce laws prohibiting the import of

Israeli goods produced in the Occupied Territories; criminal cooperation is investment in Israel which in 2012 alone rose 14.5% to $73.9 billion with American investors accounting for $19.7 billion followed by $9 billion from the Cayman Islands – a global tax shelter that serves as corporate headquarters for many companies such as Coca-Cola, Oracle and Intel; criminal cooperation is the acceptance by politicians of pro-Israel political action committee contributions which in the U.S. alone are quite astronomical. Israel's ability to bribe and corrupt politicians does not extend to the people, therefore it is up to the people to show their disapproval in the only possible and peaceful way: they must effectively boycott Israeli goods by joining the BDS campaign; they must boycott companies who invest in Israel; they must crusade against individuals or organisations that associate with, or support Israel; and they must continually lobby their politicians especially those that have accepted the accursed Israeli new shekel and demand justice and respect for the human rights of Palestinians.

Culpable complicity with Israel's barbarous criminality takes many forms including nations who either abstain or vote against UN resolutions condemning Israel's persistent persecution of the Palestinian people with the U.S. having used more vetoes on behalf of Israel than it has on behalf of itself; culpable complicity includes the provision of military-related equipment to Israel with the knowledge that it will be used for the continued oppression of the Palestinian people in the illegally Occupied Territories with such aid from the U.S. due to be increased to some $4 billion annually; and culpable complicity includes the hypocritical double standards by which Israel's criminality is either positively judged or simply ignored completely as compared to other less useful international law violators whom Western nations do not regard as being of much use or within their sphere of influence.

The time has come for the supposedly humane "Silent Majority" to finally voice their outrage – without demonstrations or violence – by repeatedly emailing or otherwise contacting their elected representatives. Lowlife, treacherous politicians who have their inboxes regularly swamped with thousands of emails will quickly realise that ignoring the will of the majority to serve minority Zionist and corporate interests alone, will not be enough to get them reelected. The long-suffering Palestinian people should not be forced to continue paying for the West's guilt complex over Jewish suffering perpetrated by the Nazis during the Second World war which incidentally also caused the estimated deaths of some 70 million other people. It should also be remembered that for example in 1960 alone, the child mortality rate – the silent killers being poverty, hunger, easily preventable illness and disease, and other related causes – was at 18,900,000, three times more than the alleged Jewish Holocaust death toll. The premise that Jewish people have a monopoly on suffering is not only false, but also – considering the barbaric persecution of Palestinian people by a racist Apartheid Jewish state in Palestine – unashamedly hypocritical.

Not surprisingly, the Israeli reaction to BDS has been to conflate it with anti-Semitism and accuse it of trying to delegitimise Israel. And this from a nation whose long history and proficiency – in delegitimising anything or anyone who questioned its diabolic policies – has included decades of self-serving delegitimisation of the Palestinian people. Though Israelis have been uncompromising on their right to exist as a nation state, they have had no hesitation or qualms about brutally denying that same right to the Palestinian people while claiming to be "defending" themselves. This ploy has become a well-practised national trait that must be challenged and exposed for the manifest criminal fraud which it is.

For Israel's claim of "self-defence" to be valid requires that it is the Israelis who are the victims of aggression and not the Palestinian people. It was the Palestinian people who from the very start were the victims of Zionist terror groups who drove them from their homes and villages, killing thousands in the process; it was the Palestinians who in their millions have been terrorised and driven from their lands; it was the Palestinians who were subjected to every form of inhumanity in violation of their natural and legal rights; and it was the Palestinians who were subjected to barbaric Israeli ethnic cleansing while more and more of their land was stolen. So when the brutally occupied virtually defenceless Palestinians people rightly resist the overwhelming odds of an occupying nuclear nation with the one of the world's largest and best equipped military forces backed unconditionally by the U.S., they are called "terrorists" while the war criminal Israelis are said to be the "victims" who are only "defending themselves."

In conclusion, it should be noted that ever since I started writing about the Israeli-Palestinian conflict I have been subjected to much Jewish hate and vitriol for my alleged anti-Semitism. For some unknown reason my "God Chosen" critics refuse to consider the possibility that rather than being "anti-Semitic," I am simply pro-human rights for all people and have in fact condemned human rights violations by all three major Abrahamic religions. The truth of course is that my Jewish critics – most of whom are Ashkenazi and not as they claim Semitic – are not actually interested in whether or not I am or am not anti-Semitic; are not interested in whether or not my articles and books are deserving of impartial judgment; and are not interested in using facts to question or disprove anything I have written. They are only concerned with silencing anything or anyone who in anyway criticises the criminal ethnic cleansing of the Palestinian people by a land and resource grabbing parasitic Apartheid colonial state. To achieve this they slander their targets with accusations of *anti-Semitism* and *Holocaust denial* while simultaneously playing the "Jewish Victim Card" whose effectiveness has now been trivialised by constant and indiscriminate use. So it is perhaps time for those opponents of the Universal Declaration of Human Rights to honestly ask themselves whether actual anti-Semitism is the consequence of an inherent and unjustified hate for Jews by non-Jews, or whether it is just a reasonable reaction to a "Jewish separateness" that promotes supremacy over, hate for, and exploitation of non-Jews that is justified by the bogus claim of having been "chosen" and "promised" Palestine by God Himself.

> *"Actually – and this was where I began to feel seriously uncomfortable – some such divine claim underlay not just 'the occupation' but the whole idea of a separate state for Jews in Palestine. Take away the divine warrant for the Holy Land and where were you, and what were you? Just another land-thief like the Turks or the British, except that in this case you wanted the land without the people. And the original Zionist slogan – 'a land without a people for a people without a land' – disclosed its own negation when I saw the densely populated Arab towns dwelling sullenly under Jewish tutelage. You want irony? How about Jews becoming colonisers at just the moment when other Europeans had given up on the idea?"*
> **Christopher Hitchens, *Hitch-22: A Memoir***

19

Monday, 28 December

Office Of The Israeli Prime Minister, West Jerusalem

The Directors of Mossad (Foreign Intelligence and Special Operations), Shin Bet (Internal Security Service), Aman (Military intelligence), and the Chief of the General Staff (Commander-in-Chief of the Israel Defence Forces), had all been summoned for a meeting with the Prime Minister at his office in the Knesset building which had just marked its 50th anniversary. The main building had been financed by James Armand Edmond de Rothschild (1878–1957) who had continued his father's support for the Zionist cause by donating six million Israeli Pounds towards its construction.

Today's meeting had been scheduled to discuss certain issues of national importance including the apparent frustration of Palestinian youth who had defied both the duplicitous Palestinian President's call for restraint and an Israeli security crackdown by taking part in violent protests in annexed East Jerusalem and the occupied West Bank. There was a risk of a full-scale Palestinian uprising – or third intifada – with an increase in out of desperation knife stabbing attacks which security forces had so far struggled to stop. Last week the Prime Minister had reminded Israelis that past uprisings had been crushed and that the current "knife terror will not defeat us now." Consequently he began the meeting by asking the Director of Shin Bet "what's being done to stop these stabbings?"

The Director explained the problem was that the stabbings were not group organised – thereby preventing the agency from monitoring and gathering intelligence about potential trouble – but were being committed mostly by "lone wolf" youths acting on their own volition. This left the Israeli security forces with no alternative other than to respond lethally with live fire and rubber bullets against demonstrators resulting in in over 20,000 Palestinians being injured. As part of that response, Palestinians were also being killed by Israeli soldiers, police, and civilians merely on suspicion that they were possibly about to carry out an attack or some other violent act. It was unfortunate but unavoidable that the disparity in the number killed on each side had led to accusations by rights groups and others that Israel was as usual using excessive force to quell the unrest.

Equally problematic, the director explained, was the posting of video clips on YouTube that showed Israeli soldiers cold-bloodedly shooting dead alleged knife attackers. The outcome of such apparent extrajudicial killings – along with increased violent harassment from Jewish settlers – had only served to galvanise more protests from Palestinian youths.

"As you know, we sent our Deputy Foreign Minister to Silicon Valley late last month to meet senior executives at Google and its subsidiary, YouTube. She told them that for the sake of peace, they must censor the growing number of Palestinian videos posted on YouTube because they encouraged violent unrest. She made it clear that we're gonna declare a war on incitement through Facebook and YouTube," the PM said. "We're also pushing for our Washington embassy's Chief of Staff to be appointed as head of policy and Communications at Facebook's Israel office. I also plan on meeting with Facebook officials sometime next year to demand that they give us more access to posts deemed as 'incitement,' which will allow us to raid the homes of Palestinian children who post on social media sites and detain them indefinitely under administrative detention orders.

"Let's be honest with ourselves," the Shin Bet Director ventured cautiously, "many of those videos are being posted by us or ordinary Israelis as proof of Palestinian violence. The Palestinians are only posting recordings of what is being done to them."

"Whatever's being done to them isn't enough!" The in denial PM snapped. He refused to accept that the escalating unrest was not because of social media, but because of the government's determination to maintain the occupation which caused Palestinians to lose all hope for a better and just future. The PM stubbornly ignored warnings that without impartial diplomacy the attacks and resistance would never end. In his and the extreme right's desperation to obscure this reality, the PM was blaming everything and everyone apart from Israel's fanatical and uncompromising ideology. Targets for such unjustified blame had included the Palestinian President; the Palestinian education system; the Palestinian parties in Israel's parliament along with human rights groups and three West Bank radio stations which were closed down; and Palestinian children who had been arrested for their posts on social media.

"I can assure you that the number of knife attacks has decreased and there's evidence of support for these attacks weakening amongst the Palestinians themselves."

"Keep the pressure up on those animals and don't you worry about what anyone thinks," the PM was adamant, "we're drawing up legislation for a law that will expand our power to label activist individuals and groups as 'terrorists.' It will have wide-reaching definitions about what constitutes 'terrorism,' a 'terrorist organisation,' and 'support' for such groups which will give us the power to criminalise even legitimate Palestinian political activity including any charities that support them."

The PM added that in the meantime far right news sites and groups should be given a carte blanche for their accusations – however false – and attacks against Palestinians. He also revealed that plans were in the pipeline to "retool Israel's occupation" with the colour-coding of "good" and "bad" Palestinians and "carrot and stick" plan that would include sidelining the Palestinian Authority in favour of a new local leadership of "notables" hand-picked by Israel; "cutting out the middle man" to open a dialogue with supposedly more responsible Palestinians such as business people, academics and mayors; and establishing a new communications unit that would speak in Arabic directly to ordinary Palestinians over the heads of the PA in the West Bank, and its Hamas rival in Gaza. The PM, his eyes filled with undisguised, fervent hatred, then changed the subject by turning to the Mossad Director and referring to a report from Mossad's Collections Department which was responsible for numerous overseas espionage assignments. "We've got a situation in London that needs attention … "

"That's right Prime Minister. Since the Labour Party's leadership election in September was won easily by a left-winger, who's an activist in the Palestine solidarity movement and supporter of the idea for a just peace in the Middle East with recognition of Palestinian rights, the issue has been firmly placed in the public domain where we don't want it to be. I mean, this guy could conceivably become Prime Minister."

"Not if we can help it he won't. What about the Labour Friends of Israel?" The PM asked in reference to the parliamentary group that – along with the Conservative Friends of Israel and the Liberal Democrats Friends of Israel – promoted support for a strong bilateral relationship between the two countries.

"They've been outflanked, as they were in the leadership election, by support for the left-winger from the party's membership and several large trade unions."

"Then it's time for our people to get off their fucking backsides and start earning their money."

The Mossad Director explained that they already had by having one newspaper claiming anti-Semitism at the heart of the Labour Party had been revealed by a devastating dossier exposing extensive anti-Jewish bigotry within Labour ranks that posed profoundly troubling questions which its leaders had to answer.

"There's also local elections in May?" The PM said.

"And an important mayoral election in London."

"I know. It's between the son of a billionaire Jew and a Muslim from some British Pakistani working-class family."

"Anti-Semitism has been mentioned and one Murdoch paper has already hinted at the Muslim's links to Islamic extremists."

"The whole Labour Party has to be attacked, not just its candidate for London Mayor. We need to do ourselves and our Conservative government friends a favour. Get our people on it without delay. Phone calls must be made, emails must be sent, and complaints to the media must be made. There has to be an outraged eruption of protest in the media against anti-Semitism in the Labour Party."

"We can start off by attacking any Labour members who have spoken in favour of Palestinian human rights and especially those supporting BDS. We can also quietly pressure those with compromising secrets such as extramarital affairs, and get the right-leaning party members to allege that there are numerous anti-Semites within the ranks."

"We have to do everything possible to help the Conservatives stay in power because we'll need their support in the EU to counter criticism when we pass our law for NGOs." The PM said in reference to the forthcoming legislation that would require non-government organisations receiving more than half their funds from foreign governments or state agencies to disclose that fact in any public reports, advocacy literature and interactions with government officials, or face a NIS 29,000 fine. The government was going to state that the law was not intended for targeting left-wing and human rights organisations which receive funding from European countries, but for increasing transparency of foreign government interference in Israeli affairs.

The Aman Director chipped in, "they've got a referendum in June about whether to remain in the EU."

"Brexit," the PM confirmed. "Can't see them leaving … But in any case we are taking positive action to bring more countries onside. I'm planning on visiting Africa next summer to meet with leaders at the counterterrorism conference being held in Uganda. I shall seek to improve not only mutual security, but also agricultural and economic relations. We Israelis have much to offer that African countries, including Muslim ones, urgently need." The PM explained that during the visit he would emphasise that the number of African countries seeking to actively cooperate with Israel would continue to increase to the extent of eliminating the so-called automatic majority against the Jewish state in international forums such as the UN. Such alliances would come about gradually and may even take a decade with some African countries already voting for Israel and not against it.

The PM's interest in fostering better relations with African nations, however, had not come about as a result of some uncharacteristic Israeli altruism or a newly discovered fondness for people with dark skins – the PM had previously expressed the view with regards to Africans that "if we don't stop their entry, the problem that currently stands at 60,000 could grow to 600,000, and that threatens our existence as a Jewish and democratic state … This phenomenon is very grave and threatens the social fabric of society, our national security and our national identity" – but out of a desperate necessity to find new friends irrespective of colour at a time when the BDS Movement, a crucial form of peaceful international pressure on Israel, had become stronger, more diverse, and increasingly effective.

Between the 1870s and 1900, Africa was subject to European imperialist aggression, diplomatic pressures, military invasions, and eventual conquest and colonisation. Though African societies had put up various forms of resistance to the colonisation of their countries, much of Africa was nonetheless colonised by Britain, France, Germany, Belgium, Spain, Portugal, and Italy. It was not until the "Wind of Change" speech by then British Prime Minister Harold Macmillan to the South African Parliament on 3 February 1960 – "the wind of change is blowing through this continent. Whether we like it or not, this growth of national consciousness is a political fact" – that African countries began to shed the yoke of colonialism: a colonialism and plunder of African natural resources that Israel had, and still was to some extent missing out on.

Israeli intelligence was for instance aware from its agents in Panama – a transcontinental country located between North and South America – that Mossack Fonseca, an offshore law firm, had for decades been helping corrupt politicians, their favoured families, and profiteering businessmen to steal billions of dollars from Africa where in 44 out of 54 African countries at least 37 mining, oil and mineral companies were connected to offshore accounts. It was estimated that tax avoidance was annually depriving African nations of more than $50 billion. This was possible as a consequence of companies being given access to lucrative extractive projects because their owners were either politically connected, or prepared to engage in questionable deals that generated quick profits for the few rather than benefiting those African societies in general.

"In the meantime," the PM said, "there are some other problems that need fixing: a couple of troublesome bitches."

"The Brazilian President and the Swedish Foreign

Minister?" The Mossad Director ventured with regards to the former's refusal to accept the PM's choice of the new Israeli ambassador because from 2007 to 2013 he managed all Jewish settlements in the West Bank of the Jordan River; and the latter for agitating for an inquiry into Israeli extrajudicial killings of Palestinians and daring to describe the Palestinians' plight as a factor leading to Islamist radicalisation.

"Have our people in Stockholm dig up some dirt, there's gotta to be something we can pin on the bitch." The PM said.

"In hand. We've already uncovered information that she may have bypassed a waiting period when renting a home from a trade union," the Mossad Director said but regretted that with regards to the Brazilian President, and despite billions being stolen from state oil giant Petrobras by private construction companies and politicians; that despite the country being rife with jaw-dropping corruption; that despite virtually the whole political class being implicated in some sort of shady deal; and that despite all the ongoing investigations into corruption, the only person that had so far managed to remain "clean," was the President.

"Even if that dago bitch is clean, the scandal can still be used to get rid of her. Remember there are more than a few businessmen and politicians who would like to see the back of her so that everything can be swept under the carpet. The country is overrun with corruption. Most senators have taken backhanders of one kind or another. Use them to impeach her and have her thrown out."

The Mossad Director was reassuring with the reply that they had at least a dozen "righteous Gentiles" – as Israelis like to call their puppets – in the Senate who could be relied upon to incite Zionist and Christian Zionist connections to overthrow the Brazilian President. The Coup-Monger-In-Chief amongst them had already been working closely with the President of the Brazilian Israelite Confederation, on raising awareness – brainwashing – amongst Brazilians about "Holocaust Remembrance Day" as well as passing Zionised "anti-terrorism" legislation that would without doubt have an Orwellian effect on the Brazilian people. Brazil's "Christian" Zionist scourge was similar to that which had infected much of America, other Western nations, and to a lesser extent Australia, Britain, and Canada. Help could also be expected from wealthy American neoconservatives.

"You can always rely on the the Americans for mischief in Latin America. All you have to do is mention the words 'communist' or 'left winger' and they're in there like a shot. If we can get 'our Brazilians' in power, we can have them regret supporting the UNESCO resolution denying a Jewish connection to the Temple Mount in Jerusalem, admit that the text was partial and unbalanced, and pledge to vote against future resolutions on the topic if its reservations are not taken into account."

"I think our main priority has to be BDS. We have to intensify the fight against the movement before next month's Knesset Caucus to Fight Delegitimisation and BDS," the Shin Bet Director pointed out, "I know we spent over a 100 million shekels on *hasbara* in 2014, but our efforts to fight delegitimisation and boycotts need to be more focused with both a legal and a *hasbara* defensive shield, especially in Europe."

"Agreed," the PM said, "we've already got the Americans, the British, and the French tightening the screw and we don't have to worry about Germans. With their Holocaust guilt complex, they're shit scared of doing or saying anything that might be seen as anti-Semitic." The PM explained that the longterm success of BDS was also going to be countered by accelerating plans for permanent settlement of territories occupied by Israel. Early next year he intended making a much publicised visit to the Golan Heights to vow that it would forever remain in Israeli hands while calling upon the international community to recognise Israeli sovereignty; would further Israel's intention to become a major global energy player by exploiting the Syrian civil war to enable expanded drilling in the illegally occupied Golan Heights, and by finalising a massive deal with Jordan so as to exploit the Leviathan offshore gas field with a massive reserve of natural gas in Israeli waters; would ensure the passing of a bill in the Knesset that would retroactively legalise all illegal settler outposts in the occupied West Bank, potentially stopping the evacuation of some 4,000 settlement units built on privately-owned Palestinian land; and would announce that the policing of the West Bank was the sole responsibility of Israel so as to reinforce the concept of a one Apartheid state regime.

"Our New York Mission is also setting up a summer conference at the UN for about 1,500 people including college students," the Mossad man said, "they'll hear speakers condemn BDS for spreading lies about Israel and for being anti-Semitic. Similar *'hasbara'* conferences are being organised across America and even here in Israel."

The PM turned to the Chief of the General Staff. "Anything on *hasbara* from the IDF?"

"Last year, Prime Minister, we paid 380,000 shekels for 'cooperation' with the children's television network Nickelodeon Israel for a series of commercials sponsored by Home Front Command that featured several of the channel's stars; for a video on self-defence during emergency situations; and for an interactive page on the channels' website. We have plans for more of the same." The Chief of the General staff also revealed that apart from allocating a large portion of its resources to documenting and distributing "news" items, photographs and videos to Israeli media outlets for publication, the IDF would also continue annually spending an average of 7 million shekels on purchasing advertorial content including the publication in newspapers of regular IDF columns in which commanders of various military divisions explained to readers the worthwhile benefits of enlisting in their units.

"Very good, but that's just one battlefront. The other is Iran and the question of whether we do, or we don't." The PM said referring to Israel's option of an attack against Iran.

"Definitely not!" The Chief of the General Staff said emphatically. Senior figures in the Israeli intelligence and military leadership had to date opposed such an attack because they regarded the PM's apocalyptic rhetoric about Iran's nuclear capability being an "existential threat" as unnecessary and self-defeating. They had begun to express their opposition to such rhetoric as early as the 1990s, but on taking office in 1996, the PM had acted to stop such talk along with his insistence that "a nuclear Iran poses the gravest threat since Hitler to the physical survival of the Jewish people." A former Major General chief of military intelligence had stated that the Israeli public's perception of the Iranian nuclear threat had been seriously "distorted." An internal Israeli inter-ministerial committee formed in 1994 to make recommendations on dealing with Iran concluded that Israeli rhetoric had been self-defeating because it had actually made Iran more fearful of Israel, and consequently more hostile towards it. The PM nonetheless regarded such views with disdain and opposed the very notion of direct negotiations with the Iranians.

In a speech to the joint meeting of the U.S. Congress in the House Chamber on Capitol Hill earlier in the year, the PM had stated that since the Iranian revolution in 1979, Iran had transitioned from a secular to religious government with the country having been hijacked by zealots; becoming a sponsor of terrorism; and playing a role in the killings of Americans in Beirut, Iraq and Afghanistan. He added that Iran's regime was not merely a Jewish problem anymore than the Nazi regime was merely a Jewish problem. When the PM then stressed that Iran's regime posed a great threat to the peace of the entire world, anyone could have be forgiven for wondering whether the he was talking about Iran or Israel.

This after all was the same PM who in a barefaced lie a few months earlier informed the World Zionist Congress that Hitler only wanted to expel the Jews, but Jerusalem's Grand Mufti – the Sunni Muslim cleric in charge of Jerusalem's Islamic holy places – convinced him to exterminate them: a claim that was rejected by most recognised Holocaust scholars. This blatantly false allegation was condemned by critics as a historical untruth, a distortion of the Holocaust, and a diminishment of the evil of Nazism. Equally critical of the PM were two active-duty IDF generals – among the army's top experts on Palestinian affairs – who publicly stated that Palestinian violence was driven to a considerable degree by anger at Israeli actions. One of the two went a step further, with the warning that only a serious Israeli diplomatic re-engagement with the Palestinians would help to quell such violence over the long term.

"Some of the motivation of the Palestinians to carry out terror attacks is due to the violence of right-wing elements in the West Bank,"
Major General Nitzan Alon, the director of the IDF operations directorate.

Despite the expression of such concerns by military and security leaders, the meeting nonetheless concluded with the general agreement that Israel's war on open discourse had to be waged not just abroad, but also in Israel with monitoring and censorship being largely derived from measures known as the "Defence (Emergency) Regulations," which came into operation in 1945 during the British Mandate and had since been adapted by Israel to include the imposition of gag orders on international journalists; the creation of difficulties for international journalists and editors to determine the extent of information worth fighting for; the use of an indefinite and broad notion of "incitement" to arrest and detain individuals for items posted on social media such as Facebook; the requirement by certain individuals to obtain the State's permission prior to posting on social media; the enlistment of social media organisations by coercing them into support for, and acceptance of Israel's criteria for what is to be censored; and finally to employ strong-arm tactics for the persuasion of other countries to unite for the formation of a consortium of watchdogs on Israel's behalf.

Israel's launching of an all out war against open discourse, however, was not intended as a means of stemming the spread of anti-Semitism, but as a ploy for silencing any political or public discourse concerning Israel's ethnic cleansing and land grabbing criminality which was otherwise gift-wrapped as a shimmering God-given Jewish right to the land of Palestine. The consciously concocted illusion of present-day "anti-Semitism" combined with the alarming allusion to the possibility of another "Holocaust" was a most powerful weapon for the imposition of global censorship of any criticism – irrespective of how justified – of Israel and its inhumane policies in the Occupied Palestinian Territories. Freedom of speech and conscientious objections to buying products from countries contravening international law were the core values of free and democratic societies that must never be surrendered in the fight for justice which is not just for the Palestinian people's sake, but for the sake of all humanity.

20

Tuesday, 29 December

Connaught Square, London, England

The house on the West side of Connaught Square was purchased in 2004 for a reported £3.5 million by then British Prime Minister Tony Blair who was considered by many Britons and others all over the world to be an inveterate liar and unrepentant war criminal. Before qualifying as a fully fledged candidate for indictment as a war criminal, Blair began his lying, war-mongering, and money-grubbing career as a shyster lawyer whose cosy, potentially corrupt, and now war criminal connection with Israel began in earnest in 1994 when he first met Michael Levy – an encounter that was probably calculated rather than fortuitous – at a dinner party hosted by Israeli diplomat Gideon Meir who, like Blair was friendly with Eldred Tabachnik, a senior barrister and Queens Council at 11 King's Bench Walk, the chambers founded by Derry Irvine where Blair had been a junior tenant on its foundation in 1981. Tabachnik was also a former president (1994-2000) of the Board of Deputies of British Jews.

Following that more than providential meeting, Blair and Levy became friends, tennis partners, and political cahoots with Levy running the Labour Leader's Office Fund to finance Blair's 1997 general election campaign which received substantial contributions from notables such as Alex Bernstein (Granada Group Chairman 1979-1996) and Robert Gavron (publishing). Generally referred to as "Lord Cashpoint" in media and political circles, Levy was the Labour Party's leading fundraiser with over £100m raised between 1994 to 2007. After becoming Prime Minister, Blair ennobled Bernstein and Gavron and made Levy a life peer whom *The Jerusalem Post* – owned by the subsequently convicted felon Canadian newspaper publisher Conrad Black – described as "undoubtedly the notional leader of British Jewry."

In 1998 Blair appointed Levy as his personal envoy to the Middle East and it is perhaps no coincidence that as a consequence of being financed and in effect controlled by Israeli interests, Blair – like the semi-illiterate President Bush in the U.S. – was inveigled into launching an illegal war against Iraq despite widespread opposition to such a conflict. The need for war was then "sold" to the British and American people on the basis of doctored intelligence reports backed by Blair's now infamous claim to Parliament that Saddam Hussein could deploy weapons of mass destruction within 45 minutes of an order to use them. It was a claim that subsequently proved to be a blatant lie because Iraq had nothing even remotely resembling a weapon of mass destruction. So once again an AIPAC-controlled U.S.-led Western alliance had been conned into waging war on Israel's behalf in what proved to be only the first of a series of regime change wars waged "enemy" Arab states whom Israel wanted destroyed along with Iran and Syria. Needless to say, as always, the cost of such wars was borne by Western nations and not by Israel.

"Lord Cashpoint" Levy, who praised Blair for his "solid and committed support of the State of Israel," maintained close ties with Israel's political leaders and kept a home in Herzliya, a city in the central coast of Israel. Daniel Levy, his son, was active in Israeli politics and at one time served as an assistant to former Israeli Prime Minister Ehud Barak and to Knesset member Yossi Beilin. Daniel – amongst other positions – was a senior research fellow of the Middle East Task Force at the New

America Foundation and director of MENA (Middle East and North Africa) programme at the European Council on Foreign Relations. It is the calculated placement of such dedicated, eager beaver people in strategic positions that enabled Israel to exert influence over Western decision-making on the Middle East.

In March 2006 it was revealed that Tony Blair's Labour Party had raised £14 million in loans from private individuals of whom some were later nominated for peerages. Levy was later arrested but released on bail pending Scotland Yard's investigation into what came to be known as the "cash for honours" controversy. In July 2007 – one month after the Jewish Attorney General Lord Peter Goldsmith had stepped down at the same time as Blair – the Crown Prosecution Service unsurprisingly announced that Levy would be neither prosecuted in connection with the affair nor face any other charges.

In June 2007, the Quartet on the Middle East – mediating the peace process in the Israeli-Palestinian conflict and consisting of the EU, the UN, the U.S. and Russia – decided that the best way to achieve peace was to appoint as their Peace Envoy the Israeli-biased, and heinous war criminal Tony Blair whose subsequent sterling and impartial "mediation" resulted in Israel's 2008 ethnic Cleansing Operation Cast Lead. The Irony of Blair's grovelling devotion to Apartheid Israel's cause, – and others of his ilk – is that they were not actually liked or respected by their Jewish masters who regarded them as exploitable fools deserving of nothing but complete contempt.

Being an Israeli stooge, however, had its rewards and in May 2009 Blair received the $1 million Dan David prize at a Tel Aviv university ceremony. Blair's office stated that 90 percent of the money from the prize – which was named after Dan David, the Jewish-born Romanian international businessman who made his millions by setting up Photo-Me booths in shopping malls around the world – would be donated to the Tony Blair Faith Foundation (TBFF).

This was followed up in September 2010 with the National Constitution Centre's Liberty Medal and $100,000 (£65,000) prize being awarded by Former President Bill Clinton to Blair. The Centre is an "independent," non-profit organisation that promotes understanding of the U.S. constitution and its relevance. Officials acknowledged that Blair, who had just been forced to cancel promotional events for a new autobiography amid protests by critics of his role in the U.S.-led Iraq war, was a contentious choice. The Centre's Jewish president David Eisner, said that "there is always an element of controversy when you pick people at the forefront of change. They are usually very controversial figures. We understand … how differently Tony Blair appears to be viewed by many people in the UK as compared with many people in the US." That was probably because the British people had not forgotten how he deliberately involved Britain in a war on the strength of concocted "intelligence."

Following the September 2014 much criticised GQ glossy magazine's "Philanthropist of the Year" award" to Blair, the Charity Commission announced that it would meet representatives of the Tony Blair Faith Foundation (TBFF) over concerns brought to its attention by a former senior employee turned whistleblower. The whistleblower – who as editor of the TBFF website for the charity analysed religious conflict – had complained about Blair's interference and effectively accused him of abusing his role as patron by using the charity as a think tank for his private office which allegedly spent large sums of money on a sizeable communications team whose priority appeared to be the protection of Blair's image, rather than the promotion of the charity. He further maintained that "the Faith Foundation is an independent charity with Tony Blair as its patron. He is not supposed to have any executive role … But it was clear from the outset that … his [Mr Blair's] reputation was to be protected at all costs."

Though the Labour Party leadership had since endeavoured to jettison the pernicious legacy of the illegal and still ongoing Iraqi conflict, Blair has stubbornly continued to maintain that he made the right decision because "if we hadn't removed Saddam from power just think, for example, what would be happening if these Arab revolutions were continuing now and Saddam, who's probably 20 times as bad as Assad in Syria, was trying to suppress an uprising in Iraq? Think of the consequences of leaving that regime in power." Anyone thinking about it – taking into account how Iraq's entire infrastructure has since been destroyed, its communities divided, and its people devastated with millions killed – would have to honestly conclude Iraq and its people were much better off under Saddam Hussein who as a war criminal was strictly an amateur when compared to the likes of Tony Blair, George Bush Jr., Dick Cheney, and numerous other Zionist neoconservatives including Richard Perle, Paul Wolfowitz, Douglas Feith, Michael Ledeen, Stephen Bryen, and Robert Kagan.

Despite his criminal role in the illegal war against Iraq – possibly due to be confirmed by the long-awaited release of the Chilcot Inquiry in the summer – Blair had called for regime change in Iran and Syria while blaming Tehran for prolonging the conflict in Iraq after the 2003 invasion; had steadfastly rejected claims that the 2003 U.S.-UK invasion of Iraq was to blame for that country's current horrendous crisis and instead categorically blamed the Iraqi government and the war in Syria; and had repeatedly called for a war against against Islam because "the threat of this radical Islam is not abating. It is growing. It is spreading across the world. It is destabilising communities and even nations. It is undermining the possibility of peaceful coexistence in an era of globalisation. And in the face of this threat we seem curiously reluctant to acknowledge it and powerless to counter it effectively."

Since Blair's resignation in 2007, a controversial and costly police presence has been maintained around his Connaught Square residence with at least four officers – being present at any given time – from the Metropolitan Police Service's Diplomatic Protection Group (DPG) which provides overt armed protection for Her Majesty's Government, diplomatic premises such as embassies, high commissions, and consular sections. Part of the house now served as an office for the pretentiously named "Tony Blair Faith Foundation" whose alleged function to "provide practical support to counter religious conflict and extremism in order to promote open-minded and stable societies," is patronised by a man whose persistent promotion of Islamophobia on behalf of Israel is surpassed only by the Israelis themselves.

More recently Blair's Connaught Square staff had been feverishly endeavouring to counter published newspaper reports – due to increased public interest over the forthcoming publication of the Iraq War Chilcot Inquiry – that during his time as the Quartet Representative, Blair had been guilty of a potential conflict of interest between his private work and his role as the Quartet representative in the Middle East.

Such indiscretions included allegations that he also used taxpayer-funded trips in his capacity as Quartet Representative for his private business; that he had been visiting up to five countries a week at a potential cost of between £14,000 and £16,000 to the public purse; that he and his wife's law firm "sniffed out" the possibility for work in one European country; that during his trips he was accompanied by a team of Metropolitan Police officers whose salary, overtime, and living expenses were paid for by the taxpayer with the more complex trips involving eight officers – not counting those protecting his homes in Britain – each of whom was likely to have been earning at least £56,000, but upwards to £70,000 with accumulated overtime; had nurtured a network of some of the world's most influential leaders and businessmen to build up a client list that payed him tens of millions of pounds for advice; had with his entourage stayed in five-star hotels around the world, with each room for his police bodyguards costing the taxpayer an estimated £1,000; had travelled on a series of private jets, in some cases belonging to clients and governments; had secured a £1 million private contract with the World Bank, while at the time working with the Bank in his role as Middle East envoy; had struck lucrative commercial deals with Abu Dhabi while he was also in negotiations with the emirate as Middle East envoy with regards to £29 million ($45 million) funding for the Palestinian Authority; had his team seek assistance from British officials so as to further his private business interests, including briefings on countries such as Albania, Canada, and Macedonia; and had on private business trips met with influential figures who also happened to be contacts with whom he had dealt in his official capacity as the Quartet envoy.

Very early on during his tenure as Quartet Representative, Blair met with the emir of Kuwait, on supposed Quartet business. But instead of being accompanied by someone from the well-staffed Quartet office, he had taken with him his former Downing Street chief of staff Jonathan Powell, then a consultant with Tony Blair Associates. Whether this meeting had anything to do with achieving Middle East peace is not known, but the eventual outcome was that the emir awarded Blair a £27 million consultancy contract.

So while war criminal Blair was almost entirely occupied with building his business empire at the expense of British taxpayers, he also did so at the expense of the Palestinian people who were themselves "forcefully occupied" in less salubrious circumstances because Blair had totally abandoned – in favour of Israel – the impartiality that his position as Quartet Representative demanded; had confirmed his lack of impartiality by accompanying his one-sided praise of Israel with outspoken attacks against Islam; had during his tenure of some eight years failed to alleviate the effects of a contracting

Palestinian economy, to heal the rupture in Palestinian-Israeli relations, or to in any way relieve the humanitarian crisis and stalled rebuilding in the Gaza Strip following Israel's 2014 Operation Protective Edge which killed thousands, injured tens of thousands, and laid waste to Gaza's already fragile infrastructure; and had forsaken the universal responsibility that each individual has for all other human beings regardless of who or what they were. One can only wonder if the English writer, Rudyard Kipling, had a character as despicable as Tony Blair in mind when he penned his *Epitaphs of the War:*

A DEAD STATESMAN

I could not dig: I dared not rob:
Therefore I lied to please the mob.
Now all my lies are proved untrue
And I must face the men I slew.
What tale shall serve me here among
Mine angry and defrauded young?

Silwan, Occupied East Jerusalem

Since the murder of his father, twelve-year-old Anton Hadawi had become sullen and withdrawn as he grappled with mixed emotions that ranged from being devastated over the sudden loss of a much loved father, and a simmering hatred for those responsible. Such hatred was neither inherent nor something he had learnt from his parents or at school, but had evolved as a result of his growing up as a child in an environment where he was regarded by Israeli Jews as an unwelcome interloper to be despised and driven out from the land of Palestine like an animal; to be deliberately targeted because of his childhood as a future threat to the "Jewishness" of a Jewish state; and to be denied all those rights which were proclaimed on 20 November

1959 in the General Assembly Resolution 1386(XIV) which formed the basis of the Convention of the Rights of the Child adopted by the UN General Assembly 30 years later on 20 November 1989, and entered into force on 2 September 1990:

Whereas the peoples of the United Nations have, in the Charter, reaffirmed their faith in fundamental human rights and in the dignity and worth of the human person, and have determined to promote social progress and better standards of life in larger freedom,

Whereas the United Nations has, in the Universal Declaration of Human Rights, proclaimed that everyone is entitled to all the rights and freedoms set forth therein, without distinction of any kind, such as race, colour, sex, language, religion, political or other opinion, national or social origin, property, birth or other status,

Whereas the child, by reason of his physical and mental immaturity, needs special safeguards and care, including appropriate legal protection, before as well as after birth,

Whereas the need for such special safeguards has been stated in the Geneva Declaration of the Rights of the Child of 1924, and recognised in the Universal Declaration of Human Rights and in the statutes of specialised agencies and international organisations concerned with the welfare of children,

Whereas mankind owes to the child the best it has to give,

Now therefore,

The General Assembly

Proclaims this Declaration of the Rights of the Child to the end that he may have a happy childhood and enjoy for his own good and for the good of society the rights and freedoms herein set forth, and calls upon parents, upon men and women as individuals, and upon voluntary organisations, local authorities and national Governments to recognise these rights and strive for their observance by legislative and other measures progressively taken in accordance with the following principles:

Principle 1
The child shall enjoy all the rights set forth in this Declaration. Every child, without any exception whatsoever, shall be entitled to these rights, without distinction or discrimination on account of race, colour, sex, language, religion, political or other opinion, national or social origin, property, birth or other status, whether of himself or of his family.

Principle 2
The child shall enjoy special protection, and shall be given opportunities and facilities, by law and by other means, to enable him to develop physically, mentally, morally, spiritually and socially in a healthy and normal manner and in conditions of freedom and dignity. In the enactment of laws for this purpose, the best interests of the child shall be the paramount consideration.

Principle 3
The child shall be entitled from his birth to a name and a nationality.

Principle 4
The child shall enjoy the benefits of social security. He shall be entitled to grow and develop in health; to this end, special care and protection shall be provided both to him and to his mother, including adequate pre-natal and post-natal care. The child shall have the right to adequate nutrition, housing, recreation and medical services.

Principle 5
The child who is physically, mentally or socially handicapped shall be

given the special treatment, education and care required by his particular condition.

Principle 6
The child, for the full and harmonious development of his personality, needs love and understanding. He shall, wherever possible, grow up in the care and under the responsibility of his parents, and, in any case, in an atmosphere of affection and of moral and material security; a child of tender years shall not, save in exceptional circumstances, be separated from his mother. Society and the public authorities shall have the duty to extend particular care to children without a family and to those without adequate means of support. Payment of State and other assistance towards the maintenance of children of large families is desirable.

Principle 7
The child is entitled to receive education, which shall be free and compulsory, at least in the elementary stages. He shall be given an education which will promote his general culture and enable him, on a basis of equal opportunity, to develop his abilities, his individual judgement, and his sense of moral and social responsibility, and to become a useful member of society.

The best interests of the child shall be the guiding principle of those responsible for his education and guidance; that responsibility lies in the first place with his parents.

The child shall have full opportunity for play and recreation, which should be directed to the same purposes as education; society and the public authorities shall endeavor to promote the enjoyment of this right.

Principle 8
The child shall in all circumstances be among the first to receive protection and relief.

Principle 9

The child shall be protected against all forms of neglect, cruelty and exploitation. He shall not be the subject of traffic, in any form.

The child shall not be admitted to employment before an appropriate minimum age; he shall in no case be caused or permitted to engage in any occupation or employment which would prejudice his health or education, or interfere with his physical, mental or moral development.

Principle 10

The child shall be protected from practices which may foster racial, religious and any other form of discrimination. He shall be brought up in a spirit of understanding, tolerance, friendship among peoples, peace and universal brotherhood, and in full consciousness that his energy and talents should be devoted to the service of his fellow men.

Only three U.N. countries have not ratified the Convention of the Rights of the Child: Somalia, South Sudan, and the United States. Though a signatory, Israel with its usual contempt for international law, simply ignores the Convention.

Children like Anton – who lived in conditions of constant political turmoil, violence, and war – have been described by child development experts as having "grown up too soon" with the consequence of having "lost their childhood." They had been forced to take on onerous responsibilities before achieving sufficient maturity which in the opinion of mental health professionals led to negative psychological consequences as a result of their being deprived of the parent-child attachment considered vital for providing a protective shield for children's psychological wellbeing when exposed to dangerous situations. A soon to be released report by the United Nations Children's Emergency Fund (UNICEF) would state that some 250 million girls and boys, one in nine children, are forced to grow up in conflict zones.

The report's revelations include the fact that during 2015

alone, 16 million babies will have been born in conflict regions; that globally, 75 million children between the ages of three and 18 cannot attend a kindergarten or school – or learn only irregularly – due to ongoing crises or catastrophes; that an average of four schools or hospitals become targets of armed attacks every day; that during 2015, Unicef registered 1,500 – only the tip of the iceberg – severe violations of the rights of children in Syria; that in 60 percent of cases, children were killed or injured by bombs in densely populated residential areas with one-third of all victims being killed on the way to school; and that many children in war zones had been unable to attend school for years because their schools had been destroyed, the route to school was too dangerous, or there had been a lack of funds for books and pens.

The psychological sequelae of political turmoil and violence on children were very serious and traumatising and while many of the injured Palestinian children had acquired a permanent physical disability, many more had developed psychological impairments with up to half of them suffering from post-traumatic stress disorder. Traumas inflicted by the Israeli Defence Force were mostly the result of Palestinian children having their homes being subjected to artillery shelling; of being exposed to and inhaling tear gas; of suffering burns; of being shot at by live ammunition; of being shot at by rubber bullets; of being shot in the head and losing consciousness; of being deprived of medical care when required; of being witness to shootings, fighting, and explosions; of being witness to strangers being injured or killed; and of being witness to family members, relatives, and neighbours being injured or killed.

There were innumerable reports backed by documentation published by international, Israeli, and Palestinian human rights and children's rights organisations that clearly demonstrate how politically motivated abuses against children are additional tools of Israel's colonial dispossession of the Palestinian people.

Being aware of the power that individual Palestinian children possess by virtue of their mere existence, Israel deliberately keeps them under the constant threat of disappearance. Within the Israeli context, Palestinian children are regarded as definite threats to security who must be denied the established and accepted framework for basic human rights. Targeting Palestinian children served to deny them the right to resist their own oppression by criminalising, demonising, incarcerating, and killing them. Despite its pious claims to the contrary, Israel targets and kills Palestinian children, not because they pose a threat as "future terrorists," but because as the next generation they challenge the blatantly false and inhumane Israeli assertion that "there is no such thing as a Palestinian people."

A Joint report by HaMoked and B'Tselem – the former is a Centre for the Defence of the Individual, and the latter an Israeli Information Centre for Human Rights in the Occupied Territories – highlights Israel's inhumane treatment of Palestinian children which included sleep deprivation, on occasion for days at a time; being bound hand and foot to a chair, with movement restricted for hours on end; being subjected to shouting, swearing, threats, spitting, and indignities; being exposed to extreme cold and heat; being fed with little and substandard food; being denied the possibility to shower or change clothes for days and even weeks on end; being incarcerated in a small, foul-smelling cells, usually in solitary confinement, for many days: and being subjected to inhuman and degrading interrogations lasting for days with interrogators working in shifts so as to deny their victims more than a few hours of respite per day while also inflicting mental and physical harm. Calls for Israel to abide by the prohibition on torture and for it to immediately cease the use of cruel, inhuman and degrading treatment, as well as the abuse and torture of detainees, are routinely ignored by the Israelis who know that the rest of the world will as usual remain silent and do nothing.

Apart from being targeted for abuse, hundreds of Palestinian children were also exploited as workers on settlement farms – in exhausting and hazardous conditions that cause health problems including severe backaches from long hours of toiling in the fields – picking dates, onions, peppers, and tomatoes in the Jordan Valley. The children, some as young as 12, are paid 70 New Israeli Shekels for an eight-hour day which is 16 shekels an hour less than the Israeli minimum wage of 25 shekels an hour. The children toil under a climate of fear where the hate-filled settler farmers frequently scream at them and threaten to fire them at will. This occurs despite the fact that employing children aged 15 in a job that could damage their health is illegal according to Israeli and International law. Employing anyone aged 14 or under, is completely forbidden.

Israel justifies its contempt for, and criminality towards Palestinians – including defenceless children like Anton – by constantly playing the "victim" and "self-defence" cards and highlighting the suffering endured by Jews during the Holocaust whose atrocities were of course indefensible and should never again be allowed against any ethnic group or individual human being. Though most people like to periodically reaffirm their own humanity by commemorating those who died in battle or as a result of genocide, they feel no such obligation to show concern for the hundreds of millions of children who have died due to indifference, neglect, hypocrisy, and double standards. An example of such double standards occurred recently when the British Prime Minister announced that Britain would put £50 million towards the construction of a "striking and prominent" Holocaust memorial that would stand beside Parliament as a permanent statement of British values. The PM's sentiment was echoed by Chief Rabbi Ephraim Mirvis who said it would "send the strongest possible message … that the lessons of the Holocaust will forever form a part of our national consciousness." A national consciousness and Holocaust lesson, however, which the Chief Rabbi hypocritically sets aside where the ethnic cleansing of the Palestinian people is concerned.

For Anton Hadawi, his sister and millions of other Palestinian children there is no hope or vision of any kind for the future and they can only gape in silent astonishment at how the rest of the world led by hypocritical political and religious leaders can stand by indifferently as Israel with its racist ideology deliberately targets them for brutal persecution. That racist ideology was aptly described by the Israeli peace activist Miko Peled – a grandson of Avraham Katsnelson who signed Israel's Declaration of Independence, and son of Mattiyahu Peled who fought in the 1948 war, served as a general in the 1967 war, and after the Israeli cabinet ignored his investigation of a 1967 alleged Israeli war crime, became a peace activist and leading proponent of dialogue with the Palestinians – who stated the following:

"De-Arabising the history of Palestine is another crucial element of the ethnic cleansing. 1500 years of Arab and Muslim rule and culture in Palestine are trivialised, evidence of its existence is being destroyed and all this is done to make the absurd connection between the ancient Hebrew civilisation and today's Israel. The most glaring example of this today is in Silwan, (Wadi Hilwe) a town adjacent to the Old City of Jerusalem with some 50,000 residents. Israel is expelling families from Silwan and destroying their homes because it claims that King David built a city there some 3,000 years ago. Thousands of families will be made homeless so that Israel can build a park to commemorate a king that may or may not have lived 3,000 years ago. Not a shred of historical evidence exists that can prove King David ever lived yet Palestinian men, women, children and the elderly along with their schools and mosques, churches and ancient cemeteries and any evidence of their existence must be destroyed and then denied so that Zionist claims to exclusive rights to the land may be substantiated."

21

Wednesday, 30 December

Little Venice, London, England

Conrad and Freya had been in a sombre mood since their return to London and it was with a heavy heart that Conrad began working on the dialogue for his documentary which would note that the long-suffering Palestinians had very few options or hopes for the future as a people with a state of their own. Theodore Herzl, the founding father of Zionism, had asserted that the area of the Jewish State stretched "From the Brook of Egypt to the Euphrates." This view was subsequently reiterated by Rabbi Fischmann, a member of the Jewish Agency for Palestine, who declared in his testimony to the U.N. Special Committee of Enquiry on July 9, 1947 that "the Promised Land extends from the River of Egypt up to the Euphrates, it includes parts of Syria and Lebanon." And more recently the incumbent Israeli Deputy Foreign Minister had imperiously stressed that it was "important to say that this land is ours. All of it is ours. We didn't come here to apologise for that."

Conrad's research had shown him that settler colonial movements – unlike other types of colonialism including direct rule, indirect rule, and corporate – were quite different and often involved the use of extreme violence towards the indigenous population including genocide as occurred to the First Nation Peoples in Canada, the Native American peoples in the U.S., and to the Aboriginal Australians; could involve forced segregation according to racial criteria, as was the case with Apartheid in South Africa; could involve extensive ethnic cleansing as was and still being carried out by Israel since 1948; and could also involve a combination of any of the aforementioned strategies.

So while most people in the world may have been conditioned by decades of Israeli atrocities, they had so far, however, been shielded from Israel's shocking story of stolen babies which was part of a deliberate de-Arabisation programme. While European colonials – such as the British, French, Portuguese, Spanish, and others – had been mainly concerned with subjugating the indigenous population, plundering the country's resources, and then eventually granting independence as occurred in Africa, the Jewish settlers had come to Palestine not simply to just colonise, but to ruthlessly replace the indigenous population. Consequently not only was the destruction of Palestinian society necessary, but also certain precautions had to be taken to avoid "contamination" of the Jewish state by anything or anyone that may be "Arabised." So while Prime Minister David Ben-Gurion recognised the improbability of being able to educate Arab Jews out of their "primitiveness," he nonetheless believed that by seizing Arab Jewish babies – an estimated 8,000 were taken – and relocating them with "civilised" European Jews, they would grow up "civilised." Such abductions to "civilise" and "tame" "savage" indigenous populations had also been a feature of colonialism in Australia and Canada.

Since Israel's establishment in 1948, successive governments and three public inquiries had so far denied any such wrongdoing with the excuse that the babies had died during the chaotic times of mass Jewish immigration. Because mothers were simply informed their babies had died either during or shortly after delivery without being shown a body, a grave, or death certificate – along with the fact that all relevant documents were to remain classified until 1971 – the only plausible explanation was that this was yet another coverup by Israeli officials well versed in the art of chutzpah deniability. The forcible transfer of children from one ethnic group to another meets the United Nation's definition of genocide.

Conrad intended highlighting the fact that despite participating in the decades-long charade of "Peace Talks" and the illusionary promise of a "Two-State Solution" – as was the original intention of the 1947 United Nations Partition Plan for Palestine – Israel had never at any time actually intended to seriously pursue or honour either of those two concepts which were incompatible with the Zionist objective for a Greater Israel with an undivided Jerusalem as its capitol. As a consequence of that objective, Israel had been instrumental in orchestrating the subversion and fragmentation of neighbouring Arab states, and of instigating the 2003 war on Iraq, the 2006 war on Lebanon, the 2011 war on Libya, the current hostilities in Syria, and the ongoing efforts to incite a war against Iran by a U.S.-led coalition of Western nations. In the meantime, such unjustified and illegal wars had served to distract from Israel's own unrelenting efforts to ethnically cleanse the Palestinian population with a view to annexing all Palestine where the rule of law and true democracy would be superseded by a racist Jewish nationalism promoted, supported, and implemented by transnational Zionism and toleration by Jews in diaspora.

Conrad now believed that the seed for a global disregard for Palestinian legal and human rights was first sowed way back in November 1917 when His Britannic Majesty's Government – being somewhat still preoccupied with the First World War and defending its own position as the world's foremost imperial power – perpetrated the first of its betrayals of the Palestinian people with the Balfour Declaration which presumptuously promised to give away a substantial part of Palestine without even bothering to consult the Palestinian people.

Following its connived conception in 1948, Israel had

deliberately and with impunity done everything conceivable to "prejudice the civil and religious rights of existing non-Jewish communities in Palestine." Such flagrant agreement violations by Israel – now well-established as the nation's hallmark – had since been tolerated, apart from a few Scandinavian nations, by an obsequious West inculcated with guilt over the Holocaust; by Arab states such as Egypt who were reliant on U.S. aid; by Gulf Sheikhdoms reliant on oil sales to the West; by ambivalent Asian countries where human rights had still to be accorded some significant degree of importance; by most European descent antipodeans whose history was rooted in criminal colonialism; and by most North Americans who had been successfully mainstream media brainwashed into believing that everything Judaic was noble and good, while anything Islamic was ignoble and evil. It was the Israeli-born professor of law and philosophy, Oren Ben-Dor, who best described Israeli statehood:

> *"Israel's statehood is based on an unjust ideology which causes indignity and suffering for those who are classified as non-Jewish by either a religious or ethnic test. To hide this primordial immorality, Israel fosters an image of victimhood. Provoking violence, consciously or unconsciously, against which one must defend oneself is a key feature of the victim-mentality. By perpetuating such a tragic cycle, Israel is a terrorist state like no other … The very creation of Israel required an act of terror. In 1948, most of the non-Jewish indigenous people were ethnically cleansed from the part of Palestine which became Israel. This action was carefully planned. Without it, no state with a Jewish majority and character would have been possible."*

The greatest betrayal of the Palestinian people, however, had been that perpetrated by their own leaders – yes, even by Yasser Arafat – most of whom were more concerned with serving their own interests while lining their pockets, than with actually representing the aspirations of their hapless and much maligned constituents. Apart from aiding and abetting such Palestinian leadership corruption, Israel had also stoked and exploited the bitter rivalry that existed between the different national and religious Palestinian factions.

On reflection, Conrad also noted that over and above the fact of having very few friends or a formidable World respected leader like South Africa's Nelson Mandela to espouse their cause, the Palestinian people were also being denied the protection of international organisations such as the United Nations and the International Criminal Court with the former being rendered impotent by U.S. vetoes of any resolutions condemning Israel, and the latter being susceptible to pressure from those who funded its existence. The release of some of former U.S. Secretary of State Hillary Clinton's emails show how the State Department was devoted to "deferring" UN action on Israeli war crimes by "reframing the debate" about the atrocities, and "moving away from the UN." Some of the messages, written by high-level State Department officials, expose the U.S. government's role in undermining the international response to the 2009 United Nations Fact-Finding Mission on the Gaza Conflict (the Goldstone Report) which the U.S. acknowledged as "moderate," but still opposed.

That "fact finding mission," led by South African judge Richard Goldstone, had accused Israel of using disproportionate force, deliberately targeting civilians, destroying civilian infrastructure, and using people as human shields. Unsurprisingly, however, Goldstone subsequently changed his mind by saying that new accounts indicated Israel had not deliberately targeted civilians. He said that if he had known then what he knew now, "the Goldstone Report would have been a different document." Mr. Goldstone did not explain what it was that he failed to learn back in 2009, which he had suddenly subsequently discovered. Goldstone's change of mind was not the first time that criticism of Israel by a Jew had been withdrawn following intimidatory Israeli pressure.

The most daunting reality of all, however, was the fact that Jewish settler colonisation of Palestine had been and still was transnational with established economic and military alliances ensuring a steady flow of support and finance from both American and European Zionist-led organisations. The principal such organisation was for example, the Jewish National Fund (JNF) which was founded in 1901 specifically as a Zionist tool for Jewish colonisation. The JFN evolved into a quasi-governmental agency responsible for collecting donations not only for settlement in Western Europe, but also for purchasing land in Palestine whose occupants were either immediately or eventually expelled to make way for the establishment of illegal Jewish settlements. The JNF's role in the 1948 establishment of Israel had been of paramount importance.

Even after the achieving their objective of an Israeli state with the forced expulsion of most of the indigenous Palestinian population, the Zionist leadership was determined to create an extensive network of international institutions supportive of Israel. Consequently Israel was now involved in numerous diplomatic, economic, intelligence gathering, and military forums; is the recipient of generous transnational corporate and government investment; and is closely allied to the superpower that emerged following World War Two.

The extent of such reliance on U.S. support was evident from the JFN-USA tax-exempt charity which worked together with the right-wing settler group Elad to evict Palestinians and take over their property. This cooperation involved the JFN confiscating Palestinian property and then transferring it to Elad so that the U.S.-based JFN-USA is irrefutably complicit in dispossessing Palestinians of their land to facilitate Jewish settlement despite alleged U.S. government "opposition" to such activity. Such connivance in dishonest and illegal appropriation of Palestinian land also involved participation by U.S. Evangelical Christian charities – such as the Christian Friends of Israeli Communities (CFOIC), the Hebron Fund, and Christians United for Israel – which bankroll illegal Israeli settlements and buildings in the West Bank. Typically and hypocritically the U.S. government has failed to take any steps to either oppose such tax-exempt organisations or to close the nonprofit loophole that facilitates their settlement bankrolling operations.

It was also manifest to Conrad that another catastrophic and insurmountable obstacle for Palestinian aspirations was the arming of Israel's military with the best available state-of-the-art weaponry by the U.S. defence corporations whom Israel payed from the more than $4 billion it was receiving annually in U.S. aid. In return for such U.S. largesse, Israel had acted both as a conduit for U.S. arms shipments to oppressive regimes in furtherance of American interests, and as a geopolitical base and surrogate for American imperialism. When Israel in the war of 1967 defeated Colonel Nasser's Egypt – regarded as the centre of Arab nationalism at the time – it also unwittingly fulfilled a long-term U.S. geopolitical strategy, which is probably why it got away with its deliberate attack on the USS Liberty and instead started receiving increased material and diplomatic support which resulted in the transnational Zionist network transferring its main reliance from Western Europe to the United States.

In 1970 the U.S. – which considered the Palestinian Liberation Organisation (PLO) to be a threat to its ally, Jordan – supported the Jordanian campaign to destroy and expel the PLO from Jordan by asking Israel to mobilise its forces on the Syrian border so as to bring about the withdrawal of Syrian forces who were aiding the fedayeen (freedom fighters) to fend off Jordanian troops. The subsequent withdrawal of

Syrian troops resulted in the U.S. military aid to Israel being immediately increased from $140 million to $1.15 billion. Israel was consequently also a beneficiary by virtue of the Jordanian massacre of thousands of Palestinians in what came to be know as "Black September." It is no coincidence that Israeli instigated violence within Syria, regarded as an ally of Iran, had included the targeting of Palestinian refugees of whom many are descended from ancestors who fled or were driven from their homes in Palestine in the 1948.

The U.S. had also been complicit in Israel's periodic assaults on Gaza – one of the most densely populated regions in the world – where U.S. supplied new and experimental weaponry was "battle-tested" on Palestinian "guinea pigs" so that Gaza had become Israel's weapons testing ground for the joint benefit of its colonial occupation and the U.S. military industrial complex. U.S. support for the illegal Israeli occupation does not simply involve the supply of deadly weapons, but also the provision of the most essential ingredient of any occupation – and that is people. Ideological Jewish Zionists from the U.S. had emigrated and illegally settled on Palestinian land so that over 70,00 of them – with no connection to Palestine whatsoever – now lived in the West Bank.

Not only had the U.S. Zionist network provided people, cash, and weapons to sustain an Apartheid Jewish settler-colonial state, but it had also guaranteed the expansion of that state by being complicit in the displacement, destruction, and denial of rights to the Palestinian people. Israel's ethnic cleansing of Palestine which has been ongoing since 1948, was now apathetically viewed by the rest of the world as being one of life's inevitabilities. Such passivity towards the desperate plight of the Palestinian people – a people who have endured almost 70 years of brutal military occupation, the longest ever – could not have been possible without the combined factors of relentless Zionist efforts to criminalise criticism of Israel in the

West, and the use of U.S. vetoes at the UN to enable Israel's avoidance of legal accountability for its barbaric violations of international law in the Palestinian Occupied Territories.

For the isolated Palestinians, therefore – faced with global indifference, inhumanity, and injustice – there were few feasible options or any realistic hope of ever shedding the yoke of Israel's illegal and parasitic occupation. Decades of rather feeble Palestinian "armed resistance" and "peace negotiations" had proved futile against one of the world's largest and best equipped armies enforcing a Zionist ideology that from the start had shunned peaceful coexistence, and instead pursued its larcenous desire for all of Palestine.

Conrad recalled that it was Mohandas Karamchand Gandhi – assassinated in 1948 – who as an expatriate lawyer in South Africa first employed nonviolent civil disobedience in the resident Indian community's struggle for civil rights. Following his return to India in 1915, Gandhi organised peasants, farmers, and urban labourers to protest against excessive land-tax and racial discrimination before assuming leadership of the Indian National Congress. He subsequently led nationwide campaigns for alleviating poverty, increasing women's rights, promoting ethnic and religious harmony, ending untouchability as practiced by the caste system, and ultimately – after British Crown rule lasting from 1858 to 1947– achieving Indian self-rule.

Palestinians, however, did not have the same degree of freedom of movement as that enjoyed by Gandhi and his followers. Palestinians were subject to cruel air, land, and sea blockades; were subject to caged checkpoints through which they were herded like animals to inflict humiliation and suffering; were subject to Apartheid separation barriers consisting of wire fencing and twenty-five foot high concrete walls; were subject to a repressed existence in towns and villages that were in effect detention centres; were subject to travel restrictions imposed by roadblocks and roads built specifically for the use by Jews only; and were constantly subject to being harassed, beaten, tear-gassed, or shot by either Israeli security forces or armed Jewish settler gangs. All such barbarous human rights violations were then candy-flossed over by Israel, Western governments, and the media to be presented as "self-defence" to the faint-hearted people of the world who were ridden with debilitating hypocrisy, selective morality, and collective preoccupation with their own survival in the rat race that is called human endeavour.

Conrad felt that because they were faced with such biased and overwhelming odds, the Palestinian people had no realistic chance of ever achieving a globally recognised and UN-endorsed statehood that would enable them to finally enjoy the freedoms and human rights that the hypocritical West claims to be upholding and fighting for, and which the swaggering racist Israelis – with Palestinian blood on their hands – audaciously demand for themselves. Numerous examples of Western hypocrisy and double standards included the fact that organised civilian opposition to Nazi occupation in Europe during World War Two was acclaimed as "The Resistance" while token Palestinian dissent against Israel's equally brutal occupation with overwhelming military might was denounced as "Terrorism."

Yet since their 1948 forced exodus, the Palestinian people have allowed their hopes for justice and freedom to rest in the hands of various leaders and factions who were unfortunately motivated by self-interest and greed. In a rare disclosure in September 2003 – suspiciously reminiscent of a Machiavellian Rothschild manoeuvre – the International Monetary Fund stated that from 1995 to 2000 Yasser Arafat had diverted more than £560 million of Palestinian Authority funds of which a sizeable portion ended up in a Swiss bank account. So not only were the Palestinian people being betrayed by Britain's Balfour Declaration and the international community, but also by many of their own avaricious and duplicitous leaders of the past and the present.

Conrad felt that it must be obvious to even the most naive and optimistic of people – as the rapacious Israelis gobble up more and more Palestinian land – that the Palestinians have no chance of achieving either justice or statehood by any tried and tested means including armed resistance. Faced with one of the world's best equipped military forces, the odds for the unarmed Palestinians were insurmountable. Even though the Israelis have made it very clear that Palestinian statehood is out of the question, the ever accommodating U.S. had nonetheless announced a $1.9 billion deal to supply Israel for defence purposes – presumably against stone throwing Palestinian children – with some 3,000 Hellfire precision missiles, 250 AIM-120C advanced medium-range air-to-air missiles, 4,100 GBU-39 small diameter bombs and 50 BLU-113 bunker buster bombs. Also included are 14,500 tail kits for Joint Direct Attack Munitions for 220kg and 900kg bombs and a variety of Paveway laser-guided bomb kits. Needless to say, the U.S. will not be supplying Palestinian children with stones with which to "defend themselves" against continual targeting by the "world's most [i]moral army."

Conrad tried to figure out what options the Palestinians had. They could either continue to stand by while their heritage, their homeland, and their hopes gradually diminished to the point of oblivion, or they could recognise and accept the historical reality that for almost seven decades they had been on their own and that it was unlikely that anyone was about to start helping them apart from themselves. But how? With all the odds overwhelmingly against them, Conrad could only come up with one feasible option which was to call Israel's bluff of a criminally concocted contention that it was "defending itself."

Difficult as it may seem, the Palestinian people would have to seriously endeavour to take control of their own despairing destiny by insisting – irrespective of cost or consequences – that all Palestinian leaders and factions without exception announce their recognition of the state of Israel within the essential borders of 1967; that they renounce the use of any and all violence and armed conflict; and that they call for an internationally supervised removal/destruction of their offensive weapons. Such unconditional Palestinian proclamations would serve to deny Israel of the deceitful "self-defence" excuse which is also routinely echoed by Western nations submissive to the Judaeo-Zionist lobby; would serve to highlight Western hypocrisy and double standards if an immediate and positive Western reaction was not forthcoming; and would serve to expose Israel's true intention of not seeking peaceful coexistence, but of maintaining an endless conflict that provided a smokescreen for its real intention of driving out the entire indigenous Palestinian population because not only did Zionist ideology deem it, but also because the majority of Israelis self-righteously believed that "this land is ours. All of it is ours. We didn't come here to apologise for that." So while admitting to having "come here," they nonetheless refused to admit that the Palestinian people were already "here" by subscribing to yet another fraudulent Zionist soundbite about "a land without a people, for a people without a land." First Israeli Prime Minister David Ben-Gurion was at least being honest when while playing the devil's advocate he admitted the following:

> *"If I were an Arab leader, I would never sign a contract with Israel. It's normal: We took their land. It's true, that it was promised to us by God, but why should they care? Our God is not their God. There were anti-Semites, the Nazis, Hitler, Auschwitz, but was it their fault? They only see one thing: We came and stole their land. Why should they accept that?"*
> **Quoted in Nahum Goldmann, *Le Paradoxe Juif (The Jewish Paradox)*.**

Would such a ploy prove successful? Conrad asked himself. *Would anything actually change,* he wondered. But after taking some time to consider the various possible reactions to such Palestinian proclamations, Conrad doubted that anything would change because as Adolf Hitler had noted, "by the skilful and sustained use of propaganda, one can make a people see even heaven as hell or an extremely wretched life as paradise." Consequently the possibility of change was an illusion because the world's mainstream media – which persuaded a credulous world that Iraq possessed weapons of mass destruction which subsequently proved to be nonexistent; which incorrectly reported that Iran was on the verge of possessing nuclear weapons; and which purveyed propaganda about Syrian President Assad's use of chemical weapons against his own people – was the same Zionist-controlled mainstream media whose so-called journalists would continue to prostitute themselves by churning out news that legitimised Israel's lies to the world. Such newshound whores were only employed after a careful selection process that eliminated those dissidents who were inclined to think critically for themselves – rather than trotting out carefully scripted government and corporate propaganda – and whose world view was not closely compatible with those in power.

Nowadays real journalists or whistleblowers who refused to descend to the truly toxic levels of printed and broadcast disinformation and instead expose the truth were fired, forced into exile, persecuted, imprisoned, or even murdered, while newshound whores – who sacrifice their own integrity and the journalistic ethicality that should "strive to ensure the free exchange of information that is accurate, fair and thorough" – were acclaimed and showered with awards by a powerful Zionist elite that had mastered the art of both media control and the believable deception. They had been able to convince the world's credulous masses that rampant destruction is actually a careful and responsible "targeted attack," and that the wanton and senseless massacre of thousands of unarmed Palestinian men, women, and children was "self-defence." But while no other nation could have possibly hoped to get away with such outrageous behaviour, barbaric Israel can and does because it controls and directs the media language that is supposed to impartially report on its atrocities: a media language that George Orwell referred to as "Newspeak."

The Israel Project's 2009 Global Language Dictionary, is for example a propaganda manual that provides instruction on how to control the reporting and discussion of Israel's ethnic cleansing of Palestinian people. Apart from providing Israeli government officials with the descriptive language that gains the Zionist government support from the majority of Americans and many Europeans, it also helps Israelis to present narratives of events that contain significant concoctions – so long as the repetition of such falsehoods served the Israeli war against its Middle Eastern enemies – being presented as "factual." The manual's objective is not the conveyance of truth, but the acquirement for Israel from a Western world support that is blinkered, emotionally-based, and unconditional. It was clear to Conrad that fair reporting by the mainstream media about the tragedy of Palestine was something that was very unlikely to happen in the foreseeable future.

One of the most cunning forms of censorship is political correctness – the art of disguising intolerance as tolerance – which was invented by a Rothschild think tank known as the Frankfurt school. The "school" had been set up in 1923 to devise a means of spreading collectivism – which holds that man must be chained to collective action and collective thought for the sake of what is called "the common good" – from which Socialism, Marxism, and Communism were offshoots. The role of political correctness is to stifle objective investigation and free speech; to eliminate criticism of the power elite under the guise of preventing racism and hate speech; and to act as part of a larger influence known as Cultural Marxism which involves the subversion of a country's culture with collectivist ideology. This form of censorship exploited guilt by shaming people into avoiding certain words and phrases – self-censorship – while using others that were allowable. Censorship is the only available means of countering the "power of truth" which governments and power elites fear will undermine their power bases. Political correctness operates on the premise that if people feel insulted, offended or upset by certain words or language, then they have the right to demand that the State outlaws such words and language.

Another impediment for the achievement of Palestinian human rights was the Balkanisation – the process of fragmenting or dividing a country or region into smaller parts that are inevitably at odds or hostile to one another – of Middle Eastern countries such as Iraq and Syria as was promoted by Zionist neoconservative hawks in the U.S. and Israel and which was anticipated by former Egyptian President Mubarak who said "we fear a state of disorder and chaos may prevail in the region." Such balkanisation of Middle Eastern countries was further inspired by an Israeli think tank, the Institute for Advanced Strategic and Political Studies, which in 1996 published a policy document entitled *A clean break: a new strategy for securing the realm.* The document was intended as a policy blueprint for Benjamin Netanyahu's incoming right-wing government and advised making a complete break with the past and instead adopting a strategy "based on an entirely new intellectual foundation, one that restores strategic initiative and provides the nation the room to engage every possible energy on rebuilding Zionism … "

The document's introduction specifically proposed that rather than pursuing a "comprehensive peace" with the entire Arab world, Israel should work jointly with Jordan and Turkey to "contain, destabilise, and roll-back" those entities that are threats to all three; changing the nature of relations with the Palestinians, specifically reserving the right of "hot pursuit" anywhere within Palestinian territory as well as attempting to promote alternatives to Arafat's leadership; and changing relations with the U.S. while stressing self-reliance and strategic cooperation.

The object of the plan was for Israel to "shape its strategic environment," starting with the removal of Iraq's Saddam Hussein who was to be replaced by a Hashemite monarchy in Baghdad which along with Jordan and Turkey would form an axis with Israel to undermine and "roll back" Syria. Jordan was allocated the task of sorting out Lebanon by "weaning" the Shia Muslim population away from Syria and Iran, and re-establishing their former connections with the Shia in the new Hashemite kingdom of Iraq. The document's conclusion was that "Israel will not only contain its foes; it will transcend them." The document's neoconservative authors – led by Richard Perle, chairman of the Defence Policy Board Advisory Committee at the Pentagon (2001-2003) – included several other Jews who were also holding key positions in Washington.

The imperious, cold-blooded logic in the "Clean Break" manifesto and a paper produced by The Project for a New American Century (PNAC) in 2000 entitled "Rebuilding America's Defences," is very clear about the need to destabilise the region with a view to both reshaping Israel's "strategic environment," and dramatically increasing the number of U.S. "forward bases" in the region to support the systematic destruction of oil-rich Arab countries such as Iraq and Libya while exploiting ethnic and religious differences in Egypt and Syria to instigate and maintain the murderous destruction for which the U.S. and Israel were now renowned. Those same neocons who while planning, agitating for, and bringing about wars, were also in the meantime advancing Israeli interests not only at the expense of America and its people, but also of the rest of the world

Israel's objective of sowing dissension between Shiite and Sunni Muslims was helped by the fact that both sects have been more or less at each others throats ever since the Prophet Muhammad (c. 570 – 632) died without having designated a successor for the Muslim community he had established at Medina. This led to a succession dispute between the "Emigrants" who had accompanied him from Mecca to Medina, and the local "Supporters" who by joining his movement had enhanced it both materially and spiritually. Though Ali, Muhammed's son-in-law, was the obvious candidate for succession, the community elders decided that Muhammed's father-in-law would become the caliph and thereby the institution of the caliphate was begun whereby the caliph acted as both the religious and secular authority.

One of the main disadvantages of having outright authority vested in one man is that his eventual death will result in considerable turmoil as claimants squabble over the succession. Further problems may also arise from having religion dominate every aspect of community life because in the event of social disaffection, such disaffection will be expressed in religious terms whereby sectarianism becomes the only recourse available to the disaffected. Though Ali's supporters, who became known as shi'at Ali, or party of Ali, did not take any immediate overt action, they nonetheless covertly laid the foundation for Islam's main division of Sunni and Shia Muslims who to this day – especially in Iraq – resort to ungodly violence towards each other. The Shias lived by a strict social code that demanded absolute obedience to their imams, or priest-kings, who were the direct descendants of Muhammed through the union of his daughter Fatima and Ali. They believed that in the coming millennium one of the past imams would return to earth as the Mahdi, or "guided one" to establish the rule of justice.

In the meantime, in order to avoid persecution while simultaneously working to undermine the orthodox doctrines of the Sunni majority, the Shias established a discipline of secrecy that required them to conceal their true religious beliefs and to outwardly conform to the state religion. In Shia Islam, this religious dissimulation – a form of deception that conceals the truth – was known as taqiyya and provided legal dispensation whereby believers could conceal their true religious beliefs when under threat, persecution, or compulsion. The concept of taqiyya was developed to protect the Shias who were usually in the minority and under threat. The Shia view was that taqiyya was lawful in situations of overwhelming danger such as loss of life or property but where danger to the religion would not occur. The term "taqiyya" did not exist in Sunni jurisprudence because denying the faith under duress was only permitted in some extreme circumstances.

Deliberate destabilisation and destruction was also being aided and abetted by private military and security companies (PMSCs) who were being increasingly hired for "security" operations in Africa, the Caribbean, Europe, Latin America, and North America. They had been integral in clandestine operations of various U.S. intelligence agencies fighting the global "War on Terror" in Afghanistan, the Gulf of Aden, Iraq, and Pakistan. Even the UN has dramatically increased its use of PMSCs by hiring them for a wide range of "security services" wherein they are given considerable influence over procedures and policies.

In the U.K., for example, the Foreign and Commonwealth Office had awarded conflict zone contracts to PMSCs worth some £50 million ($70 million) per year since 2003. This included approximately £150 million ($210 million) just for operations in Iraq between 2007 and 2012. The PMSCs' former dependency on Pentagon contracts had to some extent been replaced by new and zealous private sector clients and particularly by those involved in the extractive industries such as for oil and gas extraction, mining, dredging and quarrying. They had pursued and exploited political instability in the wake of the Arab uprisings. Use of the secretive PMSCs had increased dramatically – worth hundreds of billions of dollars – because states and corporations wanted to avoid being associated with, or held responsible for the use of violent and frequently deadly force.

The role of PMSCs in armed conflicts had also been responsible for prolonging and frequently intensifying violence. International PMSCs in Iraq and Afghanistan have subcontracted to local indigenous PMSCs who in many cases serve as fronts for other purposes including insurgencies, organised crime, and terrorism. There was also ample evidence to suggest that greater reliance on PMSCs had been responsible for compromising infrastructures in countries where governance was already inadequate and unstable. This boded ill for "failed states" where PMSCs had been contracted – particularly in Latin American regions – where states have had their power usurped by drug trafficking barons. Instead of bringing stability to those regions, PMSCs have tended to create dangerous militarised environments that destabilised instead of providing security.

Political instability and endless wars needed to be fuelled by an endless supply of deadly weapons – and to this end as the number one arms exporter over the past five years, the U.S. had impelled the global surge in militarisation by supplying at least 96 countries with deadly weaponry with the main recipients being in the Middle East where Saudi Arabia was the biggest importer. As regional conflicts and tensions continued to mount, the U.S. remained as the leading global arms supplier by a significant margin – with over 600 F-35 combat aircraft still to be delivered to 9 states – followed by Russia, China, France, and Germany. Worldwide, U.S. arms exports over the past five years were 27 percent more than the 2006-2010 level and were poised to rise even further. Such increases during a period of rising conflict and endless wars were leading to levels of human displacement not seen since World War Two. The UN Refugee Agency had estimated that currently one out of every 122 people on the planet had been violently uprooted from their homes by war and persecution; had been forced to become refugees, asylum seekers, or internally displaced people; and if all of those displaced people had formed a country, it would be the 24th largest in the world.

Apart from its past embargo breaking relationship with Apartheid South Africa, Israel had in the meantime not shied away from sharing in the death and destruction money-making bonanza and – despite unashamedly claiming to be the only democracy and a preserver of human rights in the Middle East while with its institutional racism brutally occupying Palestine – was as far back as the 1960s not only fighting a secret war in South Sudan, but was also involved in the sale of arms and military equipment despite their being used in war crimes and violations of human rights to other troubled African states. In 1989 an Israeli-produced videotape emerged showing Israeli instructors training paramilitary forces belonging to Colombia's deadly Medellin drug cartel which was killing numerous civilians, police, and government officials. Israel's history of supporting repressive regimes also included using its experience to help Mexico in suppressing the Zapatista indigenous Mayan uprisings in the Chiapas region. Not surprisingly, the Zapatistas have repeatedly expressed solidarity with the Palestinian people and following last summer's devastating attack on Gaza, condemned Israel's "war of extermination."

Israel's reasons for selling the expertise and weapons that fuelled destructive wars were not just about making money, but also about drawing attention away from its once covert but now overt official policy of implementing annexation of the West

Bank. While international law recognised the legitimacy of a situation where one power occupied a territory where a local population lived, it was nonetheless the assumption of that international law that occupation would be a temporary state of affairs with the occupier – in the meantime not being permitted to make any long-term changes to the occupied territory – being regarded as a trustee of that conquered territory until the conflict was over. Annexation on the other hand, was the one-sided takeover of a territory by a state using force which was impermissible under international law that was mostly established on the lessons learnt during the Second World War. Despite that, Israel's legal position was that the occupied Palestinian Territories were not in actual fact occupied, because they were promised to the Jewish people by the British Mandate, and of course – lest we forget – by God Himself.

For Conrad this raised the question of whether Zionism's usurpation of Judaism to attain its objective for a Greater Israel had in fact succeeded? To neutral observers for example, it may appear that such an objective – at least on the ground – had already been, or was being achieved by the gradual, if brutal and illegal, annexation of the Palestinian Occupied territories. But could such a reality on the ground be regarded as an unassailable and de facto success for the Jewish people whom Zionism was persistent in claiming to represent?

This, after all, was a nation where according to a survey with in-person interviews by the Pew Research Centre in Israel, Israeli Jews increasingly believed the West Bank settlements helped, rather than harmed, Israel's security; where nearly half of Jewish Israelis agreed that Arabs should be expelled or transferred from Israel; where a solid majority of 79 percent maintained that Jews in Israel should be given preferential treatment; and where at the same time – despite the aforementioned – a 76 percent majority of Israeli Jews said they that they viewed a state for "Jews only" as being compatible with democracy.

As to the claim of a "Promised Land," a 61 percent majority of Jews believed Israel was given by God to the Jewish people with the ultra-Orthodox and Modern Orthodox being nearly unanimous – 99 and 98 percent respectively – and 85 percent of traditional Israeli Jews agreeing with that premise. Among secular Israeli Jews, however, 31 percent agreed, 19 percent disagreed, and 50 percent said they didn't believe in God or didn't know.

Could the reality of such facts, Conrad asked himself, *be regarded as a triumph for Judaism and the Jewish people, or was it a step backwards and self-defeating?* To begin with, and unfortunately, all Israelis had fallen into the habit – without question or even token resistance – of accepting as fact outrageous Zionist propaganda statements such as that made by the president of NORAC who claimed that with nuclear weapons "Iran wants to do to the Jews in 12 minutes what Hitler did in 12 years." NORAC is a political action committee which while working to strengthen Israel's relationship with the U.S., also disburses most of the money raised by the Zionist lobby to fund the election campaigns of those candidates seeking election to Congress so long as they undertake to serve the interests of Zionism before those of the American people.

Having been constantly exposed to such paranoid statements and reminders of the Holocaust as justification for the establishment of an Israeli state, Israelis now have a mindset that believes there are "Hitlers" everywhere – who as the Israeli Prime Minister was always quick to point out – are just waiting for an opportunity "to exterminate us completely." This is what Israeli children learn in school and from visits to the death camps where the Holocaust emerges as the only means for Israel to define itself and justify its existence. The Israeli newspaper *Ha'aretz* had reported that only two percent of Israeli youth felt committed to democratic principles after studying the Holocaust which had become the only prism through which Israeli society and its leadership viewed every situation. Consequently Israeli Jews now had a distorted view of life as one unending threat of persecution and extermination: a persecution and extermination which, however, they are quite prepared to perpetrate against the Palestinian people.

22

Saturday, 2 January

Le Marais, Paris

Jews have been living in France from the time of the Romans to the present with their fate being decided by the various kings and leaders. But despite the hardships – and what was subsequently termed as anti-Semitism when in 1879 a German journalist, Wilhelm Marr, first used the term anti-Semite – Jewish intellectual and spiritual life flourished and produced some of the most renowned Jewish rabbis and thinkers. Initially Jewish presence in France during the Roman period consisted of isolated individuals, rather than established communities, but that changed following Jerusalem's conquest by the Romans when boat loads with Jewish prisoners landed in Arles, Bordeaux, and Lyons. There is also evidence of Jewish communities having existed in Orleans (533), Valence (524), and Vannes (465) when Jewish immigration increased and attempts were made to convert Jews to Christianity.

During the sixth century, Paris had a thriving Jewish community with a synagogue being built on the Ile de la Cite where it was later demolished and replaced by a church. Anti-Jewish sentiment, however, was uncommon and the seventh century killing of a Jew in Paris was avenged by a Christian mob. During the eighth century Jews became active in commerce and medicine; were involved with agriculture with some degree of domination in grapevine cultivation; and were

447

permitted by the Carolingian emperors to become accredited purveyors in the imperial court.

Though statements were made by the Crusaders in Rouen justifying the persecution of Jews throughout Europe, French Jews remained basically unaffected by the First Crusade (1096 – 1099). Following the Second Crusade (1147 – 1149), however, a lengthy period of persecution began with French clergyman frequently giving anti-Semitic sermons. Various forms of punishment were also imposed including the forced payment of a special tax every Palm Sunday; the weekly attendance by Jewish representatives at the cathedral to have their ears boxed as a reminder of their guilt; and the first blood libel in 1171 when 31 Jews were burnt at the stake.

Life for French Jews degenerated under the rule of King Philip Augustus who had been inculcated with the belief that Jews killed Christians and consequently he held an unjustified hatred for them. After only four months into his reign all the Jews in his lands were imprisoned and forced to pay a ransom for their release. He subsequently in 1181 annulled all loans made by Jews to Christians; helped himself to a percentage; confiscated all the property of Jews who a year later were expelled from Paris; and then allowed them to return in 1198, but only after payment of another ransom and the setting up of a taxation scheme to raise funds for himself.

The situation worsened when the Fourth Lateran Council in 1236 compelled Jews to wear a badge in the provinces of Languedoc, Normandy and Provence. This was followed by further persecutions under King Louis IX (1226 – 70), and in 1236 the Jewish communities of Anjou and Poitou were attacked by crusaders who tried to baptise them. Those who refused – An estimated 3,000 – were simply killed. In 1240, Jews were expelled from Brittany and in Paris the famous disputation of the Talmud began with it being put on trial and subsequently burned in 1242. Jews nonetheless managed to remain active in money-lending and commerce – and were soon joined by those Jews expelled from England – only to be once again banished in 1254 with their property and synagogues being confiscated. They were, however, allowed to return several years later.

Under Philip IV the Fair's reign, Jews were eventually imprisoned in 1305 with an estimated 100,000 being expelled, but Philip's successor, Louis X, allowed them to return ten years later. Twenty-five Jewish communities in Alsace were terrorised from 1338 to 1347 and in response to the Black Plague (1348 – 1349) massacres occurred throughout the east and southeast. The Pope's intervention, however, spared Jews in Avignon and Comtat Venaissin. In 1380 Paris and Nantes saw further persecutions which eventually culminated in the conclusive expulsion of Jews from France in 1394.

In the face of such adversity, Jewish learning nonetheless managed to survive during the middle ages with Champagne, Il-de-France, Languedoc, and the Loire Valley becoming centres for Jewish scholarship. In the north, talmudic and biblical commentary, anti-Christian polemic, and liturgical poetry were studied. Alternatively, the south witnessed the study of grammar, linguistics, philosophy, and science with numerous religious works being translated into French from Arabic and from Latin. In the mid-1500s, thousands of Marranos – Iberian Jews who converted or were forced to convert to Christianity of whom some may have continued secretly practicing Judaism – came to France from Portugal with the majority of them forsaking Judaism and instead assimilating into French society which for the first time since 1394, allowed Jews to legally live in France.

Following the 1648 Khmelnitski massacres in the Ukraine when hundreds of Jewish communities were destroyed, many Jews fled to Alsace and Lorraine with further migrations to Southeast France where the Duke of Savoy had declared Nice and Villefranche de-Conflent to be free ports.

During the 17th century in Avignon and Comtat Venaissin (Papal States), Jewish communities flourished with Jews becoming involved in commercial activity with such success spreading to other nearby areas. During the 18th century the Jews who returned to settle in Paris consisted of both Sephardic and Ashkenazi. The former, who were wealthier and descended from Bordeaux, Avignon, and Comtat Venaissin, settling on the Left Bank; and the latter who were from Alsace, Lorraine and several other cities in the north, settling on the Right Bank. Paris saw the first opening of a kosher inn in 1721, and the first opening of a synagogue in 1788. During the 1780s anti-Jewish laws began being repealed and by the time of the French Revolution (1789 – 1799) an estimated 40,000 Jews were living in France with some 500 in Paris.

French citizenship – with civic rights as individuals but with the loss of group privileges – was finally granted to the Sephardim Jews in September 1790 and the Ashkenazi Jews some six months later. The 1793 to 1794 Reign of Terror, however, caused communal organisations, religious institutions, and synagogues to close. At the start of the 19th century, Napoleon decided on creating a Jewish communal system sanctioned by the state and consequently in 1806 a Grand Sanhedrin – 45 rabbis and 26 laymen – was convened to arrange for the formation of a consistorial system with the establishment of religious bodies in every department of France that had a Jewish population of more than 2,000. This made Judaism a recognised religion under government control.

In spite of such progress, anti-Jewish laws were passed in 1808 with Napoleon declaring that all debts with Jews should be postponed, reduced, or simply annulled thereby causing the near ruin of of communities for Jews who were also placed under residential restrictions in an attempt to assimilate them into French society. Jews nonetheless played important roles in many areas of French society with the Bernhardt sisters in the

Comédie-Française; with Isaac Cremiuex and Achille Fould in the Chamber of Deputies; with Emile Durkheim, Salomon Munk, and Marcel Proust in literature and philosophy; and of course with the Rothschild and the Pereire families in finance.

Just as the situation was improving for Jews, anti-Jewish sentiment was reignited by the Damascus affair in 1840 with notable members of the Jewish community being accused of ritual murder. Further setbacks followed the 1870 Franco-Prussian War with control of the Jewish communities of Alsace and Lorraine being transferred from France to Germany. In the late 1800s anti-Semitic sentiment started to appear in newspapers and in 1886 Édouard Drumont published his 1,400 page bestseller *La France Juive* which proposed a conflict between non-Jewish "Aryans" and Jewish "Semites"; argued that finance and capitalism were controlled by the Jews; and referred to the Jews alleged complicity in the death of Christ.

With feelings still running high, Captain Alfred Drefus, a young French artillery officer of Alsatian and Jewish descent, was convicted for allegedly providing the German Embassy in Paris with French military secrets. Dreyfus, sentenced to life imprisonment on Devil's Island, had his cause championed by the influential writer Émile Zola who in his open letter *J'accuse* – which appeared on the front page of newspaper *L'Aurore* in January 1898 – accused the government of anti-Semitism. Zola was prosecuted and found guilty of libel and to avoid imprisonment fled to England, but returned in June 1899. Dreyfus was subsequently pardoned and given the Légion D'honneur with the citation "a soldier who has endured an unparalleled martyrdom."

In 1913, in response to the influx of Ashkenazi Jewish refugees from Central Europe, a decision was taken by the Russo-Polish association, Agoudas Hakehilos, to build a synagogue – the only Art Nouveau building and the last religious monument to be built in the neighbourhood – on the

Rue Pavée in the Le Marais district of Paris. When Parisian Jews were expelled from the city in back in the 13th century, they had moved to Le Marais which at that time was just outside the city wall. Following the revolution, however, much of the area was abandoned by the wealthy who were replaced by poverty-stricken bohemian arty types.

Before Napoleon III and Baron Haussmann showed up, Le Marais with its labyrinth of cobblestone alleys was what most of Paris looked like until Napoleon and Haussmann razed it to the ground. The huge avenues and gigantic squares such as the Place Concorde which now glorify Paris, were originally conceived to enable troops and artillery to easily manoeuvre around the city to keep the impoverished masses in check and to repulse any would be invaders. The other object of having such awe-inspiring features and spaces was to make citizens feel insignificant and powerless as compared to the vast civic machinery of government and its subservient army. Le Marais at one point became so squalid that it was nearly demolished by officials wanting to modernise the city with huge a avenue cutting through its centre only being narrowly avoided with the start of the World War.

With many of its pre-revolutionary buildings and streets still intact, Le Marais – more than any other area in Paris – now provided an impression of medieval Paris, and its impressive buildings and houses are an indication of its former residents' wealth. Known as the Pletzl (Yiddish for little Place) Le Marais became host to the largest Jewish community in Europe as a result of immigration from Eastern Europe and North Africa. Thanks to the Vichy government collaboration with the Nazis, however, some 75 percent of that community tragically perished in Nazi concentration camps.

The heartbeat of Le Marais was now the Rue des Rosiers (Rosebushes Street) which despite losing some of its former Jewish character to art galleries and designer shops, had still retained some of its Jewish bookshops, patisseries, delis, East European Jewish restaurants, and at least half a dozen falafel establishments.

Rue de Rosiers, Paris

The weather In Paris was dry but overcast with a temperature of around 40°F and the Rue de Rosiers was as usual bustling with its falafel establishments doing brisk business and the biggest and most boisterous of them boasting a queue of well over a hundred people. The time was just after 12:30 p.m. when not far away on the Rue de Rivoli, Aziz Gharbi and his brother Rachid sitting behind him were riding westwards on their Japanese scooter. After passing Saint-Paul Metro station they turned right and northwards onto Rue Pavée, past the synagogue which was being guarded by three heavily armed French soldiers, and then turned left and westwards onto the Rue des Rosiers. Both had their helmet visors pulled down and were clad in jumpers, jeans, black leather driving gloves, trainers, and navy blue trench coats. They had deliberately bought continental size 56 coats – instead of their actual size 46 – and had removed the right hand pocket linings so that they could thrust their hands through and grasp the pistol grips of the VZ58 assault rifles that were slung around their necks and hidden underneath their coats with steel stocks folded.

When they got to about halfway along the queue outside the falafel restaurant, they stopped, flipped aside the lower parts of their partially unbuttoned coats, shouted "Allahu Akbar," and with the gun barrels resting in their left hands, opened fire on the wall of huddled people in the queue who being only a couple of metres away with no cover or means of escape, panicked with uncontrollable hysteria. Consequently at almost point-blank range the 7.62x39mm calibre bullets tore into their defenceless bodies causing lacerations and wounds as they crushed and pushed aside anything in their way while simultaneously creating cavities 30 times wider which in less than a second closed behind the bullets' path of penetration whose shock waves also damaged nearby tissues, organs and bones. The calamitous chaos, the desperate cries of the wounded and dying, and the strewn bloodstained bodies resembled the aftermath of a battlefield. After expending all 60 rounds of their first magazine in a matter of seconds, the brothers – inculcated with the same fanatical hatred that most Israeli Jews reserved for the Palestinian people – quickly reloaded with their second magazine which they also emptied before speeding off to more shouts of "Allahu Akbar" and veering right and northwards towards the Rue des Francs Bourgeois to make good their escape.

The gunfire and terrified shrieks had been heard around the corner by the three soldiers who after momentarily hesitating decided that one of them would remain on guard at the synagogue while the other two ran to investigate. As they turned into the Rue des Rosiers they were confronted by a carnage that illustrated the satanic depravity pervading much of humanity: an unspeakable depravity that gloried in mindless and destructive violence. It mattered not what nationality or religion the victims were because irrespective of who or what they were, people the world over – misinformed and aroused by the West's mainstream media's hypocritical hystrionics – would give vent to their moral indignation with double standard condemnation of Islamic terrorism while conveniently forgetting the crimes against humanity instigated by Western governments against millions of Muslim civilians in places, to name but a few, such as Afghanistan, Iraq, Libya, Syria, and Yemen. It was the late British politician Tony Benn who sagaciously observed that "there is no moral difference between a stealth bomber and a suicide bomber. Both kill innocent people for political reasons."

Meanwhile at the corner of Rue des Francs Bourgeois, the brothers had abandoned their scooter – which had been specifically selected, periodically checked on in its parking spot, and then stolen the previous day – and walked briskly around the corner to where as prearranged Malek would be waiting for them in the also stolen white panel van. They climbed in through the van's back doors which Rachid shut behind them while Aziz went forward to knock on the back of the driver's cabin to let Malek know that they were on board and that he could drive off.

Unbeknown to them, however, Malek was not in the driver's seat, but some 100 metres behind them waiting and watching from the corner of the Rue Vieille du Temple with a mobile phone held in his left hand. On seeing the brothers get into the van, he immediately dialled the fatal number resulting in the van and its occupants being violently blown apart and engulfed in dense cloud of smoke and rising flames. The reasoning behind the plan was that the authorities would consequently conclude that the brothers had accidentally detonated the bomb themselves. As Malek turned and walked away from the scene of the devastation, he did so with another rush of adrenalin and the satisfied certainty that flying shrapnel from the explosion would cause secondary damage to nearby vehicles, buildings, and innocent bystanders while the Gharbi brothers would be on their way to meet with Satan in hell.

The Arab Quarter, Paris

It took Malek Bennabi about 45 minutes to get back to his Arab Quarter studio apartment where he immediately followed his usual procedure of ensuring that everything was as he had left it and that there was no sign of anyone having been there while he was out. As he was still pumped up from repeated rushes of adrenalin that had accompanied his detonation of the bomb and his subsequent rapid departure from the scene, he took several long, deep breaths to help him calm down before taking off his coat, throwing it on the bed, and switching on the television. News of the shootings was already dominating most channels who described the attack as a massacre and reported the disbelief and panic that followed the carnage caused by the militants including a car bomb which police were still investigating.

Malek curbed the urge to applaud and instead went to the small kitchen where with joyous anticipation he took down a wineglass from the overhead cupboard, opened the fridge, smiled, and took out the half bottle of champagne which he had bought specially to celebrate the success of his first major operation in Europe. He popped the cork, poured, and allowed the first bubbly and satisfying sip to swirl around his mouth. While alcohol was of course forbidden to Muslims, in Malek's case this was not a problem because he was not a Muslim.

Despite his hard-earned credentials as an Arab pro-Palestinian activist, Marek Bennabi was neither Algerian nor Muslim, but in fact an Israeli born Jew of Iranian descent whose family, like some 60,000 other Iranian Jews, had emigrated to Israel and North America following the 1979 Islamic Revolution – led by the supreme religious and political leader, the Ayatollah Khomeini (1902 – 1989) – that toppled the government of U.S. puppet Mohammad Reza Shah Pahlavi.

Malek's parents had chosen to live on a hardcore settlement deep inside the Israeli-occupied West Bank where he was born in 1984. By the time he had turned 16, Malek had become involved with a group of boys whose restless disenchantment was subsequently given purpose years later following Israel's 2005 disengagement from the Palestinian territory of Gaza which it had been occupying and had since persisted in blockading as an alternate form of occupation.

The government's forceful evacuation of some 8,600 Jewish settlers – the majority of whom resisted nonviolently – led to a generational split amongst the settler movement because while settler elders had vowed that God himself would prevent the Jewish state's army from forcing them to give up their settlements in what they regarded as being the biblical Land of Israel, the youngsters felt betrayed by their elders when God failed to deliver on that promise.

So while some of them including yeshiva dropouts and girls roamed the hills of the West Bank, others had become students of Rabbi Yitzchak Ginsburgh of Od Yosef Chai yeshiva in Yitzhar. Ginsburgh – a prominent scholar of Kabbalah and a member of the Chabad-Lubavitch Hasidic movement – who had attracted that disillusioned younger generation of Jewish radicals by devising a devilish ideological concoction comprising of mystical admonitions to live in nature and Kabbalah-based rationales for Jewish racial superiority and violence against Arabs.

Ginsburgh's racist ideology was reinforced by two other prominent Od Yosef Chai rabbis whose 2010 book *The King's Torah* read like a rabbinic instruction manual for scenarios where the killing of non-Jewish babies, children and adults, was quite acceptable because the prohibition of "thou shalt not murder" applied only "to a Jew who kills a Jew." Furthermore non-Jews were dispassionate "by nature" so that assaults on them would "curb their evil inclination," with it being permissible to kill the infants and children of Israel's enemies, since "it is clear that they will grow to harm us."

Now known as the hilltop youths – and living away from their parents on surrounding hilltop settlements – these young radical Jewish settlers in their teens and early 20s were responsible for the so-called "price tag attacks" against Palestinians, Arab-Israelis, Christians, left-wing Israeli Jews, the Israeli police, and Israeli Defence Force. The group's main objective was to "exact a price" from either the local Palestinians or from the Israeli security forces for any action taken which may compromise or oppose Jewish settlement activity.

Price tag attacks had included acts of vandalism directed mainly against Palestinians with attacks on their villages and property in retaliation for Palestinian resistance and for the Israeli government's demolition of structures in Jewish West Bank settlements and the removal of outposts which were either unauthorised or illegal. The group also targeted the Israeli army and security services, Christian and Muslim places of worship, and left-wing organisations that criticised the settler movement. B'Tselem – whose stated objectives were to document human rights violations in the occupied territories while combatting denial and helping to create a human rights culture in Israel – had documented many such acts with random violence including attacks against Palestinian civilians, burning of mosques and fields, stone throwing, uprooting trees, and raiding Palestinian villages and agricultural land.

Despite having missed out on becoming a hilltop youth, Malek Bennabi's upbringing – like that of most Israeli Jewish children – had nonetheless included an avid inculcation of a hatred for Arab Palestinians coupled with a jingoistic military indoctrination that included being taught the use of weapons at a very early age. In his book *You Gentiles,* Maurice Samuel, the Romanian-born Zionist Jew, provided a penetrating analysis of the Jewish psyche while making the important point that Jews were altogether so superior and spiritually advanced compared to gentiles that there was no possibility of coexistence between the two groups. Due to the baser nature of the gentiles, and the reality that they did not revere God as seriously as the Jews, it was inevitable that Jews and gentiles would be at loggerheads for ever. Samuel also stressed that "we Jews, we the destroyers, will remain the destroyers forever. Nothing that you will do will meet our needs and demands. We will forever destroy, because we need a world of our own, a God-world, which it is not in your nature to build."

Unfortunately in building a "God-world of their own" with the consistent establishment of illegal settlements in the West Bank, Israel had been violating the laws of occupation. The Fourth Geneva Convention prohibits an occupying power from transferring its citizens into the territory it occupies and from transferring or displacing the population of an occupied territory within or outside the territory. The Rome Statute, the founding treaty of the International Criminal Court, established the court's jurisdiction over war crimes including the crimes of transfer of parts of the civilian population of an occupying power into an occupied territory, and the forcible transfer of the population of an occupied territory.

Israel's confiscation of land, water, and other natural resources for the benefit of settlements and residents of Israel also violated the Hague Regulations of 1907, which prohibit an occupying power from expropriating the resources of occupied territory for its own benefit. Furthermore, Israel's settlement project violated international human rights law, in particular, Israel's discriminatory policies against Palestinians that govern virtually every aspect of life in the area of the West Bank under Israel's exclusive control, known as Area C, and that forcibly displace Palestinians while encouraging the growth of Jewish settlements. Though the ICC has jurisdiction over crimes committed in or from the territory of the State of Palestine, it had so far failed to do so.

Bennabi's transition from an Arab Palestinian-hating settler youth steeped in the religious Zionist ideology that encouraged illegal settlement, to an Arab Palestinian-killing Israeli warrior enforcing the occupation through ethnic cleansing, was facilitated by three years military service with the IDF which also offered an escape to horizons beyond the restrictive limits of orthodox settlement life. After completion of his military service, Bennabi had applied to join Mossad "to see the invisible and do the impossible" and was in due course accepted.

Mossad had its beginnings following the end of the British Mandate in 1948 and the establishment of the State of Israel in Palestine. Among the various government agencies to emerge was an intelligence and security unit called the *Sherut Yedioth* (information Service) or simply Shay. Shay, which as Haganah – the intelligence arm of the Zionist terrorist paramilitary force during the time of the British Mandate – had begun operating on a worldwide basis when the Jewish Agency was founded in 1929 at the Zionist Congress in Zurich, Switzerland. The Jewish Agency – which was then comprised of Zionists and non-Zionists including a substantial number of American Jews but was effectively under Zionist control – while having been ostensibly created to aid and sustain Jewish communities in Palestine, actually served as a cover for Shay's extension of covert operations in Western Europe and the United States.

Shay's objectives between 1923 and 1948, were to promote the establishment of an independent Jewish state; to penetrate Mandatory installations in order to keep the Zionist leadership informed about British viewpoints and planned future actions; to gather political intelligence that would be useful for Zionist propaganda; to infiltrate Arab and anti-Zionist organisations in Palestine and neighbouring nations; to monitor and control all extremist Jewish groups in Palestine and abroad; to provide security for smuggled arms and the illegal immigration programs; and to obtain information about Nazi Germany so as to provide security for Jewish underground and escape channels throughout Europe before, during, and after World War Two.

The service components of the Shay organisation included Political Intelligence; Counterespionage and Internal Security; Military Intelligence; Police Branch of Military Intelligence;

and Naval Intelligence and Security, which all worked independently on behalf of the different ministries to which they were attached. The independence of these various service units – with all of them represented in the main West European capitals – coupled with postwar chaos, inevitably meant that they often acted independently and competed amongst each other.

By April 1951, the Israeli Prime Minister and cabinet – profoundly concerned by the prevalent covetousness, mutual mistrust, and escalating costs of uncoordinated efforts between the service units – decided on a complete overhaul of Israel's intelligence and security community. Consequently, under the forceful direction of Reuven Shiloah, the services were reorganised according to functions and responsibilities with an established mechanism to coordinate operations. The Naval Intelligence and the Security Service were integrated; the embryonic air intelligence unit became a part of Military Intelligence; the Ministry of Foreign Affairs retained Research Division; Shin Bet remained intact apart from internal changes; and the Political Intelligence Service became independent from the Ministry of Foreign Affairs and was reorganised as the Secret Intelligence Service or Mossad.

Mossad's initial principal objectives had included targeting the Arab states with regards to their capabilities and intentions toward Israel; their relations with the USSR and other major powers; their official facilities and representatives throughout the world; their leaders and their internal and inter-Arab politics; general morale, military preparedness, unit formations, and equipment for the military forces; obtaining information on secret U.S. policies or decisions that might affect Israel; acquiring scientific intelligence from the U.S. and other developed countries; ascertaining the nature of East European government policies toward Israel and their position on Jewish emigration; close monitoring of anti-Zionist activity throughout the world; and getting political and economic intelligence in other areas of possible interest such as in Africa. Extra special efforts were also made to counter Arab propaganda and to neutralise anti-Zionist activity. More recently, extra operational activity – covert political, economic and paramilitary action programs – had been devoted to combating Arab terrorism which was the result of Israel's illegal and repressive occupation of the Palestinian Territories.

The main thrust of Mossad's activity was concerned with the acquisition of positive foreign intelligence, the initiation of robust political action, and the employment of ruthless counterterrorist operations. Mossad's acquisition of positive intelligence required conducting agent operations against Arab nations, their official representatives, and their installations throughout the world with particular emphasis on Western Europe and the U.S. where Arab national interests in the Near East were in conflict with those of Israel. Collection of information was not only on the disposition, morale, armaments, equipment and quality of leadership of every Arab Army that may become involved in future conflicts, but also on Arab commercial activity regarding the purchase of Western weaponry and the recruitment of economic, military, and political experts. As to the Arab recruitment of experts, Mossad endeavoured to recruit such experts as Israeli intelligence agents or at least dissuade them from either helping the Arabs or to establish their precise functions.

Another Mossad responsibility was to instigate squabbles and rancour amongst the Arabs so as to reduce Western sympathy for them; to monitor and counteract Arab propaganda; to detect and thwart Arab terrorism; and go on the offensive against terrorists especially in the Near East and Western Europe. Having a mixed Christian, Druze and Moslem population consequently made Lebanon an attractive arena for Israel's mischievous intelligence and military operations where covert assets were employed to assist with mounting paramilitary and executive action operations against Palestinian terrorist leaders, personnel, and installations in Lebanon. Israel also provided support – as was the case in the Sabra and Shatila massacre of Palestinian refugees – for Christian rightists in the Lebanese civil war.

In addition to its operations against the Arabs, Mossad acquired economic, political, and scientific intelligence in both the Eastern and Western worlds with a view to protecting the State of Israel and Zionism in particular, and Jews in general. Counterintelligence efforts – including the use of tactics to silence anti-Israel criticism and factions in the West – were concentrated in the Soviet Union, the United States, Europe, and at the United Nations where negative policy decisions could hinder Israel's Zionist goals.

Malek Bennabi did not particularly enjoy the initial stages of his training which for officer candidates incorporated a compulsory Basic Operations course for recruits and lower ranking personnel; an Operations course; and a Field Operations course. Completion of the entire training program took almost two years and was usually given to classes of around twelve recruits. Most of the training occurred within Tel Aviv and surrounding areas with a combination of instructors consisting of some on permanent assignment, intelligence officers on temporary tours of duty, and personnel from headquarters including the Director of Mossad and department directors, who occasionally gave lectures on their areas of expertise.

An advanced services school in Jerusalem offered specialised two to three month courses on world political affairs, Israel's economic and political objectives, newly developed technical operational aids, and up to date information on foreign intelligence services. Some of the younger officer recruits – who were not up to scratch in certain areas of higher education or languages – were sent to universities abroad, where their pursuit of advanced degrees also served as cover for their extracurricular Mossad activities. One of the established requirements for Mossad intelligence officers was fluency in Arabic with a nine-month, intensive Arabic language course being available. Mossad officers who were destined for Arab operations received further training with work in the Administered Territories – such as the Sinai where they combined running the of Bedouin agents into Egypt with Military Intelligence – for several years so as to sharpen their language skills before being posted abroad.

Other tasks of vital importance for Mossad were its establishment of special relationships with both highly-placed individuals and government offices in every country of importance to Israel; liaising with Zionists and other sympathisers – who could support Israeli intelligence efforts – within Jewish communities throughout the world; carefully grooming such contacts to serve as channels for information, disinformation, propaganda, and other functions; directing covert operations throughout Africa, Europe, the Far East including South East Asia, the Near East, North America, and South America. Covert operations were generally conducted through official and semiofficial Israeli establishments, deep cover companies and organisations of which some were especially created or adapted for specific objectives, and infiltration of non-Zionist national and international Jewish organisations such as the International Jewish Anti-Zionist Network (IJAN).

Responsibilities for intelligence officers working under cover of diplomatic establishments was to facilitate exchange of information with local service officials, manage communications, provide accommodation addresses and finance channels, and identify targets of interest for agents. Official organisations used for cover included Israeli Purchasing Missions, Israeli Government Tourism, El Al and Zim offices (shipping agents), Israeli construction companies, industrial groups, and international trade organisations. For activities in which the Israeli Government can never admit involvement, use was made of deep cover or illegal individuals who employed a more subtle and distant approach infiltrating their targets. This was particularly true in Arab countries because many Israelis had come from Arab countries where they were born and raised and consequently appeared more Arab than Israeli in attitude, demeanour, and speech. By providing well researched backgrounds and CVs, forged passports and identity papers of Arab and Western nations, Mossad had managed to successfully operate with agents in Arab nations with Israelis disguised and documented as Arabs or citizens from European nations.

Because of Israel's Law of "Return" there was no shortage of Jewish emigrants to Israel with both language skills and knowledge of their former countries of residence who could be useful to Mossad in helping to analyse intelligence information that would contribute to the overall operational efficiency of its agents. Such people were equally useful for passing themselves off as citizens of their respective nations of origin with the assistance of Israel's penchant for counterfeiting and forging identity documents.

Mossad was also dependent on a variety of Jewish communities and organisations overseas for the recruitment of agents and the gathering of relevant information. Zionism's aggressive ideology – which stressed that all Jews belonged to Israel where they must return – had created some difficulty for getting support for Mossad's intelligence operations from anti-Zionist Jews, but this had been mostly countered by ensuring that Mossad agents operated with discreet and utmost tact within Jewish communities so as to avoid either embarrassment or repercussions to Israel.

One important role played by Mossad was to assist Israel to quickly accelerate development of its technological, scientific, and military capabilities by exploiting scientific exchange programs with naive and trusting nations such as the United States. Apart from the overt large-scale acquisition of published scientific papers and technical journals from all over the world, Israel also devoted considerable intelligence resources to covertly obtain scientific and technical information by gaining access to various classified defence projects in the United States and other Western nations.

Another major Mossad target for infiltration – using diplomatic and journalistic cover – was the United Nations which not only sponsored international exchanges in all fields, but was also of importance in the settlement of disputes between Israel and Arab nations. Agent recruitment was almost exclusively from people of Jewish origin despite the occasional conflict between individual dedication to the Zionist State of Israel and loyalty to a Jewish homeland. Recruitment of Gentiles was a comparative rarity.

Assistance from Arabs – whether directly or indirectly – was usually due to some financial inducement which caused the Israelis to regard such sources as being unreliable. Mossad found it easier to recruit Palestinians over whom they had more control either because of unjustly imprisoned relatives under Administrative detention orders, or of bank assets frozen by Israel following the Nabka in 1948. In such cases the release of relatives or bank assets was made in exchange for providing information or other assistance to Mossad.

The agency was also always ready to exploit any weakness or motivation of potential agents or collaborators with blackmail, bribery, and bullying being standard methods of persuasion; by taking advantage of vulnerabilities such as fear, jealousy, rivalry, and political dissension; and even by false-flag recruitment tactics whereby citizens of Western European nations under the cover of a national NATO intelligence organisations are employed for operations in Arab target countries.

Following intensive evaluations of his suitability as a clandestine combatant during a two-year training period, Malek had initially been sent to Beirut in March 2012 and by October of that year had successfully completed his first assignment with the car bomb explosion – in a majority Christian neighbourhood – that killed eight people and wounded 118 including the head of the Information Branch of Lebanon's Internal Security Forces, who was the actual target of the deadly attack. Angry crowds had taken to the streets blocking the main roads leading into Western Beirut with burning tires to protest the assassination. Clashes had ensued on the dividing line between Sunni and Alawite neighbourhoods in the northern Lebanese city of Tripoli resulting in security forces being dispatched to restore order. As had been the intention of the bombing, former Lebanese Prime Minister Saad al-Hariri accused Syrian president Assad of orchestrating the assassination. It was the the assassination of Saad's father and former Lebanese prime minister Rafik Hariri that sparked the 2005 Cedar Revolution which demanded the withdrawal of Syrian troops from Lebanon and an end to Syria's meddling in Lebanon's affairs.

The explosive-laden car's blast had rocked the city's Sassine Square in the predominately Christian Ashrafieh neighbourhood during rush hour when many students were leaving school. At least seven cars had been set on fire by the blast and many more were damaged by falling bricks and masonry with considerable damage to the surrounding buildings. Human body parts were scattered on the roads and the wounded included children. The operation was part of a much wider campaign to blame Syria and fuel its ongoing multi-sided armed conflict with international interventions that had started the previous year within the context of the of the Arab Spring. Nationwide protests against President Bashar al-Assad's government had been met with violent crackdowns by the armed forces. The unrest developed from mass protests to sectarian conflicts with Alawite-dominated government forces, militias and various Shia groups, fighting primarily against Sunni-dominated rebel groups resulting in the country's destruction.

After being withdrawn from Beirut, Malek was sent from Tel Aviv to London – with a genuine Israeli passport bearing his real name of Barak Golestan – for four weeks to familiarise himself with the the city and its Muslim community before making the two and a half hour journey on the Eurostar to Paris through the Channel Tunnel with a cloned British passport of an Algerian living in London's Stoke Newington. The forged passport was given to Malek by a Mossad agent operating from within the Israeli Embassy and its details had been illegally obtained by a sayan from that city's Jewish community of more than 172,000 who were mostly of European descent. Malek's assignment for Paris was to find accommodation, employment, and to infiltrate the Arab community, but to initially remain as a sleeper agent with no immediate mission in mind. His patience had finally been rewarded some months earlier when he had been put in contact with Pierre who as an experienced katza was to direct a false flag operation involving an attack on an ostensibly Jewish target which would attract negative media attention and create White French population hostility towards North African Muslim emigrant communities. Malek, who was now satisfied with the operation's success and was anticipating with relish his next assignment, was not a religious person with a belief in a God who had promised Palestine to the Jewish people, he just took a sadistic pleasure from being what he was and doing what he did, which was to cause death and destruction with his government's surreptitious sanction and support.

23

Sunday, 3 January

The Corniche, Beirut, Lebanon

Mark Banner settled for a light breakfast of toast and several cups of black coffee as he checked his inbox and online news sources. The latest national news, as it had been of late, was not good. Lebanon with its high literacy rate and instinctive flair for a mercantile culture had traditionally – in spite of its small size – been an important commercial hub for the Middle East. Because of its uniquely complex communal make-up and its location which bordered Israel and Syria, however, it had also frequently been at the centre and receiving end of Middle East intrigues and conflicts.

Prior to the eruption of the Syrian civil war, there had been high hopes that the nascent revival of Lebanon's tourism industry would lead to economic recovery so that by 2010 tourism accounted for a fifth of Lebanon's economic output. The fighting in Syria and the associated resurgence of sectarian tensions in Lebanon had, however, severely curtailed tourist numbers visiting the country and diminished hopes of a return to the cosmopolitan prosperity of the 1950s and 1960s.

So as neighbouring Syria had begun its Israeli instigated descent into civil war in 2011, deadly clashes in Tripoli and Beirut between Sunni Muslims and Alawites – a branch of Islam centred in Syria who followed the Twelver school of Shia Islam but with syncretistic elements – raised justifiable fears that the conflict would spill over the border so that Lebanon's already fragile political truce would yet again collapse as a result of sectarian strife. The subsequent overwhelming influx of refugees fleeing the Syrian conflict meant that by April 2014, Syrian refugees were estimated to make up some 25 percent of the population thereby placing a severe strain on the country's resources and eliciting a warning from Lebanese foreign minister that the refugee crisis was threatening the country's very existence.

The news today, however, was dominated by reports of yesterday's terrorist atrocity in Paris where in spite of investigations being still in the early stages, Western politicians had nonetheless wasted no time in climbing on the bandwagon of media orchestrated sanctimonious public outrage with the French Prime Minister already reportedly condemning the attack as an "act of war" perpetrated by the Islamic State (IS) militant group. Mark, however, retained a more cautious approach as there was always the possibility that the attack had been another Israeli false flag operation. He would therefore wait for more information to become available before drawing any premature conclusions. He would in the meantime check on his latest article which was currently appearing in several newspapers.

Happy New Year Palestine: But Don't Expect Any Change In Your Status Quo

Mark Banner
Sunday, 3 January

It is a New Year certainty that there will be no change in the Palestinian people's perilous plight because Israeli police, soldiers, and Zionist zealots have continued to extrajudicially brutalise and murder Palestinians with impunity. The majority of Israeli Jews had for example also just confirmed that dehumanising Palestinians – by describing them as "beasts," "cockroaches," or "snakes," while regarding them as expendable inferiors – had been the main unifying factor for most of them irrespective of their ideological, political, or religious background. This racist perception was reiterated by the Israeli Prime Minister when he expressed the view that "at the end, in the State of Israel, as I see it, there will be a fence that spans it all … in the area that we live, we must defend ourselves against the wild beasts."

Another indicator of "no change" has been the expression of outrage by Israelis over the arrest of an IDF soldier for "finishing off" an alleged Palestinian attacker – who had already been shot and was lying wounded and motionless on the street – with a bullet to the head in what was a clear case of coldblooded murder. According to a poll conducted for Israel's Channel 2, 57 percent of Israelis opposed the soldier's arrest, while 42 percent described his actions as "responsible." Only 5 percent of those polled said they would describe the shooting as murder.

The world's terrified tolerance for Israel's insane criminality was also recently evident at the UN when the Security Council rejected a Palestinian resolution calling for peace with Israel within a year, and an end to Israel's occupation by 2017. The draft resolution called for two sovereign Israeli and Palestinian states living side by side; the ending of Israeli occupation and the establishment of the Palestinian state within a time frame of no more than three years; East Jerusalem becoming the capital of the Palestinian state which would be established on 1967 borders; the settling of the refugee question according to UN resolution 194; and the ending of settlement activities in West Bank and East Jerusalem accompanied by the release all Palestinian prisoners in Israeli jails. Even if the UN Security

Council had voted for the resolution it would still have made no difference because it would have been vetoed by Israel's superpower lapdog – that principled and supreme upholder of democracy and international law – the United States of America.

A reminder of the unchanging Palestinian reality will also come from a soon to be released report by the Palestinian Detainees' Committee and the Palestinian Prisoners' Society (PPS) revealing that Israeli soldiers have kidnapped around 1,000,000 Palestinians, including tens of thousands of women and children, since occupying the West Bank, the Gaza Strip and East Jerusalem in 1967. In the report which will mark the April 17 Palestinian Prisoners' Day, the Detainees' Committee and the PPS state the Israeli army – since the start of the "Al-Aqsa Intifada," in late September 2000 – had kidnapped, more than 90,000 Palestinians, including 11,000 children, 1.300 women and girls, and 65 elected legislators and government ministers. Also to be revealed was the fact that Israel issued some 15,000 Administrative Detention orders to imprison detainees for months, and in many cases for years, without charges and with the current number held in 22 prisons, detention and interrogation centres being no less than 7,000 individuals. "These abductions targeted children, elderly, youngsters, men, women and mothers, teachers, journalists, writers, artists and workers … " During a recent six-month period, 4,800 Palestinians, including 1,400 children, mainly from Hebron and Jerusalem were kidnapped. The registration of Palestinians in Hebron's Old City with numbers next to their identity was reminiscent of Nazi Germany.

So despite recent encouraging recognitions for a potential "Palestinian state" by parliaments in some European countries, forewarnings that the status quo for the Palestinian people would remain unchanged came from various sources including the UK Prime Minister, who during a visit to Israel in march last year had taken Western leaders' obsequious and mandatory Knesset-grovelling to new heights by confirming that very determined and insidious "friends of Israel" lobby groups would continue to successfully corrupt and exert influence over Western governments irrespective of what the people themselves may want as was the case in the lead-up to the Iraq War:

> *"I will always stand up for the right of Israel to defend its citizens, a right enshrined in international law, in natural justice and fundamental morality* [which is not applicable to the Palestinian people because their lobby is nowhere near as powerful as yours], *and in decades of common endeavour between Israel and her* [bought and paid for political] *allies. When I was in opposition, I spoke out when – because of the law on universal jurisdiction – senior Israelis could not safely come to my country without fear of ideologically motivated court cases and legal stunts; when I became Prime Minister, I legislated to change it. My country is open to you and you are welcome* [as are your shiny Jewish lobby shekels] *to visit any time."*

Not to be outdone by his British counterpart, the Prime Minister of Canada – a country which cut funding to the United Nations Relief and Works Agency (UNRWA) that provides clothing, food and health services to approximately 4.7 million registered Palestinian refugees, and where the word anti-Semitism it is now primarily invoked to uphold Jewish/white privilege – in the first ever speech delivered by a Canadian Prime Minister to the Knesset, rhetorically and unashamedly brown-nosed his audience on behalf of the Canadian people:

"Shalom. And thank you for inviting me to visit this remarkable country [that can get away with endless crimes against humanity]*, and especially for this opportunity to address the Knesset* [which owns so many Western politicians] ... *Some openly call Israel an apartheid state* [but who cares about truth and reality]. *This is the face of the new anti-Semitism* [an ingenious invention with which to silence your critics] ... *Through fire and water, Canada will stand with you* [because thanks to you and me, Canada has lost its moral compass] ... *I believe the story of Israel is a great example to the world* [and that is why we must all lie, cheat, steal, and murder with impunity]."*

Such British and Canadian prime ministerial admiration was enthusiastically delivered in spite of Israel's flagrant crimes against humanity during past assaults on Gaza and following the Israeli Knesset's Jewish nation-state bill which affirmed "the personal rights of all [Israel's] citizens according to law," but reserved communal rights for Jews only. This meant that while individual Arabs would be equal in the eyes of the law, their communal rights would not be recognised by an Apartheid state whose racism reigned supreme.

Furthermore, as a consequence of last year's increased public sympathy for the Palestinian people, Israel has ramped-up its propaganda through Zionism's reliable army of selfish, self-serving, sleazy, sewer-scavenging, slime ball supporters – time to abandon political correctness and unjustified respect – whose leading lights include renowned war criminals such as Britain's former Prime Minister Tony Blair who while masquerading as "Middle East Peace Envoy" was pocketing millions. Such lowlife paid for recruits contaminate not only politics, but also the mainstream media which helps to plant the seeds of support for Israel by expurgating the news we hear, read, and watch. While speaking at a conference in Jerusalem last month, the director of the Israeli-biased BBC Television said: "I've never felt so uncomfortable being a Jew in the UK as in the last 12 months," and that rising anti-Semitism had made him question the long-term future for Jews in the UK.

It had obviously escaped this director's Zionist-focussed mentality that what he refers to as anti-Semitism in Britain, may in fact be the British people's exasperation with continually seeing images of Israel's barbarity against a defenceless people who only want to be left alone to enjoy their inalienable human rights in an unoccupied Palestinian state. How can this individual and others of his shameful ilk be made to understand that the general public's revulsion and condemnation resulting from seeing images of Palestinian children burnt to a crisp with limbs blown off, is not in any way anti-Semitic but simply empathy for fellow human beings whose savage persecution has been ongoing for more almost 70 years.

Unmitigated Zionist arrogance – with its inherent Ariel Sharon belief that "Israel may have the right to put others on trial, but certainly no one has the right to put the Jewish people and the State of Israel on trial" – presumes to tell the rest of the "unchosen" goyim world what it can and cannot do; presumes to condemn the European parliaments that finally took a moral stand and voted to recognise a Palestinian state; presumes –after the Palestinians signed up to join the International Criminal Court (ICC) – to issue the threat that Israel would take "steps in response and defend Israel's soldiers"; presumes that it has a right to special trade agreements and dispensations whose conditions it routinely violates; presumes that it can take what it wants without giving anything in return; and presumes in accordance with its self nomination as "God's chosen people" that it has a supremacist entitlement to treat all non-Jews as contemptible individuals to be used and exploited.

Further proof of an unchanged Palestinian status quo for the forthcoming year came after the first step was taken to join the ICC with the U.S. state department – an Israeli mouthpiece – releasing a statement condemning what it called "an escalatory step" on the part of the Palestinians and that negotiations between the two sides were the only "realistic path towards peace … today's action is entirely counter-productive and does nothing to further the aspirations of the Palestinian people for a sovereign and independent state."

It is hard to comprehend how after decades of "peace talks" anyone can still believe that peace is achievable through negotiations. The Israeli position of insisting that only through negotiations can an agreement be reached is a ploy that always includes the deliberate Israeli intent to sabotage such negotiations so as to prolong the status quo and thereby enable Israel to continue with its illegal settlement building and gradual expropriation of more Palestinian land by means of ethnic cleansing. Israel does not want peace. Peace would mean an end to its gratuitous persecution of the Palestinians and the larcenous plunder of Palestinian land and resources.

Even before the UN Security Council vote Israel considered the resolution to be a diplomatic declaration of war with the Intelligence and Strategic Affairs Minister calling for drastic measures if the Palestinians did indeed make the move: "A vote at the UN is expected on the aggressive, hostile and one-sided resolution regarding a Palestinian state. We must not let it pass quietly," he declared, "in my opinion, if such a resolution is accepted by the UNSC we will have to seriously consider the dismantling of the Palestinian Authority."

Another ill omen for Palestinian hopes for justice and a better life was the UK Government's announcement that it would be setting up guidelines to prevent public bodies from supporting – through their procurement and investment policies – the legal and human rights of the brutally persecuted Palestinian people. This is despite the fact that the Boycott, Divestment and Sanctions (BDS) campaign – similar to the sanctions tactic successfully employed against Apartheid South Africa – is a peaceful and effective method of forcing the Israeli Government to cease its arrogant disregard for international law.

The hypocrisy and double standards of most Western leaders is not a phenomenon that evolved by chance, but is one that came about as a result of well-financed and organised Zionist Jewish lobby groups that exist throughout Australia, Canada, New Zealand, the United States, and Western Europe. Yes, there is even a SAIPAC (South African Israel Public Affairs Committee) in Cape Town. Such parastatal organisations and faux-NGOs routinely exploit lawfare to illegitimately subvert domestic and international law to discredit and criminalise individuals or organisations by spreading propaganda and/or influencing public opinion with a view to forcing their respective countries of residence to embrace the Israeli narrative and stifle any public debate whenever the subject of Israel's criminality is raised.

The lawfare tactic is supported by a worldwide network of Israel's diaspora allies and helpers known as sayanim – local Jews in their countries of residence – who having received email alerts from the Israeli Foreign Ministry, will take all necessary steps to intimidate, pressurise, or simply bribe individuals in the media and politics to adopt pro-Israel positions that are neither moral nor in the best interests of their own countries. By distorting and suppressing any criticism of Israel, they pre-empt the potential implementation of any initiatives that might undermine either Israel's economy or the world's perception of Israel as an innocent victim just defending itself. Needless to say, the hawkish and less than honest Israeli Prime Minister – never one to miss an opportunity – drew parallels between efforts to boycott Israel, the long history of anti-Semitism, and the international community's alleged anti-Israel bias. He also emphasised his gratitude to Britain by stating that "I want to commend the British government for refusing to discriminate against Israel and Israelis and I commend you for standing up for the one and only true democracy in the Middle East." The one and only true democracy in the Middle East? How is that for fascist chutzpah?

This intended British government directive is no doubt an effort to keep in step with recent legislation in the U.S. where some states have made it illegal to either divest from Israel or to promote a boycott of Israeli products. A trade pact with Europe will also stipulate – at the instigation of the American Israel Public Affairs Committee (AIPAC) – that the U.S. is obliged to take retaliatory action against any European country endeavouring to boycott Israel including the West Bank settlements which the empowering legislation views as part of Israel proper. Apart form committing $25 million to a new anti-BDS task force – an admission of the BDS campaign's effectiveness – Israel is also working to create a mechanism for global internet censorship with a ban on any material critical of its criminal policies with such criticism being euphemistically branded as "incitement." Consequently Facebook and other social networking sites have started deleting from their sites any "hate speech" or "terrorism" related material including criticism of Israel which is of course "anti-Semitic."

Policing of the internet will be maintained by ever-watchful Zionist organisations including the Zionist Federation of

Australia; the Britain Israel Communications and Research Centre (BICOM); the Centre for Israel and Jewish Affairs (CIJA) in Canada; the Conseil Representatif des Institutions Juives de France (CRIF) in France; the Zionist Federation of New Zealand; and AIPAC in the United States. The financial and political power of such groups should not be underestimated and their access to government policy making ensures protection of Israel which for example in France has included legislation of hate crimes that while *de facto* protecting Jews, also limits French citizen ability to criticise Israel. This has led to a French court declaring that a peaceful protest promoting the BDS campaign against Israel was illegal. So much for France's motto of *"liberté, égalité, fraternité."* He may have been a white nationalist, a Neo-Nazi, Holocaust denying white separatist, and associate editor of *National Vanguard*, but American Kevin Alfred Strom nonetheless had a valid point when in 1993 he suggested that "to learn who rules over you, simply find out who you are not allowed to criticise."

All of which reminds me of the famous and provocative poem by Pastor Martin Niemöller (1892 – 1984) about the cowardice of German intellectuals following the Nazis' rise to power and the subsequent purging of their chosen targets:

> *"First they came for the Socialists, and I did not speak out –*
> *Because I was not a Socialist.*
> *Then they came for the Trade Unionists, and I did not speak*
> *out – Because I was not a Trade Unionist.*
> *Then they came for the Jews, and I did not speak out –*
> *Because I was not a Jew.*
> *Then they came for me – and there was no one left to speak*
> *for me."*

It is time for people in the West to face up to certain inescapable realities: the first is to honestly recognise and accept that Israel is a Zionist Apartheid warmongering state bent on driving out the indigenous Palestinian people so as to grab their land irrespective of cost or consequence; the second is that Western political leaders cannot be relied upon to unconditionally insist on justice for the Palestinian people including Israel's withdrawal to the 1967 borders which would enable the establishment of a Palestinian state; the third is that they cannot rely on those same political and religious leaders to force Israel to respect international law relating to the rights of others; and finally, that they must take upon themselves the responsibility of peacefully resorting to the types of boycotts that successfully ended Apartheid in South Africa. By simply observing an all out boycott of anything Israeli, or Israel-related through the current global Boycott, Divestment and Sanctions Movement, they would make Israelis realise that there was no option other than to accept that even as "a God chosen people" they are still subject to an unconditional obligation to respect both the ethical and moral principles of international law, and the inalienable rights of other human beings. Before embarking on such a humane, noble, and imperative task, however, many Westerners might do well to heed the advice of Wendell Berry, the American environmental activist, cultural critic, essayist, poet, and prolific author:

> "We must not again allow public emotion or the public media to caricature our enemies. If our enemies are now to be some nations of Islam, then we should undertake to know those enemies. Our schools should begin to teach the histories, cultures, arts, and language of the Islamic nations. And our leaders should have the humility and the wisdom to ask the reasons some of those people have for hating us."

24

Monday, 4 January

Champ de Mars, Paris, France

Malek Bennabi stood looking up at the *Monument des Droits de l'Homme* in the Champ de Mars park where Pierre had arranged to meet him. Inaugurated in 1989 by the City of Paris to celebrate the bicentenary of the French Revolution – when the Rights of Man and Citizen, was drawn up at the Chateaux Versailles in 1789 – this somewhat intriguing "Rights of man" monument by the Czech sculptor Ivan Theimer, owed its distinct esoteric symbolism to Michel Boroni the former Grand Master of the Grand Orient Masonic Lodge who was responsible for organising the anniversary. The monument was a small stone temple featuring mostly Egyptian and Masonic motifs including a sundial, pyramids, triangular obelisks, and solar images as well as other astrological and esoteric symbols. The side of the monument overlooking the park featured four statues of figures clad in togas including one of a small boy in a cylindrical cap who no doubt represented apprenticeship in knowledge.

Malek did not have long to wait before Pierre turned up and dispensed with formalities. "Let's walk," he said, motioning towards the Eiffel Tower at the other end of the Park.

"Is there a problem?" Malek asked anxiously.

"Not at all. There's couple of new assignments for you."

"So soon?"

"First, there's a small matter needing immediate attention

in London where a piece of shit needs to be taken care of. You will be staying with one of our people who will fill you in and see that you have everything you need. Then you will leave immediately for Brussels for a few months."

"What's so important in Brussels?"

"You may remember late last year the European Union decided that goods produced on territories we've occupied since sixty-seven must now have a 'made in settlements' label."

"Yeah, some Knesset members said it was like European Jews having their storefronts daubed with yellow stars during the Holocaust."

"Exactly. But it's been decided to go further than our usual diplomatic objections and threats of repercussions," Pierre said and proceeded to explain that the EU's decision to proceed on the proposal's guidelines – which had taken years to produce – had come about despite fierce lobbying by Israel and intervention by a group of AIPAC-led U.S. congresspeople. Though the EU was Israel's top trading partner, only one percent of Israel's $13 billion in annual exports to the bloc's 28 countries consisted of products from the occupied West Bank, the Golan Heights and East Jerusalem. So while the immediate economic impact was expected to be minimal, there was nonetheless much concern that the concept behind the mere labelling of such products could expand into also targeting the numerous businesses that had operations or affiliates in the contested areas.

Israeli banks that provided mortgages to homeowners in the West Bank could for example become vulnerable to divestment from Europe; retail chains with outlets in illegal settlements could be barred from the continent; and manufacturers using parts produced in occupied territory factories could be subject to labelling or sanctions. There was even the possibility that Jewish settlers could lose the privilege of being allowed to travel to Europe without a visa as Israeli citizens. Consequently

Israel's response was intended to intimidate the Europeans into either not going further down that route, or into slowing the process as much possible because at the very least it could prove troublesome, or at most – devastating.

Pierre cited the Israeli government view that since the recent formal or symbolic recognition of an independent Palestinian state by the EU parliament and some of its member states, there had been mounting European frustration over the stalemated peace process and the growing political pressure on leaders in countries with large Muslim populations sympathetic to the Palestinian cause.

Though a spokesman for the European Commission had stressed that the decision had in no way changed the bloc's stance on the peace process or Israel's special treatment in European markets wherein "Made in Israel" products were subject to little or no tariffs, products coming from occupied territory settlements would not benefit from such preferential treatment.

Pierre stressed the fact that there were "at least 1,000 Israeli companies operating in over a dozen industrial zones in West Bank settlements, and some 25,000 acres of Jewish-run farms producing fresh fruit and vegetables, honey, olive oil, eggs, poultry, organic products and even cosmetics … Our wineries in the Golan Heights have gained international recognition."

"So what do you need me for?"

"You are to go to Brussels and check into this Hotel," Pierre said as he handed Malek an envelope with all the details. "You will be contacted by someone claiming to be your cousin Walid, the son of your uncle Idris in London. You will be briefed, provided with everything you need, and introduced to a group of radical Muslims in the borough of Molenbeek."

Malek knew that apart from having a thriving middle-class with well kept bourgeois villas and green spaces, Molenbeek was also in parts a run-down borough with large Moroccan and Turkish communities which had not fully integrated within

Belgium society. The borough was now identified with European jihadism and almost invariably whenever an "Islamist" atrocity occurred on the continent, attention was always focused on this area on the north-western fringes of the Brussels' city centre.

"Memorise the envelope's contents and then get rid of it," Pierre said, "these Europeans have to be taught a lesson … One they wont forget in a hurry."

Malek nodded his head and smirked malevolently as he pocketed the envelope.

Pierre shook Malek's hand and wished him "good luck," as they parted. He did not, however, tell him that the targets for the attacks were to be Brussels' Zaventem Airport, to the north-east of the city centre, and the Maalbeek metro station located under the Rue de la Loi/Wetstraat, which was renowned for the numerous official buildings of the European Parliament, the European Union, the European Commission and the Belgian Government. Plans for the attacks were well advanced with the attackers having already been selected. Malek's function was to coordinate the attacks and carry out any necessary "mopping up" afterwards.

Security at Brussels Airport was handled by the aviation and general security company International Consultants on Targeted Security (ICTS) which was established in 1982 with former members of Shin Bet, Israel's internal security agency, and and El Al airline security agents. ICTS – which used the same security system as employed in Israel with passengers being profiled to assess the degree to which they posed a potential threat on the basis of certain indicators such as age, name, origin and behaviour during questioning – was also involved with airport security operations in Germany, Italy, Japan, Netherlands, Portugal, Russia, and Spain.

The Chairman of the Supervisory Board at ICTS, Menachem J. Atzmon, was one of the Likud party members – including his co-treasurer Ehud Olmert – involved in the Likud fundraising scandal which culminated in his 1996 conviction for fraud and embezzlement. As party treasurer, Olmert was indicted in the Likud crimes but received special treatment and was subsequently acquitted. Despite their involvement in the scandal, Olmert went on to become Israel's Prime Minister in March 2009, and Atzmon became the founder and head of ICTS which owned Huntleigh USA, the airport security firm that ran passenger screening operations at the airports of Boston and Newark on 9/11.

United Flight 175 and American Flight 11, which allegedly struck the twin towers, both originated from Boston's Logan Airport, while United Flight 93, which purportedly crashed in Pennsylvania, departed from the Newark airport. Some 9/11 victims' families initiated lawsuits against Huntleigh USA for negligence, but Huntleigh, along with two other foreign security companies, was granted protection in 2002 by a U.S. Congress under the control of AIPAC and will consequently not in any way be made accountable in a U.S. court. ICTS' responsibility for Boston's Airport security on 9/11 was a conspicuous indication – completely ignored by authorities and the mainstream media – of Israel's involvement in the terror attacks that became the excuse for the so-called "War on Terror" from which Israel had so far been the only beneficiary.

ICTS had also come under scrutiny for other security "lapses" which apart from managing to miss several of the alleged 9/11 hijackers – who where said to have flown out of Boston's Logan airport on September 11th 2001 – also included allowing Richard Reid, the seriously deranged shoe bomber, to board his Miami-bound flight from Paris; being responsible for the London bus networks security during the July 7, 2005, "suicide" bomb attacks; and the bizarre case of the "underwear bomber," Umar Farouk Abdulmutallab, who was allowed to board Northwest Airlines Flight 253 to Detroit carrying explosive materials on Christmas day 2009.

Abdulmutallab – unlike the usual patsy Muslim terrorists who carried their passports with them during suicidal attacks and then conveniently left them at the scene for police to find – arrived at Schipol Airport to board his flight to the US with a one way ticket but no luggage or passport. His boarding of the flight was apparently facilitated by a mysterious smartly dressed man who spoke to the security management.

The events of 9/11 were an uncanny answer to the prayers of the Project for the New American Century (PNAC) – a neoconservative think tank that focussed on U.S. foreign policy – which was co-founded in 1997 by the Zionist Jews William Kristol and Robert Kagan with the latter being married to Victoria Nuland, the Assistant Secretary of European and Eurasian Affairs in the current U.S. administration.

In June 1997 the PNAC issued a statement of principles whose aims were to to shape a new century favourable to American principles and interests; to achieve "a foreign policy that boldly and purposefully promotes American principles abroad"; to "increase defence spending significantly"; to challenge "regimes hostile to US interests and values"; and to "accept America's unique role in preserving and extending an international order friendly to our security, our prosperity, and our principles": all of which was in reality a blueprint for Israeli controlled U.S. global domination. Of the 25 people who signed the PNAC's founding statement of principles, ten – including Dick Cheney, Donald Rumsfeld, and Paul Wolfowitz – went on to serve in the administration of President George W. Bush and to instigate a regime change with the removal of Iraq's Saddam Hussein.

Occupied East Jerusalem

In a sharp rise over the past years, four out of five Palestinians (82 percent) in East Jerusalem were now living in poverty with the separation wall – along with an upsurge in violent disturbances and a lack of welfare benefits – being cited as the main factor for the growing impoverishment. The daily disturbances occurring at the most bitterly contested and incendiary of holy sites had been the consequence of an increased number of incursions by religious Zionist activists – with their fanatically irrational yearning for a Third Temple – deliberately overstepping the line between peaceful presence and physical provocation. Attendance by the police clad in bullet-proof vests and armed with stun grenades and tear gas, had so far failed to prevent violent confrontations especially when white-clad Jewish men prostrated themselves at the site in an overt and inflammatory act of worship that is prohibited to Jews on Haram al-Sharif/ Temple Mount. The result was usually an ill-tempered brawl between Israeli forces and a group of incensed Muslim men who were either arrested or simply forcibly removed from the site.

It was former Defence Minister Moshe Dayan who – ten days after the holy site's capture by Israeli soldiers during the 1967 Land Grab War – brokered the agreement which allowed Jews to freely visit the Jordanian Waqf administered holy site where only Muslims were allowed to worship. The agreement was subsequently firmly established in the 1994 peace treaty between Jordan and an Israeli government keen on subduing Arab unrest in its newly occupied territories despite strident Jewish voices calling for the right to pray on the Muslim site.

More recently, however, thanks to an intensive long-term PR campaign, the Israeli public's perception of the ban had become increasingly mainstream with the encouragement of cynical tongue in cheek calls for "religious freedom" and "human rights": commendable concepts which those same Jewish people were brutally denying the Palestinians. Such overt yearnings for Jewish Prayer on the Mount – once taboo and limited to extremist politicians – was now being supported by an increasing number of political and religious leaders not wishing to appear out of step with the settler movement whose increasing influence over the government prevented action being taken against the Jewish extremists who attacked Palestinians and their property.

It had also become public knowledge that the Israeli border police had often been briefed to initiate "friction activity" so as to deliberately provoke a violent Palestinian reaction in occupied East Jerusalem that would provide an excuse for the customary disproportionate Israeli response. Reports from police individuals present during these "clashes" all contained use of the same term "friction activity" which included deployment in the streets and on rooftops of Israeli Occupation forces who haphazardly fired tear gas canisters and potentially lethal bullets "at resident's homes and vehicles" to provoke a reaction.

Such provocations were – in keeping with Israel's ploy of laying the blame on its victims – accompanied by the usual ministerial invective against perceived enemies with the "hate deranged" Prime Minister ignoring Israel's criminality while bombastically referring to Israel as "civilisation's front line against barbarism." He described Iran – a country that unlike Israel had not in recent history invaded any of its neighbours – as "a dark theocracy that conquers its neighbours … Unleashed and unmuzzled, Iran will go on the prowl, devouring more and more prey." He yet again condemned the nuclear agreement with Iran as a "a very bad deal," with the "world rushing to embrace and do business with a regime openly committed to our destruction."

So while portraying Israel as a victim country at risk, betrayed by the world, and under attack by enemies at home and abroad, this disreputable excuse for Prime Minister, let alone a human being – who if there is any justice will be charged with war crimes by the ICC – disregarded the fact that Israel had systematically violated all agreements with the Palestinians including the 1993 Oslo Accords which it had effectively annulled by increasing the number of settlements and by failing to open a free passage between Gaza and the West Bank.

In October, UNESCO had adopted a resolution condemning what it called "Israeli aggressions and illegal measures against the freedom of worship and Muslims' access to their holy site, the al-Aqsa Mosque." UNESCO not only decried "the continuous storming of the mosque compound by Israeli extremists and uniformed forces," but also called on Israel "to cease the persistent excavations and works in East Jerusalem particularly around the Old City" where repeated Israeli provocations fuelled the current outbreak of violence.

Despite all the provocations against them – and what they have had to endure under occupation – the majority of Palestinians had refrained from violence and attacks on Israelis were relatively infrequent when compared to having lived for almost seventy years at the mercy of soldiers and armed settlers who while committing vile crimes against Palestinians were nonetheless immune from prosecution or punishment by the so-called Israeli "judicial" system.

Israel's determined policy of displacing the indigenous population by encroaching on Palestinian land with illegal Jewish settlements was matched by an equal determination to keep out "undesirables" by erecting security fences along its boundaries with Lebanon and Syria, and by building a wall along the Jordanian border because according to the prime Minister "we must control our borders against both illegal immigrants and terrorism … To the extent that it is possible we will encompass Israel's borders with a security fence and barriers." The concept of a fenced-in and isolated territory with a ghetto mentality was something that non-Zionist Jews had long ago predicted would be the consequence of establishing a Jewish state on land that had been inhabited by Palestinians for centuries. It was felt that in endeavouring to survive, Israel would be forced to become a fortress state reliant on fortifications for its security. That prediction had now become very much a reality for Apartheid Israel.

A few of the media's more courageous columnists such as Mark Banner had recently expressed the view that after centuries of past persecution, the playing of the "victim card" by Jews may have been justified, but that Jews must now accept they can no longer play the role of "the victims" while actually now being the persistent perpetrators whose illusion of moral superiority to others was in effect Jewish "chosenness" and tantamount to Nazi narcissism. Furthermore, the portrayal of Israel as "a poor little Jewish state defending itself" was no longer compatible with the fact that Israel – with its nuclear weapons and more than $4 billion in annual U.S. military aid – was the dominant power in the Middle East; that it was Israel that had invaded neighbouring Arab countries; and that it was Israel that had illegally occupied the lands of the Palestinian people while deliberately displacing them and denying them their legal and human rights.

Israel's heinous crimes against humanity which are perpetrated with an arrogant impunity facilitated by endless reminders of the Holocaust and the constant portrayal of Jews as the perennial victims of racist anti-Semitism had resulted in the former victims of Nazi fascism becoming Nazi fascists themselves. In his book *Balaam's Curse: How Israel Lost its Way, and How it Can Find it Again,* author Moshe Leshem, asserted that the expansion of Israeli power was commensurate with the expansion of "Holocaust" propaganda:

> *"Israelis and American Jews fully agree that the memory of the Holocaust is an indispensable weapon – one that must be used relentlessly against their common enemy … Jewish organisations and individuals thus*

labour cut continuously to remind the world of it. In America, the
perpetuation of the Holocaust memory is now a $100-million-a-year
enterprise, part of which is government funded."

Office Of The Israeli Prime Minister, West Jerusalem

The Prime Minister and his Chief of Staff were busy discussing the schedule for meetings with the leaders of other political parties – apart from the coalition of four Palestinian parties known as the Joint List – whose support was required for the forthcoming and controversial legislation that would provide the Knesset with a draconian new power enabling a three-quarters majority of its members to expel an elected politician if they disagreed with his or her views. The legislation was designed to restrict the rights of Israel's Palestinian minority and to curb their dissent by intimidating them into either being silent or remaining within the boundaries dictated to them by the Israeli Jewish majority. Such legislation would be at variance with all principles of democracy including the stipulated requirement that minorities should be represented.

The law would specify that when the Knesset decides on an expulsion, the statements of the "suspect" Knesset member would also be examined and not just their aims or actions; that a member's expulsion would last for the full period of the Knesset's remaining term; that the commencement of expulsion proceedings would require the support of 70 Knesset members, including a minimum of 10 opposition members; and that suspension proceedings may not commence during an election campaign.

Enactment of this law would confirm the evolution of a disturbing national tendency during the past few years – including numerous attempts to disqualify Arab Members of Knesset and Arab party lists from participating in the elections – that witnessed the outlawing of the Islamic Movement along with other laws such as the "Electoral Threshold Law" (that raised the electoral threshold from two percent to 3.25 percent); the "Nakba Law" (which fines bodies who openly reject Israel as a Jewish state or mark the Israel's Independence Day as a day of mourning): and the "Boycott Law" (that penalises individuals or organisations calling for the boycott of Israel or the illegal settlements), all of which were intended to silence the Arab voices and support for the Palestinian cause. The claim that Israel was "the only democracy in the Middle East" was about as deceitful and delusional as the assertion that God chose the Jews and promised them Palestine.

Dirksen Senate Office Building, Washington, D.C.

Senator Edward Wright had so far managed to obtain pledges of support from over 80 of the 100 sitting Senators and had this morning received from AIPAC the draft of a letter to be co-signed by the Senators and sent to the President. The letter started by referring to the Paris terrorist attack – whose perpetrators were alleged to have connections with Iran – and urged the President that in view of the rising threat of Islamic terrorism and "Israel's dramatically rising defence challenges, we stand ready to support a substantially enhanced new long-term agreement to help provide Israel with the resources required to defend itself and preserve its qualitative military edge by having defence-related aid increased with the signing of a 'robust' commitment to help combat its mounting security challenges … Unfortunately, Washington's staunch Mideast ally faces a variety of threats which require increasing the resources devoted to its defence against extremist groups such as Hezbollah whose positioning of up to 150,000 rockets and missiles was threatening Israel's north while the Sinai has become a 'lawless haven' for militant Islamist groups."

Since being blackmailed with the video recording of

his sexual gymnastics with Sally Berkley, Wright's usual philandering bravado had deserted him. At least before he had been heartened by having some semblance of choice, but now that thin veneer of having options had been suddenly wrenched away from him along with the illusion of his being dignified and beyond reproach. A dark cloud of apprehension had engulfed him and for the first time in many years he yearned for the love and security to be found in the bosom of his family and despite being a religious sceptic, he had even sought some solace from silent prayer. This morning, Senator Wright, the Chairman of the United States Senate Committee on Foreign Relations was feeling sorry for himself, sorry for his family, and sorry his country. It was a country where virtually all American people were also living under the illusion of choice: a choice of being governed by either the Democrats or Republicans who were both marching to the rhythmic but oppressive beat of Zionist jackboots.

That rhythmic beat's oppression of freedom of speech and expression was not, however, limited to America but also echoed in neighbouring Canada, and across the Atlantic Ocean in Europe. The mounting harshness of Zionist censorship had matched that of the Nazi Party as was implemented by the Minister of Propaganda, Joseph Goebbels with all media – literature, music, newspapers, and public events– being ruthlessly censored. The extent of the current censorship had become more evident as a result of Zionist Israel's determined efforts to shut down the BDS Movement by having its peaceful activities criminalised with the result that people everywhere were being denied their will while their right and freedoms were being eroded.

Censorship was also rampant in the "Promised Land" where more than 50 laws and an Israeli social structure discriminated against, and disenfranchised non-Jews. The reality of Israel's inability to exist in its present form without institutional Apartheid was confirmed by an Israeli Supreme Court Chief Justice who declared that the "human rights [of the Palestinians] cannot be a prescription for national suicide." Consequently in order to maintain its existence by depriving the indigenous Palestinians of their own existence – by means of dehumanisation, dispossession, and displacement – Zionist Israel had to silence criticism of its abhorrent Apartheid activities.

Doing so had so far required a global "war on criticism" which the Israeli government was now intending – with hyper-exceptionalist rhetoric – to intensify by seeking to develop "legislation in conjunction with European countries" to create a world coalition that would force social media platforms such as Facebook, YouTube, Twitter, and others, to accept responsibility for the content posted on their sites. Though the Israelis were endeavouring to disguise their proposal as a means of preventing Palestinians posting "violence promoting material" on the Internet, it was transparently evident that such legislation would provide censors with a far wider scope to effectively silence criticism of Israel on a global scale.

The "war on criticism," however, was to be all inclusive with Israeli social media activists and bloggers being required to submit "security-related material" for approval prior to posting. In other words, any Israeli Jew in "the only democracy in the Middle East" with a troubled conscience regarding Israel's Apartheid policies would now have to abide by the censorship conditions as set out for the Israeli media by the Israel's military censor. This blatant denial of Israeli citizen rights to express opinions and openly debate issues pertinent to the questionable character of the Jewish state, was justified by the cleverly couched contention delivered with diabolical "Newspeak" as follows: **Censorship: The Freedom To Speak Responsibly."**

25

Tuesday, 5 January

King David Street, West Jerusalem

Yaakov Katzir had as arranged picked up Abe Goldman from his Talbiyah apartment at 6:45 p.m. and driven him to the nearby King David Street for an after-hours appointment at 7:00 'p.m. with an antique dealer. The antiquities business in Israel was sufficiently significant to warrant a special government unit within the Israeli Antiquities Authority (IAA) to investigate theft and prevent important artefacts from being taken out of country. Overseeing the antiquities trade, however, was not an easy task because with some 30,000 known antiquity sites in Israel and the Occupied Palestinian Territories – mostly in open and unguarded areas – such sites were regularly plundered with the plunder then being sold on to middlemen. More often than not, it was the middlemen who financed the illegal nighttime digging with excavation tools and metal detectors being used to uncover rare coins and other valuable artefacts which the middlemen then resold to merchants and specialist collectors.

In recent years the illegal antiquities trade had proliferated as a consequence of ongoing conflicts in the Middle East with archaeological sites in ISIS-controlled areas of Syria and Iraq being illegally looted on a massive scale. Much of this loot was turning up in Western antiquity markets such as London and it was commonly known that Israel was also a regular recipient of pillaged artefacts. There had been no shortage of evidence regarding Israeli support for terrorist rebels in Syria and it was not by coincidence that neither ISIS nor Al-Nusra had attacked Israel, even though the latter was operating very close to Israel's border in the Golan Heights. Furthermore, not only have Israel and Al-Nusra avoided attacking each other, but Israel had even taken wounded terrorists across its border for medical treatment. So while pursuing its policy for a destructive regime change in Syria, Israel was also benefitting from the theft of antiquities dating from the ancient civilisations that once flourished in Mesopotamia.

Recently there had been some justified suspicions over "finds" in circumstances which stretched the imaginations of even the most gullible of people with the IAA claiming that a hiker while walking in Israel's eastern Galilee region had by chance discovered a 2,000-year-old shiny gold coin which was one of only two – the other being in the British Museum – to be known in existence. The coin, dating from the year 107 CE, bore the image of Augustus, the first emperor of the Roman Empire, and was part of a series minted to honour Roman rulers.

Other such fortuitous Israeli state finds – without archaeological digs or excavations – have included amateur scuba divers discovering approximately 2,000 gold coins just lying on the ocean floor, some twelve metres deep, in the harbour of what was once the ancient port of Caesarea which was built by Herod the Great sometime around 25–13 BCE as the port city Caesarea Maritima. This was shortly afterwards followed by a hoard of valuables being discovered in a cave in northern Israel by three members of a spelunking club. Though the location of the cave was not disclosed, it was, however, reported that the hoard included rings, bracelets, earrings, and coins minted during the reign of Alexander the Great with one side of the coins featuring an image of Alexander, and the other portraying Zeus sitting on a throne.

Questions had also been raised as to the provenance of

2,500-year-old Iraqi cuneiform tablets on display at Israel's Bible Lands Museum. The tablets' Israeli owner claimed to have purchased them in the 1990s but refused to divulge from whom. All of these events had occurred at a time when archaeological sites in Iraq and Syria were being despoiled to a supply a $7 billion black market trade in antiquities. Whenever asked about provenance, the Israelis always had a ready but invariably disingenuous answer.

The Israeli penchant for looted antiquities had been pioneered by Moshe Dayan – the Israeli military leader and politician whom the world came to regard as a fighting symbol of the new state of Israel – who in Gaza used the might of the Israeli army to pillage countless artefacts dating from the Ottoman era to the time before Christ in an effort to erase Palestinian history. There once was some 12,216 archaeological sites in Palestine, thousands of which were destroyed and looted as a result of the occupation. One such site and considered one of the most important in the Middle East was the monastery of St. Hilarion who was the disciple of St. Anthony the Great, the father of monasticism. The monastery, located in the middle of the Gaza Strip, had a mosaic floor dating back to the Byzantine era, parts of an ancient monument, a basilica-style church with three corridors, and the tomb of St. Hilarion, which was a pilgrimage destination.

When Israeli forces entered and occupied Gaza for few months in 1956, the stealing of antiquities was an Israeli priority. After 1967, the looting of antiquities became the standard practice of the occupation with the largest number and most prominent artefacts being stolen by Dayan who took thousands of pieces, including four Pharaonic clay coffins from Deir al-Balah in the Gaza Strip. *Time Magazine* subsequently published a photograph of Dayan standing triumphantly among the coffins which now reside in an Israeli Museum after being purchased from Dayan's wife. The extent of Dayan's pillaging

– not much known or discussed outside of Israel – was quite breathtaking with thousands of stolen pieces being shipped to Israel.

This evening's somewhat cloak-and-dagger meeting had come about at the request of the Israeli Ministry of Religious Services after Goldman had been recommended as the ideal negotiator by a fellow member of the Hiramic Brotherhood. According to the Ministry, the word was that this particular dealer was acting as agent for the sale of a fluted gold jar dating from between 15th and 13th centuries BCE – a time when the region was being fought over by the rival empires of Hittites, Egyptians, Assyrians, and Mitanni – that was recently discovered in Syria.

Goldman and Katzir were greeted by the theatrically ingratiating dealer and a baldheaded man with a scar on his forehead whom Katzir judged – from the slight bulge under the armpit of his jacket – to be carrying a shoulder holstered weapon. They were invited to sit around a Moorish hand-crafted console table inlaid with mother-of-pearl and the dealer began by explaining that for obvious reasons he was not in possession of the actual Jar. He did, however, have photographs of the artefact showing its excellent condition on his laptop which was open for them to view. The jar, they were told, was 16 inches high, 12 inches in diameter around the centre, and eight inches in diameter around the open neck.

Goldman pulled the laptop towards him and took his time zooming in on the photos and examining them more closely. "Provenance?" He eventually asked.

"It was discovered in Syria but definitely Egyptian from a time corresponding with what we call the Late Bronze Age of between the 14th and 13th centuries BCE, " the dealer said and then added that at that time Egyptian-Mesopotamian relations included frequent trade and of course occasional wars. The politics were fairly confused with lots of goings-on between middlemen and clients. But basically the period from the 16th to 12th centuries BCE was a three-way struggle for influence between Egypt, a succession of Mesopotamian powers such as Assyria and Babylon, and the Hittites. In between were a number of client states with shifting allegiances and for a while the powerful Mitanni kingdom played a prominent role. Essential diplomatic contacts were dominated by a system of gift exchange between the ruling elites, and this jar would have been one such gift. "There's no doubt about it … It's kosher, and I'll stake my reputation on it."

"There had better be no doubt, 'cos it's more than just your reputation that's at stake." Goldman's warning was matter of fact rather than threatening. "How much? He asked

"One point two million."

"Shekels?"

"U.S. dollars," the dealer said with a smile that that partly disguised a scowl.

"That's a bit steep."

"Maybe. But it's the seller's reserve price."

"I'll have to speak to my people." Goldman said getting up from the table.

"Do that," the dealer said tapping the side of his nose with his forefinger to indicate he knew who the potential buyers were.

"Just one thing," Goldman said, "any transaction between the parties would have to include a confidentiality agreement which if broken … "

"Don't worry. Complete confidentiality is also in my client's best interests."

As they were ushered out, Goldman thought the cost would be worth it because if the secret tunnelling under the Dome of the Rock were to locate the hoped for Well of Souls or some other comparable space, then this artefact could be "discovered" as possibly being the golden jar which contained the mana in the Ark of the Covenant. After all, it would not be the first time that provenance had been altered or an artefact's site of discovery been "relocated" to serve a political purpose. Recently an archeologist who had been excavating at the City of David archaeological site for almost 20 years, claimed to have found the legendary citadel captured by King David in his conquest of Jerusalem. The uncovering of a massive fortification of five-ton stones stacked 21 feet (6 metres) wide at the site was said to be perfectly consistent with the biblical narrative. The fortification would have been built some 800 years before King David captured it from its Jebusites, and that the biblical narrative of David's conquest of Jerusalem provided clues that indicated that David's entry point into the city had been at this particular fortification.

Though the claim had been met with a great deal of criticism that rekindled a longstanding debate regarding the Bible's use as a field guide for the identification of ancient ruins, the claim was generally accepted and joined a string of other announcements by Israeli archaeologists claiming to have unearthed palaces of the legendary biblical king – who despite so far eluding historians looking for clear-cut evidence of his existence and reign – was nonetheless revered in Jewish religious tradition as having established Jerusalem as Judaism's central holy city.

As Goldman was getting into Katzir's car, he figured that in the case of this jar, there would be no need to definitively claim it was the actual jar from the Ark because the mere well publicised suggestion that it may have been would be enough to implant the notion in the public's mind. As the erstwhile Nazi Minister of Propaganda Joseph Goebbels once said, "If you tell a lie big enough and keep repeating it, people will eventually come to believe it."

26

Sunday, 10 January

Hôtel Matignon, Paris, France

The French Prime Minister issued a warning from his official residence that the Islamic State (ISIS) will carry out another "major" terror attack like the one in Le Marais. "We are at war with terrorism; we need to be sincere with our people and we need to tell them there will be other attacks, major attacks. This is something we know for sure … Hundreds and thousands of extremists are infiltrating European countries as refugees … Often these people are from a different culture and hope to get benefits while doing nothing. There is a real threat of the destruction of a single economic space followed by cultural space and even the very European identity." Like other Western leaders he also pledged to commit military power to fighting ISIS and along with the ever obliging media helped to whip up Islamophobic hysteria. Thankfully, however, there were still a few newspapers prepared to publish alternative viewpoints by writers such as Mark Banner.

The U.S. and Israel: A Clear And Present Danger To All Humanity

Mark Banner
Sunday, 11 January

In their self-serving and apparently endless wars against humanity, the U.S. with its weapons industry and Zionist Israel with its desire for all Palestine have resorted to barefaced lies and the concoction of existential threats that require a "War on Terror." Being excessively intoxicated by the misconception of their own "exceptionality" and "chosenness," they have contrived to unleash the might of the American-Zionist-Military Industrial Complex in wars that are crimes against humanity. While the U.S. has been pursuing its goal for global hegemony under the disingenuous pretence of spreading democracy, Zionist Israel has been busy "defending itself" by ethnically cleansing the indigenous Palestinian population whose land and resources it has been – and still is – stealing with undisguised hateful rapaciousness and brutal force.

During the 11th century when Pope Urban II was itching with the imperious requirement for the amassment of greater riches, he set he sights on the Holy Land but was obliged to disguise his actual materialistic motivation. Consequently in 1095, he made one of the most influential speeches of the Middle Ages, when – to the contrived cries of "Deus vult!" or "God wills it!" – he called for a Christian Crusade to reclaim the Holy Land from the Muslims. To encourage knights and noblemen to undertake such a hazardous task, the Pope gave them an incentive to become "Soldiers of Christ" by assuring remission of their sins and the saving of their souls. Being thus incentivised, these "Soldiers of Christ" went to the Holy Land and waged wars whose barbarity in the name of God, knew no bounds. One contemporaneous report stated that after laying siege to Jerusalem for one month, the Crusaders rode into the city with their horses "knee-deep in the blood of disbelievers." Jews were herded into their synagogues and burnt alive, and on the following day Christian knights slaughtered "a great multitude of people of every age, old men and women, maidens, children, mothers with infants, by way of a solemn sacrifice" to Jesus.

Just as was the case back in 1095, today's Zio-American imperialism also requires a crusade which in this case involves opposition to radicalism with the proverbial War on Terror that by design must never end. Consequently in the U.S. – in whose footsteps Europe obediently treads – the AIPAC-controlled government calculatingly promotes anti-Muslim hatred and hysteria in response to the conflicts they have themselves created.

American imperialism – the economic, military, and cultural influence of the U.S. on other countries – is to a great extent based on American exceptionalism which is the presumptuous belief that the United States is different from other nations because of its specific mission to spread liberty and democracy to the rest of the world. It was during the presidency of James K. Polk, that the concept of American Empire became a reality throughout the latter half of the 1800s when industrialisation required new international markets for corporate America's goods. Furthermore, the increasing influence of Social Darwinism – which held that the social classes had no obligation towards those unequipped or under-equipped to compete for survival – led to the belief that the U.S. was inherently responsible for bringing concepts like industry, democracy, and Christianity to less scientifically developed, "savage" societies.

The combination of such views along with other factors led the U.S. to dramatically expand its sphere of influence. One of the earliest and most notable examples of American Imperialism involved the annexation of Hawaii – because the military significance of Hawaiian naval bases as a way station to the Spanish Philippines became the main consideration – where in 1898, the possession of all ports, buildings, harbours, military equipment, and public property that had previously belonged to the Hawaiian Islands Government came under U.S. control.

Zionist Israel's calculated but illegal annexation of Palestine was also in need of justification by a crusade shrouded in fabrications and falsehoods which included the claim that God promised Israel to his chosen people, the Jews; that all the Jews in the world had a right to Palestine; and that Israel was living in danger of annihilation with the threat of Jews being "driven into the sea." To begin with the narrative of a God "chosen people" being promised the land of Palestine, is just that – a narrative concocted by Jewish scribes – but without substantiation from any other source.

Furthermore, most Zionist leaders such as David Ben-Gurion – though not particularly religious despite their Jewish ethnicity – nonetheless cynically exploited the "promised land" narrative with even Theodor Herzl, an avowed atheist who certainly did not believe in the existence of a God, getting in on the act. Secondly, very few Jews have any biological/ancestral connection with the ancient Hebrews. And thirdly, Israel's existence has never been seriously threatened by Arab forces seeking its annihilation because right from the very start of the 1948 War – even before Israel acquired nuclear weapons – Israeli forces were superior in number and far better equipped.

All of this land and resource grabbing chicanery with gratuitous violence against mostly innocent civilians including children – who are simply written off as unavoidable collateral damage – is facilitated and justified by an unscrupulous brainwashing industry consisting of unprincipled experts, media flunkies, sleazy lobbyists, public relations pimps, and prejudiced think tanks who spread and implant neoconservative warmongering disinformation into the public consciousness.

A good deal of this disinformation has been directed at the Middle East which unfortunately due to its vast and much sought after oil resources, unwittingly became of vital strategic importance to the interests of those who wore the mantle of "exceptionality." Because the concepts of "exceptionality," "a master race," or a "chosen people" are all by their very nature irrefutably racist, Muslims in general and the sovereignty of their countries in particular, became subject to disparaging contempt and high-tech military aggression which whenever justifiably opposed or resisted was immediately given the propagandised label of "Islamic terrorism."

Following the 2015 attack on the offices of *Charlie Hebdo* weakly satirical magazine in Paris, Rupert Murdoch, owner of the disgraceful and infinitely biased Fox News, suggested that all Muslims share the guilt of terrorism by stating that "maybe most Muslims are peaceful, but until they recognise and destroy their growing jihadist cancer they must be held responsible." If Mr. Murdoch was an impartial media mogul, which he is definitely not, then he could have also said that "maybe most Jews are peaceful, but until they recognise and destroy the growing Zionist cancer that is ethnically cleansing the Palestinian people, they must be held responsible."

Without the spectre of Islamic terrorism and the inculcated need for a crusading war against it, crimes against humanity could not be committed with impunity and the Anglo-American-Zionist-military industrial complex could not survive without the trillions of dollars it makes from providing the weaponry for the destruction of humanity. It was Robert Jackson, the lead American prosecutor at the Nuremberg trials, who described that conflict's atrocities as being "so malignant and so devastating that civilisation cannot tolerate their being ignored, because it cannot survive their being repeated." Despite recognition of that fact resulting in the Nuremberg principles – a set of guidelines for determining what constitutes a war crime – the U.S. and Israel as a matter of routine indulge not only in war crimes, but also in crimes against humanity which unlike war crimes can be committed during times of either war or peace.

Crimes against humanity include government-initiated or assisted policies or practices resulting in murder, massacres, dehumanisation, extermination, forced disappearances, unjust imprisonment, extrajudicial punishments, death squads, torture, and political, racial, or religious persecution. With reference to the last-cited crime, the United Nations General Assembly declared in 1976 that the systematic persecution of one racial group by another – as for example practiced in Apartheid – to be a crime against humanity. Given the existence of such internationally legalised prohibitions, how have U.S. and Israel managed to escape without being made accountable for decades of international law violations?

They have done so through the malicious undermining of such laws by claiming the real existential threats of present day Islamic terrorism have dramatically changed conditions in a troubled world wherein laws intended for our protection had become counterproductive because they tied the hands of those entrusted with providing that protection. Consequently with the help of the tireless brainwashing industry, supposedly civilised societies now believe that the trillions of dollars/euros/pounds spent on wars that dehumanise, displace, and decimate the lives of millions of people, are wars that are necessary for their safety and protection.

While such reasoning may appear to have some superficial merit, it does not stand up to closer examination. If for example death tolls resulting from terrorist atrocities are compared either individually or together – be they in the tens, hundreds, or very occasionally thousands – with those caused by the U.S. and Israel, they would still never come anywhere near close to matching the millions killed in conflicts instigated or conducted by those two rogue nations. What is astounding is the fact that Israel – a state which claims to have been established primarily as a refuge for Jews – has since its inception been disregarding with contempt the very laws that came into being mostly in response to the deplorable persecution of innocent Jewish civilians by the Nazis.

It must now be apparent to any reasonable and moderately intelligent person that the gradual but incessant and successful criminalisation of criticism, or opposition to Apartheid Israel – initiated by Jewish lobby groups that operate throughout the world but more so in the West – has without doubt not only infringed on the basic right to free speech, but has also Zionised the perceptions of most Western so-called democratic governments where the phantom of anti-Semitism has become the ultimate zionist weapon in coercing most of them to remain subservient and silent over the reality of Israeli crimes against humanity.

The irrefutable facts are that Israel will not be satisfied until every drop of drinkable water which it has not already stolen, becomes too contaminated for Palestinians to drink; that Israel will not be satisfied until its air, land and sea blockade of Palestinian Territories – that prevents the import of vital food and medical supplies – has induced malnutrition, disease and death amongst the imprisoned and persecuted population; that Israel will not be satisfied until all Palestinian children have been traumatised by the experience of seeing their parents being hounded, humiliated, imprisoned without due process,

507

and in many cases simply murdered; that Israel will not be satisfied until those same children are further traumatised by being arbitrarily arrested, interrogated without adult or legal council support, beaten, terrorised, and forced into signing confessions (written in a language they do not understand) that incriminate parents and relatives who are then held indefinitely under the misused Administrative Detention Order; that Israel will not be satisfied until every Palestinian home, hospital and school has been reduced to rubble with bombs supplied by courtesy of U.S. taxpayers; and that Israel will not be satisfied until every drop of Palestinian blood has soaked into the stolen Palestinian lands on which more illegal Jewish settlements will be built.

> *"Give me the liberty to know, to utter, and to argue freely according to conscience, above all liberties."*
> **John Milton,** *Areopagitica.*

What is even more astounding is that Israel's total abandonment of both the Jewish people's "never again" resolve, and the core ethical teaching of Judaism that it is an "ethical monotheism" – a religion based on a concept that there is a single incorporeal God who gives commandments which constitute a moral law for all humanity – has been, and still is being either tolerated or actively supported by the majority of Jews in diaspora. Pointing out the discrepancy between the much hyped principles and values that Jews claim to aspire to and the reality of what they either tolerate, support, or do, is not anti-Semitic, but a sincere regret that a people with so much potential that could be employed to help improve the state of humanity, is instead being used to push it towards Armageddon.

Since the inception of Israel as a nation on the back of blackmail, bribery, and bullying at the UN and in the U.S.,

Israeli Jews and their supporters in diaspora have lived on yet another barefaced lie with regards to the hypocrisy of 1948 Declaration of Israel's Independence:

> *"THE STATE OF ISRAEL will be open to the immigration of Jews from all countries of their dispersion; will promote the development of the country for the benefit of all its inhabitants; will be based on the precepts of liberty, justice and peace taught by the Hebrew Prophets; will uphold the full social and political equality of all its citizens, without distinction of race, creed or sex; will guarantee full freedom of conscience, worship, education and culture; will safeguard the sanctity and inviolability of the shrines and Holy Places of all religions; and will dedicate itself to the principles of the Charter of the United Nations."*

Despite the Declaration's yet to be fulfilled promise of having "full social and political equality of all its citizens, without distinction of race, creed or sex," the reality is that from the outset David Ben-Gurion and other Jewish leaders faced the dilemma of whether to uphold such democratic principles and offer full freedom to all citizens regardless of race or religion, or to recognise the probability that the presence of a Palestinian "citizens" would represent a lethal threat to the Zionist cause which by nature was racist, and by intent rapacious. In his letters and diaries, Ben-Gurion repeatedly considered either depopulating Palestine of its Palestinians, or simply expelling them because he recognised that they would reject being subservient to the newly arrived Jewish colonists and perhaps even fight against them. In the "Ben-Gurion letter" – written when he was head of the executive committee of the Jewish Agency – he informed his son, Amos, that "the Arabs will have to go, but one needs an opportune moment for making it happen, such as a war." Consequently Israel has continued "making it happen" either by its own direct action, or by instigating Western nations to do so on its behalf as is the case in Syria where while seeking regime change, the West is obligingly destroying for Israel what was once the cradle of civilisation.

In keeping with its Arab land grabbing policy, Israel in 1981 formally annexed the 580 square mile section of Golan that it occupied. Though the illegal annexation was condemned by the UN, the U.S., and most European powers, Israel with its usual arrogant disregard for international law thumbed its nose at all concerned and held on to the Golan with more than 50,000 Jewish settlers in in some 41 subsidised settlements who replaced the expelled 130,000 Druze and Arab inhabitants. Israel's intention was recently confirmed by the Prime Minister when he informed Russia's President that Israel would never return the Golan to Syria: an intention he subsequently reiterated in a speech by not only vowing that Israel would hold on to Golan for "all eternity," but also by admitting for the first time that Israel had made "dozens" of cross-border attacks on Syria. All of which is in keeping with Ben-Gurion's stated view that the state of Israel is a work in progress and its borders should not be fixed or even defined.

Ben-Gurion's zionist perception of prioritising the establishment of Jewish nationalism within its own state while relegating the importance of human rights for all individuals was confirmed when he said "If I knew that it was possible to save all the children of Germany by transporting them to England, and only half by transferring them to the Land of Israel, I would choose the latter, for before us lies not only the numbers of these children but the historical reckoning of the people of Israel."

Since then, Zionism's continuous entrenchment and enlargement of that state has been relentlessly facilitated by maximising Israel's appeal to the Jewish people who have been force-fed the premise that a real-time threat of a second Holocaust is ever present. Consequently any terrorist incident targeting Jews is immediately ceased upon by Israeli leaders to substantiate the the notion that only in Israel can Jews be safe as was recently reiterated by the Israeli Prime Minister:

> *"The State of Israel is not just the place to which you turn in prayer. The State of Israel is also your home. This week, a special team of ministers will convene to advance steps to increase immigration from France and other countries in Europe that are suffering from terrible anti-Semitism. All Jews who want to immigrate to Israel will be welcomed here warmly and with open arms. We will help you in your absorption here in our country, which is also your country."*

In order to provide a "safe national home" for Jews, Zionism has had to ethnically cleanse an indigenous population, embrace Apartheid, and enforce oppression by very brutal military means. Consequently as Zionism becomes more representational of all Jews in diaspora, those Jews have themselves inevitably become associated with the crimes against humanity that Zionism is perpetrating in their name and on their behalf.

So, as Zionism's criminality with impunity becomes unavoidably apparent and more difficult to conceal; as Israel perseveres with its cycles of state-terror to tyrannise the Palestinian people; and as Israel maintains its persistent claim to be acting on behalf of all Jews, then inevitably Zionism – the purported solution for anti-Semitism – will become the driving force behind negative feelings by non-Jews towards Jews in Israel and diaspora.

In the event of that happening, Zionism would not be at all bothered, but would in fact be jubilant because anti-Semitism validates Zionism's raison d'être and serves as its ultimate weapon. The continued use of "anti-Semitism" as a weapon against its critics – even to the extent of the recent invention of the "New anti-Semitism" – is essential for the survival of Zionism because it serves to deflect attention from its own lying, cheating, stealing, murdering, war profiteering, blatant violations of international law, and barbaric crimes against humanity. Yet despite such overwhelming and irrefutable evidence of Israel's unabated criminality, Jews everywhere who while tolerating and even actively supporting Israeli policies, continue to do so while disingenuously insisting they are not Zionists.

In the meantime the corporate mass media continually refrains from unconditionally reporting the facts; so-called political leaders continue with blinkered eyes to fawn over and commend Israel's ethnic cleansing of the Palestinian people; and as for the most of the rest of us, by quietly accepting Israel's propaganda lies, we become complicit in its crimes while obediently supping from a Zionist trough that is overflowing with Palestinian blood. Those Jews and their deluded double standard supporters who seek to silence and criminalise justified criticism of Israel should instead try to be honest with themselves and face up to the irrefutable reality of their own shameful complicity in Israel's barbaric land grabbing crimes against humanity.

Recognition of this fact is now beginning to gain ground in Israel where an organisation of intellectuals – "Save Israel,

Stop Occupation" – is preparing to appeal in an open letter to all Jews in diaspora to end the occupation for Israel's sake because the prolonged occupation is inherently oppressive for Palestinians; fuels mutual bloodshed; undermines the moral and democratic fabric of the State of Israel; hurts Israel's standing in the community of nations; harms Israeli society; and harms Jews around the world. The estimated 500 signatories will include some 48 winners of Israel's most prestigious awards (the Israel Prize and the EMET Prize); seven high-ranking IDF officers; twenty former Israeli Ambassadors, ministers, senior government officials and Members of Knesset; and160 professors in Israeli universities.

Such sentiments now emanating from many concerned Israelis would appear to confirm the reality that majority of people supporting Palestinian rights are not anti-Semitic, but rather human beings with a moral responsibility and democratic right to free speech which the Israeli lobby is relentlessly trying to snuff out by conflating opposition to an inhumane Zionist Apartheid regime with anti-Semitism, a ploy that could have dangerous consequences. For the sake of all humanity – Jews and Palestinians included – that must never be allowed to happen and Israeli Jews can help in this regard by recalling the words of Yehoshafat Harkabi – Chief of Israeli Military Intelligence (1955-9) and subsequently a professor of International Relations and Middle East Studies at the Hebrew University of Jerusalem – who in his book *Israel's Fateful Hour,* called for Israel's withdrawal from the occupied territories and warned as follows:

> *"We Israelis must be careful lest we become not a source of pride for Jews but a distressing burden. Israel is the criterion according to which all Jews will tend to be judged. Israel as a Jewish state is an example of the Jewish character, which finds free and*

concentrated expression within it. Anti-Semitism has deep and historical roots. Nevertheless, any flaw in Israeli conduct, which initially is cited as anti-Israelism, is likely to be transformed into empirical proof of the validity of anti-Semitism. It would be a tragic irony if the Jewish state, which was intended to solve the problem of anti-Semitism, was to become a factor in the rise of anti-Semitism. Israelis must be aware that the price of their misconduct is paid not only by them but also Jews throughout the world. In the struggle against anti-Semitism, the frontline begins in Israel."

Little Venice, London, England

Conrad and Freya invariably skipped breakfast on Sundays, preferring instead the enjoyment of a chilled bottle of dry white wine with their brunch a little later in the day. Most of their morning was spent lounging on a couch while pouring over the newspapers that were delivered regularly every Sunday. Conrad was particularly interested in the news that a hospital in northern Yemen near the border with Saudi Arabia and supported by the medical charity Doctors Without Borders – whose emergency care for Syrian families fleeing to Iraq Conrad had already documented – had come under an attack that killed at least four people and destroyed several buildings.

Fierce fighting along the frontier between Saudi troops and Yemen's Houthi rebels had devastated many border towns and displaced thousands of people. Attacks on clinics and hospitals had left the province with only one major medical facility, forcing the sick and the wounded to travel for hours in order to receive even basic treatment. Such attacks on the charity's medical facilities were a regular occurrence despite the charity regularly providing all warring parties – including the Saudi-led coalition – with GPS coordinates of the medical facilities where its doctors were working. The U.S.-backed Saudi-led coalition had already been criticised the previous week for dropping cluster bombs – designed to kill personnel and destroy vehicles – on Sana, the Yemeni capital, despite the Convention on Cluster Munitions (CCM) which as an international treaty prohibited the use, transfer and stockpile of cluster bombs.

Another item of interest was the revelation by a New York based strategic security firm that "weaponisation of sectarianism" was fuelling the divide between Sunni and Shia Muslims while causing the "greatest threat facing the Middle East." In a region already beset by persistent and widespread problems – ranging from absolute monarchies, military dictatorships, corrupt governance, limited career opportunities and freedom of expression, violent extremism, devastating wars, and scarcity of resources – the one threat that stood out above the rest with regards to potential for destabilisation, destruction, and denial of human rights – was the exploitation of sectarianism as a geopolitical weapon.

Conrad shared the view that sectarianism encouraged the extremist rhetoric and violence which served to distract populations from economic and social priorities by providing an expedient enemy on which to focus the blame. Conrad noted that while the Sunni-Shia divide had existed since the death of the Prophet Mohammed (632 CE), the current divisions were being driven far more by regional rivalries and political shenanigans – of which Israel was the principal instigator – than by religion which nonetheless remained as one of the primary factors. As the leader of the Sunni sphere of influence, Saudi Arabia shared Israel's animosity towards Iran's Shiite theocracy which was suspected of trying to expand its influence in the region. As far as Conrad was concerned, America's supportive supply of weaponry to Saudi Arabia for its war crimes in the Yemen, merely confirmed a previous assertion by his father in an article titled *The Real Axis of Evil: United States, Israel, and Saudi Arabia.*

Current sectarian enmity had been further exacerbated by Saudi Arabia's recent execution of a Shiite cleric whose only crime appears to have been speaking out against the Saudi Kingdom's oppression of the Shiite minority. Though Saudi Arabia's deputy crown prince – the man who wielded power behind the throne of his father, King Salman – had promised painful economic restructuring, he had done so without offering any prospect of political, religious, or social change in a country where intolerance persisted with one blogger calling for open debate regarding the interpretations of Islam being sentenced to ten years in prison and 1,000 lashes; where two females arrested for defying the driving ban for women were to be tried in a special court for terrorism suspects; and where the human rights record was still one of the worst in the world.

For her part, Freya was especially sympathetic towards Muslim women in the Middle East who apart from having to cope with the region's turmoil, were also challenged by the necessity of remaining devout Muslims – but within a kinder environment with equal opportunities – while also endeavouring to emerge from the repression that had them living invisibly in the shadow of the men in their society. In Saudi Arabia for example, it was not until October 2013 that the first female lawyer was licensed to practice.

Many Muslim women were also subject to the contentious and barbaric tradition of Female Genital Mutilation (FMG) which posed immediate risks to the health of its victims with severe pain and bleeding, difficulty in passing urine, infections, and even death due to hemorrhagic or neurogenic shock. Other effects included long-term scars, post-traumatic stress disorder, chronic pain, HIV infection, cysts, abscesses, genital ulcers, difficulty and pain during sexual activity, and an increased risk of complications affecting menstrual cycles that could result in infertility. The disturbing extent of this barbarity had been made apparent by a UNICEF study showing that at least 200 million girls and women alive today had undergone such ritual mutilation.

After carefully analysing and discussing the veracity of the mainstream media's main news items – which they knew had been doctored under pressure mostly from the American Central Intelligence Agency (CIA) and pro-Israel media monitoring groups to sell the need for war and curtail criticism of Israel – Conrad and Freya focussed their attention on the less vexing subject of what accompaniment to have with their wild Alaskan salmon fillets which Freya intended to bake.

"How about a Béarnaise sauce," Freya finally asked, "but you'd have to get some fresh tarragon."

Conrad smiled. "I think I can just about manage a trip to the supermarket."

She took his hand as they both got up together and walked to the hallway where he held her in his arms gently but with an intimate closeness that enhanced the love instinctually radiating between them. They affectionately caressed each other and lingered in the warmth of their embrace without uttering a single word. Words alone could not have explained their predestined friendship, their attraction for each other, or the uncanny understanding between them. The mental and physical compatibility of their relationship had long since been transcended by a spiritual love that reached to the core of their souls, forming a mental-physical-spiritual bond that was unbreakable even when they were apart from each other. Finally – and with some reluctance – he let go of her, kissed her on the forehead, turned, and picked up the car keys from the hallway table as he headed for the front door. She watched him leave and close the door behind him with a love that had been fully fulfilled by a midweek pregnancy test confirmation that she was now carrying his child.

Moments later the canal-side's omnipresent tranquility was shattered by the deafening sound of a reverberating rumble that presaged a horrendous doom. Apart from being terrified by the effect of the invasive explosion, Freya also shuddered involuntarily as she was overcome by an overwhelming sense of foreboding that prompted her to let loose a long, desperate, and shrill "no" that as a heartfelt appeal fell on the invariably deaf ears of all the Gods and other supposed celestial powers. Her panicked rush from the kitchen to the front of the house sitting room window to find out what had happened, only confirmed her worst fears … The shell of Conrad's burnt out car was the epicentre of a charred and now silent and still devastation that had transformed the neighbourhood's sheltered serenity into yet another war zone.

27

Thursday, 5 May

Holocaust Remembrance Day, Israel

In a speech for Holocaust Remembrance Day, IDF Deputy Chief of Staff Major General Yair Golan said that he identified processes in Israel today that were similar to those that took place in Europe prior to the Holocaust. In a strongly worded speech uncommon for a military commander – subsequently condemned by the Prime Minister who said "the comparison which rises from the Deputy Chief of Staff's words is outrageous, and factually wrong. They should not have been said." – Golan warned against trends of growing callousness and indifference towards those outside of mainstream Israeli society, and called for a "thorough consideration" of how society treats the disadvantaged and "the other" in its midst.

> *"The Holocaust must lead us to think about our public life, and more importantly, it must lead everyone who can, not merely those who want, to carry public responsibility. If there is something that frightens me about the memory of the Holocaust, it is seeing the abhorrent processes that took place in Europe, and Germany in particular, some 70, 80 or 90 years ago, and finding manifestations of these processes here among us in 2016 … The Holocaust, as I see it, must enable us to deeply reflect on the nature of man. It must bring us to deeply reflect on the responsibility of leadership and the nature of society, and it must enable us to think fundamentally about how we, here and now, are conducting ourselves toward orphans, widows and their like …*

Indeed, there is nothing easier than to simply hate the other, there is nothing easier than to provoke fears and strike terror; there is nothing easier than barbaric behaviour, moral corruption and hypocrisy … On Holocaust Remembrance day, it is appropriate to discuss our abilities to extricate from among us signs of intolerance and violence, signs that we're heading towards self destruction and down the road to moral depravity. In fact, Holocaust Remembrance Day is an opportunity for self-examination. If Yom Kippur is a day for personal self-reflection, then it is appropriate, and even absolutely necessary, that Holocaust Remembrance Day, will also be a day of national self-examination, and in this national self-examination we must consider the effects of those who seek to disrupt the peace."

Maj. Gen. Yair Golan's heartfelt appraisal was met by immediate condemnation from some right-wing cabinet ministers with the Minister of Culture and Sport calling for Golan's resignation due to it not being "the IDF deputy chief of staff's place to interfere in social matters" including the use of "severe words" in his speech. The PM said that "the comparison that was made in IDF Deputy Chief of Staff Major General Yair Golan's remarks about processes that characterised Nazi Germany 80 years ago is infuriating. The remarks are fundamentally incorrect. They should not have been made at any time, much less now. They do an injustice to Israeli society and belittle the Holocaust. The deputy chief of staff is an outstanding officer, but his remarks on this issue were utterly mistaken and unacceptable to me."

Such outspoken remarks were not restricted to the domain of IDF officers, but were also a common feature of among the retired chiefs of the Israeli Internal Security Service, Shin Bet, which as the backbone of the occupation is admired by Israelis and dreaded by Palestinians. It would appear that the paradox of security chiefs becoming spokesmen for peace is due to the fact of their having been in direct, daily contact with Palestinians whom they arrest, imprison, interrogate, torture, and endeavour to recruit as informers. Consequently their close involvement with Palestinian society results in the more intelligent amongst them coming to the conclusion – a conclusion that evades most Israelis and their politicians – that the Palestinians are a people in their own right with no intention of disappearing, and every intention of having a state of their own.

This apparent contradiction is also rife amongst Mossad chiefs who as part of Israel's external intelligence service were charged with fighting against Arabs in general, and Palestinians in particular. Yet as soon as they retire, they become "peace" and "two-state solution" advocates at variance with government policies.

In Dror Moreh's 2012 documentary film *The Gatekeepers,* six former chiefs of the Shin Bet and Mossad were asked for their opinions regarding a solution to the conflict. They were all commendably candid about their involvement over the past 45 years in the war against terrorism where according to one of them there had been "no strategy, only tactics," and another who said "forget about morality."

The former chiefs were articulate with their viewpoints including the fact that the intransigence of pig-headed politicians on both sides had created the possibility that while Israel may be winning every battle, it could end up losing the war; that the conduct of Israel in the West Bank was comparable to that of the Nazis towards the non-Jewish civilian population of occupied western Europe during the Second World War; that they felt nothing but contempt for the Israeli right-wing bomb-throwing extremists who wanted to blow up the Dome of the Rock which could lead to the world's Muslims going to war against Israel.

By being outspoken in his views, Major General Yair Golan was merely echoing the concern of other top Israeli security chiefs and military leaders who had recently been at odds with the PM's flagship policies with warnings that the direction in which he was leading the country – particularly his refusal to engage in talks with the Palestinians and his push for military action against Iran – was leading to a dangerous situation that was not caused by "Israel's external enemies, but rather its own democratically elected leader … "

28

Saturday, 7 May

South Bank, London, England

Mark Banner could not recall such a concerted kerfuffle by the pro-Israel Jewish lobby to have a public performance banned since 1987 when Jim Allen's stage play, *Perdition,* was due to open under Ken Loach's direction at London's Royal Court Theatre. The play, based on the allegation of Zionist collaboration with the Nazis – Zionism offered to fight on Germany's side if after a German victory the the Zionists would be given Palestine as was documented in Lenni Brenner's *51 Documents: Zionist Collaboration With The Nazis* – was controversially cancelled just 36 hours before the first performance.

Brenner, who was also the fearless author of *Zionism in the Age of Dictators,* revealed disturbing new evidence that Zionists had a long history of unashamed cooperation with the Nazis, especially after Adolph Hitler had came to power in 1933. The Zionists were also cosy with the World War Two's "Axis of Evil" which included Benito Mussolini's Italy, and Tojo Hideki's Japan. Following the enactment of the Nuremberg Anti-Jewish Race Laws in September 1935, only two flags were permitted to be displayed in all of Nazi Germany. One was the Swastika, and the other was Zionism's blue and white banner. The Zionists were also allowed to publish their own newspaper with the reason for such Third Reich-sponsored favouritism being the fact that the Zionists and the Nazis shared the common interest of wanting to make German Jews emigrate to Palestine.

Despite the Jewish lobby's best endeavours, however, a capacity crowd of 450 people – including academics, celebrity supporters of human rights, and pro-Palestinian activists – attended the premiere of *The Promised Land and Ezekiel's Temple Prophecy*. Mark Banner introduced the occasion by speaking briefly and warmly about his late son whom he eulogised with Ernesto "Che" Guevara's assertion that "we cannot be sure of having something to live for unless we are willing to die for it"; by thanking the now six-months-pregnant Freya Nielson for her courage and commitment to the completion of Conrad's documentary as a tribute to his memory; and finally by recalling the words of Desmond Tutu, the South African social rights activist and retired Anglican bishop who during the 1980s became renowned worldwide as an opponent of Apartheid:

> *"It means a great deal to those who are oppressed to know that they are not alone. Never let anyone tell you that what you are doing is insignificant."*

29

Thursday, 25 August

CCR, New York, NY

In its legal briefing *The Genocide of the Palestinian People: An International Law and Human Rights Perspective,* the Centre for Constitutional Rights – which is dedicated to advancing and protecting the rights guaranteed by the U.S. Constitution and the Universal Declaration of Human Rights – stated that "while there has been recent criticism of those taking the position that Israel is committing genocide against Palestinians, there is a long history of human rights scholarship and legal analysis that supports the assertion. Prominent scholars of the international law crime of genocide and human rights authorities take the position that Israel's policies toward the Palestinian people could constitute a form of genocide. Those policies range from the 1948 mass killing and displacement of Palestinians to a half-century of military occupation and, correspondingly, the discriminatory legal regime governing Palestinians, repeated military assaults on Gaza, and official Israeli statements expressly favouring the elimination of Palestinians." The briefing pointed out that the term "genocide" had both a sociological and legal meaning and was first coined in 1944 by the Jewish Polish legal scholar, Raphael Lemkin who explained that "the term does not necessarily signify mass killings":

> *"More often [genocide] refers to a coordinated plan aimed at destruction of the essential foundations of the life of national groups so that these*

groups wither and die like plants that have suffered a blight. The end may be accomplished by the forced disintegration of political and social institutions, of the culture of the people, of their language, their national feelings and their religion. It may be accomplished by wiping out all basis of personal security, liberty, health and dignity. When these means fail the machine gun can always be utilised as a last resort. Genocide is directed against a national group as an entity and the attack on individuals is only secondary to the annihilation of the national group to which they belong."

In 2013, the professor of international law Francis Boyle testified that "The Palestinians have been the victims of genocide as defined by the 1948 Convention on the Prevention and Punishment of the Crime of Genocide":

"For over the past six and one-half decades, the Israeli government and its predecessors in law – the Zionist agencies, forces, and terrorist gangs – have ruthlessly implemented a systematic and comprehensive military, political, religious, economic, and cultural campaign with the intent to destroy in substantial part the national, ethnical, racial, and different religious group (Jews versus Muslims and Christians) constituting the Palestinian people."

As to Israel's so-called "Operation Protective Edge" – the most recent military offensive launched against Gaza in the summer of 2014 – the CCR briefing also cited the expression of concern by prominent human rights authorities who felt that the campaign constituted a violation of international humanitarian law as contained in the Geneva Conventions:

★ *Amnesty International issued a statement proclaiming "an International Criminal Court (ICC) investigation is essential to break the culture of impunity which perpetuates the commission of war crimes and crimes against humanity in Israel and the Occupied Palestinian Territories. The case for such action is made all the more compelling in the light of the ongoing serious violations of international humanitarian law being committed by all parties to the current hostilities in the Gaza Strip and Israel."*

★ *The ICC has jurisdiction over genocide, and the U.N. Special Advisers on the Prevention of Genocide issued a statement two weeks into the 2014 offensive that they were "disturbed by the flagrant use of hate speech in the social media, particularly against the Palestinian population," finding that "individuals have disseminated messages that could be dehumanising to the Palestinians and have called for the killing of members of this group," while "remind[ing] all that incitement to commit atrocity crimes is prohibited under international law."*

★ *Al-Haq, the oldest Palestinian Human Rights organisation, found that serious violations of international law were committed in the course of the 2014 Israeli offensive against Gaza. Al-Haq, along with other Palestinian human rights organisations into the crimes against humanity and war crimes committed during the course of Israel's 2014 Gaza offensive. The crimes suggested for prosecution by these human rights organisations include genocide.*

★ *Dozens of Holocaust survivors, together with hundreds of descendants of Holocaust survivors and victims, accused Israel of "genocide" for the deaths of more than 2,000 Palestinians in Gaza during the 2008-2009 Israeli military offensive against Gaza, "Operation Cast Lead."*

★ *Others who have charged that Israel committed genocide during Operation Cast Lead include Bolivian President Evo Morales, who recalled that country's ambassador from Israel. He stated, "What is happening in Palestine is genocide."*

★ *Author and activist Naomi Wolf wrote, "I mourn genocide in Gaza because I am the granddaughter of a family half wiped out in a holocaust and I know genocide when I see it."*

The briefing finally noted the fact that the public calling for action against the Palestinian people by prominent Israeli politicians had unequivocally met the definition of genocide under the 1948 Convention and cited the example of Israeli Justice Minister Ayelet Shaked who posted a statement on Facebook in June 2014 claiming that "the entire Palestinian people is the enemy" and called for the destruction of Palestine, "including its elderly and its women, its cities and its villages, its property and its infrastructure." Her post also called for the killing of Palestinian mothers who give birth to "little snakes."

The CCR's briefing ended with the assertion that "prominent human rights advocates and scholars have argued that the killings of Palestinians and their forceful expulsion from mandate Palestine in 1948, the Israeli occupation of the West Bank, East Jerusalem, and Gaza, and the violence and discrimination directed at Palestinians by the Israeli government have violated a number of human rights protections contained in international human rights law, genocide being among them."

Other important CCR briefings on its website include a *Letter to Claremont Colleges in Southern California Regarding Repression of Palestinian Human Rights Advocacy on Campus; The closure of Gaza is persecution; Palestine Legal, Centre for Constitutional Rights Warn State Lawmakers Anti-Boycott Bills Unconstitutional; Rights Groups Issue Statement in Support of Students' Right to Speak on Palestinian Human Rights; The Palestinian Right of Return: A Legal and Political Analysis; CCR and Palestine Legal Submission to UN Special Rapporteur on the situation of human rights in the Palestinian Territory occupied since 1967; Palestinian Human Rights Delegation Meets with Hague Court Prosecutor, Delivers Victims' Submission of Israeli Crimes in Gaza; False Accusations of Anti-Semitism Used to Silence Advocacy for Palestinian Rights on U.S. College Campuses; Letter to University of California President Advising Him of Need to Protect Pro-Palestinian Speech on Campus; Palestinian Group Slams*

New York Governor over BDS 'Blacklist'; Escalating Threats Against Palestinian NGO Representative to the ICC; Palestine Legal and CCR Release First-of-Its-Kind Report Documenting Efforts to Silence U.S. Supporters of Palestinian Rights; Rights Attorneys Urge International Criminal Court to Investigate Persecution of Palestinians in Gaza; Centre for Constitutional Rights Condemns Mass Killing, Collective Punishment of Palestinian Civilians in Gaza; A New Report Shows That the Palestinian Movement is Under Attack in the U.S.; and much more.

30

Wednesday, 9 November

Washington, D.C.

In a defiant declaration regarding the definitive decline of their already amoral democracy, the American people have elected as their president, an apparent illiterate and dangerously deranged dummkopf whose proudly proclaimed understanding of democracy and human rights is limited to his avowed and widely publicised pledge to simply "grab them by the pussy."

"Donald Trump shattered expectations on Tuesday with an election night victory that revealed deep anti-establishment anger among American voters and set the world on a journey into the political unknown. The Republican nominee has achieved one of the most improbable political victories in modern US history, despite a series of controversies that would easily have destroyed other candidacies, extreme policies that have drawn criticism from both sides of the aisle, a record of racist and sexist behaviour, and a lack of conventional political experience."
Britain's *The Guardian* newspaper

"GOD BLESS AMERICA" … AND THE REST OF HUMANITY.

31

Friday, 23 December

UN Headquarters, New York, NY

The United Nations Security Council (UNSC) passed a relatively mild non-binding – under Chapter VI of the United nations Charter – resolution by 14 – 0 and one U.S. abstention concerning Israeli settlements in "Palestinian territories occupied since 1967, including East Jerusalem." Resolution 2334 stated that Israel's settlement activity constituted a "flagrant violation" of international law and had "no legal validity." It also demanded that Israel stop such activity and fulfil its obligation as an occupying power under the Fourth Geneva Convention.

Asking the Jewish state of Israel with its "chosen people" to abide by international law was of course an outrageous request which was rightly described as "shameful" and condemned with Israeli prime ministerial histrionics and heated rhetoric including a reprimand for the Ambassadors of the Security Council members which voted for it; the recall of ambassadors from several countries; a promise that Israel would reassess its ties with the UN; the stopping of some $60 million in funding to five UN bodies that are especially hostile to Israel with the threat of more to come; and a phone call threat to New Zealand's foreign minister: "This is a scandalous decision. I'm asking that you not support it and not promote it … If you continue to promote this resolution from our point of view it will be a declaration of war. It will rupture the relations and there will be consequences."

All this rage and threatening vitriol was despite the fact that the resolution merely reaffirmed the international law principle of the inadmissibility of the acquisition of territory by force. It also reaffirmed its own previous resolutions including Resolution 242, which was passed after the 1967 war, and called for the withdrawal of Israel's armed forces from the territories it had "occupied in the recent conflict" and Resolution 338 which was passed on October 22, 1973 and called for an immediate ceasefire in the Yom Kippur war.

Israel, however, refuses to accept the fact that the Geneva Convention applies to the Palestinian Territories because it clings to its fictional narrative that it is not "occupying" but actually "returning" after an absence of some 2,500 years. Israel's refusal to abide by the 4th Geneva Convention – passed in August 1949– is at the very least both regrettable and reprehensible because the Convention was passed as a result of the treatment of the Jewish population in the countries the Nazis or their satellites occupied. So despite asserting that it is a Jewish state, Israel had failed to learn from the crimes of the Nazi state, and was instead hell-bent on following in its jackbooted footsteps. Furthermore, Israel's hysterical reaction will only serve to reinforce the country's status as a rogue state.

The UNSC's apparent small step forward towards enforcing some human rights for the Palestinian people was, however, preceded earlier this month – as a consequence of Zionism's frenetic response during the past year to the success of the BDS movement – with some major setbacks that heralded the fast approaching demise of democracy with its right to free speech and the prerogative of social justice movements to continue employing the already proven tactics of boycott, divestment, and sanctions in their global struggle for justice.

Having been encouraged back in February by the introduction of bills in Congress seeking to authorise state and local governments to divest assets from and prohibit investment in any entity that "engages in a commerce or investment-related boycott, divestment or sanctions activity targeting Israel," many states have since introduced anti-BDS legislation that criminalises the right to boycott which leading international legal experts regard "as a lawful exercise of freedom of expression": a lawful exercise, incidentally, which Western governments – led by the U.S. – were quite happy to encourage, support, and uphold against a far less barbaric form of Apartheid in South Africa.

American democracy had been further eroded at the end of November when in a move intended to dramatically broaden Department of Education probes of colleges and universities who tolerate criticism of Israel by students, the Senate unanimously but surreptitiously passed the AIPAC-supported Anti-Semitism Awareness Act without any debate or fanfare. The bill aims to instruct the Department of Education on the use of the State Department's definition of anti-semitism, which broadly includes criticism of Israel or attempts to "delegitimise" Israel's status as a Jewish state, or even "focusing on Israel" for human rights investigations or urging peace. In America, urging peace is now a crime.

Though the pro-Israel lobby led by AIPAC continues to have a stranglehold on Congress, its hold on the American people is slipping. According to a national poll published by the Brookings Institute, the number of Americans who support imposing sanctions on Israel over its defiant settlement policies had shot up ten percentage points to 46 percent. This would seem to suggest that nearly half of the American people support the Palestinian demand for an end to Israel's military occupation, a move which would probably require the dismantling of all those illegal West Bank settlements and an end to the blockade of the Gaza Strip.

Not to be outdone by their southern neighbours, earlier this month the Ontario provincial legislature passed a symbolic motion condemning the growing BDS movement which Palestinian rights activists in Canada claim was aimed at stifling criticism of Israeli human rights violations. The motion stated that the provincial legislature stands against any position or movement that promotes "any form of hatred, hostility, prejudice, racism and intolerance in any way" – abhorrent characteristics of which Israelis are of course entirely blameless. The motion was also endorsed by the Ottawa Protocol on Combating Antisemitism, which Canada signed during the tenure of former prime minister Stephen Harper, a nauseatingly subservient and staunch supporter of Israel.

In its relentless "war on truth," the pro-Israel Jewish lobby along with its bought and paid for Western politicians, its media lackeys, and other sundry blinkered individuals and organisations, has just notched up another victory – in Britain – in its efforts to silence the voice of Western conscience.

The "bold as brass" British Prime Minister Teresa May announced at the biggest ever Conservative Friends of Israel (cfi) Annual Business Lunch that Britain was adopting the broad definition of anti-Semitism as drawn up by the International Holocaust Remembrance Alliance (IHRA) which according to its website is "an intergovernmental body whose purpose is to place political and social leaders' support behind the need for Holocaust education, remembrance and research both nationally and internationally." The IHRA hopes that its definition – whose eleven examples of anti-Semitic motivation include seven that relate not to Jews as Jews, but to the state of Israel and its violations – will be adopted globally with a view to no doubt shielding Israel and its foundational Zionist political philosophy, rather than actually protecting Jews.

The so-called British Prime Minister, unashamed, unblinking, and with unmatched political temerity said that Israel is a "remarkable country … We have, in Israel, a thriving democracy, a beacon of tolerance, an engine of enterprise and an example to the rest of the world about how to overcome adversity and defying disadvantages." To add insult to the unjust injury of the Palestinian people, the Prime Minister then volunteered the hard to believe assertion that "for it is only when you walk through Jerusalem or Tel Aviv that you see a country where people of all religions and sexualities are free and equal in the eyes of the law."

So while hypocritical Western legislators with yellow streaks down their backs continue to subserviently prostrate themselves before the pro-Israel Jewish lobby and sanctimoniously condemn the "hatred, hostility, prejudice, racism and intolerance" of those seeking justice for the Palestinian people, they – along with mainstream media whores – religiously avoid discussion of any negative news about Israel. Such Israeli instigated censorship also aids and abets the hypocrisy of those who while wearing the mantle of hifalutin moral superiority will nonetheless turn their backs on the reality of Israel's Nazification as a Jewish state and its barbaric ethnic cleansing of Palestine.

"I swore never to be silent whenever and wherever human beings endure suffering and humiliation. We must take sides. Neutrality helps the oppressor, never the victim. Silence encourages the tormentor, never the tormented."
Eliezer "Elie" Wiesel (1928 – 2016), writer, professor, political activist, Nobel Laureate, and Holocaust survivor.

There can be no greater threat to free speech than a "gagged" mainstream media combined with puppet politicians who criminalise criticism of, or activism against the inhumane violations such as those being perpetrated in the illegally occupied Palestinian territories. The most tragic aspect of such censorship with its threat of prosecution and possible imprisonment is that it will be this generation's legacy to the next which will in turn also cringe at the prospect of being subjected to shrill and irrational accusations of "anti-Semitism" and "Holocaust denial." Jews everywhere should be unreservedly ashamed and troubled by Israel's racist nature, its ignoble conduct, and its irrefutable crimes against humanity the amoral diaspora Jewish toleration of which represents an unforgivable betrayal of every single Jew who perished in the Holocaust: the same Holocaust that continues to be callously exploited as justification for the displacement of an indigenous Palestinian people to facilitate the existence of an Israel whose Prime Minister defined as being "the nation state of one people only – the Jewish people – and of no other people."

"Cowardice asks the question – is it safe? Expediency asks the question – is it politic? Vanity asks the question – is it popular? But conscience asks the question – is it right? And there comes a time when one must take a position that is neither safe, nor politic, nor popular; but one must take it because it is right."
Martin Luther King Jr. (1929 – 1968)

32

Sunday, 8 January

London, England

While Israel's historic subversion of Western democracy had been clearly evident to anyone with a modicum of intelligence, those in the mainstream media who supposedly championed the five core principles of ethical journalism – Truth and Accuracy, Independence, Fairness and Impartiality, Humanity, and Accountability – had left it to Al-Jazeera to investigate how the Israeli government was in the midst of a brazen covert campaign to shape Britain's foreign policy and influence its perception of Israel.

During a six-month investigation, undercover reporter Robin (an alias), met with members of Britain's lobby network which enjoyed strong Israeli government support by way of the Israeli embassy in London. Robin had posed as a graduate activist strongly sympathetic towards Israel who was keen to assist in combating the Boycott, Divestment and Sanctions movement which was prominent and gaining ground in Britain.

Al-Jazeera's four-part series *The Lobby* (available online and a must-see for anyone interested in the illusionary concept of British democracy) makes it abundantly evident that the main objective of the Labour Friends of Israel (LFI) – and other pro-Israel groups in the UK working with the Israeli embassy – was to smear pro-Palestinian activists and organisations with charges of anti-Semitism and other equally villainous claims that deliberately created crises for political ends. At a private meeting held during the annual Labour Party Conference last September, Mark Regev, Israel's ambassador to the UK – known to millions as the mealy mouthed liar who as the former spokesman for Israel's Prime Minister pugnaciously defended Israel's endless criminal violations – advised key activist leaders of Labour's pro-Israel contingent on strategy and talking points as follows:

> *"Why are people who consider themselves progressive in Britain, supporting reactionaries like Hamas and Hezbollah? We've gotta say in the language of social democracy, I think, these people are misogynistic, they are homophobic, they are racist, they are anti-Semitic, they are reactionary. I think that's what we need to say, it's an important message."*

Part of that strategy was to "take down" anti-settlement British politicians such as UK deputy foreign secretary Sir Alan Duncan who in 2014 had said that while he fully supported Israel's right to exist, he believed settlements on occupied Palestinian land represented an "ever-deepening stain on the face of the globe." He also likened the situation in Hebron in the occupied West Bank to Apartheid.

Al Jazeera's Investigative Unit also revealed that Israel was influencing student, activist, and parliamentary groups in the UK by offering financial and strategic assistance in order to gather support among young organisers with a view to moulding British politics in favour of Israel. Such efforts also included targeting students to boost support for Israel as a counter to the BDS movement; having pro-Israel groups – such as the Union of Jewish Students (UJS) comprising 64 Jewish societies at British universities which received money from the Israeli embassy – attempting not only to influence the National Union of Students (NUS) presidency election, but also of trying to oust Malia Bouattia following her victory as the first Muslim president of the NUS to identify as a Black British; and sending "pluralist" Fabian Society think-tank analysts on paid trips to Israel.

While the British government's response was a characteristic and cowardly reaffirmation of support for Israel, the British people's reaction to that Apartheid state's arrogant assault on their "British democracy" was conspicuous by its mute indifference as they busied themselves with prioritised concerns over the fate of their favourite characters in television soap operas such as *Coronation Street;* with being mesmerised into a silent stupor by the mainstream media's mendacious mind-washing mediocrity; and with religiously checking their lottery numbers for the win that might possibly free them from the bondage of their android existence. In fairness to the British people, however, their irresponsible detachment – from the cataclysmic reality of what was occurring around them – was no different to that of other subdued subjects especially in North America and Europe, but also to varying degrees on other continents where Israel's Machiavellian subversion of human and democratic rights was just as debilitating and rampant.

"Every time we turn our heads the other way when we see the law flouted, when we tolerate what we know to be wrong, when we close our eyes and ears to the corrupt because we are too busy or too frightened, when we fail to speak up and speak out, we strike a blow against freedom and decency and justice."
Robert F. Kennedy (1926 – 1968)

Epilogue

"This is, in theory, still a free country, but our politically correct, censorious times are such that many of us tremble to give vent to perfectly acceptable views for fear of condemnation. Freedom of speech is thereby imperilled, big questions go undebated, and great lies become accepted, unequivocally as great truths."
Simon Heffer, British journalist, author and political commentator.